'Plenty of action, some well-wrought characterisation and nice evocations of the Marlborough Sounds make for a good solid Kiwi book.' *New Zealand Listener*

'The characters work, the plot is cleverly executed and the sense of place is visceral. There's touches of humour and self-inflicted jeopardy which are perfectly justifiable … an absolute stand-out book …' *Australian Crime Fiction*

"Chester is a brilliantly realised flawed protagonist, inflected with the direct wit of northern England … The writing is extremely vivid in its evocation of scenery and character. At times this makes for disturbing reading, not because of gory detail, but because the characters are so well rendered that we can't fail to feel the cost of the violence. This establishes a momentum that makes the book hard to put down. *Marlborough Man* is crime fiction at its best.' *The Australian*

'A well written, tension-filled and accurate portrait of a man struggling with his past …' *Otago Daily Times*

'*Marlborough Man* is an unrelenting, incredibly readable book that will hold you through a whole day … Carter has paced this novel brilliantly, and when Nick Chester's nightmare moment arrives, the crescendo is breathtaking.' *Bookoccino*

'Carter is back to his best …' *Herald Sun*

'… a roller coaster ride of false leads and red herrings … Carter draws the reader to his characters, flaws and all …' *Fremantle Herald*

'What makes a great thriller is nerve-wracking plotting, rich atmospheric settings, and complex characters – *Marlborough Man* has the lot …' *Kiwi Crime*

'This is a cracker of a novel, pacey and sharp … compelling from start to finish. Highly recommended …' *Landfall Review Online*

'Carter is a first-class wordsmith with a particular talent for authentic dialogue. The novel's setting wholly embraces the people and action, and the overall effect is powerful and persuasive.' *Ngaio Marsh Award judges*

'The crime aspects of the novel are well handled, with dogged police work inching the team ever closer to catching the killer. But it is the human aspects of the story that make you understand the characters and care about them.' *New Zealand Review of Books Pukapuka Aotearoa*

'This is a story of perversion and vengeance, made more gripping by the fact that it is set in one of the most beautiful places on earth … It is a fascinating mix that only a skilled writer should attempt. Alan Carter succeeds admirably.' *Queensland Reviewers Collective*

'Carter's laconic style and small-town chills are excellently placed to ease you into a long winter in front of the fire.' *Readings*

'*Marlborough Man* weaves local politics, culture and crime into a story that is gripping and at times brimming with Kiwi humour. The scenery, so beautifully described, could almost be a character in the story.' *Writing WA*

ALAN CARTER
MARLBOROUGH MAN

 FREMANTLE PRESS

Alan Carter was born in Sunderland, UK. He immigrated to Australia in 1991 and now lives in splendid semi-rural semi-isolation south of Hobart, Tasmania. In his spare time he follows the black line up and down the local swimming pool or drags on his wetsuit and braves the icy waters of the D'Entrecasteaux Channel. He is the author of seven previous novels: the Fremantle-set DS Cato Kwong series *Prime Cut* (winner of the Ned Kelly Award for Best First Fiction), *Getting Warmer*, *Bad Seed* and *Heaven Sent*. His New Zealand-set *Marlborough Man*, featuring Sergeant Nick Chester, won the Ngaio Marsh Award for Best Novel. Its sequel is *Doom Creek*.

For Kath, my beautiful muse and soul mate.

PROLOGUE

He is well overdue for a treat. He has been very patient but temptation is everywhere. The woman in the next car looks at him a second time, not in an unfriendly way. He smiles back, rolls his eyes: chauffeurs, that's all we are. Today? Swimming lessons. She's waiting too. Smooth skin but the neck showing signs of those creeping years. Perhaps a little more jowly than she should be. Her fingers play with her fringe as she checks herself, yet again, in the mirror.

They're coming out.

The parents who went inside are now zapping the locks, throwing in school bags and swimming gear, kids clambering inside, some with junk food in their plump little hands. Some whining because they're overtired. Others nattering ten to the dozen, their faces animated, bursting with life, curiosity, wonder.

A blonde girl climbs into the next car. A serious thing, pinched face, feeling neglected no doubt, like her mother. She too will grow up needy for attention and reassurance, unable to distinguish between the good men and the bad. Mum gives him a last lingering look, hoping maybe for something more than the complicit smile of another long-suffering overcommitted parent. She wants the flash of danger and passion that's missing from her existence. You won't get that from me, he thinks. Loving mothers aren't on my radar. He winks at her. It makes her day and she pulls out of the parking space to go home.

And there he is. The treat. Father is away, trying to pay their mortgage from a mining camp in Western Australia. His mother still at work in the real estate office in the city. Their only child.

Roll out of the parking space and pull up at the bus stop. The car door opens. He speaks the child's name.

The child looks up from his daydream, not expecting anybody to be there for him. But there's always a first time for everything. A smile of recognition.

'Hop in.'

'I'm meant to get the bus. Stranger danger.'

'But I'm not a stranger, surely?'

The little boy climbs in.

PART ONE

1

It's the third night running that car has been past. Same time, around ten. A low rumble, the occasional cough, missing a beat.

It could be pig hunters looking for the track just up the road that takes you into the forest on the far hill. People don't come down this road for no reason or by mistake; it doesn't go anywhere. It stops about five ks up from here at Butchers Flat. The full moon slips behind the clouds and the silhouettes of the hills fade into the background dark. I can hear the river down below, rushing over the rocks.

It could be campers heading back to their tents at Butchers after a few beers in town, but it's too damn cold for camping. It could be scavengers after some firewood from the recently logged hills. It's meant to be spring but it still gets down near to freezing and there's no dry wood left in town. Besides, who's got two hundred bucks for a trailer-load when every other bastard is on the dole, and surely it's got to get warmer soon. In winter, the wind roars up from the South Pole across the Antarctic and Southern Oceans, dusting the Alps with snow and ice, snaking through the green fjords and lonely valleys, under the door and into your bones. It will freeze your core and consume your heart if you let it. If it wasn't for the fact that New Zealand is so bloody beautiful, there are days when you could happily shoot yourself.

I live in a two-storey timber house perched on the side of a steep hill that plunges down to the river. In summer it's a trickle but in winter it boils. If the Wakamarina isn't flooded and the land hasn't slipped, my house can be reached by a narrow road winding up the valley, but the bitumen stops well before that – we're not just off the grid, we're off the tarmac. The valley is a good place to hide, whether from the toils and tribulations of the modern world, or from real people and real threats. We're adjacent to a tectonic faultline which is statistically due for a catastrophic seismic event – any day now, according to the doomsayers and geologists. That's okay, I've been expecting a catastrophe ever since I got here.

It could be those weekend miners down from their day jobs in the city, here to work their claim on the hundred-and-fifty-year-old scratchings in the riverbank that never turned a profit back then either. It's not about the gold they say, it's about history, tradition and mateship. And an escape from whatever ails them in the big smoke.

But it's not them. I know who it is. It's Sammy Pritchard. He's finally found me and this is his way of letting me know. His reach is long, even from maximum security.

'Come back to bed.'

'Yes, pet.' I look at Vanessa lying there, sleep-gummed and irritable. I think of Paulie asleep downstairs. I wonder if Sammy will just come for me and let them live.

No. Of course he won't.

*

The phone goes shortly after six thirty.

'You're wanted down at the marina, Sarge,' Latifa says.

'Murder?'

'Vandalism. A boat belonging to Mr McCormack.'

'You're getting me out of bed at this hour for vandalism?'

'Special request from the District Commander. Him and Mr M play squash together in Nelson.'

We all know who Mr M is, and that he owns half of Marlborough.

'You're five minutes away, Latifa. It'll take me half an hour.'

'You want to live up there with the hillbillies, that's your business. Anyway, speed's not the point here.'

'What is?'

'McCormack's a willy-waver. He wants the top man on the job. That'd be you.'

'Tell the DC I'm on my way.'

I grab a mug of tea and try to kiss Vanessa but she pulls the blanket over her head. It's been happening a bit lately. She doesn't like New Zealand; maybe she's stopped liking me too.

The Toyota coughs into life and I back out onto the gravel driveway. There's a blur of black and rich blue as a tui flits into a nearby silver beech, beeping and whirring. I wonder about that car from last night. Will they return and slaughter my family while I'm out?

No, Sammy would want me to watch. They'll wait for my return.

*

At Havelock Marina, the sun washes the green hills across the water and glints off the rows of pleasure craft. A tall man with short greying hair is stamping his feet to ward off the chill. It's McCormack and he's dressed for a day on the boat. It's only Tuesday, alright for some. His companions, a man and two women, sit in a white BMW parked nearby, sipping takeaway coffees and looking bored. The boat is big and has an extra half-berth at the rich end of the marina away from the riffraff. I glance at the damage: spray paint on the starboard hull of his treasured catamaran. Where once it said *Serenity II* it now says *Smaug*.

'Smaug, sir?'

He looks at me like I'm a moron. 'The evil dragon in *The Hobbit*. The Desolation of.'

I take out a notebook to seem interested. 'Why Smaug, sir? Do you think someone might have some sort of grudge against you?' Like maybe half the population of the top of the South Island? I've seen his handiwork on the drive down the valley road to the marina: logged hills shaved into sad submission, once-stunning landscape become devastated moonscape.

'Try that hippie chicken farmer up your way.'

Up my way? I'm thinking. How do you know where I live?

He shoves an iPhone in my face. 'He's been sending me threatening emails.'

'*Die, you rapacious cunt.*' I nod. 'Rapacious. He knows his way around a dictionary then.' I tell McCormack to forward the email to us, and he does so with a few finger prods. The wind changes and for a moment I catch the rotten odour of bad breath. All that money and he can't even floss regularly.

'What's that accent of yours?' asks McCormack.

'Geordie. North-east England.'

'Dark satanic mills and all that stuff?'

'Not anymore, they closed them all down. Lovely and green now. Like here.'

A sniff. 'Maybe you should have stayed there.'

'Then I wouldn't have had the pleasure of meeting you, sir.'

Behind me the car window rolls down. A weary drawl from one of McCormack's travel companions, a smooth-faced man with blond hair that flops in his eyes. 'Let's just forget it, Dickie – back to the shack for brekkie, yeah?'

'This has ruined our day,' says McCormack, pocketing his phone. 'Sort that greenie prick out.'

'Leave it with me, sir. I'll have a word with him and see if he knows anything about it.'

'A word? Just arrest him.'

All around us there are cameras and signs saying twenty-four-hour surveillance. That's the kind of service you can command when you own a big flash boat. This shouldn't be too hard, Havelock isn't known for the quality of its criminals.

'I'll keep you updated on the progress of our inquiries, sir.'

'You know I play squash with your boss, don't you?'

'Yep. Me too,' I lie. 'I think it's his backhand that lets him down.'

*

Latifa Rapata hands me a cardboard cup of coffee as I walk through the door. Two years out of police college and she has the jaded air of a thirty-year vet. 'The DC phoned five minutes ago. He'd like a word.'

McCormack didn't waste time whingeing to his squash pal.

'Nick,' says the DC. 'What the hell are you up to?'

'The pursuit of justice, sir.' My coffee is good and strong, from the bakery down the road. 'Without fear or favour.' Try changing the subject. 'Any news on that missing kid?'

'Nothing. It's been a week. Thin air. Look, Nick, give me a break, mate. McCormack's a dick but it's not just me he knows. He hangs out with all those government and public-service wankers in Wellington. Those people are reviewing my budget as we speak.'

There's a memo on my desk, calls for voluntary redundancies and early retirements. I can't afford that, not yet.

'Three per cent efficiency dividend. You know what that means, Nick. It means station closures, rationalisations, all that palaver.' A studied pause. 'How is that boy of yours? Paulie? Must be eleven by now?'

Subtle, I'm thinking. Really subtle. I know he doesn't mean it, he's just reminding me of the quid pro quo. 'Leave it with me, boss.'

*

Latifa is in the driving seat as we wind our way back up the valley.

'So McCormack is blue blood is he?' I ask.

She nods and changes down for a steep, sharp turn. 'Fifth-generation Scot, and an arsehole from way back.'

'You're not in his fan club either then?'

'Why would I be? His great-great-whatever grandfather stole a big block of land from mine two hundred years ago and he hasn't said sorry yet.'

I gesture at the scenery. 'He owns all this?'

'Bought and paid for.' Back up to fourth for the straight, and nudging a hundred before the next hairpin bend. 'That hill over there is next for the chop.'

A mountain of pine heading for matchsticks. 'It's like the fucking *Lorax*.'

'What?'

'A Dr Seuss book, I read it to my boy.'

'Soows, boowk. I love that accent of yours, Sarge. If you weren't already married I'd probably find you sexy or something.'

Latifa missed the police college class about how to talk to your superiors. 'Your turn to buy the fush and chups today,' I tell her.

'At least I belong here.' She lifts her chin. 'Charlie the Chicken Man is next on the left.'

He lives on the same valley road as me but eight kilometres away. I must have passed his gate a thousand times and we've never even met. We pull up at a functional – dare I say, ugly – box of a house with open paddocks either side and a half-cleared pine hill looming behind. Chickens clucking in the field – that ticks the free-range box – and a rooster cockadoodling way beyond dawn. In the other paddock some recently shorn alpacas are chewing on straw bales. In front of me stands Charlie the Chicken Man. He is short and hairy, buttoned neck to toe against the sandflies, and his gumboots are caked in grey mud. He holds his hand out, a welcoming smile on his face.

'Charlie Evans.'

'Nick Chester, Havelock Police.'

'I've seen you around but I don't think we've actually spoken.'

'You must've been keeping out of trouble, then.' I let Latifa explain the McCormack situation to him. She needs the practice on her people skills.

'McCormack.' Charlie snorts. 'Piece of work.'

Latifa shows him the email on her iPad. 'Did you send this?'

Charlie reads it. '*Rapacious cunt*: yeah that was me. And he is.'

'Did you do this?' She shows him a photo of the vandalism.

He grins. 'Smaug. I like it.'

'So did you?'

'No.'

'Can you account for your movements over the last twenty-four hours, sir?' Latifa says sir like she doesn't mean it. I know from experience.

Charlie can account for himself and does. He worked the farm, fed the chickens and alpacas, and looked after his bedridden wife who's dying of cancer. 'Pancreas,' he says. 'Anything else you wanted to ask?'

I look at his boots. 'Where's the grey mud from? All I can see around here is brown.'

'Follow me.'

So we do. Trudging up the back of the paddock as the wind picks up, a bellbird chimes, and the alpacas bray. I slap a sandfly or two off my neck but I know they'll itch like crazy later. We're heading towards the bottom of the logged hill and a culvert channelling the run-off. Charlie turns and waves his hand at the hill behind.

'McCormack's handiwork. Bastards cleared this half about a month ago.'

'Harvested,' says Latifa. 'His trees, his harvest, his right. No law against it.'

'Bloody should be.' Charlie points down into the culvert, clogged with grey mud from the hillside. 'In the big rain a fortnight ago, this lot came down and clogged my drainage channel so the slurry spread all over my pasture and ruined the grass. Now I have to buy in straw to feed the alpacas. That's half my income from the chickens gone,' he snaps his fingers, 'like that.'

'Did you talk to McCormack about it?' I ask.

'Not interested.'

'Maybe try getting in a lawyer or something?' Latifa says.

'His will be bigger and better. He's got money to burn. They're clearing the other half in the next month or two.' Charlie gives the blocked culvert a last sad look. 'Maybe this is what they mean by the economic trickle-down effect.'

Latifa hands him our business card. 'Can you think of anyone who might have wanted to damage Mr McCormack's boat?'

'Join the queue,' he says, pocketing it.

*

The rest of the day is spent doing paperwork. Reports, budgets, circulars and such, and answering more emails than a man should receive in a place like this. Havelock, population around five hundred, is the greenshell-mussel capital of the world according to the sign just outside town. That's pretty much the economy here: mussels, farmed salmon, sheep and logging. You could boil the population down to two personality types: those who like nature and those who would happily shoot it and skin it. Havelock is a two-cop station, a quaint little white weatherboard shack on the main street. Most of our work concerns bad or drunk drivers and their consequences, or bad drinkers and their consequences. Everybody knows it doesn't really need a sergeant in charge but I wasn't going to drop a pay grade to come and hide here, so that's that.

In theory, my chain of command goes east via Picton, the ferry port, then south through Blenheim, the capital of Marlborough, then west over to district headquarters in Nelson. Follow the dotted-line track and it looks like a man lost in the desert. In practice, I pretty much work to the DC in Nelson because the fewer people who know about me the better. The Tasman Police District covers the whole of the top of the South Island. It has to be one of the most spectacular beats in the world. There's a sprinkling of small towns and a couple of places that call themselves cities. There are remote farms, vineyards, pristine beaches, a thousand coves and bays: a bonanza of boltholes and last resorts. The compact fjord-like coastline of the Marlborough Sounds adds up to nearly two thousand kilometres, that's like two-thirds of the way across America. As befits a land that markets itself as Middle Earth, it is peopled by industrious and good-hearted hobbits, some fierce grumpy dwarves, haughty elves, and a smattering of orcs to keep the weekend patrols busy. For the most part, it's a stunningly beautiful and peaceful place to hide.

As I turn the last corner on the unsealed section leading to our home, the sun drops behind the hill. A dun-coloured weka darts from the undergrowth out across the road. Pulling into the driveway, I see a dark blue ute with a couple of bull mastiffs caged in the back. Pig dogs. They set up a frenzy of barking and I hope the cages are locked; I've seen what they can do to a fully-grown hog. In the ute tray there's a collection of guns and knives and tools, a chainsaw. Cold with dread, I unclip my Glock and head for the front door.

2

Sunderland's motto is *Nil desperandum auspice Deo*, or loosely translated, *Never despair, trust in God*. With the unemployment statistics, real or imagined, rarely dipping below twenty per cent for the last three generations, you need something like that to cling to. Or a win on the pools. The shipyards and coalmines that once defined the place are long gone, replaced by Poundland, and Gregg's the Bakers. But in this mock-Tudor mansion behind a tall fence in the select and secluded suburb of Cleadon, such grimy realities are out of sight and out of mind.

'Marty, get this lad a Stella.'

For a man who's a millionaire several times over and hangs out with captains of industry, Sammy Pritchard is a man of simple tastes. There's nothing he likes more than a hot curry and cold lager in South Shields every Friday, a season ticket to watch Sunderland at the Stadium of Light where the score is depressingly predictable. Sammy's gang. I'm looking at them now: a motley collection of beer guts, dead eyes, and cruel mirth. Sammy keeps a few of us lads close: some are hard men, like Marty, and some are clever or useful to him, like me. Some are just useless twats who are always good for a laugh.

Tonight is film night, the first Thursday of every month, unless business prevails. We gather in Sammy's basement den with its big screen, surround sound, comfy chairs and a full fridge. Sometimes it's comedy: Sammy can't get enough of *Blazing Saddles* – he loves the campfire farting scene and the one where the horse gets punched. Sometimes it's porn: Sammy keeps these old VHSs from the 1980s when the hair and mos were as big as everything else on the screen. Mostly we hoot at them but some of us go home with a stiffy later. Vanessa likes those nights.

And then there's Sammy's absolute all-time untouchable favourite.

Marty hands me that beer and winks. 'Y'alright there, Nicky?'

'Aye, mate.' I pop the tin and lift it in salute. 'Cheers.'

His look stays on me a second longer than it should. According to the intelligence file, Marty Stringfellow is the Godfather-in-waiting and he's down for at least three murders and several serious woundings. Two of the murders were street dealers caught skimming. Sammy runs a tight ship and he wasn't having any of that – people might start thinking he's soft. So he sent out Marty, who's very handy with a knife. The dealers were butchered and dumped at the town tip. The third was a teenage Ukrainian girl whom Sammy had gifted to a Newcastle businessman to sweeten a property deal. She ran away: embarrassment all round. She was found on display, throat slit, in a toilet cubicle in a city centre nightclub. No more runaways since. There's no proof on Marty yet, but I'll find it. I hope.

How come I'm in Sammy Pritchard's inner circle? He thinks I'm a bigwig in the Prisons Department. And so I am, showing up most days to earn my crust like I've done for the last twelve months we've been running this operation. I first met Sammy on the Whitburn golf course one brisk spring morning and cheekily challenged him to a bet; letting him win the hundred quid, not by much, so he'd think he earned it. Since then, in my capacity as a supposed logistics guru for Prisons, I've helped Sammy get some contraband and favours for friends inside, hurt some enemies, and moved guards and prisoners around at will to further Sammy's aims. And he pays me well – pity it all goes back into the evidence drawer. He also seems to really like me.

There's a lot of work gone in to trapping Sammy. He's flagged as a level three. SOCA – the Serious and Organised Crime Agency – want him locked up for a long time. I was perfect for the job: on the fast track at Greater Manchester Police and fresh back from a training course with the FBI. It's years since anybody in Sunderland ever heard of me, and even then I was just a pisshead student on the tap. And, last but not least, I went to the same school as Sammy: Monkwearmouth – the Monkeyhouse. I was five years behind him so he doesn't remember me but that connection is enough. It's noted in the file, quote: 'For a nasty piece of work, Pritchard can be remarkably sentimental and trusting.'

'Put the DVD in, Marty, there's a good lad.' We all know Marty is ambitious, and Sammy is jerking his leash. He turns to me. 'How's that lad of yours, Nicky?'

He means Paulie. Yes, that's how low I can go. I'm using my own Down's syndrome son to build my undercover legend in order to entrap a shitty Sunderland gangster who'll be replaced by ten others the day he goes down. 'Aye, champion, Sammy. Thrilled to bits with the season ticket. He's looking forward to the Man U game on Saturday.'

'We'll get hammered.'

'He doesn't care. As long as he's got his Bovril and pie he could be anywhere, he could even be watching Newcastle United.'

'The Mags? Fuckin' hell. Little twat does that, I'll have the season ticket back.'

'And I'll have his Bovril and pie an' all.'

Sammy lifts his Stella and grins.

Movie time. I've been in the inner circle for about six months and we've already watched it five times. Sammy could recite the dialogue by heart and often does, under his breath; lips moving, face twitching. The movie is *Bring Me the Head of Alfredo Garcia*. It's by Sam Peckinpah, the Sultan of Splatter. Here's the synopsis: an American bartender and his prostitute girlfriend go on a road trip through the Mexican underworld to collect a million-dollar bounty on the head of a gigolo. I sometimes wonder if Sammy's fixation on it is just because it's made by another Sammy P. No, there's more to it than that. Violent retribution is his guiding mantra. Legend has it that when he was a lad in the 1970s, he ran with the Seaburn Casuals, Sunderland's football hooligan hordes, and excelled himself by thumbing out the eyes of a Newcastle supporter. Sammy would have been about fifteen at the time.

The lights go down and we settle in.

All through the movie, Marty Stringfellow is casting glances my way. Sizing me up. We're about the same age, same height, same build. I reckon I'm better looking though. He's been to uni as well – Leicester. If he wasn't an enforcer for Sammy Pritchard he could have been a middle-manager by now. He doesn't trust me. He identifies with the bounty-hunting bartender. Me? I'm with Alfredo Garcia, the ill-fated gigolo.

3

New Zealand police don't routinely carry firearms but I've got special dispensation – well, a nod and a wink from the DC, really. I slip the safety off the Glock and slide the screen door open. A shape moves in the gloom.

'Dad!' Paulie gives me a hug. He looks down at the gun in my hand, purses his lips and shakes his head. 'I'd put that away if I were you. You know what Mam's like.'

He leads me back into the kitchen. There are two blokes with their backs to me and Vanessa is looking happier than I've seen her in ages. They turn and smile. Two big Maori lads, forties, nudging fifty maybe, they rise to shake my hand.

'Steve,' says one.

'Gary,' says the other. My hand is intact, but only just.

'Tea?' says Vanessa, pulling a mug towards the pot.

'Sure.' I take a seat beside her.

'Steve and Gary were wondering if the cabin was available for rent.'

We could do with the money, we both know that. Our rainy-day fund for Paulie. 'What's your line of work?' I ask Steve.

'This and that,' says Gary for him. 'We've just done five years in Perth, FIFO, but now they're laying people off. Lovely place, nice beaches, but expensive.'

'And too fucken hot,' says Steve. He realises his mistake. 'Sorry, missus. Sorry about the language.'

Vanessa finishes pouring my tea. 'We've heard worse.'

'Fucking right,' says Paulie, lifting his can of Coke Zero.

It breaks the tension. Everybody laughs, even me. 'And now?'

Gary again. 'Odd jobs, fixing stuff, fencing, chopping down trees. Whatever's going.'

I drink some tea. 'The guns and the dogs?'

'We hunt sometimes. People buy the meat.'

'We were thinking a month or two,' says Vanessa. 'See how we go.'

We? 'Was that you guys driving up and down the road the last few nights?'

'Yep,' says Gary. 'Sorry if it spooked you. We've been camping up at Butchers Flat but we heard about this place.' He nods at the badge on my uniform. 'Took a while to get our nerve up.'

I'm relieved. Me and my paranoia. Vanessa seems happy enough with the idea and the extra presence might be good if Sammy Pritchard does send somebody. I thumb over my shoulder. 'I don't want dogs or guns on the property.'

'No problem. There's someone we can leave them with, down the road.'

'They can take the dogs but they can't take you?'

'Their property isn't as grand as yours,' says Gary. 'Not enough room.'

We agree a price and shake on it. Gary hands over the first month in cash. I shove it in my wallet. 'Receipt?'

'No need,' says Gary.

'What's your surnames? I'll need them for my tax return.' It's a lie and we all know it.

'McCaw,' says Gary, and spells it out.

'Lomu,' says Steve, doing the same. McCaw and Lomu, All Blacks rugby legends, household names. Their eyes twinkle. Say it ain't so.

We've swapped lies. I leave it at that. 'If it doesn't work out for any reason you'll get a refund.'

'Seems fair,' says Gary.

They leave to drop off the dogs and guns and pick up their bags.

'Nice eyes,' says Vanessa.

'Steve or Gary?'

'You,' she says, squeezing my hand. We plonk Paulie in front of the Play Station and head upstairs to bed.

*

The phone goes early again. If it's about McCormack and his damn boat, I swear blood will be spilt.

'You awake?' says Latifa.

'What is it?' I growl.

'The DC wants you to come in.'

'McCormack?'

'Not this time. They found the missing boy this morning. The one from Nelson.'

'Alive?'

'No. They found him on our patch. By the shoe fence just outside town.' Her voice cracks. 'Somebody messed him up badly.'

*

A couple of kilometres south as you drive out of Havelock on State Highway 6 – the road to Blenheim and the vineyards – there's a stretch of fence on your left. Three wires strung between pine posts, sheep in a paddock and green hills all around. The fence itself probably runs maybe a kilometre along the road but the shoes hang off just a one-hundred-metre stretch: little kids shoes with pink stars and sparkly bits, trainers, wedding shoes, dancing shoes, Sunday best, footy boots, you name it. There must be a thousand pairs, all hanging by their laces. I don't know the story of how it all started. Maybe there was a car crash and some people died on this notorious stretch of road, and maybe a pair was left in memory. Maybe others were left there later to share the sadness of that day. Maybe even more were left to mark other people's sadnesses. But most likely they're there for no reason at all, just to be part of the crowd, some kind of belonging: Havelock's answer to Facebook.

There's a white tent erected halfway along and crime-scene tape flapping in the breeze. Uniforms are guarding the perimeter and blocking the road, and Latifa is telling some gawpers to get lost. There are forensics people in their zip-up jimjams sifting the ground and taking photographs. There are detectives with clipboards talking to locals or trying to get signals on their mobiles. They'll be lucky, it's pretty patchy out here. The sun is somewhere behind rain clouds; another hour and everyone will be shrugging on the wet-weather gear. Even the DC is here, his prop-forward shoulders straining his police windcheater. He summons me over to talk to one of his detectives.

'Nick, this is DI Marianne Keegan. Wellington office sent her. She's running things.'

Wellington? I'm thinking. All the detectives in Tasman and Marlborough on holiday, are they? We shake hands and say hello. She has strong features and looks like she does stuff to keep fit. Her hand is cool and smooth, the grip firm. She seems destined for the big league in a few years and the DC can't be too far from retirement now. She thanks me for having my team – that's me and Latifa – help out, and asks for a list of locals we should be talking to, either because they're gossipy know-it-alls or because they're possible suspects. 'Living round here,' she says, 'a lot of people have to be hiding from something.'

I detect the hint of a Liverpool accent from way back. 'Scouser?'

'Yes, I was, but I'm a detective now. The list asap, hmmm?' She walks away to issue instructions to a flunky.

'Found the boat vandal yet?' asks the DC.

'No. How much do we know about this kid?'

'Jamie Riley, six. From Stoke, other side of Nelson. Good family, nice boy by all accounts. He didn't come home after a swimming lesson out at Richmond, Monday before last. We've looked into the parents and relatives and associates and so far all clean as a whistle. They're genuine, absolutely devastated. Don't know what's hit them.'

'How did he die?'

'Neck snapped. But there was other damage too. Somebody has had him for a week now.' He turns to me, he looks angry. 'Anybody round here top of your list?'

'Nobody jumps to mind. There's a few sniffers and flashers but I don't recall any with violence flags on their record.'

'Pull them in anyway. Maybe they know something. Maybe they've graduated.' He examines the screen on his warbling mobile. 'And keep me in the loop on the vandal thing.'

I spend the next couple of hours in the office drawing up a list of sad bastards and busybodies for Detective Inspector Keegan, zapping it through to her email. I offer to have myself or Latifa accompany her team if any local liaison is deemed necessary. She says thanks. By lunchtime I'm peckish and twiddling my thumbs. It's not what I expected on a day when a child is found murdered on my patch. The phone goes.

'Sergeant Chester?'

'Speaking.'

'Jessie James from the *Journal*. Latifa said I should call you?'

'What about?'

'Well, the murder obviously.'

'You need to talk to Police Media.'

'I'm not after a story, silly. I've got a tip-off for you.'

'Go ahead.'

'There's a bloke out on the Sounds. You can only get there by boat. He's got a past.'

'What kind of past?'

'Kids. In Australia. He's from Perth.'

'How do you know about him?'

'My boyfriend works on the mail boat. He's from Perth as well. A few months ago now he thought this guy looked familiar. He checked the name on the letters and then googled him. He got a result. After this morning, I thought you might like to know.'

I reach for a pen. 'Tell me.'

*

That rain rolled in and the wind revved up. The police boat came over from Picton to pick us up and now we're out on the far reaches of Pelorus Sound bumping through the waves on a wet Wednesday afternoon. There's Marianne, two of her detectives, a handful of ninjas from the Armed Offenders Squad, and there's me. Coves and islands rear out of the water, sanctuaries for threatened prehistoric lizards and birds that never learned to fly. As we draw near Patrick Smith's secluded cove, a pod of dolphins skips alongside, and a chopper hovers over the bach, a weatherboard cabin nestled into the folds of a hill.

Patrick is there on his jetty to greet us with a black hairy pig beside him sitting at heel like a dog. Smith doesn't look particularly like a child molester, no more so than anyone else in Marlborough anyway. I wonder whether the tactical firearms guys were really needed but the Perth police assured us he has a temper. Or maybe they were having a laugh.

'Patrick,' says Marianne stepping onto the jetty. He holds out his hand but she ignores it. I don't blame her. You never get used to the idea of shaking hands with a known kiddie-fiddler.

Having made sure that Smith didn't go anywhere until we got there, the chopper departs to another job, or a nice hot cup of tea back at base.

'You'll be wanting to come in out of the weather,' says Patrick. Middle-aged and nondescript, he looks and sounds like a private school teacher, which is what he was. Twenty years in one of Perth's most prestigious; all those parents paying big money to have Patrick buggering their little boys. Over the years a few complained but the school hushed them up until finally they had to let Patrick go, with a nice payout. If it hadn't been for the Royal Commission he wouldn't have had to come here to hide, and Jessie James' boyfriend wouldn't have recognised him. The allegation of rough play by one victim has piqued Marianne's interest. She stalks off towards the bach and the big pig munches on a biscuit, slobber dripping from its bristly gob.

'He answers to Ginger,' says Patrick, following my gaze.

'But he's black,' I say.

'He doesn't know that. He's not burdened by other people's expectations.'

'They're waiting for you inside.'

We sit around a pine kitchen table in a cosy, cluttered room with a view over to the nature reserve. A log burner crackles away and the kettle is on but nobody wants anything. The tactical guys are outside having a smoke.

'We need to take you into the station, Patrick. Get some samples of your spit. Ask a few questions.' Marianne gazes around the room. 'You won't mind if we take a look around?'

'Do I have a choice in the matter?'

'Not really.' She gives him a chilly smile. 'You might want to pack an overnight bag.'

She designates me to supervise his packing while they tear the place apart. The rain pounds the windows as I watch him fold a couple of shirts.

'Even somewhere like this, you can't escape your past,' he says, putting some undies, socks, and toiletries into a holdall.

'Yep,' I say.

'If you don't mind me saying, you seem a bit old for this.'

'Old for what?'

'Nursemaiding me while they do the real cop work.'

'Familiar with this routine, are you?'

'Every few weeks in Perth I'd get the treatment. Then it followed me to Adelaide. Then Hobart.'

'Looking for sympathy?'

'No. But usually it's one of the younger ones that watches over me.'

I step closer to him. 'Finished packing?'

'It must be hard not being at the centre of things anymore.' He zips up his bag. 'I feel for you.'

*

By the time we get back to Havelock, it's late afternoon and growing dim. They've taken Patrick to the lock-up thirty-odd ks away at Blenheim for questioning. Just before finishing for the day, I run my tenants Gary McCaw and Steve Lomu through the system and – guess what? – they don't exist. So why did I let them move onto my property? Vanessa likes them and it seems I will do anything, any stupid thing, to keep her happy. I set off home for the eighteen-kilometre drive back up the Wakamarina Valley. There is a police house available in town but I choose not to use it and now it's Latifa's. If I do need to stay overnight for any reason, there's a room at the motel or the camp bed and sleeping bag at the office. At the turn off at Canvastown, so named for the old gold rush mining camp, a few cars are parked outside the Trout Hotel. A *For Sale* banner has been hanging off the front for over a year now.

I pass Charlie Evans tending his alpacas and breaking up straw bales. We exchange a wave. The further you go, up past the hobby farms and weekenders, the more remote, beautiful and feral it gets. Finally, turning into the drive, I see the dark blue ute parked outside the cabin and wonder again whether it was such a good idea to invite Steve and Gary into our lives. They're cooking something out the back on the barbecue and sinking a beer and they give me a nod. Inside, Paulie is watching a *Spongebob* cartoon on TV and Vanessa is humming to herself while she boils soup on the stove.

'Nice smell.' I slip my arm around her waist and she lets me.

'Thanks. The soup should be good too.'

'How's it been around here today?'

'Quiet. Paulie's been hanging out with the guys. Gary's going to show him how to trap eels tomorrow.'

'Is that a good idea?' Eels around here can be as thick as your arm and twice as long. Paulie gets squeamish and it bothers him and us for days afterwards.

'Gary's good with him. He's got a brother the same.'

'Okay.' I study her. 'You seem happy.'

'It's a bit of a worry, a tick on the calendar two days in a row.' She's right. It's been nothing but crosses since we arrived. There they sit in the top left hand corner of each day square, two years' worth of calendars, two years' worth of crosses. 'What about you? I heard it on the news: the little boy, those poor parents.'

'Nasty. We've picked somebody up but I doubt it's him.'

'Who?'

'A bloke out on the Sounds. He has a history back in Oz.'

'Be good if it was him. It'd be over soon.'

'That'd be nice.'

'Why don't you think he's your man?'

'Too much of a sad bastard. The bloke that's done this, he's a lot colder.'

She casts a warning glance Paulie's way. 'We need some wood chopped for the stove. Make yourself useful.'

Outside to split some logs. After I've chopped a wheelbarrow load there's a crunch of gravel behind me. I whip round. It's Steve. With a knife. My hand grips the wood axe tighter, I'm gauging distances, swing arcs.

'Can I ask a favour?' In the other hand he's got a whetstone. He rubs the knife on it.

'Go ahead.'

'We're out after a pig tonight. Wondering if it's okay to gut and skin it out the back in that empty shed?'

I think of Paulie accidentally wandering in on the scene. 'I don't think so, mate. The boy.'

'Your missus mentioned he'll be at school tomorrow. We can padlock the door overnight. We'll have it cleaned up, hosed out and away before he comes home.' A pause. 'She seemed okay with that.'

'I'll be out at work.' I shrug and nod. 'If Vanessa is happy, then I am.' But I'm not, and he knows it. I don't like being played off against my wife. Is it my imagination or does he seem to find this all a bit amusing?

'Cheers, Nick,' he says. 'Appreciated. There'll be a bit of pork in your fridge when you get home tomorrow night.'

'Thanks.'

'Bad business in town, I hear.'

'Yeah.'

'Catch the bastard soon, eh? We can set the dogs on him.'

'I'll see what I can do.'

'These people keep on getting away with it.' He strolls off, slapping the knife against his thigh. 'That Latifa? She reckons you're all right.'

A tick of approval from my junior. I'm blessed. 'Glad to hear it. How do you know her?'

'Latifa knows everybody.'

*

In the middle of the night I hear the ute pull up out by the shed. Low murmurings and grunts as a weight is lifted. A curse and a chuckle. The clink of chain against roof beam. I hear, or I imagine, a tear and a wet slop as the pig guts fall to the floor. The hosepipe. The shed door padlocked against idle inquiry by Paulie. I spoon into Vanessa and she presses back into me, clutches my hand to her breast. When I close my eyes again, I see blood dripping from the pig's torn throat.

4

About a hundred million years ago, New Zealand broke off from Gondwanaland and drifted away on its own scrap of geological flotsam. It lodged itself in a cold corner of the South Pacific, unmolested by the predatory mammals that evolved back on the super continent. Birds never learned to fly because they didn't need to. Tuatara skittered around the undergrowth unaware that their fellow dinosaurs perished millions of years earlier under that rogue meteorite. Snails and beetles grew as big as your fist. New Zealand was a Noah's Ark of weird critters long before Noah. Then, about eight hundred years ago, man arrived and things went downhill. As a destructive and relentless predator, we take a lot of beating. I reflect upon this, driving back down the valley past the cleared hills softened by the drizzling rain. I reflect upon it as I imagine that pig hanging up in my shed with blood seeping into the soil below. And I reflect upon it coming back into mobile range and my phone beeps with a missed call from Marianne Keegan who's been up all night grilling Patrick Smith.

'Nothing?' I say, returning her call.

'Nothing. Clean house. Clean computer. And, so far, no traces linking him to the scene. Some dodgy stains on the bedsheets but I could say the same about my fourteen-year-old.'

'And he can account for himself in the timeframe?' We have drive-by witnesses who can narrow the dumping of the body down to a couple of hours before dawn yesterday, and others who saw Jamie Riley up until around four thirty that fateful Monday afternoon at swim squad at Richmond Pool.

'No, but he doesn't really have to, does he? It's up to us to put him in that frame.'

Why is she telling me, the hick cop from Havelock?

'Are you releasing him?' I ask.

'Not yet. We've still got some science to run. And maybe a witness will come forward to answer our dreams.' She sniffs. 'According to the post-mortem, there was enough Rohypnol in the boy to stun an elephant. Hopefully he was sedated for those last few dreadful days of his life.'

Small mercies. I can't hold it any longer. 'Why are you telling me?'

A pause. 'You knew straight away, didn't you? You knew it wasn't Smith.'

'It's not rocket science.'

'I looked you up, got a colleague to do it in Wellington.'

'And?'

'Nothing. You don't have any history. But you walk from nowhere into a two-bit shitsville station and command a sergeant's salary.'

'You can't put a price on quality.'

'Are you a test?'

'What?'

'Are you testing me?'

You get that when you work in a big office in a place like Wellington: an inflated notion of self. I want to tell her the world doesn't revolve around her, that she should leave the paranoia and sociopathy to the crims. 'Like I said, it's not rocket science. Just a lucky guess on my part.'

'I'm going to find out who you are.'

The phone goes dead, the rain stops, and the sun comes out.

*

Two of Marianne's Wellington minions are waiting for me at the station, prematurely balding and podgy. They introduce themselves: Benson and Hodgson. They lodge in my brain as Benson and Hedges and I know I'll never get rid of that thought. Marianne wants me to go with them to check out the sad bastards and busybodies on the list I gave her. She wants me busy and under her proxy supervision. I'd do the same if I was poisoned by office politics and thinking her dark thoughts. So it's back out onto the highways and byways of western Marlborough. I can't decide who I don't want to talk to first – a saddie or a busy – but Benson has decided for me. There's a woman who lives up behind the school in Havelock and works part-time at the information centre. Good place for her too.

'Christine, got a moment?'

She's got the kettle on like she's been expecting us. I introduce her to Benson and Hedges. She gives us a cuppa and an Anzac and some tittle-tattle about who's selling drugs and who's hunting illegally on McCormack's forestry company land.

'But you already know all about that, don't you?' she says to me, pointedly.

Steve and Gary. She's got their number already.

'No strangers in town who've been asking weird questions at the info centre?'

'Sadly, no. We get weird questions every day but nothing that's made me shudder lately.'

'No rumours or theories from your network of informants?'

'If anything comes to mind I'll call you.'

So, apart from letting me know that she doesn't approve of my new tenants, Christine from the information centre proves useless to the inquiry. After that, we drive west past Pelorus Bridge and out towards the Rai Valley. Tourists are taking happy snaps of each other at the spectacular gorge.

I decide to be sociable. 'You know that scene in *The Hobbit 2* where the dwarves float down the rushing river in barrels? That was shot here at Pelorus Bridge.'

Hedges looks at me in the rear-view. 'Where's that accent from? I didn't understand anything there apart from "Hobbit" and "Pelorus".'

'Dudn't you? Sorry.'

We drive on in silence.

Perilously close to the school lives Rai Valley's own little Gollum. Michael Flower. His name only adds to the creep factor. Michael has form for photographing up the skirts of schoolgirls on public transport in Nelson and Christchurch. He has a neat disinfected house and a computer screen saver of the little girl from *ET* touching fingers with her alien friend. He also has alibis for the timeframe: visiting Mum in the aged-care home in Christchurch when Jamie Riley was taken, and sailing on the Bluebridge ferry back from Wellington when Jamie was found.

'Haemorrhoids,' he says, shifting in his seat. 'The doctor's going to sort them out next week. Round 'em up, brand 'em, and herd them back into the paddock.'

'Surely they can do that locally?' says Benson. 'Don't need to get on a boat to have your grapes harvested.'

'Long waiting list. I'm going private. Mum's paying.'

And the day goes on like that. Saddies ticked off, busybodies probed, petrol consumed. Last on the list for the day is a volunteer who works at the nature reserve out on the Sounds, trying to keep some flightless bird from the brink of extinction. And we strike gold.

'Yep, I was camped overnight waiting for an egg to hatch. It didn't. But I did see lights and boat movement over at Paddy Smith's jetty.'

'What time?'

'Around four in the morning. He's not normally an early riser.'

'You take that much notice of him?'

'I've been waiting six weeks for that fucking egg to pop. Not much else to look at, is there?'

*

Marianne Keegan is pleased with our work – it adds to another little breakthrough she's had today – and she sets about Patrick Smith with renewed gusto. She might be right after all, and I might be wrong. How good can it get? She's brisk, alert and pert, and I find myself admiring her posture – this dangerous woman who has declared her intention to dig up my secrets. As a special treat she even allows us to watch on the video link in the next room. Benson and Hedges decline, they've got stuff to be getting on with. I unwrap a sandwich from the canteen and make myself comfortable in the TV room. By now Patrick has a lawyer beside him, a young woman from the community legal centre – a nice-enough sort. The recording equipment is on and there's a minion taking notes. Marianne glances one last time at her file before closing it.

'Mr Smith, the night before last, about four in the morning, there was a boat at your jetty. Tell me about it.'

He shrugs. 'I haven't a clue. I was fast asleep.'

'There were lights. People moving about. Your bach is less than fifty metres from the jetty.'

'I'm a deep sleeper.'

'The noise and activity were noticed by someone over five hundred metres away.'

'Like I said.'

She slaps a printout on the table. 'This is the boat that was seen departing from your jetty at around four a.m. Can you read the name and registration number?'

'*Caravaggio*.' He reads the number. 'That's my boat.'

The lawyer frowns. 'Remarkable eyesight your witness has, seeing the boat number from five hundred metres, in the dark.'

'He's a bird watcher. He has binoculars. And there were lights on the boat.' Marianne turns back to Patrick. 'Where is it now?'

'I don't know. People borrow it from time to time. We're like that out on the Sounds. We help each other.'

'Anybody regularly borrow your boat?'

Patrick throws her a couple of names. The minion writes them down.

The lawyer stifles a yawn. 'Is that it? Only, you've been holding my client for nearly thirty hours and he's fully cooperated and answered all your questions.'

Marianne smiles. 'Bear with me a while longer.' She flicks through the file again and draws out a sheet of paper. 'Mr Smith, do you know a boy by the name of Denzel Haruru?'

'Boy? He's fifteen. He shaves. He's built like a prop forward. And ...'

'He's underage.'

'And, as I was about to say, he's exploring his sexuality.'

'Like all those boys at that fancy school of yours, hmmm? If I had a dollar for every time I've heard someone like you say something like that.'

The lawyer shakes her head. 'This is an ambush. I'm advising my client to say nothing further.'

Patrick pats her arm and nods at the file. 'What about him? What is he saying?'

'He says you sexually assaulted him and threatened him with further violence if he told anyone. He says you told him you'd done it before and would do it again.'

Patrick barks out a laugh. 'The boy can take care of himself. If I tried to touch him uninvited he'd break my neck. How absurd.'

'He said, you said.' The lawyer gathers her things and stands to leave. 'This is ridiculous. We're out of here.'

Patrick shrugs and smiles. 'As advised.'

'Sit down, both of you. I'm not finished.'

They sit. The lawyer has her coat and briefcase on her knee. She's making no attempt to take any more notes.

Patrick still seems amused. 'Just so you know, I'll be a "No comment" from here on in.' He nods at his lawyer. 'Again, as advised.'

Marianne squints at the clock on the wall. She's run out of steam. I'm disappointed. I was expecting a bit of Wellington wizardry. 'You're free to go for now, Mr Smith.' She turns to the brief. 'We will be talking to your client again, very soon.'

'I'll watch this space,' says the lawyer.

*

By the time I'm on the way home, it's dark. Moths and other insects flit in the headlights. The rain has stopped but there's still a strong wind shaking the trees. Frogs hop on the road and a couple of branches have blown down. Rounding the last bend, I hear the river below. The lights are on at home and in the rented hut. When I stamp my boots on the mat and slide the door open I hear Paulie crying.

'What is it?'

Vanessa is crouching in front of him, comforting him. She turns. 'They caught an eel today in the river. Paulie saw Gary getting it ready for dinner. Bit of a shock, wasn't it, love?'

Paulie nods and heaves a couple of brave shaky breaths.

'I knew this wouldn't work.'

'What?'

I thumb over my shoulder. 'The guys. We don't need this.'

Vanessa looks at me like I'm an idiot. 'Steady on, love. Worse things happen at sea.'

'Yeah,' says Paulie, looking at me like I'm that same idiot. 'Steady on, Dad.'

There's a rap on the screen door behind me. It's Gary, looking worried. 'Paulie, you okay, mate?'

'Fine, bro,' says Paulie.

Gary grins. 'That's good. Give us a yell or a knock next time before you come in the hut, yeah? No surprises then.'

Paulie gives him the thumbs up. 'Sweet as.'

I step out the back with Gary. 'You caught your pig then? I heard you come back last night.'

'Yep, and all cleared up, like it never happened. Wanna check?'

'I believe you.'

'The butcher is turning it into patties. You'll have a boxful in a few days.'

'Great.' I nod back towards the house. 'Paulie's taken a shine to you.' Vanessa too, I'm thinking.

'He's a great kid.'

'He's very trusting.'

Gary smiles. 'Doesn't get it from his dad, does he?'

'No, he doesn't. But you're still here and we're still talking, so that's good, isn't it?'

'One day at a time, eh?'

He goes back into the hut and there's a muffled conversation with Steve. A short harsh laugh at the end. What's so fucking funny all the time?

In the night I hear the wind tearing at the tin roof and the rain pounds down. I can't sleep and still can't rid myself of the thought that Sammy Pritchard has found me and sent out his emissaries. Gary and Steve: harmless wayfarers or lethal cuckoos in the nest? At one point Vanessa moans in her sleep. I can't tell whether it's from pleasure or pain.

5

The hills around here make their own clouds. The vapours rise from the trees to join the sky and it's like they live and breathe before your eyes. When I first came here, the pine-clad hills were part of the outrageous beauty and serenity of this land I'd fled to. How lucky it felt to be taking refuge in such a place. Now I am watching them being systematically reduced to debris and dust. A life force extinguished. These days I look at a view and wonder how long it will last.

Latifa digs deep for some sympathy. 'Yeah, must be tough, eh?'

We're on a boat headed out into the Sounds again. No detectives this time, just Latifa and me and some begrudging volunteers from Search and Rescue.

'You reckon?' I want to know what Latifa really thinks, I can tell she's just being polite this morning, which is not really like her.

'Yeah, having your lovely view spoiled just so someone can make a living.' She blows out a breath. 'Sucks.'

As we approach Patrick Smith's jetty, the smoke is still rising where his bach once stood. The driving rain has pretty much put the fire out but the emergency services volunteers set about finishing the job for sure. Patrick is sitting cross-legged on the ground beside what remains of Ginger.

'They shot my pig,' he says bleakly.

'Small towns can be rough when word gets out,' I say.

'Yeah,' says Latifa. 'I'll head over and supervise the volunteers while you fellas chat.'

'Where will you go?' I ask Smith, not really that interested.

He shakes his head. 'I'm not going anywhere.'

'This won't stop. You know that.'

He strokes Ginger's lifeless bristles. 'I'm tired of running away.'

Over at his charred house, some volunteers are grinning at the destruction.

'Nobody will help you rebuild, no tradies, no post, no deliveries, nothing. If I were you I'd pack my bags, call it quits.'

He blinks up through the rain. 'But you're not me, are you?'

There's a crash as the remaining wall of the bach caves in on itself. A desultory cheer from the workers.

Latifa returns, pen and notebook in hand. 'Ready to make a report, sir? For insurance, or something?'

*

Back at the station there are two messages waiting for me. District Commander Ford would like a word, as would Jessie James the Journo. I decide Jessie will be marginally more fun right now and, besides, I have a bone to pick with her.

'What's your boyfriend's name, again? The one on the mail boat?'

'Sergeant Chester, thanks for calling back.'

'I've just returned from the scene of a crime. We don't need vigilantes around here. We've already got enough on our plates right now.'

'D'you reckon he did it?' She laughs. 'When the mail boat's not running you can't get him out of bed before eleven. Nah, try Denzel and his mates. Much better bet.'

'You rang?' I growl, thinking she's probably right.

'Yes, I was after a comment.'

'Comment?'

'Mr McCormack, local businessman, major employer, supporter of local charities and community groups, and biggest advertiser for our paper ...'

'What about him?'

'He says you're not doing your job properly and wonders if you're in with the greenies. Care to comment?'

'No. Talk to Police Media.' I can half-guess what the DC wants now.

'I did. They put me back onto you.'

'Again. No comment.'

'That's fine, we can run with that. Police Media said they didn't have a photo of you on file, which is strange, but don't worry we snapped a couple off when you came back in on the boat today.'

'Don't –' But the phone is already dead.

I pray that Sammy Pritchard doesn't have some facial-recognition computer program trawling the net in search of me. Next, the DC.

'What's happening with Patrick Smith?' he says. 'When's he going?'

'He's not. He's staying put.'

'Then you'd better dampen down the fires of wrath and vengeance over there unless you want the extra paperwork.'

'I'm onto it.'

'DI Keegan isn't too impressed with you. What have you done to piss her off?'

'Nothing. I just guessed before she did that Smith is probably a dud.'

'She's digging dirt on you. You've made an enemy.'

'Maybe you can tell her I'm not part of some HQ boys' club conspiracy to bring her down.'

'That's what she thinks?'

'So it seems.'

'She might be touchy but she's good. Organised, methodical. You could learn from her, Nick. Try being nice. Try not being too smart.'

'What's to learn? I don't have any ambitions beyond making it to retirement age.'

'So try being nice anyway. Enemies don't make for a quiet life.'

'Fair point. Anything else?'

'Another enemy: McCormack. Again, try being nice. Find his vandal and grovel a bit.'

The DC is one of the very few people who knows about me, knows where I came from, knows why I'm hiding. If I'm going to have to be nice, I need a favour from him in return. 'The *Journal* is running a story about me, with pictures. We need to squash it.'

'Leave it to me.'

Just fifteen minutes later Jessie James is back on the phone and seething. 'Who *are* you?'

'What?'

'Who the fuck are you, getting my story spiked?' The phone dies. I imagine it being hurled across a room.

*

Out at the shoe fence they're dismantling the outer perimeters of the crime scene, although the body tent is still up and the numbered plastic markers remain in place. The road has reopened, in one lane anyway, and there's a queue of half a dozen cars waiting for the sign to spin from *Stop* to *Go*. The rain has cleared and the wind has dropped. Marianne Keegan breaks away from talking to a colleague and comes up to me.

'What are you doing here?' she says.

'I'm here to apologise, I think we got off on the wrong foot.'

'And?'

'And I was wondering if there was anything I could do to help.'

Marianne scrutinises me. 'Why?'

I decide honesty is the best policy, up to a point, and invite her to take a wee walk with me. 'I'm not on file because I'm in a kind of witness protection, it's an old and long story. That's the only reason. Nobody has sent me to white-ant you.'

'I know.' She lifts a palm. 'Not the whole tale. But the DC invited me to back off.'

I offer her my hand. 'Friends, then?'

She shakes it. 'For now.'

Her hand feels warmer today and I have this weird urge to hold on to it for longer than I should. I nod at the crime scene. 'Any developments?'

'No. Doorknocking is an epic undertaking in these parts. As usual, the only people coming forward after the media appeal are fruit loops.' She steps closer. There's a hint of tobacco and mints on her breath. 'We're focusing back in on family and friends. Neighbours, teachers, sports clubs. Whatever.'

'Good luck.' And I mean it. 'So, anything I can do?'

She looks at me appraisingly. 'Some extra help on the canvassing will always be welcome but everything is pretty much covered. Otherwise I'll let you know if I think of something specific.'

The DC will be proud. I seem to have been nice and undone at least one enemy – maybe too diligently; I'm not obliged to fancy her. There's definitely an attraction, like a possum to a gin trap, or a wasp to a bait. I start to leave.

'It was interesting though,' says Marianne, lighting up a ciggie.

'What?'

'My colleague in Wellington who looked you up. He's in IT, so he knows this stuff.' I wait for her to go on. 'He said someone else had been following your trail recently.'

'Who?'

'Dunno, but when he looked at the numbers and codes it seemed to be coming from the old country.'

'The UK?'

Marianne blows out some smoke. 'That's what he said, yeah.'

*

The sun pokes through as I wind back up through the hills driving full tilt Latifa-style. My first instinct was to phone home and tell Vanessa to get Paulie and just go, now, anywhere. But I resist. If they're that close, Vanessa won't be hard to follow and find. I've called the DC and brought him up to date, and he's promised to look into it. Sammy Pritchard can pay people, even official police people, to look for me. All I need to know for now is just how far behind they are.

Down to my right the river shimmers and birds dart among the trees. Sheep, cows, deer, and alpacas graze like nothing has changed. Pulling into the driveway, smoke curls from the chimney. Vanessa is hanging out some washing in the rare and probably brief sunshine.

She's pleased to see me. 'What are you doing home so early?' But then she looks at me again. 'What's wrong?'

I tell her. 'Where are the guys?' I ask.

'Up the valley. They got a job.' There's a fresh pile of firewood, neatly chopped and stacked by the back door. 'Gary did it,' she says. 'This morning, after breakfast.' She shakes her head and hurries indoors, waving sandflies from her face. 'What happens now?'

'I don't know. We're trying to find out more. Whether it's something or nothing.' I look around the house, fresh cut flowers in a vase on the table, newly filled jars of jam waiting for their lids to pop and seal. 'Maybe you and Paulie should go somewhere for a while until we know.'

She laughs, short and bitter. 'I knew it couldn't last.'

'It might be nothing.'

She lifts her eyes to me, blazing and tearful. 'It usually is. You've been looking over your shoulder ever since we got here. You keep a gun under your pillow. You jump at sounds in the night. You're suspicious of good people. You're poisoned, Nick.' She waves her hand out the window. 'You can't even enjoy the fucking view. You're just waiting for someone to take it away from you. And you wonder why I put crosses on the calendar and why Paulie is so fragile.'

She storms to the bedroom, grabs a case and starts packing. I follow her. 'I'd love for this to be yet another false alarm but I can't take that chance. The police have a safe house in Nelson. A week or so. Then ...'

'Then what?' she says, taking the address from me. 'More of the same?' She gets a bag for Paulie too. 'I'll pick him up from school and go straight on from there.'

I follow her out to the car. She slams the door and winds the window down. 'A week. Sort it out, or sort yourself out, for all our fucking sakes.'

6

It's a summer's evening, sunny but cold, and still light at nine o'clock. I'm in the back of Sammy's Audi with Marty, and he's taking up more room than he needs. We're off for a curry in South Shields, it being Friday and Sammy being a man of strict habits. Vanessa is getting sick of me spending all this time with Pritchard and his crew, and she let me know as much before I came out tonight.

'How long do we have to put up with this, Nick?' She pokes my recently acquired beer gut. 'Hanging out with those sleazy, drunken thugs. Coming home at all hours smelling like a pub ashtray, and for what?' Paulie is in the background playing with his iPad and trying not to listen in to yet another of our simmering rows. 'They're scum, Nick. The world is full of them and you're not going to change that. They'll never go away.'

'It's my job, love. It's what pays the bills.'

I shouldn't have said that, she's already pissed off at having to go half-time at the school to take up the extra childcare load with Paulie while I fraternise with society's worst.

She opens a kitchen cupboard and rattles some pots and pans. 'Use the spare room when you get back, and keep quiet. I need a good night's sleep bringing up Paulie on my own.'

The coast road is busy with people heading out on the weekend lash. The North Sea is calm and unusually blue, and seagulls wheel and settle on the limestone stacks at Marsden. Sammy is in the front seat next to his driver-cum-bodyguard, a muscly Indian lad who's done one of those specialised defensive-driving courses. Sammy has been quiet, which is not like him at all; usually the prospect of chicken vindaloo and a cold

Stella has him bubbling over. Like many men of his age up here, life revolves around his growing stomach as the adventures and distractions of youth recede. I glance down at my own recently poked belly and wonder how much of it I can blame on the undercover job.

'Pull over, Vikram,' says Sammy.

The driver pulls up in the car park at Marsden Grotto. Sammy gets out and we all follow. He waves Marty and the driver away; he only wants to talk to me. I see a smirk cross Marty's face as he leaves. Sammy strolls on a few more yards, then plants himself next to the low fence overlooking the sea stacks and those squawking gulls.

'Fucken hate scenery, me. Happy to drive past it, like.' He turns to me. 'You?'

'Aye, I don't mind it, Sammy. Bit of fresh air and that. Smashin'.'

'Our lass loves it. She wants me to buy a cottage in the Lakes.'

'What did you say to her?'

'Fuck off, pet.' He shakes his head. 'Remember when this was just the old proper Marsden Rock?'

'Aye,' I say.

The sea stack collapsed in on itself a few years ago. People accommodated the transition. They just called it Marsden Rocks for a while instead of Marsden Rock. Resilience and adaptability, it's the key to survival in the north-east. Then when they demolished the smaller pile a year later it went back to being one diminished Marsden Rock again. Geologically speaking, it was all a bit of a non-event.

'Not the same is it?'

Well, no. I can see people on the beach a hundred feet below, kids scrambling on the shingle. Sammy nudges me, his arm drifts up around my shoulder. One good shove and I'm gone. He takes a step forward and brings me with him.

'Everything alright, Sammy?' I try to make it sound like a casual inquiry from a mate.

'You grow up, and life throws these uncertainties at you. Does she fancy me? Will Sunderland avoid relegation again? Who'll be their manager this year?' His hand slides from my shoulder to the back of my neck. 'Who's with me, who's not?'

My eyes are watering with the chill wind. I wonder how many seconds it takes to go from up here to down there. 'Death and taxes, Sammy.

44

Somebody said they're the only certainties.'

'Aye, and with the right accountant you can even beat one of them as well.'

'I didn't know Alfie was *that* good.'

Sammy laughs. 'Twat.' He turns to face me. 'I always thought Marsden Rock was one of those certainties. Or maybe I didn't. But once it collapsed I realised I'd been taking it for granted all these years. Know what I mean?'

'Like the Berlin Wall–type thing?'

He prods me in the chest. 'Spot on.'

'Cold for July,' I say. 'Are we going for that curry or what?'

He steps closer. His face fills my vision. 'Marty doesn't trust you.' There, it's out.

'Aye?' I say. 'Marty doesn't trust any bastard though, does he?'

'He thinks I should send you packing.'

A seagull rides the updraft, screeching, and a wave breaks on the beach below. 'And what do you think, Sammy?'

He claps me on the shoulder again. 'I think Marty's a miserable twat. Loyal, like a poodle, and just as fucken vain.' He chortles. 'He's jealous. He was the only pretty boy around here. Then you come along looking like you belong on a horse with one of them ten gallon hats. Square jaw, shoulders like a swimmer on steroids. Fucken Cowboy Joe. No wonder he thinks you're a cunt.'

As we reverse out of the car park I notice Sammy staring out of the windscreen at Marsden Rock. We head off for that curry.

7

Steve and Gary are bemused by the turn of events.

'Bit sudden?' says Gary who comes bearing a bag of lemons from the farm down the road. He's looking around the room as if I'm kidding and Vanessa's going to jump out from behind a door.

'Tell the truth, we had a bit of a row.'

'Ah,' says Steve.

'They for us?' I say, pointing at the lemons. 'Thanks.'

He hands them over. 'Yeah, sure. Anyway we'll leave you to it, eh.'

They back out and I pour the lemons into the fruit bowl. There's more murmured conversation and that low harsh laugh again. I'd love to send them packing but when, if, Vanessa comes back, she'd be furious.

I bring in the washing that Vanessa hung out earlier and fold it and put it away. There's some leftover soup in the freezer. I get it out to thaw. Stuff needs fixing: a broken venetian blind, a screen door that keeps coming off its runner, paint chips, a loose board in the balcony rail. I put the radio on and twiddle the dial but it's all static and crackle up here. And no mobile signal. We've got satellite internet at unearthly prices so if Sammy's men come calling I can send an email: *Help :(* Or post an update on Facebook: *They found me LOL.*

The sun drops behind the hill and the river changes colour. It's a beautiful view but Vanessa's right; I'm just waiting for someone to take it away from me. Paddy the Paedo's got more balls than me. He's made his life out on the Sounds and he's not going anywhere.

There's a rap on the flyscreen. It's Steve. 'Gary's cooking up a couple of patties. Want one?'

You're suspicious of good people.

'That'd be great.' The frozen soup goes back in the fridge. There's a bottle of Pinot Noir in there from down south. 'Do you guys drink wine?'

Steve grins. 'If we have to. Just to be sociable, like.'

The patties are good and the view seems even better from their hut. The sandflies and mosquitos are bearable. The wine goes down well and we push on with a few beers. Gary and Steve explain the intricacies of pig hunting to me, how the dogs work together and how it's all done on GPS.

'What about the old traditional ways?' I'm mildly disappointed and my voice is a bit louder than usual. I'm getting steadily pissed.

'Like a noble savage?' says Gary. He pokes the spatula at the barbie where more patties sizzle. 'Time and place for all that. Right now we just want to eat, right?'

'Right.' The second pattie melts in my mouth.

We talk about women and how it's all really complicated and that. They praise Paulie, and Gary tells us a little bit about his kid brother.

I'm nodding in recognition. 'Man, we had all these dreams, and then, bang.' Looking out at the view my eyes have blurred. 'I mean yep, we love him of course and he's really great but, you know.'

'No buts, mate,' says Gary. 'You can't afford to have any buts. Does your head in.'

'Yeah.' I take another swig of beer and feel like hugging him.

A few more beers later, I stumble back to the house, vaguely aware that I might have invited myself along on their next hunting trip. Slug back two large glasses of water and hope for the best in the morning. I climb into our big cold empty bed and stay there pretty much the whole weekend.

*

On Monday morning driving back down the valley to work, I still haven't heard anything from Vanessa. In mobile range, I try her number but it goes through to messages, again. There's a yellow sticky note on my desktop, a missed call from Dickie McCormack. I'm just about in the mood for him.

'Sergeant Chester, Havelock Police, returning your call.'

'I'm impressed. Not everybody can pull enough strings to bury a *Journal* story. That's more my territory. Maybe I've underestimated you, Sergeant Chester.'

Stay friends. You don't need any more grief right now. 'I'm sorry for the lack of progress on the vandalism inquiry, Mr McCormack. That dreadful murder has been occupying most of our resources, as I'm sure you'll appreciate.'

'Yes, of course.'

'But now that the investigation is in hand, I'm able to give your matter due priority.'

'Fantastic. Much appreciated. I understand the strain you're under these days.'

I explain my conversation with Charlie Evans and how I don't think he did it because he's constrained by his housebound and terminally ill wife.

'It hasn't stopped him making trouble before.'

There's obviously no point in appealing to his empathy. 'Anybody else come to mind?'

He tuts. 'Forget it. These things have a way of working themselves out.'

I want to give him the lecture about not taking the law into his own hands, but I know it will only inflame things and he'll ignore it anyway. 'As you wish, Mr McCormack. We'll continue our inquiries and keep you notified of any developments.'

'Yeah, right.'

Not quite entente cordiale. More like a fragile ceasefire.

The phone goes, it's Latifa, short on breath and running. 'Coming your way, All Blacks beanie, camo t-shirt. Get outside and stop him!'

All Blacks beanie and camo t-shirt? That's half the population of NZ. I run outside and there he is: two metres tall and a hundred kilos. Raging Bull, coming right at me. 'Stop!' I say. 'Police.'

He fields me away with a face palm and I land in the camellia bush as Latifa streaks past. 'Denzel. Fucken stop, now.'

He doesn't.

Latifa is in range and brings him down with a textbook rugby tackle. He screams in agony.

'Get it off, get it off!' Denzel is pulling at his pants, trying to undo them.

'What the fuck?' says Latifa. 'Stop it! That's disgusting!'

There's a nice smell coming off Denzel while he's screaming: herbs, gravy, sage and onion stuffing. When his pants are finally undone, we see that there's a crushed hot chicken in there and the gravy has scalded him.

'He nicked it from the supermarket,' says Latifa, unnecessarily.

Jessie James pulls up on her Vespa with her iPhone ready. 'Denzel, dude. Legend. Nice wee smile for the camera?'

*

Denzel Haruru has been sent to the nursing post to have his burns checked. We'll charge him later. I might have a word too about the attack on Patrick Smith's property. The DC calls. He wants to know how things are going.

'Okay.'

'That's good. No word on the trace yet. We've been in contact with your former colleagues at SOCA and they're onto it too.'

'They'll need everything in triplicate just to make a phone call these days. While we're all ferreting around in cyberland, somebody in the real world is heading my way.'

'I understand your frustration and your concern, Nick.'

No, he doesn't, but I don't say it. Instead I thank him and tell him I've made peace with Marianne and, up to a point, with McCormack. 'Anything from DI Keegan on the Riley case?' I ask.

'Nothing. This guy's ghosted in and dumped the kid there with no trace, no sightings, zilch.'

Another statistic. Another pair of shoes on that sad fence. Ford promises to be in touch about any developments on the computer track. I try Vanessa again but she's still not picking up so I call the officer in charge of the safe house.

'Yeah, they're both fine as of the last check-in fifteen minutes ago.' Maybe he can pass on my message for her to call me back? 'Absolutely,' he assures me.

Latifa pops her head around the door. 'Denzel's back, the injuries aren't as serious as we hoped. Wanna talk to him?'

Denzel is in the interview room with a responsible adult, Uncle Walter, who seems too old to be Denzel's actual uncle. Maybe it's a generic wise-old-man title. Denzel is sore and feeling sorry for himself. Latifa has already formally charged him on the shoplifting matter. He can expect a summons either to the children's court or juvenile justice team some time relatively soon. I want to talk to him about Patrick Smith.

'That old pervert? What about him?'

'A few nights ago his house was burned down and his pig got shot.'

'Good,' says Denzel, and Uncle Walter nods in agreement.

'Did you have anything to do with it?' I specify the day and time range.

'Nah. I was at home. Asleep in my bed.'

There's amusement in his eyes and we both know it was him and his mates. Uncle Walter is staring at the wall high behind me. Maybe he was there too.

'No more,' I say. 'It stops now.'

Denzel lifts his chin at me. 'Look after your own, you lot, don't you?'

'You've had your fun and made your point. I don't need the extra grief and the work. You make life hard for me, it'll come back on you.' I give Uncle Walter a look. 'We all want an easy life, don't we?'

He knows what I'm on about. He nudges the boy and there's a nod of acknowledgement.

Latifa throws me a wink as they leave. 'You did well there, Sarge.'

*

When I get back to my phone there's a message from Vanessa.

'We're fine. They're looking after us well here.' A pause. 'Look, I think it's best if you don't come over, not yet anyway. Paulie's out of sorts and I need some time to think about all of this.' A slight crack in the voice. 'Let me know once you've found out what's going on. We'll talk then.'

I try calling her but it's back on voicemail.

She's right of course: we need time out. Until I know who's behind the attempted trace on me and what, if any, significance it has, we're in limbo. I can't make everything better in a snatched half-hour reunion with police bodyguards looking on and Paulie needing his share of attention. I am poisoned. Sammy's men don't even need to find me. We're already fucked, my family is imploding. It's been a slow burn ever since I went undercover and started acting like those people I'm paid to despise. Sure it's not the kind of vengeance that Sammy Pritchard wants, where only blood will do. But this is no kind of life. We were on the fast track back in the UK, and I was seen as a rising star. Now here we are half a world away in the backblocks waiting to die.

Speak for yourself, I can almost hear Vanessa say. Speak for your damn self.

I step outside the station for some air. It doesn't know whether to rain or shine today. The wind shifts and changes, one moment a refreshing breeze, the next snapping at you irritably. The clouds are in a hurry. Maybe there is more rain due. I haven't checked the forecast in a few days. Usually it's part of the routine when there's little else to do. Our work is tied closely to the weather: traffic accidents, flash floods, landslips, stealing, domestics. Firewood and food thefts are our winter trade, domestics come when the weather is too warm, or too cold, too anything in fact.

I'm feeling cornered and I want to lash out. I want to go out and find Sammy Pritchard's men. Front up.

Do it, then, I'd say to them. Do it now, do your worst. Or fuck off and leave me alone.

But it's me that's the problem. Me and what's inside my own head. I can't run away from that, and it won't let me be. I need something to numb it down, dissolve it.

A drink would be good.

I check my watch: too early.

Marianne Keegan calls to let me know they found Patrick Smith's boat in Okiwi Bay on the outer edge of the Sounds. 'Burned out.'

And there's a road back from there into town. 'Any worthwhile traces?' I ask.

'No. But there's a few empty beer cans in the near vicinity and some weed roaches.'

'Denzel?'

'It's a possibility. When it comes to mention of him and his family, people seem to clam up.'

'They're very influential.'

'Well, just thought I'd keep you in the loop.'

'Thanks.'

'We're winding things back a bit here in Blenheim. The main incident room's in Nelson, given that's where the kid's from. We'll base everything back there.'

'Shipping out, then?'

'Blenheim was always going to be temporary and Havelock doesn't have the facilities.'

Why's she justifying this to me? 'Makes sense.'

Her voice drops a notch. 'Fancy a farewell drink before we close shop in Blenheim?'

The wind changes again. 'Yes. Why not?' I say.

8

I wake up in a motel in Blenheim with Marianne Keegan's smell on me and a guilt as crushing as my hangover. Of DI Keegan, there is no sign. I fuzzily recall mention of a scheduled early-morning Skype appointment with her angry, boring, disappointing husband. Her Scouse accent thickening as she did hilarious impressions of him, and her laugh getting louder and dirtier as the wine went down. A button slipping open on her shirt. Her noticing me looking and not minding when I undid another.

I shower and dress gingerly, then leave the motel, wondering where I parked my car. Down the road, I remember now, outside the Thai place. Beyond the fact that I've betrayed my wife of fourteen years, I do have a vague recollection of last night being refreshingly carnal.

'This is a really bad idea,' I told her as she slipped her key into the door of her room.

'Yes,' she said, pulling me in, tugging at my belt and buttons. 'It is.'

I lifted her shirt and my hands slid up inside. 'Really bad.'

'Shush.' She pushed me back on the bed and climbed onto me.

Folded into each other with an intensity and abandon I haven't felt in so long. Mine borne out of fear and recklessness. Hers. God knows where hers came from.

I'm not convinced that I wouldn't do it again, given the opportunity. And so ends another cop marriage. I buy a can of sugary L&P and chuck it down. I can't turn up at work looking like this, so I phone in, citing private business, and head home for a change of clothes and a shave. There are no messages on my mobile. Vanessa is sticking to her guns and it would seem there are no developments on my phantom tracker from the UK. At home is a note from Gary saying they're out on a job and there's some leftover dinner in the fridge if I want it. Quick check.

It's fish. My stomach lurches.

Another shower, a shave and a change of clothes later, and I'm back on the winding road down the valley. The road is wet and wind buffets the car. As I pass Charlie Evan's place, he waves me down.

'You look shocking,' he says.

'Touch of flu.'

The wind tears at his hat and he needs to blink against the rain. 'One of my alpacas got shot last night. With a crossbow.' He wipes the rain from his face. 'She was still alive when I found her this morning. All that time in so much pain.'

'Now?'

'I've put her down.'

'Get the vet in, keep the bolt. Photograph and document everything.' I gun the car.

'That's it?'

'I can stand here in the rain and sympathise. I can call the vet myself if you like and requisition a forensics team who probably won't make it out here for a few days. Or I can go and see the bloke who did this.'

'McCormack?'

'I'll keep you informed of the progress of our inquiries.'

*

The offices of McCormack Forestry are in Trafalgar Street in Nelson, seventy-odd ks west of Havelock. It's a winding road, even for these parts, and it's not a good idea to go the speed I'm going in this kind of weather but I keep my foot down anyway.

Nelson is a nice enough little town, a port on a big tidal bay, surrounded by mountains which are snow-capped for half the year. What's not to like? McCormack's got a suite above a bank with a view over the river. Somebody has taken a permanent marker and inserted 'DE' before the 'Forestry' on his sign. His receptionist is not sure about me.

'Send him in,' I hear him say on her telephone. She does. He's drinking a bottle of mineral water and looking out of his window. 'Don't tell me, you've found the vandal?'

'Somebody shot one of Charlie Evans' alpacas last night. With a crossbow.'

McCormack winces. 'Nasty.' But he's wearing that same half-buried smirk Denzel had when I asked him about Paddy Smith's place. Two of a damn kind. 'Well, thanks for the update,' he says. 'I'll be sure to tell your boss you're excelling at the PR these days.'

On his wall are pictures of him with government ministers, with one of the All Blacks, and with some kids from a community project holding a big cardboard cheque. Among them, a younger Denzel with a big cheesy grin. Surprise, surprise.

'Tell my boss whatever you like,' I say over my shoulder, 'but I'm going to fucking have you.'

On my way out through reception I find myself in one of those annoying dances where you're trying to get past somebody but you both move the wrong way to try and make way for the other. My dancing partner has a twinkle in his eye and a name badge that says Feargal.

He grins. 'If you like, I'll be the lady and you can lead.'

He's lucky I don't punch him.

*

In Nelson I drop by HQ. I feel the need to say something about last night. Marianne Keegan has a recently bedded look about her which stirs up a nice memory. She takes me down the road to a coffee shop and we scurry in out of the rain. She makes it clear she's only got about fifteen minutes. I'm not sure where to start, so we talk about anything else for a while, moving the air around.

'Don't worry about it,' she says, finally. 'It was nothing.' She gets a dirty little half-smile on her lips. 'Well, not quite nothing.' She sips her flat white. 'These things happen sometimes.'

I nod. 'Yeah.' Tap my teaspoon on the rim of the cup. 'So how'd the Skype call go with your hubby?'

'I failed the performance appraisal. Got a list of KPIs to address before I go home for the weekend. Anything else?' she says, checking her watch.

Something is ticking in my brain but I can't grab hold of it through the fog of my hangover. 'How's the investigation going?'

She shrugs. 'One of the boy's uncles has a Social Services flag on his file but he lives up on the North Island and hasn't been to visit in years. There was a teacher at the boy's school last year who had an allegation made against him but it's pretty flimsy. We'll be talking to both of them.'

'Anything like this happened anywhere else? Young boys, the Rohypnol and that?'

'We're trawling the archives.' She pats my hand. 'It was nice you dropped by.' A mischievous look. 'If you ever find yourself in Wellington at a loose end.' A wink and she's out the door.

*

It doesn't take long for the DC to come after me. I'm driving past Rai Valley school on the way back to Havelock and my mobile goes during the brief pocket of coverage.

'Nick, that wasn't helpful.'

'McCormack?'

'He's not worth winding up. He's a vengeful and malicious man. He actually makes time for his grudges. He enjoys them.'

'He arranged to have some livestock shot on my patch. Payback to the bloke he thinks vandalised his boat. We can't make exceptions on the vigilante stuff. If it's not okay for Denzel and his mates, it's not okay for McCormack either.'

'Yeah, sure, but hopefully that's an end to it now?'

'Hope is a wonderful thing.'

Ford takes a deep breath. 'Hold that thought because I've some bad news on your cyber stalker.'

'Tell me.'

'SOCA traced the anonymous inquiry to a computer in Northumbria Police HQ. The access code was bogus. It had been hacked. Then they traced it back to some student who lives in Newcastle upon Tyne. A so-called "hacktivist" doing some freelance work to supplement his grant or whatever it is they have over there.'

'Loans,' I say, watching the rain dot my windscreen. 'Student loans.'

'Right. They kicked his door down and asked him who he was working for. He didn't have a name but he recognised a photo they showed him.'

'Go on.'

'Martin Stringfellow: you'll know him of course.'

'Yes. We go way back. How much did the hacker know?'

'He had your name, address, and the photo from the ID card we issued you. He had your driving licence details.' There's a pause. 'Nick. You still there?'

'I'm here.'

9

We've all had way too much to drink by the time we leave the Shagorika Indian Restaurant at Seaburn. Wind gusts off the beach over the road and there's sand in it. The North Sea is in the air we breathe: salt, oil, a hint of sewerage. Marty wants to go on to the house in Hendon where they keep some of the girls they've trafficked. There's a new one from Moldova he's taken an interest in. He wants me to come along.

Sammy shakes his head. 'Leave him alone, Marty. He's got family.'

Marty puts his arm around my shoulder. Speaks softly, cajoling. 'Arse on it, and only fourteen. Ha'way man, I tell you, you don't know what you're missing.'

I'm really looking forward to putting Marty away. Even more than Sammy. A plan is slowly taking shape. Slowly, because Sammy is so, so careful. Nearly all his business interests now are legit: the sex trafficking we can't track anywhere nearer to him than some Polish bloke in Manchester he occasionally uses for labour subcontracting. In the last few years he's dropped the drugs and leaves that to the riffraff on the estates, although he is believed to make the odd investment in a consignment via a six-link chain that would evaporate in court. No, we need nothing less than Sammy on tape ordering a murder.

We've been grooming a lad from Middlesborough who's hard, knows no fear, and is cocky enough to think he can topple Sammy. He's not clever enough to share and cooperate as Sammy has learned to do. We've been helping the lad along, feeding him a few victories and successes: putting some of his smaller rivals either out of business or behind bars, allowing some of his drug shipments through and blocking those of his competitors. We've also been putting malicious words in his ear about Sammy: the lack of respect thing always works well. And vice versa. Sammy is rattled enough to want to do something, and Marty has been egging him on, nettling him. Sometimes the way Marty is, I wonder if he's working for our side as well and nobody has told me.

'Nah, thanks mate, I'll leave that to you.' I extricate myself from his grip. 'Enjoy yourself.'

'She must be worth it, this lass of yours. Vanessa?'

'Marty.' A warning growl from Sammy.

'You'll have to introduce me one of these days, Nicky boy.'

Sammy's driver pulls up to take him home. 'Need a lift?' Sammy is offering me a way out.

'Ta, mate but I can walk from here. It's just up the hill.'

He gives Marty a look. 'Be good. See you tomorrow. Nine sharp. Got some heads to crack.' The Audi disappears up the coast road.

'Looks like it's just you and me, Nicky.' Marty is back in my face. 'Sure you don't want to come down to Hendon? It's free. On the house.' There's Stella and lamb gosht on his breath. A glint in his eye.

Maybe I could just do him now. A nut in the face. A stamp on the head. Call in some backup to finish him. Dump him in a builder's skip and blame it on the lad from Middlesborough. He knows I'm thinking such things, he knows I want to hit him. Go on, his eyes say, try it.

'Spit it out, Marty. What's your problem?'

'Problem?'

'With me.'

'Wrong end of the stick, bonny lad. I'm everybody's mate.' He lights up a ciggie. 'What about you? You my mate?'

'Nah, I think you're a twat. But I'm staying civil for Sammy's sake.'

'No need. Sammy's a big lad. He can look after himself. He's the one keeping you in one piece, more like.' He steps forward. 'Gan on, have a pop if you like. I won't tell.'

And potentially blow a two-year operation.

Big picture, bigger fish. 'Some other time, maybe.' I start to walk away.

'Aye, back home to the bosom of your family, bonny lad. Enjoy them while you can.'

I turn. 'Meaning?'

He pulls me into a drunken hug. 'Exactly what I said.' And he plants a lagery kiss on my lips.

A car pulls up, someone I've never seen before. 'Put him down, man, Marty. You don't know where he's been.'

Marty jumps in the passenger seat. 'Oh, I think I do though.' He winks and cocks his thumb and forefinger at me. Fires an imaginary gun and blows the smoke from the end.

10

Driving back over Pelorus Bridge I think again about *The Hobbit 2* and those dwarves in their bobbing barrels at the mercy of the tumbling currents and natural forces way beyond their control. By the time I get back to Havelock the rain has ceased but the hills are still shrouded in mist.

The DC has promised to move Vanessa and Paulie to an even more secure place: a self-contained apartment within police HQ normally reserved for visiting brass, high-risk politicians and VIPs, or occasions exactly like this.

'But it's just a temporary measure until we get you out of the country.'

'No,' I hear myself say.

'Leave it to us, Nick. We'll arrange everything.'

'No.'

'That's not your call, mate. We decide what's going to happen.'

'Get the family safe but I'm not going anywhere.'

'This isn't *High Noon*, Nick.'

'It isn't going to stop, wherever we go.'

'We'll talk about this later. Go home, pack a bag, and get back over to HQ before dark.'

No, I say again in my own mind. 'Right. Okay.'

Back at the station I grab some paperwork and sign out one of the bigger guns from the cabinet.

'What's up?' Latifa says.

'Nothing.'

'Liar.'

But I've got a job for her. 'Pay Denzel a visit. If he's got a crossbow, take it off him. Bring him, and it, into the station. Tomorrow'll do.'

Up the valley towards chez nous. Passing Charlie Evans' place, I see the vet's car is at the gate and two figures are crouched in the far corner of the paddock. Back home, Steve and Gary are there, off work because the weather is shit. I feel obliged to tell them to leave, and why. They see the look on my face and sit me down.

'Beer?' says Gary.

'Got any L&P?'

He hands me one and I tell them pretty much the whole tale. 'You guys might be best moving on. You don't need this kind of grief.' I shrug. 'Sorry.'

They're taking the story in. '*Bring Me the Head of Alfredo Whatsisname*? Awesome. Have to check it out.' Steve seems to find it all very entertaining. 'And this Sammy bloke is in prison now?'

'Yep.'

Gary is pensive. 'And this other bloke, the two IC, is coming after you. Marty, you say?'

'Stringfellow,' Steve adds.

I nod and sip from my can. 'Sammy pulls the strings, decides how and when, and Marty does his bidding.'

Gary leans back in his chair. 'And so far this Marty's killed a sixteen-year-old girl and a couple of junkies.'

'Has he ever been in a proper fight?' asks Steve.

'Stringfellow.' Gary snorts. 'Sounds like he should be wearing bells on his shoes.'

'And green tights,' says Steve. 'Court fucken jester.'

'This bloke isn't funny,' I say. 'He'll bring some nasties with him.'

'Yeah, Bigfellow!' says Steve.

Gary is chuckling. 'And Longfellow!'

'Not forgetting Baaaadfellow!'

I find myself laughing with them. Bravado does that to you. It blinds you to reality.

*

We've agreed it's probably worth them bringing the dogs back up here, and the guns. Their ute is parked across the gate and the black mastiffs, Sonny Boy and Richie, are caged up in the back, having been quieted by Steve. The shit weather has passed through. It seems unlikely that anything will happen so soon but already I feel comforted. There are more pork patties on the go. We're on the back verandah and the river is rushing below, swollen by the rain.

'You don't have to do this,' I say again, cramming the meat into a bun.

'We know that,' says Gary. 'But we've been up and down this valley for weeks. There are plenty of spare cabins but you're the only one who let us have one.'

'To be honest that was down to Vanessa. If it had been up to me …'

'She's a good woman,' says Steve. 'Doesn't matter if you're a cunt, we'll do this for her. And the boy.'

'Cheers,' I say.

'*Kaitiaki,*' murmurs Gary.

'What?'

'Guardians. Keepers.' Steve lifts his mug of tea. 'Goodfellows.'

Darkness creeps in and the sandflies fall away. The trees are full of noise and my jumpiness returns. I try to keep it in check. 'How do you guys know each other?'

They share a look. Steve nods permission for Gary to speak. 'We were in prison together.'

Hence the false names. The cop in me can't help himself. 'What for?'

'Gang stuff. When we were younger. North Island.'

'What changed?'

'We got too old for it. Got out.'

'How long ago?'

'Ten years, fifteen?' Gary squeezes some sauce on his pattie. 'Worked the fishing boats for a while. Then the FIFO in Oz. And now we're here.'

The dogs are growling. We tense up. Steve wanders over to check. All around us is the blackness of night in the country. I unclip my gun. Gary chews on his bun. Relaxed. Too relaxed. It doesn't seem right. All of a sudden the dread and suspicion returns. Have I got him and Steve badly wrong? There's a scrape of gravel behind me and adrenalin jolts through my system.

'Dogs must've scented a boar,' says Steve. 'They're fine.'

This could go on for days, weeks, months. A time of Sammy's or Marty's choosing.

11

The next morning is bright and sunny with a wreath of low, wispy white cloud around the hills. Steve and Gary have some fences to mend down near Okaramio on the way to Blenheim. We agree that waiting around on tenterhooks for Marty Stringfellow is not practical. We have jobs to do, lives to live. So I head into the office for another chat with Denzel, who once again has Uncle Walter with him. Latifa is on my side of the desk.

'Alpacas?' Denzel acts confused. 'Me?'

'Same bolts you use in your crossbow, Denzel.'

'Same bolts everybody uses in their crossbow.'

'We've got forensics people who can match a particular bolt to a particular weapon.' That's if we get around to taking it that far.

'Lots of people use it,' he says. 'It's like what you call a community resource.' A street lawyer at fifteen. Uncle Walter looks proud.

Already I feel the day slipping away from me. 'School not on today?'

He coughs. 'Got the flu.'

'Richard McCormack is a bad sort.'

'Who?' says Denzel.

I try appealing directly to Uncle Walter. 'He might pay well when he wants to, but he uses people. He's trouble.'

Uncle Walter leans forward. 'We've been dealing with trouble for a long time, Sergeant. We can take care of ourselves.' He spreads his big hands on the table between us. 'We don't need to be told how to live our lives. We've tried trust and cooperation and you lot always let us down. We've learned to make our own luck.'

There must be about two hundred years of history crammed into his words but I'm more concerned with the here and now. I fix back on Denzel. 'Paddy Smith was strike one, the alpaca is strike two. No more,

Denzel, or I'm coming down hard on you.'

Latifa lifts her head from her notepad. 'You forgot about the hot chicken, Sarge. That's strike three.'

I look at Denzel. 'You're on borrowed time, mate.'

Him and me both.

*

The DC is on the phone and wants to know why I didn't return to HQ last night as instructed.

'It's complicated.'

'No, it's not. Get your arse over here.'

I tell him relations with my wife are strained. Close proximity in protective custody will only make things worse.

'I go home to that every night. Toughen up.'

'I can't keep running and hiding. The best way to end this is for me to stay in plain sight and let him come and get me. If we get in first, it's game over. If he gets in first, then the same. Either way.'

Silence. He's thinking. 'I might need you to sign a waiver or something. Occupational health and safety, mate. It's getting like that these days. Even in New Zealand.'

'Happy to.'

'But we're still keeping your family under lock and key.'

'I'll talk to Vanessa.'

'I already did that. She's cool. You must have really pissed her off.' There's the sound of rustling at his end. 'She's made a list of things she needs. Wants you to bring them over. Good opportunity for you guys to have a big talk?'

'Yeah.' I ask him to read out the list but he says life's too short and he'll email it instead. 'Tell her I'll bring it over tomorrow. I'll phone ahead.'

'Make sure that talk is a good one, Nick. "Tell *him* this, tell *her* that." I'm not really up for being a go-between. Below my pay grade.'

I promise him my best endeavours. 'Is there a way of getting advance warning of suspicious people coming into the country?'

'You've got to be joking. We put the welcome mat out for hunters and psychos. We've got people coming from all over the world to kill things here. Think you're special?' Ford realises he might have gone too far. 'Sorry. Not funny. I'll see what we can do.'

Latifa, standing in my doorway, is bursting with curiosity. She cares, and she deserves more, so I invite her down the road for a walk.

'I made some enemies in my last job. It's possibly caught up with me.' I give her the lowdown.

'Shit,' she says mildly, as if I'd just told her I had a flat tyre. 'You mean like *Donnie Brasco*?'

'Who?'

'Johnny Depp and Al Pacino, Johnny's in the FBI, he infiltrates the mob. Al Pacino, the Godfather dude, treats him like the son he never had.'

'Yeah, something like that. Look, you might have to manage a bit more of the day-to-day for a while.'

'Easy.'

I change the subject. If everyone knows my life story, half of Marlborough will be ringing Sammy Pritchard to see if there's any work going. 'That was quite a speech by Uncle Walter. What do you make of him?'

'Oh, he's alright. All bark and not much bite. He's bitter.'

'Anything specific?'

'A son in prison, a daughter in the psych ward, family tragedies over the years. It gets to you after a while.'

'It would.'

'He's a good friend but a fierce enemy. Watch yourself.'

'How's he related to you?'

She bristles. 'He's not. We're not rabbits you know. They're just neighbours. Same iwi.'

'And you know Steve and Gary too?'

'Again: good friends, fierce enemies. Watch yourself.'

'Same iwi?'

She rolls her eyes. 'No, they're from up north. They're hiding as well, like you.'

'Who isn't?' I wonder out loud.

'Me,' says Latifa, proudly. 'I'm not.'

*

We walk the length of the marina, past McCormack's catamaran, which has a tarp over the offending graffiti while he awaits the attentions of a master craftsman to restore it to its full beauty. Circling back around on to the main drag, I call into the petrol station to arrange an overdue service on my car. In the magazine rack there's a choice of lad mags plus *Logger* and *Hooked on Boars*. I ponder briefly on that welcome mat for the world's hunters and figure that if I was Marty I'd be thinking along those lines too – whoever you send, all they need to do is merge in with the crowd. I opt for a pie from up the road at the bakery and take it back to my desk to plough through some paperwork for the next couple of hours. Charlie Evans has lodged his complaint and evidence about the dead alpaca, and the bolt has gone off to the labs for testing against Denzel's crossbow. It'll be given a low priority. There's been a spate of firewood thefts as winter lingers and spring teases. A fight in the Havelock Hotel last night resulted in a man needing stitches after a bottle was smashed over his head. Even though there were only six people in the bar, nobody saw anything. The CCTV was on the blink. A shadow falls across my desk.

'Patrick. What can I do for you?'

'Do you have the application forms for a gun licence?' There's a redness about his left cheek. Perhaps the beginnings of a bruise.

'Constable Rapata can probably get you one at the front desk.'

'I asked to speak to you.'

I dig around in the filing cabinet behind me and find a form. 'You can do it online these days.'

'Not out on the Sounds, you can't.'

We go through the checklist. 'Any criminal convictions?'

'No,' he says firmly.

'Purpose of licence?'

'Hunting and pest control.'

'Don't do anything silly, Patrick.' I hand the form over and gesture at his swelling face. 'What happened?'

'I got slapped in the supermarket.'

There's a large bundle under his arm. 'What's that?'

'A tent. From Blenheim. Nobody would sell me one here.'

'You're going to live out on the Sounds in a tent?'

'Nobody will help me rebuild.'

'You can't say I didn't warn you.' Over his shoulder, Latifa is taking a great interest. 'It'd be easier all round if you moved on, mate.'

'I'm sure it would. But life's not always about the easiest option.'

'Bring the form back when you're ready and with the appropriate fee.'

He starts walking out the door.

'Patrick?' He turns. I'm tempted to say good luck but I remember those kids whose trust he betrayed. 'Be careful.'

*

The afternoon drifts by like any other during midweek and I slip back up the valley and pack the things on Vanessa's list. After a long hard day on the fences, Steve and Gary are stuffed and opting for an early night. We agree that being slaughtered in our beds tonight mightn't be the worst thing that could happen. Blasé? Maybe, or plain fatalistic. It's not easy remaining on high alert 24/7.

I've put a pile of Vanessa's and Paulie's things in an open suitcase. It feels like the end of a marriage. Hardly sudden, she's been unhappy ever since we had to leave Sunderland. That evening, after the shit had just hit the fan.

'That's it? That's all you've got to show for two years of cosying up to Mr Fucking Big? And now we spend the rest of our lives looking over our shoulders?' Paulie followed us along the beach at Seaburn, our words mercifully whipped away by the biting winds as he chucked a ball for Buster. Vanessa shook her head. 'What a waste.'

'What's done is done. We need to focus on the future.'

'What future? Tell me what it is we have to look forward to, Nick.'

But I didn't know then because I hadn't been told.

And here we are now today – a headlong dive into yet more unknown. I try to imagine the practicalities of a life of separation, of custody visits with Paulie. The worry about what will happen to him when we're dead and gone seems even more acute tonight. That rainy-day fund we've set up for him, which drives us to take in lodgers and scrimp and save and stick with this job when something different and lower profile would be safer. But being a cop is all I know and being a security guard or some other loser is shit money.

I think about my mad night with Marianne Keegan. What possessed me? I know I've pressed the self-destruct button. I'm feeling terrified and sad and out of control. But there's something else in there too. Liberation? Excitement? Hysteria, more like.

I finish packing Vanessa's stuff and close the case.

12

Sammy's driving like a madman. He's got the lad from Middlesborough trussed up in the boot. We're in the lad's car, a Mitsubishi Magna, and Vikram is following in Sammy's Audi.

'Piece of shit,' snarls Sammy.

'The car or him?' chortles Marty from the front passenger seat.

'Shut up.' Sammy reaches down to change gears, forgetting it's an automatic. 'Fuck.'

I've never seen Sammy like this. After eighteen months I've begun to kid myself that he's not that bad, and that Marty is the real vicious piece of work. And Marty is of course, but this Sammy I'm seeing tonight is the one we were warned about. The real Sammy. Dangerous and unpredictable. Looking from the back seat into the rear view I see his eyes, small and black and mad.

'Fuck you look'n at?' Sammy has clocked me.

'Nothing, mate. You sure you want me along on this? I mean …'

'Yes, I am sure.'

Marty twists his neck like a boxer entering the ring. He seems happy tonight. He reaches for the dashboard. 'Music, Sammy?'

'Fuck off.'

We're heading south towards Seaham, along winding country lanes. They used to lead to the pit villages that have given way to soulless housing developments. They might have cleaned the old black beach up now that the coalmines have closed, and for coastal property it's pretty cheap, but really it's still as shite a place as it always was.

'Where are we going, Sammy?'

He barks out a nasty little laugh. 'Cunt in the back. Might be based in

Middlesborough but he's a fucken Monkeyhanger.'

Hartlepool: a bit further south. That's where we're going. The story goes that during the Napoleonic Wars with France, a ship got wrecked off the north-east coast and the only survivor was the ship's monkey. The good citizens of Hartlepool, having not ever seen a monkey before, tried and hung the creature as a French spy. Daft sods. We've never let them forget it. I wonder if the lad in the back faces the same fate.

'Monkeyhanger. Monkeyhouse.' Marty can hardly contain his mirth. 'You've all got something in common.'

'Pull your head in, Marty.' Sammy doesn't like his old school being taken in vain. It was hardly Eton or Rugby but, to him, Monkwearmouth School is a place of character-formation and kinship. Marty starts to hum the theme tune from *The Monkees*. Sammy snarls again: 'Shut it.'

We pull into a lay by. It's dark, there's nobody around and Sammy wants me out of the car. A cow moos in the adjacent field as Marty joins us. Sammy presses the key fob and the boot clicks open.

'Take a look,' says Sammy.

'What?'

'Take a good fucken look.' Sammy grips the back of my neck, wrenches the boot open and presses my head down towards the bloody mess and the stench of piss and shit. Even though he's still alive, there's a deadness about the eyes of the Middlesborough lad. There's no fight or spirit left in him, he's lost the will to live. Brendan's his name. Brendan's face has been sliced repeatedly by Marty's blade, and there's so much blood on him it's impossible to distinguish the actual wounds. All I care about right now is whether or not Brendan knows who I am. He shouldn't, others are running him. But you never know.

'What's your point, Sammy? What's this got to do with me?'

He leans in close to join me in the gore. His teeth an inch from my ear. 'It's a message, son. Nobody should ever take me for granted.'

'Nobody does, Sammy. Least of all, me.'

Sammy presses my face right up to Brendan's. I can smell the fear on the wretched lad's rank breath. 'This cunt did. And there's others out there. Lining up for a pop at me.' The grip on the back of my neck tightens. I think I can feel vertebrae fusing. He's rubbing my nose in this poor bastard's blood. 'Marty reckons you should be in there with Brendan. That right, Marty?'

'Aye, Sammy.' Marty chuckles. He's loving this and I realise I've blown it. Sammy really does not trust me any more.

'But I like you, Nicky. You do your job, and no matter how hard we look we can't find anything on you. That right, Marty?'

'Aye, Sammy. So far.'

'I love that little lad of yours, and Vanessa, she's a canny lass, and I really can't believe that anybody would do anything to put them in harm's way. You wouldn't be that stupid.' He twists my head around so I can see him. 'Would you?'

'No way, Sammy. Fuck's sake.'

Brendan's blood-filled eyes stare back at me from point blank. As long as I'm getting the grief, he's not.

'As I thought.' Sammy releases me and slams the boot lid down on Brendan. 'We'll just drop this lad off and then home again, home again, jiggety-jig. Fancy a Stella back at the ranch after?' A shaky nod and smile from me. He chucks the keys to Marty. 'You drive.'

Marty salutes. 'Monkey see, monkey do.' He is extra cocky tonight. Pushing his luck. Maybe he senses what we all do: the beginning of the end of Sammy Pritchard.

We leave the Mitsubishi in a car park down the sea front in Hartlepool. I breathe a sigh of relief. The lad in the back has been badly hurt but hopefully he'll survive. Sammy's driver Vikram takes us home.

The next day I learn that Sammy, through an intermediary, had paid some kids to set fire to the car overnight.

No survivors.

13

Thursday, and I decide to get the Vanessa thing over quickly. Is that what it's become? The Vanessa Thing. She's waiting for me as I step out of the lift on the top floor of police HQ and walk through the plain double doors that lead to the apartment suites. I hand over the suitcase of clothes and the box of books, laptop, DVDs and video games. She looks a million dollars, freed from the burden of me and my fears. There's a grace and confidence about her I haven't seen for a long time. She hugs me but it feels sisterly.

'DC Ford tells me you're staying put.'

'Yep,' I say.

We go into the kitchen, which is kitted out with expensive appliances and has a great view out over the port. I say yes to a coffee.

'Is that a good idea?'

'The coffee? Yeah, I think so. It's my first today.'

She smiles. 'Dickhead.'

It's nice to see her smile. 'I'm sick of hiding. You're right, it's no life for us. It's led to this.' My hand flaps at the space between us. 'Us.' I run out of words.

She looks at me sadly. 'I think the way we are has been a long time in the making. Long before we went into hiding.' She stirs milk into the coffees. 'But you're right, it didn't help.'

'So what now?'

'Why's that up to me, Nick? I haven't a clue.' She stands with the kitchen counter between us. She's looking fantastic and I feel lost. 'The DC says we can stay here for a month. We'll get a specialist tutor in to help out with Paulie.'

'How is he?'

'Upset. Out of sorts. He's at school today.' She sees my look of alarm.

'With minders.' She pulls up a chair. 'We'll be fine for that month. After that we need to make a decision about where to go. What to do.'

'What are you thinking?'

'I'm not thinking anything. Maybe in the coming month you'll have sorted this thing out. Or you'll be dead. Either way, we'll cross that bridge.'

She's harder than I realised. Or maybe just pragmatic. 'Can I call during that time?'

'Sure. I may or may not want to talk to you but there's no harm in trying, is there?

I'm feeling resentful now. The traffic seems all one-way and I say as much.

'Welcome to my world, Nick.'

*

It's early afternoon by the time I get back from Nelson to Havelock. There's a package waiting on my desk. A USB drive and a handwritten compliments slip: Derek from Marina IT, apologising for the late arrival of the CCTV material. Apparently my request for footage from the twenty-four hours preceding the vandalising of McCormack's boat was superseded by, and confused with, DI Keegan's request a day later in connection with the discovery of Jamie Riley's body. During his scheduled fortnightly email-tidy, Derek found my original email and promptly rectified the mistake. Where would we be without the Dereks of this world? I study the footage and, even though there are comings and goings at the marina, none of them seem related to the vandalism of *Serenity II*. That's strange. How can the cameras not have caught somebody coming in with a spray can that previous night and doing their worst? Maybe it was done much earlier but not noticed, the boat being at the far end of the marina. Or maybe they kayaked in under cover of darkness on the camera's blind side? Should I request CCTV going back further? No matter, McCormack has had his justice even if Charlie Evans and his poor animal had nothing to do with it. Let sleeping alpacas lie.

Outside across the road there's a green and purple Jucy rental campervan parked outside the Blue Moon backpackers. A young bloke sits in the driver's seat sipping a takeaway coffee. He notices me and lifts his cup in salute. I nod in reply. I'm twiddling my thumbs again. Maybe I should tidy my emails? No. I'm being hunted by ruthless gangsters and their hired assassins. I've let my marriage crash and burn. I've had a tempestuous one-night stand with a colleague. All in less than a week. I am not the kind of man who tidies his emails.

The rest of the afternoon is spent tidying my emails, and my desk, the filing cabinet, the office. Latifa comes to lean in the doorway and watch me. She lets me know the excitement is all too much and she's contemplating putting in a transfer request.

*

Back up the valley road I drop by and let Charlie Evans know what's happening.

'Thanks,' he says. 'But Denzel's not the one who should be getting into trouble for this.'

I shrug. 'Que sera. Maybe he'll dob on McCormack if things look too sticky?'

'And we'll be tangled up by his lawyers for the next two years.' He shakes his head. 'Anyway, these things all get worked out.'

That sounds suspiciously like more tit-for-tat. Sometimes the police seem an unnecessary frivolity around here. 'How's Mrs Evans?'

'Beatrice? Today's a good day. She likes to look out the window at the sunshine.' He's adrift, broken his moorings. 'It's our anniversary. Thirty-five years.'

'Congratulations.'

'She never wanted to come here. She's a city girl, Christchurch. Hated it for the first two years, couldn't make friends. She's from a clever family. Used to talking about big stuff, you know? Politics, art, literature. Not much call for that around these parts.' He smiles sadly. 'I don't know why she married me.'

'You're a good man, Charlie. A catch for any girl.'

'You reckon?' He takes off his beanie and rubs his brow. 'She did settle though. Made the best of a bad lot.' His eyes fill. 'Been lucky, I guess, haven't I?'

On up the valley there's a lamb standing in the road, squeezed out between the wires with its mum bleating on the other side of the fence. I stop the car, hop out and try to shoo it back but it runs off in the wrong direction, even further away. I leave it to its own devices and drive off.

There's no sign of Steve or Gary or the dogs. Somebody else has been here though and made no attempt to disguise it. The lid of the mailbox is open, the toolshed door is ajar. I unclip my Glock and go to take a look. The door creaks. It's dim inside. I'm not the most handy of men so I can't tell if the tools have been tampered with, although even I wouldn't have left that many lying around on the bench. And I'm pretty sure the fishing rods were on the hooks on the wall. Now they're on the floor. Kids? Thieves? The lawnmower is still there, and the weedeater. The big plastic storage boxes have been rummaged through, lids left askew.

Back outside. It's still light but the sun is about to disappear behind the hill. The wind has picked up and across the river the pines are swaying like a gospel choir. The door to the cabin is also open and I peek inside. The place is a mess but I don't know whether that's Steve and Gary's doing, or someone else's. The main house is locked. When I look around inside, it seems untouched. Have some scungy campers from Butchers Flat had an opportunistic look around the place and found nothing much worth stealing? Maybe. But your average camper these days is either Gen Y or Grey Nomad, both often with more money than sense and no need to do this shit. Real low-lifes? Ten kilometres up the valley road is too much like hard work for them. Am I letting my paranoia get the better of me? Well, not really. Marty Stringfellow has paid someone to find out where I live. Fact.

Gravel crunches on the road outside. A vehicle comes to a stop. Another Jucy rental van. The window slides down.

'Hi.' It's the same guy who was drinking coffee outside the backpackers this afternoon. His companion is another male about the same age.

'Hi,' I say.

'Butcher Flat. Is this way, yes?' A German accent, I think.

'Yeah, about another five kilometres up. Can't miss it. The road stops there.'

He waves at the scenery. 'Beautiful here. Beautiful evening, too.' You're right, I'm thinking. There's Charlie Evans down the road with his own worries and still able to reflect on how lucky he is. Maybe I could learn from him. I nod as the window whirrs back up. 'Great,' he says. 'Thank you.' The camper makes dust on the unsealed road. Mountain bikes hang from the back, they look top of the range. That's Gen Y for you.

Steve and Gary pull into the driveway. 'All this traffic. Like rush hour in Nelson,' I say.

Steve nods at the departing dust trail. 'Who was that?'

'Tourists. Germans. Looking for Butchers Flat.' The guys look tired. 'Tough day?'

They nod. Gary lets the dogs out of the cages for a stretch. 'Clearing a section the other side of the river, down near the hotel.'

'Forestry?'

'Yep.'

I tell them about the tool shed and about their digs. Is that mess theirs? Steve isn't impressed. 'No, mate, we learned to stay tidy in prison.' He nods inside the cabin. 'Somebody's been in.'

'Kids? Campers?'

'They'd have to be game,' says Gary. 'We've put the word around that we're here and they know we're not to be messed with.'

'But campers?'

'They've usually got more money than us but you never can tell, can you?' He summons the dogs and pats them back up onto the ute tray and into the cages.

'Maybe we need to be a bit more on our toes tonight?'

'Maybe,' says Gary, pulling his dirty shirt off. 'I'll just have the one beer.'

*

There's no light pollution up here so there's a million stars and they're bright as hell. Steve pointed out Scorpio, his sign, before heading off for his sleep shift. Gary has been snoring for a few hours now. So it's me and the dogs, Sonny Boy and Richie, who give off the occasional low growl but I'm learning not to get too excited by them.

I'm parked on the front verandah with a shotgun, facing the road, lathered in insect repellent and with a thermos of coffee on the go. If anybody comes I think it's unlikely they'll do so from the other side, which is too steep and too hard. Unless of course they're seasoned professional hunters and they just love that shit. But I'm also hoping the dogs will kick up a fuss whatever direction these people come from. It's three a.m. The guys gave me the last pre-dawn shift because they figured I needed the sleep if I'm to fulfill my duty as an officer of the law, but I barely slept anyway.

So why the deliberate declaration of intent? No attempt to hide the fact they'd been here. Part of the mind games? Let him know you've been, I can imagine Marty saying. Wind the bastard up. Turn the screws. The dogs growl again. The scent of a boar? They don't stop. One of them changes to a short bark of warning. The second follows suit. The cabin door opens and Steve is there with his hunting rifle, Gary close behind with the axe.

'What's up?' he says.

'Dunno.'

Gary shushes the hounds and we all strain to see and hear whatever or whoever might be out there. Seconds go by, a minute. Nothing. Then I become aware of a dancing red light at the corner of my vision. I yell out a warning but it's too late and a crack rings out. We've all hit the deck. Laser sights, probably night-vision too, we're utterly exposed. I'm bracing, holding my breath, waiting for a bullet to tear into me.

'Gary, Gary, you okay? Steve?' A grunt and a curse; it's Steve. But where's Gary? 'Gary, you okay?'

'Fucken bastards, why'd they have to do that?'

He's standing on full display by the ute tray, and he doesn't care. I see now – or rather, I hear. Only one dog is barking. Gary pulls open the cage and flicks on a torch. Sonny Boy's brains are all over the place.

14

None of us slept for the rest of the night but we weren't shot at anymore. He'd made his point. Night-vision, laser sights, cool as fuck. And no sounds of a departing vehicle. He must have tramped through the bush into his position. As the sun rose, Gary and Steve took turns digging a hole in the back paddock and they laid Sonny Boy in it. Now we're having breakfast on the balcony looking out over the river.

'Nice view,' says Steve, putting down his cereal bowl.

Gary hasn't said a word. It's a reversal of roles and Steve seems comfortable stepping up. He's right, it's a glorious morning and the river is green and so clear you can see the bottom from here.

'It's not too late to move on,' I say. 'These people mean business. It's not your fight.'

'It is now,' says Gary.

I throw up my hands. 'It's hopeless. He can just sit in the bush at night and pick us off one by one. That's what he's telling us. That's what he's telling you. He's giving you a chance to get out while you can.'

'What would *you* do?' Steve takes a spoonful of corn flakes.

That safe house in Nelson HQ is looking better by the minute. I'm realising the futility of my *High Noon* stance. But he's not asking what *will* I do, he's asking what *would* I do, if I were him. Not the practicalities or the realities, but the principle. It's a good question. I hardly know these blokes. Would I put myself in the firing line for them? They hardly know me, and they did exactly that.

'Well?' says Gary.

'I'd bugger off on the next plane to South America and leave you guys high and dry.'

'That's not very nice,' says Gary, grinning for the first time since his dog died.

'Yeah,' says Steve. 'Hurtful. Disappointing.'

'Sorry.'

'Good job we're doing this for your wife and kid and not you.' Gary lifts his coffee mug. 'Pour us some more.'

By now it's lukewarm sludge but he doesn't seem to mind. 'The fact remains. He or they are still out there, ready and willing to do us damage.'

'I think that's the problem.' Gary drains his cup and chucks the dregs over the rail. 'We're hanging about letting the enemy control everything. If people give me the shits, I usually go looking for them.'

*

Steve and Gary have packed up the ute as if they have taken the hint and are shipping out. Ostensibly they've gone, along with the surviving dog. It's me on my lonesome. Just the way Marty and Sammy would like it. I head off down the valley for a day at the office.

Patrick Smith is waiting for me with his gun-licence form and his money.

Latifa shakes her head. 'I advised the gentleman that I could deal with the matter but he insists on talking to you.'

I nod and go through to the other side of the partition. 'Patrick.'

'No offence to your colleague, it's just ...' He looks rattled, there are bags under his eyes.

'Where are you sleeping these days?'

'On the jetty. But somebody's doused that in petrol too. Probably be gone by the time I get back.'

'Denzel?'

He nods. 'Sometimes he sails by and yells abuse or fires off a couple of shots in the air. Other times it's his mates. It's open season.'

'I can't control these people, you know that. It'd be best if you just went away.'

He nods but the answer is no. 'How long before I get the licence?'

'I'll get back to you as soon as possible. We need to run the usual checks.' Something nags at me. 'Were you and Denzel ...' I search for the word, '... close, in the past?'

'Yes.'

'He doesn't seem to like you very much now.'

'No.'

Latifa is pulling faces in the background. I give her a job to do which necessitates pissing off somewhere else. Then I turn back to Paddy. 'How did it happen?'

'You really want the details? Is this you being prurient or is it relevant to my gun licence?'

'I don't know. You keep asking for me every time you come in here. So indulge my curiosity.'

He pulls up a seat. 'Denzel was always hanging about out there on the boats with his grandad. The boy was never at school. Sometimes I'd wave as they were passing, tell him to get back to school and stop wasting his life.'

'And?'

'They'd both laugh. Tell me to eff off.' A glance into the distance. 'Denzel started bringing biscuits for Ginger. Sometimes the old man would drop him at the jetty and go off fishing, pick the boy up on the way back.'

'That's when you got ... close?'

'We got talking. Yes.'

'What about?'

'His life. Mine. Mainly his, kids are pretty self-focused aren't they?'

'Go on.'

'He's got a lot of anger in him. I think Walter is an angry man too. He's passing it on.'

'And one day?'

'He was very sad, I comforted him, it led from there.'

'You're a fifty-year-old man, Patrick.'

'You don't understand.' He looks reproachful. 'You asked me to indulge your curiosity. I just did.' He allows himself a smile. 'And that's what Denzel asked me to do for him.' He seems to be enjoying the memory.

'And now?'

'Now he's even angrier.'

No shit. 'What was he sad about in the first place?'

'It was an anniversary. Some family member, a young cousin I think, drowned or something like that.'

Latifa returns and fixes Smith with a frown. 'You're still here?'

'I'd better be going,' he says.

The door closes behind him. 'It's not going unnoticed,' says Latifa.

'What?'

'Giving him the time of day. Town like this, people expect you to take sides.' She can see I'm not in the mood. 'Just sayin'.'

*

I phone the DC and tell him about last night.

'They shot a dog?'

'Yes.'

'So you don't need any more persuading to get yourself in here.'

'That wouldn't change anything. They'll be waiting when I come back out again.'

'Wrong. Next time you come out you'd have a new name and a new country.'

'What's the choices? Australia: too obvious. Canada: too cold and polite. America: too gun crazy. True, they like their guns here too but not in that same weird fetishistic way. Anywhere else speak English?'

'England. Oh, wait.'

'So you get my point.'

'The Falklands. Hong Kong. Look Nick, everywhere speaks English these days. Just be an expat somewhere.'

'And within six months another whizkid with a laptop has found me and it all starts again. The only way to stop this is to stop them.'

'You're going back to Sunderland?'

'Not a bad idea, but I want to try something else first.' I explain the half-baked scheme to him.

'Waste of time. It'll never work.' A pause. 'Anything I can do to help?'

I ponder the matter. 'A heads up on any undesirables who've recently arrived would still be welcome.'

'I'm onto it.'

'By close of business?'

An audible sigh, and the phone dies.

*

Ford comes up with the goods by four thirty on Friday afternoon.

'We've only let about sixty undesirables into New Zealand in the last two weeks or so. Not bad going, considering.' There's a tapping of keys as he scrolls through his list. 'Most of them are Aussies, mind you, or returning Kiwis. But these two look like contenders.'

A Russian couple in their early forties. He's ex-army and now runs some import-export business. His name has been flagged on international databases for links to far-right groups, connections with Russian gangsters, and unproven accusations of war crimes in Chechnya.

'He's still allowed to fly around the world?'

'Nothing proven,' says Ford. 'The Hague takes decades to try war crimes and most of the Russian political hierarchy has links either to far-right groups or gangsters. Come to that, so do the Aussies and the Poms.'

'You reckon he's the assassin type?'

'Doesn't say so here but he certainly loves his hunting. Lots of photos of him on Facebook next to big dead animals.'

Sammy and Marty and the business chain back to trafficked Russian girls. It adds up. 'And they're in the area?'

'Flew into Auckland last week, shuttled to Wellington beginning of this, took the Interislander ferry the day before last. Hired a vehicle at Picton. I'll send you details and pictures.'

*

'Russian assassins?' says Gary.

'Awesome,' says Steve. 'That is just so fucken awesome.'

We're grabbing a beer in the Havelock Hotel and finalising strategy. I show them my laptop. 'They're staying at the Beachcomber Inn, Picton.'

'Nice,' says Steve.

'Armed, we assume. And dangerous?' Gary is sticking with L&P. He wants to be sober to avenge Sonny Boy.

'They have all the permits and all the gear, apparently.'

'Plan, maestro?'

'The Picton cops tell me they're still in situ in the hotel. She's having an aperitif and sunning herself on the balcony.'

'And your cop mates over there don't mind about our plans?'

'They don't know about them. But they'll be called away on a job by my boss in good time.'

'Sweet,' says Steve.

As the gateway to the Marlborough Sounds, the Queen Charlotte Drive has to be one of the most magnificent road journeys in the world. It snakes forty kilometres between Havelock and Picton, and around every hairpin bend there's another stunning vista of blue waters and green hills. Think Norway, think Vancouver Island, no – think Marlborough bloody Sounds. With the sun falling and shadows growing, the landscape seems all the more dramatic. Picton nestles near the mouth of Queen Charlotte Sound where the ferries come in from the North Island. With its docksides stacked with pine logs and its marinas clogged with gin palaces, I once again remember to appreciate humble little Havelock. I've never been a great fan of ostentatious wealth – it comes from growing up in Sunderland maybe – and Picton feels like a rich boaties' town. The guys seem to like it though.

'Pretty,' says Steve. 'Wouldn't mind living here myself, if I could afford it.'

'Yeah, nice,' says Gary, ratcheting his shotgun. 'For some.'

We park down the street from the Beachcomber. According to their credit card records, Andrei and Svetlana have taken a shine to the seafood place just round the corner from where we are parked. Going off the receipt timings, they tend to finish eating around ten-ish. Even cosmopolitan Picton will be quiet by then, and dark. We've borrowed a Kombi van from a mate of Steve and Gary; the one further down the valley who had room for their dogs and guns but not them. At just after eight, Andrei and Svetlana head to dinner, walking past the Kombi with arms around each other's waists and not a care in the world. They're fine and fit-looking specimens if you're into 1990s style and glamour, well-muscled beneath their tight-fitting couture.

'Fuck me,' says Steve, admiring Svetlana. 'Will you look at that.'

'Are they packing?' wonders Gary.

'Svetlana isn't,' says Steve.

I confirm that it doesn't appear so, with either of them.

'Crap assassins,' says Gary.

'Good,' I say. 'We're going to need all the luck we can get.'

At ten fifteen they come back and we jump out, push guns in their faces, and bundle them into the van. Nobody has heard or seen a thing. So far so good.

＊

Deep in New Zealand's lakes and along its meandering rivers, lives a monster. The New Zealand longfin eel is the largest freshwater eel on earth. They grow to two metres in length and weigh up to forty kilos. They have leathery skin, embedded with hundreds of tiny scales and covered with a thick layer of slime. They are extremely efficient hunters, relying on a hypersensitive sense of smell rather than sight to locate their prey. Their olfactory ability is several times better than the great white shark. Scientists have calculated that if just one teaspoon of blood was tipped into a lake fifty times the volume of Lake Taupo a longfin eel would be able to detect it. Eels, like their reptilian counterpart the crocodile, are classic ambush predators, concealing themselves and lunging at victims as they pass. To dismember a large animal, a longfin will first clamp onto a carcass with rows of small extremely sharp teeth, using the force of its jaws to achieve a vice-like grip. It then spins its body, twisting and rolling until a mouth-sized lump of flesh is torn away. Its stomach is highly extendable, and eels will feed until gorged.

'A real *taniwha*. A monster. Impressive, eh?' Gary puts the book down and smacks a mosquito on his neck. 'Good eating, too.' The beam from his headtorch dances over the bowed heads of Andrei and Svetlana who are kneeling shivering in the Wakamarina River with Steve standing guard over them. Their hands are bound behind them with cable ties.

'You are making a very big mistake,' says Andrei.

He's been remarkably calm throughout all this. Before we left Picton, I took their hotel keycard and grabbed their guns and passports and wallets and crammed them into a couple of cases. We dropped the guns down a ravine somewhere along Queen Charlotte Drive and Gary is going through Andrei's wallet now.

'Took me best part of a year to train up Sonny Boy. Best pigger on the South Island, I reckon.' He pulls out a wad of notes. 'That's going to cost you, mate.'

'We are tourists. Here for hunting and to look at real estate.'

'Anything take your fancy?' asks Steve.

'Take the money and let us go. We are not your enemies. We will not inform on you.' Andrei lifts his head and looks at me as, by the light of my own headtorch, I examine their passports. He must have guessed this is more than just your average stick-up.

'Who hired you?' I say.

'Excuse me?'

Svetlana says something to him in Russian, low and urgent. She's seen Gary pull a net out of the river. 'Oh, my god.'

An eel. I don't know if it's a longfin or a shortfin but it really is a monster. Meanwhile Steve is walking round them, shottie in one hand and a pan of pig's blood in the other. He's pouring the blood over their heads.

'You are crazy,' growls Andrei. 'What do you want from us?'

'Who hired you?'

'Nobody hired us, we are tourists. Like we said, here for hunting and to look at real estate.'

'This thing's a bit slippy,' says Gary. 'Can I let it go yet?'

'I know you are hunters. You killed his dog last night and you have been sent here to kill me.'

'Who killed a dog?' says Svetlana. 'Bastards.'

Andrei looks at me out of an eye dripping with pig blood. He seems amused. The eel is thrashing to be free. 'If I was here to kill you, you would already be dead. I am on holiday, my friend. You have the wrong people.'

Svetlana mutters to him again in Russian.

'What is she saying?'

'She is saying she wants to go home.'

'Why are you so calm, if you are not a killer? An innocent man would be tearing his hair out and pleading for mercy.'

He smiles. 'I was a prisoner in Chechnya for three months until they rescued me. Guns, cold rivers and threats are nothing new.'

I'm beginning to believe him. He is a killer but he's not my killer. Lights appear through the trees down the valley. Flashing and blue. How do they know we are here? Except, of course, it's the river below my property and this could only be DC Ford.

'GPS,' says Andrei, lifting his bound hands behind him. 'In my watch. If I don't respond twice a day it alerts my friends. Kidnapping is a big problem in Russia.' He nods at the approaching cars on the road above. 'You have some explaining to do.'

'Oh, shit. Better let the eel go, then eh?' says Gary. 'And here's that money back, mate. Sorry.'

Steve helps Svetlana up off her knees out of the river. 'Alright there, missus?' There's a stream of what I take to be Russian invective and she snaps her head back and butts him in the face. Steve drops, dazed, with a bloodied nose. 'Awesome.'

There are cops around us, Armed Offenders Squad, and this time it is us on our knees with guns at our heads.

The Russians are swaddled in blankets and led away.

'The eel,' says Andrei. 'Nice touch. You would have done well in Chechnya.'

15

'He laughed all the way back to Picton, apparently. Good sort, for a Russkie.'

It's Saturday morning and I'm in the DC's office, having spent a night in the cells at Nelson. Steve and Gary have been released and they're waiting for me at a cafe down the road. The Russians aren't pressing charges because they think it's a great dinner-time story. They've already posted on Facebook to that effect, along with a pic of them and the Armed Offenders Squad, and attracted over two hundred likes in the first hour. The DC and the security agencies are relieved. While it would be easy to scapegoat me, as I was behind the devilish plot, I couldn't have done it without the information supplied by them.

'You weren't really going to do that thing with the eel were you?'

'It was just meant to scare them.'

'Yeah, that worked well. And you still don't know who shot the dog.'

I have my suspicions and I'll pursue them later. 'Sorry for the trouble this will have caused, sir.'

He shrugs. 'I think we'll be taking a hands-off approach with the information flow from here on in.'

Fair enough. Change the subject. 'Have you seen anything of Vanessa?'

'I dropped in first thing this morning. I didn't mention your little misadventure. She's got enough to worry about.' He uncaps a bottle of water and takes a swig; it's his new regime he tells me, less coffee. 'Did you have your big talk?'

'Yes.'

'Went well?'

'Not as such. But we understand each other.'

He reaches for the bottle again. 'Fight for her, Nick. Don't throw it away. Too many cop marriages fail and it's too easy to blame the job. Give up, and it's another victory to the scumbags.'

I tell him I'm not ready to give it away yet, and I surprise myself because I mean it.

*

Latifa comes over to pick us up. We drop Steve and Gary off at the valley. They look like they need a good sleep. I tell them we've got a few things to sort out later this afternoon and they perk up. Then it's back down the valley road, Latifa-style.

'What the heck are you playing at, Sarge?' She's been talking to her Nelson colleagues who attended last night and she's angry. 'Russians.' She taps her temple. '*Porangi*.'

I'll look it up later but I'm guessing it means crazy. I grab the cissy-handle as she takes a tight turn at seventy. I'm not the only one who's *porangi* around here. 'Ease up.'

'Why don't you trust me? I'm not a kid.'

'What?'

'If there's people out to get you, ask for my help. You'll get it.'

'Okay. Sorry.'

'I could have helped ladle the blood.' She bursts into a laugh. 'Eels. Jesus.'

I decide there and then to let the guys have their sleep this afternoon. Latifa and I can deal with outstanding matters. 'Any other business overnight, or this morning?'

'Jessie James called wanting to know what the ruckus was up your way, last night.'

'What'd you say?'

'No comment.' She drops down to sixty for the next hairpin. 'And Paddy Smith on the phone, whingeing and wanting his licence.'

'Think we should give him one?'

'He *is* a citizen, I suppose.' She swerves to avoid the same lamb I encountered yesterday. 'Careful, baby, or you'll be on the dinner table sooner than you think. Go back home to mama. Maybe Paddy'll shoot himself. Do us all a favour.'

'Unchristian of you.'

'What he does is unchristian.'

'You said something yesterday about people expecting me to take sides. Anything specific, or just a generic warning about dealing with the likes of Paddy?'

We slow briefly at the Canvastown junction with SH6 before she turns right and guns it for Havelock. 'You should sit down and have a talk with Uncle Walter someday.'

No time soon, I fear. Life's too short to be glowered at.

*

We take two police vehicles and we do it in broad daylight.

Latifa hauls the shotgun out of the steel cabinet in the boot. Being a rural cop where guns proliferate, she's allowed to keep one near for occasions just like this.

'I hope you've got this right, Sarge.'

'Yep, me too.'

I'm pretty confident, and a rental firm background check plus a glance at their social media pages tells me all I need to know. Precious few hunters these days don't post their successes on Facebook. But these guys? Not a peep. They're either remarkably modest, or it's not animals that they hunt.

We've left the cars blocking the only track in and out, and walked the last fifty metres, hugging the shade. I have my pistol at the ready and Latifa wields the pump action. It's a beautiful day, bright and cool and just a soft wind. There's only one vehicle parked here, it's still early in the season. Birds twitter and we can hear the river beyond the trees.

As we approach the van, there's a scrape from inside and a figure rushes through the doorway. Latifa is immediately in hot pursuit. I'm about to shout a warning to her when a second figure emerges, sleepy, tousled. He feels my gun in his neck and lifts his hands.

'Oh, fuck this,' says Latifa, halfway across the paddock and puffing under the burden of her shottie. She stands her ground. 'Police! Stop or I will shoot you!'

The other figure slows to a halt. Turns.

'Hands behind your head, kneel on the ground.'

No movement.

'Now!' Latifa advances, gun levelled.

The hands go up but one seems to be reaching back over the shoulder, fingers curled.

Latifa takes another step forward. Even from this distance I can see her grip tightening around the trigger. 'Last chance.'

There's a burst of guttural sounds from my prisoner and Latifa's quarry does as he's told.

They are brothers, Joachim and Tobias Otto from Aachen, according to their papers. Cleanskins. No flags on their records and their weapons and hunting permits are all in order. Joachim is the one who spoke to me outside my home and waved his coffee cup at me when parked outside the backpackers hostel across the road from the station. The mountain bikes are propped against a nearby tree. Dusty, no doubt, from the track through the pine forest across the way from my home. Under the bench seat in their Jucy rental van are two hunting rifles with laser sights and night-vision and dum-dum bullets that explode on impact. Latifa is kneeling on the back of Tobias, cuffing him, having taken the hunting knife from the scabbard he had down the back of his shirt. Meanwhile I cuff Joachim.

'What is this about? You are mistaken.'

Not this time.

On Joachim's iPad is an email from Marty Stringfellow asking for an update. I give him one:

> They're shite, Marty – amateurs, just like you. I don't know where you found twats like these – all gadgets and no bottle. You might know where I live but that works both ways. Take the spoils and move on – or I'll come looking for you.

And I send him a photo of the boys trussed up like turkeys, with Latifa and me standing giving the thumbs up, like a pig hunter on a magazine cover. We drive to Nelson and hand the lads over to DC Ford for processing and prison or deportation. The Jucy rep will come and collect the van tomorrow. Steve and Gary are a bit disappointed to have missed out but I tell them it had to be official this time.

We crack open the Speight's and cook up some patties for dinner. Latifa joins us but sticks with L&P.

'To Sonny Boy.' Gary raises his bottle. 'Mission accomplished.'

16

Sammy pours me a whisky from the other side of his new kitchen table. It's expensive Norwegian wood, specially carved by some ancient revered craftsman up a fjord somewhere. He raises his tot and we clink glasses. 'Ha'way the lads.'

'Ha'way the lads.' I down mine in one. It burns my throat and stings my eyes.

'Steady on, marra. It's vintage stuff, made even before Sunderland won the FA Cup and that's a fucken long time ago.'

'Quality's wasted on me, Sammy. I'm a philistine, no class. Give me a Stella any day.'

He swirls the amber fluid around in his glass. 'You're a good lad, Nicky. Solid. That's important to me.'

I have just lined up a man to be murdered by Sammy. Well, actually by Marty, on Sammy's orders, but I'm the one facilitating it.

That's the term my bosses use: facilitating.

They're just hurting each other, Nick, they say. Not civilians. Why should we care?

Until now I've facilitated some nasty bashings and woundings. We even facilitated putting that poor incinerated Middlesborough lad in Sammy's line of sight a few months ago. But I never envisaged directly facilitating a murder.

Still, it's the key to putting Sammy away, because I've recorded him asking me to do it and making all the arrangements in detail. The kind of detail a jury will love and his defence team will hate. Marty is inside now on remand. He allowed himself to get caught doing something silly so he could be near the target. This is a job that Sammy will trust only Marty to do.

I've arranged for Marty and the prospective victim to be on the same wing. The victim isn't even that bad a lad, not ambitious or hard, just stupid. So stupid he's serving six months for nutting a copper when he could be back out there muscling in on the outer fringes of Sammy's turf. Really, he's no significant threat but these days Sammy is lashing out in all directions. We've staged a few disasters and his empire is crumbling. A fortnight ago we closed down his proxy sex-trafficking operation after somebody finally snitched on his Polish mate in Manchester. We're hoping he'll snitch further up the chain and give us Sammy. We sent Immigration in to raid the house in Hendon and free the trafficked girls and women. There was one missing: Marty's Moldovan favourite. God knows what happened to her. Meanwhile the tax office has auditors combing through Sammy's businesses – determined grudge-bearing grey men and women who don't know when to stop, and lack the manners and good graces that Sammy has become used to.

'Some twat even burnt down that new holiday home in the Lakes I bought for our lass. Keep her sweet, like.'

'Bastards.' I shake my head.

Sammy feels the world closing in, a loss of control. Have you ever seen the bag jerk when you chuck it in the river and the cat inside realises what's going on? Frantic, man. Vicious. That's Sammy Pritchard.

'Tough times, Sammy but you'll pull through. You'll show them.'

'Fucken hope so. Can I ask you a question, Nicky?' He refills my glass. Ardbeg. Supposed to be good stuff.

'Fire away.'

'D'you reckon Marty's doing this?'

'Doing what, Sammy?'

'Trying to bring me down.'

'Marty?' A thoughtful sip. 'I can't deny I think he's an arsehole but I can't see him having the bottle or the brains.'

'Don't underestimate him, Nicky. He might be a twat but he's a tricky one.'

'Loyal though, eh? Surely?'

'That's what Julius Caesar thought about Brutus, Othello thought about Iago.'

'You went through to upper sixth with Miss Brown as well, then?'

'Smartarse. So I shouldn't have Marty topped?'

'Your call, mate. Two birds, one stone. Let him do that job for you inside and then see him on his way. I can understand the temptation.'

A laugh. 'You should be in fucken politics.'

I've arranged for a notoriously bent screw who is in Sammy's pay to be on shift. All of it has been done in such a way as to keep me at arm's-length and squeaky clean so as not to taint my testimony in court. It's a fine balancing act and you have to choose your words carefully for the tape. I'm not aiding and abetting, not offering to help, I'm even sounding cagey; it's all a nod and a wink which won't get picked up on the audio tape. To really nail it, Marty needs to succeed, to think he's got away with it, and be allowed out on bail to celebrate with Sammy and for that also to be recorded. A man needs to die on my watch and this has been approved at a very high and very secret level.

'I'm worried about you, Sammy. You're losing weight, not that you didn't need to, you fat cunt. But you know what I mean.' I dip a cracker into some of his fancy pâté. 'Four blokes hospitalised in the last few weeks, lads you used to have around on film night. Everybody's scared shitless, mate. Treadin' on eggshells.'

A narrowing of the eyes. 'What's your point, Nicky?'

'Where does it stop, and when?' Another bite of the cracker. 'Perpetual war. Can't be good for business.'

He shrugs. 'I'm well set up. Money isn't the issue any more. Did I ever tell you my dad worked at Wearmouth Colliery? Forty years. He was on the picket lines at the end there in eighty-four. Marched back with the lads after twelve months of living on fuck all and gettin' smacked every week by the cops. Best year of his life he reckoned. Two years later he'd taken his redundancy and drank himself to death.'

Pride. That's what drives Sammy.

Of course the defence lawyers are going to want to know who I am and what my role has been. They'll be looking for evidence of entrapment. And they'll want to know how and why it was allowed to go so far when I had recorded evidence of evil intent. It wasn't meant to happen, we'll say. Our operative – that's me – was going to tip us off. Then the masterstroke. Unfortunately I will be attacked by persons unknown, possibly connected with Pritchard, and hospitalised before, during, and after the tragic occurrence in Durham Prison. I will never have got the chance to pass it on to the relevant authorities. Tragic, but there you go. Some of the lads from Northumbria's finest will give me a beating at a time of our choosing and, hey presto! I'm not really looking forward to the 'hey presto' bit, but I'm a consummate professional and ambitious as hell. It's not the worst crackpot scheme I've come across, but it's up there. The thing is, it's the only plan we've got because, try as we might, we just can't land a decent blow on Sammy Pritchard. It's like he's untouchable.

Sammy refills my glass. 'Happy days.'

'Aye, Sammy. Happy days.'

17

A fortnight has gone by since we dispatched the German boys. No telecommunications traffic from Marty. No notice of a diplomatic incident from the Russians. No noises in the night. Steve and Gary have a block of work lined up on a salmon farm out on the Sounds. We've given Paddy Smith his gun licence. The lab has confirmed that the bolt that killed Charlie Evans' alpaca was fired from Denzel's crossbow. And Dickie McCormack keeps on cutting down trees. The weather is more settled the further we get into spring. Everybody is expecting a hot, dry summer because of El Niño – which means little to me but I'll take their word for it. We operate on tank rainwater so I've shortened my showers and flush the toilet less. I say we, but it's still me. Vanessa and Paulie haven't left the safe house at police HQ even though all signs point to Sammy and Marty backing off.

'We've got two more weeks and then some bigwig is coming in from China and needs extra protection. According to David.' David is DC Ford. Vanessa and he are on first-name terms now. And why not, she sees him a lot more than she sees me. She's granted me a phone call today. I've had a chat with Paulie who wonders when I'm coming back from my trip away, but is keen to return to *Spongebob* so he's put his mum back on. 'You sound a lot more positive, these days, Nick. That's good.'

Maybe I should roll over and you can tickle my tummy. Behave, Nick, you're committed to saving your marriage. 'Yeah, I'm feeling it. I think the boil has been lanced.'

'Euuwww,' says Vanessa with a laugh in her voice.

'And I think it helps having the guys around. Steve and Gary, they're good people.'

A pause. Have I overdone it? Laid it on too thick? 'Good, love. That's great,' she says.

'So when do you reckon you'll be back home?' I try to keep the plea out of my voice.

'Like I said, David says we have this place for two more weeks.' I can hear Paulie in the background, chuckling at the TV. He's an adapter, that boy, more resilient than I give him credit for. 'It's been useful, the time apart. I've been able to do a lot of thinking.'

'And?'

'I haven't finished thinking yet.'

*

I put the phone down on Vanessa and find Uncle Walter standing in front of my desk. 'If this is about the crossbow charge, Denzel will just have to work it through with the juvenile justice team.'

He shakes his head briefly. 'The girl said you wanted to talk?'

Latifa puts her head around the partition. 'Eh! That's *Constable* Rapata to you, old man.'

I don't remember wanting to talk to him. 'Remind me?' I say to Latifa.

'Taking sides in the community.' She looks at me expectantly. 'I recommended you talk to Uncle Walter. Remember?'

I do now but I don't recall any intention of actually following it up.

'You can buy me a cup of tea down the road,' he says, turning towards the door. 'And a date scone.'

We find a table by the bakery window and look out on to the main drag in Havelock. There's nothing much going on but we're both looking at it and not saying anything. The tea and scones arrive. Uncle Walter digs in and so do I.

'So what is it you want to tell me?'

He wipes some crumbs from his chin. 'What is it you want to know?'

This could take a while. 'Damned if I know. Latifa reckons I can learn from you.'

'Learn what?'

I recall my conversation with Patrick Smith. 'Why is Denzel so angry? Why are you so angry?'

He looks at his watch. 'Got a while?'

'No, I've got about another twenty minutes.'

Walter sips his tea. 'Denzel used to be a good boy.'

'What went wrong?'

The old man sizes me up. Wonders, perhaps, if I'm worth the bother.

'He had a cousin. Prince, we called him. You might think that's a stupid name but he really was one. Angelic and dignified, you know?'

'Go on.'

'The boy was my daughter's, Denzel's Auntie Deborah.' His eyes turn cloudy. 'Denzel was about ten at that time.'

I recall more of the Patrick Smith conversation: Denzel sharing his sadness with the older man and earning a cuddle. 'Is this the boy that drowned? When was it?'

'Five years ago last summer. That's what's on the record. He was found facedown on the beach out just past Linkwater.'

A well-heeled weekenders holiday community on that winding road through the Sounds over towards Picton. 'But?'

'The medical report says there was some terrible stuff, injuries.' He looks around the cafe and drops his voice. 'Private, you know?'

'He'd been abused?' A nod. 'It wasn't investigated?'

'What's an eight-year-old boy doing alone in fucking Linkwater? His home is over thirty kilometres away.' Walter pushes his plate and cup away. 'You want to impress me? Try reading your own files. Try doing some damn work.'

*

Back at the office I drag up whatever is on the database regarding eight-year-old Prince Haruru; his mother never marrying, keeping her birth name. There's not much. The boy was found at Linkwater Bay one morning in summer at low tide. The investigating officer concluded death by drowning. There are photos attached. A pale little Prince, face down in the mud flats in close-up, wide, and at various angles. The face seems vaguely familiar, then I realise it's the family resemblance to Denzel. The autopsy report confirms death by drowning and notes fingermark bruising on the back of the neck, along with anal tearing. It also finds a high level of alcohol and sedatives in his system. I note the investigating officer's name and look him up: a Blenheim man, retired. I phone Human Resources in Nelson and they suggest talking to Wellington. So I do. I lie and say I'm connected to DI Marianne Keegan's investigation and after some tutting, key-tapping, and checking of name spellings – his and mine – they tell me he's living in a bach on the east coast in Kaikōura.

Should I hand this over to Marianne? So far it does look promising for the Jamie Riley case but it's also, in its own right, a test set to me by Uncle Walter. If I pass it over it might just get buried again, particularly if it proves irrelevant to their investigation. I claim it as my own for now. It's my chance to rebalance my karmic accounts ledger.

*

A cool, bright sunny day and the road to Kaikōura hugs the coast, winding along the side of steep hills, taking you past grey-black volcanic beaches, glistening masses of brown kelp, and fat fur seals basking on the rocks. Today the Pacific Ocean is freezing blue and calm, on others it can be shark-grey, tearing at the land with the rage of the suddenly bereaved. Kaikōura is a tourist stopover based around whale-watching, surfing, and the eating of crayfish. As I drive into town, the snow-capped Kaikōura Ranges rear up to my right. It looks a lovely place to retire to.

Ex-detective sergeant Desmond Rogers lives alone in a brightly coloured two-bedroom bach down a lane off the main drag. There's a rusty corrugated iron lean-to off to the side, bigger than the bach itself, with a dust-covered 4WD that hasn't moved in months. I knock, and his door opens with a sour waft of old tobacco. He is a stout man barely fifty, turning to fat, with a Canterbury Crusaders shirt and trackie bottoms, home-knitted TV socks and a mug of something brown in his fist.

'Mr Rogers?'

'Who's asking?' he says.

I introduce myself.

He nods. 'You're the one that took my job.'

Not to my knowledge. He explains that he was forced to take early retirement from Blenheim and the bloke that got his job was the last officer in charge at Havelock, and then I filled that vacancy. This man blames all the way down the chain.

'Nice place you've got here,' I say, looking over his shoulder at the pigsty. 'Can I have a word?' This is a bloke who doesn't get many visitors. He'll talk to me even if he decides he hates my guts.

'Coffee?'

'Great, thanks.' I try to recall if my jabs are up to date.

'Greyyt, thanks. Aye, well I'll mek you one then, lad.' Des is taking the piss out of the way I speak. Some people – you let it pass. Him? He'll keep.

He spoons instant coffee from a jar of supermarket own brand while the kettle finishes boiling, slops some milk into a chipped mug with a kiwi on it. Hands it over. I take a sip – not as bad as I feared. I explain my interest and Des shakes his head. 'Prince Haruru. These people and their fucken names. Yeah, I remember him, little Maori kid. Drowned.'

'The autopsy mentioned high levels of sedatives and alcohol in his system. And bruises on the back of his neck.' I mime the pushing down of a head under water. 'And there was the anal tearing. Rape.'

He looks at me over the rim of his mug. 'It's what these people do. They drink. They take drugs. They fuck each other. Young and old.'

'So you think the abuse happened at home?'

'What I said.'

'Did you investigate the matter?'

'Kid's dead, what's the point?'

'He was found at Linkwater, quite a distance from his home, some thirty-odd ks.'

'Yeah.'

'That didn't interest you?'

'They like fishing. Got boats with the loans the government gives them. Musta fallen overboard.'

'Case closed?'

'Far as I'm concerned.' A gleam comes into Des Rogers' eyes. 'That mother still around?'

'Psych ward, I hear.'

'What a waste. She was a looker.'

I give him my business card in case he remembers anything useful, then I leave. I'm needing a shower and wondering if I can arrange for Denzel and his mates to come and burn this place down and shoot the pig inside.

*

It's dark by the time I get home. On the way back I've picked up a couple of crays at Nin's Bin just north of Kaikōura and chucked them on the barbie. Steve and Gary are out on the Sounds until the weekend so I'm all alone. This would be a good time for Pritchard or Marty to send in some more clowns. There have been some feral cats around lately, big muscly bastards with bullet heads, and I know Vanessa likes the bird life around here. I've dragged the trap out of the shed and I now shove some leftover bits of shellfish in there and set it.

It's a clear sky and the stars are luminescent. The Southern Cross is up there and I can make out Scorpio further west. The bush is alive with bird sounds and rustlings. It's a strange country. Some days the beauty of it is breathtaking, yet some days its ugliness steals your breath away. Des Rogers is a piece of work, his soul as black as Kaikōura sand. No wonder Uncle Walter is angry.

18

In the morning there's a cat in the cage, clawing and hissing. It reminds me of the last days of Sammy Pritchard. I take it down to the river and drown it and set off for work. I'm feeling calmer these days, less afraid, less watchful and wary. It could be a good sign, or it could be a dangerous illusion.

Charlie Evans is at his gate, tightening some wires where two fence posts meet.

'Nice day for it,' I say.

'Some rain due later. That'll be good.'

There's somebody working back up the paddock: breaking up straw bales for the alpacas. 'Is that Denzel?'

'Restorative justice, they call it.'

'But he hasn't even had his case conference yet.'

'Uncle Walter dropped him off yesterday. He's the one making him do it.'

Quid pro quo. The ways of the valley: I'm doing something for Walter, so he's doing something for Charlie. 'Looks like he's enjoying himself.'

'You never know until you try.'

At the office Latifa is checking the overnight log of incidents in the region. 'Break-in at the tennis club, a nasty crash in the ranges near Nelson last night. Tourist camper went down a ravine. No survivors. Swiss family.'

'Anything else?'

'A raid on the bikies in Nelson netted the usual: few pills and a couple of guns. They'd get more if they kicked down the doors of some of the pig shooters over here.' She keeps on scrolling. 'Uh-oh.'

'What?'

'A break-in at the offices of your old mate McCormack.'

'Anything taken?'

She studies the report. 'Doesn't look like it. Place was trashed a bit. Maybe it's those environmentalists. Out of control, they are.'

'Insurance'll cover it.' I tell her about Denzel being at Charlie Evans' place.

'Yeah, Uncle Walter did that.'

'So I hear.'

'You'll be wanting to talk to Deborah next, I guess?'

'Hmmm?'

'Prince's mum. After talking to that prick in Kaikōura you need to hear her side of the story.'

'Is there anything you don't know about my movements?'

'My cuz sold you the crays. Why else would you be over there?'

'How does she know what I look like?'

'I pointed you out last time she was in town. She reckons if you weren't already married and a bit old, she'd be in your pants, quick-fast.'

I dimly recall the woman who sold me the crays. A shudder passes through me. 'And you already knew where Rogers lives?'

'Yeah. All you had to do was ask.'

I shake my head. 'Yes, I'd like to speak to Prince's mum. Can you set it up?'

'Already did.' She gives me the details.

*

It's an iwi-run halfway house on the southern outskirts of Blenheim. The street is quiet, a mix of art deco bungalows and weatherboard cottages. Latifa is with me to smooth the way. We've driven through industrial-scale vineyards to get here. They fill the horizon and belie the wine labels that always seem to depict a picturesque slice of rural paradise. We're in the back garden of the hostel and Deborah Haruru has a rug around her shoulders. She and Latifa exchange some words in Maori while I try to absorb the thin sunshine and act like I'm not really there. Finally Latifa lifts her chin at me. 'Go ahead.'

'I want to talk about your little boy. About what happened when he … died.'

'Murdered. What do you want to know?' Deborah pulls a pack of cigarettes out from under her blanket and lights up. There are scars on her arms and wrists. She's looking anywhere but at me.

'Tell me about that day.'

She exhales a plume. 'Some pakeha found him over at Linkwater. The police came and told us.'

'You'd reported him missing?'

'Course. What do you think?'

'How long had he been missing?'

'Four days. We told the cops by the end of the first day. They didn't give a fuck.'

'The day he went missing. Tell me about that.'

'I told all this to the cops already.' Latifa says something to her in a calm voice and she nods irritably. 'We were out at French Pass camping for a few days. He and Denzel, my brother's boy, and a whole bunch of other kids were messing about. On the beach, in the bush, in the paddock. All over. We just let 'em run, you know?'

I tilt my head to show I'm listening.

'It's getting dark and I call him over for his tea. And he doesn't come.' Her eyes fill. 'That's it.'

'The kids didn't see anything? Denzel? Nobody saw anybody hanging around?'

'Nah.'

'What did the police say?'

'He's a kid, messing about. Had I smacked him or anything, made him run off? Told me to call them when he comes back.'

We break for a few minutes while Deborah is given some tablets to swallow.

'Me happy pills,' she says. 'Take a while to kick in.'

We jump forward again to the investigation after her son's body was found.

'Investigation? There wasn't one. That detective reckoned somebody at the marae had been messing with my boy. Pretty much said it was my fault, the way I live.'

Latifa sits stock still, angry. I can tell she wants to comfort Deborah but she's holding back. Something is building. For the first time Deborah is looking at me.

'I'm not a slut and I wasn't then either. I don't drink and I didn't then.'

I looked after my boy and I never had bad people in my home.' She glances around the backyard at the camellias and rhododendrons, the assortment of sad, messed-up women receiving visitors in the afternoon. Taking their medication. 'Look at me now.'

She lights up another cigarette, reaches into her pocket and pulls out a photo. It's of her and her little boy when he would have been maybe three or four. 'Princey. Isn't he gorgeous? He would have grown up into a fine man, I reckon. A leader. *Amokapua.*'

It's a lovely photo. Deborah was a striking-looking woman. Happy. Proud. Strong. The kid has the same qualities, along with mischief and laughter. Snuffed out. There's still a tingle of recognition, that resemblance to his cousin Denzel. Deborah and Latifa talk some more. Low and urgent. Latifa is encouraging her, looking at me, nodding my way. Tell him, she's saying, go on.

'That Rogers bloke, the detective? You've talked to him.'

'Yes.'

'We were in this room at the cop station in Blenheim one time. He keeps on wanting to ask me questions even though he does fuck-all about them. It's like he just wants me there, for him to look at.'

'Go on.' I'm beginning to guess. 'Please.'

'I'm sad, start crying. I'm feeling so alone. So he comes round the table and gives me a hug.' She draws long on that cigarette. 'It felt nice for a moment. Comforting. Somebody caring.' She looks into the middle distance. 'Then I feel his hand up between my legs.'

Latifa sits back and takes a breath, like it's her that just told the story.

Deborah throws away her half-smoked cigarette. 'And that dirty old bastard is still drawing a police pension.'

*

Driving back through the vineyards and past the blossoming cherry orchards my fists are tight on the wheel. Des Rogers and Patrick Smith: peas in a pod. Except thinking about Rogers makes me feel angrier and dirtier.

'She's tried to kill herself three times,' says Latifa. 'But she's not very good at it.'

'Maybe there's a life force in there somewhere. A will to live.'

'Outlasting Des Rogers. That'd be motivation.' She turns to me. 'So what are you going to do with all that knowledge?'

Good question. There's enough there for me to feed it through to Marianne Keegan for the Riley investigation. And yet. Will it just get buried under the rubble of police bureaucracy? I imagine clowns like Benson and Hedges tramping in to interrogate Deborah Haruru. Shutters coming down. But it's not my decision. That's for seasoned professionals like DI Keegan and DC Ford to deal with.

'I'll pass it on to the Riley investigation.'

'You have to be joking.'

'No, I'm not.' I explain my rationale. 'But I'll keep my eye on things and keep digging if I think fit.'

'If I think fit.' She does a passable imitation of me. 'I'll tell Uncle Walter the good news.'

We're driving past the shoe fence. The crime scene paraphernalia has gone but a mini shrine has appeared in honour of Jamie Riley. I pull over and we take a look. I scan the area for the CCTV camera that will be monitoring the site, just in case it catches the killer's return. It's perched on a telegraph pole across the road, powered by a cable running down to a junction box. The shrine has the usual: flowers, teddy bears, cards and messages of condolence. Why here, I'm thinking. Why leave the body here? What's this bloke saying?

Latifa must be thinking the same. 'You reckon they're linked? Prince and Jamie?'

'Both got sedatives or whatnot inside them, both missing for a few days. Both had some internal damage.'

'Prince was drowned. Jamie had his neck broken.' She blinks against the strengthening wind. There's dust in the air. 'Five years between them. It's a long time to wait.'

'Maybe there's others,' I say.

'Yeah. 'Spect so.'

*

We spend the afternoon visiting local schools and ensuring they're geared up for National Earthquake Drill Day, which is next Thursday. While we're there we remind the kids that it's bad to take drugs and steal. Today is Friday and I'm on drunk duty this weekend so I'll be using the camp bed in the office. At the end of the day Latifa reminds me to call anytime if I need help subduing dickheads. I thank her.

'What's your plans for the weekend?'

She frowns. 'Got an assignment due in Monday, probably working on that. And maybe a swim at Blenheim Pool.'

'Assignment?'

'Law degree. Online. Except for the odd tutorial over in Nelson.'

'You never mentioned.'

'You never asked.'

Off she goes. I ring Marianne Keegan, intending to pass on the Prince Haruru stuff, but they tell me she's gone back to Wellington for a weekend with family. I feel unjustifiably jealous. I leave a message for her to ring me about the Riley case. Outside, day is giving way to night and the pub is getting busier. I hope for no fights and no car accidents. Make up the camp bed and flick the kettle on for yet another cuppa. There's a red dot on my desktop screen and it reminds me of the laser sight the night the dog was shot. It's a new email, from an unknown sender.

Hey, Marlborough Man.
Gr8 to hear from you. Showed the picture of you and the krauts
to Sammy. Good laugh. Just to let you know we're still thinking
of you. Maybe we should catch up, talk about old times.
M.

19

Sunderland, England. Two years earlier.

It didn't go as planned. Marty bottled out, or twigged to the set-up, and the lad didn't get killed. At least it saved me a staged beating from my colleagues. With nothing else on the horizon, we proceeded with a prosecution of Sammy for conspiracy to a murder that never happened. Far from satisfactory, the operation had been a huge investment in time, money and manpower for negligible return, and I know SOCA wanted to blame me. The court case only just scraped through. The defence team savaged us, particularly me, but we did get Sammy sent down for ten. After remission and good behavior it could be half that. As he was led from the dock Sammy gave me this look: how could he have got me so badly wrong? A sad shake of the head as he disappeared from view.

Marty stepped into the breach to run things while Sammy was inside. He escaped the conspiracy charge because it's only Sammy we had on tape, not him. He was able to run the line that he was just serving time for his offence and no way would he have gone looking for more trouble, whatever Sammy Pritchard might have said on the tape. That's another thing that surprised us about Marty: his loyalty to Sammy. He's not made a move, yet anyway. It seems he's just minding the shop. He was in the courtroom and his eyes never left me for the full two weeks of the trial.

On the last day, while the jury deliberated, I was taking a piss and admiring the graffiti on the wall in front of me.

'Nicky.'

I turned my head, zipping up at the same time. Marty was standing by the wash basins checking himself and me in the mirrors – nobody else around. I had to get past him to get to the door. He reached inside his jacket and I launched myself at him. He nimbly sidestepped, like a matador with a wounded bull, and he had me face down in the sink with my arm up my back and his knife against my ear.

'I could do you now, Nicky. Push this through like a shish kebab and you're gone.'

I thrashed and struggled. Furious with myself. 'What's stopping you, Marty?'

A prick of pain on my ear lobe, a warm trickle down my cheek. 'Consequences. I need to be out and about, keeping Sammy's business going. Besides, I like the idea of you never knowing where or when we'll come for you.' He twisted my arm higher, near to snapping. 'Mark my words, Nicky. I am coming after you.'

I'd love to know how he got that knife through the metal detectors, maybe it was pre-planted. 'How about I have you arrested right now?'

'What for, where's the witnesses?' He turned the tap on and cold water gushed over my face. 'Need to clean yourself up, mate. It's nearly time for the grande finale. The jury's coming back soon, I hear. You'll want to look your best.'

'It works both ways, Marty. We can keep after each other for years to come or we can get on with our lives.'

'That's what I said to Sammy. I said, mate, cut your losses. Forget the bastard. But you've hurt him, Nicky. You got him to trust you and like you. Now he's a jilted lover. Heartbroken.' A knife caress down my neck. 'Does Vanessa know how good you've become at the lying game? I'd be worried if I was her.'

And all of a sudden he was gone again and I was left looking at myself in the mirror, face flushed, hair sodden, blood on my collar. A short, sharp taster of the days, weeks, months, and years to come.

*

At home, the temperature has been frosty since the court case and now that we know where we're going, it's dropped a few degrees further.

'New Zealand?' says Vanessa. 'Jesus, Nick. I've got a good job here, there's a deputy head retiring soon and I'm up for it. Paulie's only just settled into his new school. And Mam gets her diagnosis next week. You can't do this to us.'

'I'm sorry. How many times do you want me to say it? But the alternative is worse, love. Much worse.' I'm thinking about bodies in the boot of a burning car, about people chopped up and left on display on the town tip, about the missing Moldovan girl, and about Marty's knife blade in my ear.

We'll keep our given names but we'll change the family name. Trying to change too much else will just blow Paulie's mind. From now on we're no longer Burgess, we're Chester. And I want to carry on being a cop somewhere to make sure there's some good money coming in for the Paulie Fund.

'Chester,' we drum into Paulie. 'Chester.'

'Chester,' he says. 'Not Burgess.' A frown. 'Will Buster be coming?'

'No, pet,' says Vanessa. 'Nana and Grandad'll look after him.'

While my mam makes a fuss of Paulie and the dog, my dad pulls me aside. 'It makes you easier to track down, keeping the same Christian names and the same kind of job.' He's a retired cop and he's worried for us. I acknowledge he's right. He knows my reasons though and he lets it go. He knows also that we can't have any more contact, ever. 'Your mam and me. We'll miss you.' His shoulders shake when we hug.

I know we haven't covered our tracks anywhere near as much as we should. It's like I'm almost willing them to find me eventually. Unfinished business.

When we arrive in New Zealand it's wetter than a Sunderland summer's day.

20

I didn't get to bed until after midnight. There was a fight in the pub: a local and a backpacker with their eyes on the same woman. It was pretty much over by the time I arrived. Meanwhile she had gone back to the hostel with her girlfriend. And a car crashed into a culvert on the way out to Pelorus Bridge. Bruises and scrapes but nothing permanent, except the write-off to the vehicle. And even though I was in my camp bed by twelve thirty I didn't get to sleep for a few hours more. Marty and his mind games. So what will he do now? Hire a better class of killer? Maybe. But knowing him and knowing Sammy, I think not. They may as well stop wasting their money on amateurs, and I'm sure Marty himself will want the pleasure.

The camp bed has left a crick in my neck. I have the sour taste of late-night coffee in my mouth. The kettle goes on while I brush my teeth at the tiny kitchen sink. The sun is streaming down outside and the main drag is waking to the Saturday morning shoppers and strollers. The phone goes. It's the DC.

'You've been talking to a retired officer, Des Rogers. That right?'

'Has he made a complaint?'

'Not exactly. He was found hanging in his shed this morning.'

'Why call me?'

'Your business card was in his pocket.'

*

When I arrive at the DC's office in Nelson, he's got DI Marianne Keegan with him. Straight-backed, frowning at something on her smartphone, not interested in saying hello. She's probably not happy to have her weekend interrupted. Or is she? Summoned away from the family home with your marriage going down the toilet?

'You told Records you were on my team so they'd give you Rogers' address.' She's acting severe but her eyes aren't cold enough.

'Sorry.'

'So spill,' says the DC. 'What's going on, Nick?'

I tell them: Uncle Walter, Denzel, Prince Haruru, his mum, Deborah. The lot.

'And when were you planning to pass all this on to the task force?' says Keegan.

Task force. That sounds impressive. 'I left a message for you yesterday. Assumed we'd talk on Monday. So you're getting it two days early.'

'But you've still had this for what, three or four days already?'

'It only crystallised after I spoke to the mum yesterday.'

'Crystallised,' says the DC, nodding.

'Any further details on Rogers?' I ask.

The DC flicks his eyes at his computer screen. 'Looks like suicide. Hanging from a hook on the shed wall.'

'He didn't strike me as suicidal. Seemed too bitter or lazy to bother.'

'Maybe you were the tipping point,' says DI Keegan. She arranges for me to brief Benson on my inquiries to date. 'In the absence of any other similar cases, this could be useful.' She packs some things into a bag. 'Don't ever try to pass yourself off as a member of my inquiry team again.'

I promise not to. After she leaves, I tell the DC that Marty has been in touch.

'So it's settled. We'd better get you and the family moved on then.'

'We've got, what, two weeks left before your Chinese bigwig comes to town?'

'That's right but I don't want to piss about anymore. We've tried your way and it hasn't worked.'

'One way or another I reckon it'll all be over by then.'

He sighs. 'Tell me.'

I tell him about the way Sammy and Marty work and think. Sammy relies on Marty, so Marty is the key; he'll want to get up close and personal and he's already hinted in his email to that effect. Now we know who is coming, it's a matter of looking out for him. Waiting, watching, and pulling him in when he makes his move. 'With them both locked up, that's the end of it.' Simple really. Fingers crossed.

The DC is thinking. 'It would be a shame to lose you.'

'To Marty? Yeah, my thinking too.'

'To some other force, dickhead.'

He gives me the fortnight but insists anyway on setting the wheels in motion for an evacuation and new life elsewhere, if required.

'Vanessa?' He lifts an eyebrow. 'Is she in on your decision?'

I smile reassuringly. 'She seems happy where she is for the time being.'

*

Step one is to knock off a reply to Marty.

> *Marty. Ball in your court bonny lad. Better be quick though.*
> *They're getting antsy here. Moving on soon, 2 weeks max.*

I'm counting on him not being the master criminal he thinks he is. Counting on him having an ego as big and empty as the stadium in Sunderland on a week day. Counting on him doing exactly what I want and need him to do. And hoping to hell that I'm not wrong.

Downstairs to brief Benson on the Prince Haruru case. Benson would have liked a weekend home with the family in Wellington too, but his rank doesn't allow it. He taps away on his keyboard, with an MP3 recording as backup, while I narrate.

'So it's a similar case but still no suspects or useful witnesses,' he concludes.

'Yep.'

'And it doesn't get us any further forward.'

'Unless you re-interview the witnesses on record, and find some new ones, and look for points of correspondence with the Riley case.'

'Oh, yeah.'

'And maybe compare whatever forensics there are, and the post-mortems.'

He looks at me. 'And you just a sheep-shagging sergeant from the hills. Who'da thought?'

'I'll leave it with you, then?'

'You do that, mate.' His eyes never leave the screen. 'Stay in touch, won't you? You're an asset to the task force.'

Marianne intercepts me in the corridor on my way out. 'You spoiled my weekend.'

'Sorry.'

She notices the car keys in my hand. 'Make up for it, drop me at my hotel. I came here straight from the airport.'

'Sure.'

She loads her case in the back and hops in. 'You've been a busy boy. The handover to Benson go okay?'

'Fine.'

'So now I've got an afternoon to fill in Nelson.' Her hand rests on my knee. 'Any thoughts?'

'I don't think that's a good idea.'

'No?' Her hand glides along my thigh. 'That's what you said in that motel room in Blenheim, too.'

'I'm sorry, I shouldn't have, but ...'

A caress. 'But here you are anyway, stiff as a board. Ready to abandon yourself once again.'

I shift in my seat. 'No.'

A shake of the head. 'You want it both ways. You want to think of yourself as a good family man and if it wasn't for fickle fate: drink, temptation, job stress, whatever, you'd never stray. Would you?'

'Marianne, I ...'

She takes her hand back. 'Me? I know I'm a lost cause as a wife and mother and I can live with that. You? Maybe you spent too long undercover, Nick. All that time pretending to be something you're not.' She nods out the window. We've arrived at the Rutherford. 'This is me.'

'I'll call you on Monday. About the Rogers stuff.'

She slams the boot down. 'Yeah, Nick. Speak to you then.' A playful smile. 'No hard feelings.'

*

Back at the office I draw the curtains and endeavour to catch up on some sleep ahead of what might be a busy Saturday night. It's been warmer than usual today, high twenties at least. For some that's a great excuse to drink more. But of course sleep eludes me. I lie and think of Marianne's hand on my leg, her words dissecting me. And then there's ex-detective sergeant Desmond Rogers. Was it me that drove him to suicide? I'd like to think so, but I doubt it. I don't recall him putting my business card in his pocket but I do recall him staring at it contemptuously where I left it lying on that greasy table of his. So he picked it up and kept it close to his person. Did he have second thoughts? Was there something more he wanted to tell me? What else could he possibly have to offer? He never investigated Prince's death, he didn't give a damn.

The camp bed creaks and the frame digs into my side.

Let it go. It's down to the Riley Task Force to take it further. I drift off to sleep with flashbacks to a motel room in Blenheim and dangerous thoughts about Marianne Keegan, drowsily weighing the pros and cons of my own failing marriage.

*

It's late afternoon. I've managed to snatch a couple of hours kip and it's taken the edge off. After a shower, I wander over the road to the cafe for some early dinner. At this time on a Saturday the choice isn't great and they're getting ready to close. I treat myself to a Red Bull and a burger. Another two weeks of this and I'll be too fat to save my marriage, but maybe Marianne Keegan will still have me, blubber and all. On the cafe noticeboard, Charlie Evans has pinned up a petition against McCormack Forestry and he's trying to crowdfund some kind of legal action. If I didn't have the Paulie Fund to think about, I'd chip in.

The rest of the evening involves several drives up and down SH6 and pulling people over for speeding and/or drink driving. The pub stays trouble-free after a terse talking-to last night. The licence is up for renewal at the end of the year and they don't need me objecting or seeking to vary the conditions. Things quieten down by about eleven and I'm back at base shortly after. There's another red dot flashing on my computer.

Marlborough Man.
Looking forward to the reunion. Been a while.
M.

21

'Get your essay done?'

'Yes, thanks. Had a good swim at the pool, too. You?'

'Same old, same old.' Late on Sunday, Steve and Gary got back from the Sounds. It looks like they've earned some good money. They've brought back a new fishing rod and eel net, and in the fridge there's a carton of Speight's plus some fresh salmon from the marine farm. I'm glad to have some company, waiting for Marty's next move. They were too stuffed for the gory details so I promised to fill them in after they've had a good sleep.

Latifa has just read the Monday morning round-up of the weekend incidents. She's going to be shirty with me because I never mentioned the Des Rogers thing over the weekend. So I mention the Des Rogers thing now.

'Good riddance.'

'That's it?'

'Want me to cry or something?' Latifa asks me if I passed on all that Prince stuff to the Riley inquiry.

'Task force,' I correct her.

'La-di-dah.'

'Yes, they've got everything. But as we don't have any viable suspects or witnesses in either case, it's still not much further forward.'

'But the likes of Deb, Uncle Walter and so on. They can expect a visit from your ...' she does air commas with her fingers, '"task force"?'

'Probably.'

She nods. 'I'll warn them. Tell them to cooperate, for what it's worth.'

'For a twenty-four-year-old you seem to wield quite a bit of influence.'

She lifts her chin. 'Bother you?'

'Nah.'

'Maybe I'll be your boss, one day. After I get my law degree, eh?'

'Wouldn't be surprised.'

'My tutor in Nelson reckons I'll make the big time.'

'I didn't know there was a law school over there.'

'There isn't. He's just a casual supervisor, more like a mentor. The faculty down in Christchurch arranged him. He's been up in PNG. Reckons I could make waves there.'

'Rising star, huh?'

'That's me. So watch yourself.' She grins and turns to answer the ringing phone. A moment later the grin has gone. 'Deb's taken an overdose.'

*

Deborah Haruru is hooked up to a respirator in Nelson Hospital, as the hospital in Blenheim didn't have the necessary equipment available. Her chances are fifty-fifty.

'What's she taken?'

The doctor tells me the name of the drug and I'm none the wiser. 'A bottle full of the anti-depressants she was on at the hostel,' she clarifies.

'The happy pills?' says Latifa. 'Deb should be on cloud nine.'

'Plus something we're still trying to identify. We'll have a better idea by the end of the day.'

'Suicide attempt?' I ask.

'Looks like it.' The doctor checks her file. 'There's a history.' She pats Latifa on the arm. 'I'm confident your friend will pull through. We got to her in time.'

It's nearly lunchtime. We drive down to Trafalgar Street and grab some Malaysian takeaway from a street corner stall. A block down is McCormack's place and I see him exit the building, mobile phone glued to his ear, and hop into that flash car of his. There's somebody in the passenger seat but I can't see who.

'You talk to Des Rogers, and now Deb, and they're wantin' out of this world. It can't be coincidence.' A mouthful of noodles. 'Sarge.'

'They're both messed-up people.'

'They both must know something. Or knew, in Rogers' case.'

'If Deborah knew something she would have told us, wouldn't she?'

Latifa taps her chopsticks pensively on the food box. 'Maybe Deb doesn't know that she knows?'

'We'll ask her if and when she wakes up. But let's not get too Miss Marple here.'

'Who?'

'She's a ... '

'Just jokin'. Sheesh.'

*

Driving back from Nelson to Havelock, I'm thinking about those coincidences while Latifa negotiates the hairpins in her inimitable way. I can believe Deborah Haruru would be suicidal, but Des Rogers? Not for a second. Going through Rai Valley, we're blessed with a brief mobile signal so I call Marianne Keegan and bring her up to speed.

'Two in as many days. You have the touch of evil.'

'That's what my colleague said.' I can see Latifa out the corner of my eye, looking smug. 'Any more details from the Kaikōura crew on Des Rogers?'

'I'll look into it and c.c. you. But don't go running off anymore without keeping me informed.'

The signal cuts out and we cross Pelorus Bridge on the home stretch. The car park is chock full of tourists and there's a tailback blocking the main road, which means we need to slow down for a few seconds. Latifa mutters under her breath, 'Fucking hobbits.'

Just past Canvastown the police radio bursts into life with a report of a shooting incident in the Wakamarina Valley. Normally that wouldn't mean much. In rural New Zealand, calling police out at the sound of shots fired is like calling them out for the sound of cows mooing. Usually you need to specify ill intent, human on human. Which is what we have here. AOS tactical are on their way in a chopper. Latifa chucks a kamikaze U-ey as a log truck bears down.

I recheck the property number in the report. 'It's Charlie Evans' place.'

Latifa tuts.

When we pull up I see McCormack's BMW parked across the Evans driveway and two men crouched behind it. One of them is McCormack and the other is vaguely familiar. On the other side of the locked gate is Charlie Evans with a shotgun, raised high, eyes sighted along the barrel. A further hundred metres away Denzel sits on a quad bike, arms folded, head down, an alpaca nudging him affectionately.

'Mr Ryan! What are you doing here?' Latifa seems to know McCormack's companion.

'What's going on, mate?' I say to Charlie Evans.

The shotgun is lowered, marginally. 'Trespassers.'

McCormack splutters. 'He's a lunatic. We were trying to serve him some legal documents, that's all.'

'Did you shoot at them, Charlie?'

'Only over their heads.'

Turning back to McCormack. 'What papers?'

'Sorry, but that's a private matter.' I recognise the voice of the companion. It's the bloke in the car on the morning of the boat vandalism report. *Can we go and get brekkie, Dickie?* Or something like that.

'And you are?'

'Sebastian Ryan. Mr McCormack's legal consultant.'

'And my tutor,' says Latifa, proudly.

'It isn't private anymore, Mr Ryan. The police are involved. What's it about?'

Ryan throws me this amused, patronising look that sets my Sunderland-bred hackles rising. I'm downstairs, he's upstairs. Good old-fashioned class warfare. 'Cease and desist. It's a prelude to an injunction.'

'Cease and desist what?'

'The petition against the logging,' says Charlie. 'And the crowdfunded class action.' He glares at McCormack. 'Whatever happened to democracy and free speech?'

'They run secondary to free enterprise.' McCormack comes out of his crouch and dusts himself off. 'So are you going to arrest him, or what?'

I turn to Charlie. 'Sorry, mate. By your own admission you've discharged a firearm in a threatening manner. You'll have to come with us.'

'Get them away from my property first.'

The chopper is approaching. Armed Offenders Squad: men in black with machine guns. I point them out to McCormack. 'This is going to be all over the *Journal*. Do you want that kind of publicity?'

McCormack ducks into the beemer. 'Good to see you doing your job for a change, Sergeant.'

Ryan gets a parting wave from Latifa and returns it.

Something occurs to me. 'Who made the emergency call? Those guys wouldn't have had a mobile signal.'

Evans thumbs over his shoulder at Denzel. 'The boy, probably. On the landline. He'll have meant well, stop me from killing somebody.'

We take Charlie's gun off him, put him in the car, and radio the chopper that it's all over.

*

Charlie is charged and will be summoned to a court appearance at a later date. As he's leaving the office I ask after Mrs Evans.

'Not good. She can't keep any food down.' He squints against the late afternoon sunlight. 'The boy is good with her, though. They get on like a house on fire.'

Not the best analogy after Denzel's last outing to Patrick Smith's place on the Sounds. 'That's great,' I say. 'Look after yourself and stay out of trouble, mate.'

He cocks his fingers into a gun shape. 'Lawyers at forty paces.'

'What about that cease and desist order?'

Latifa sniffs. 'I checked it. You could drive a horse and cart through it. I really would have expected better from Mr Ryan.'

What with an attempted suicide and a shootout at the Evans' corral, it's a relief to wind the day down with email circulars, health and safety surveys, and a log of expenses. As we're closing up, the phone goes. It's the doctor from Nelson Hospital.

'We identified that other drug in Deborah Haruru's system.'

'Yep?'

'Rohypnol.'

*

When I get home, Steve and Gary have cracked open the Speight's and thrown some salmon on the barbie. I've passed the Rohypnol news on to DI Keegan. Having Deborah Haruru poisoned by the same drug that was in Jamie Riley's system is one coincidence too many.

'You're a dangerous man to know, Nick Chester,' Keegan told me.

I bring the guys up to speed about the latest threat from Marty and once again offer them an out. 'It's not your fight. Really, it isn't.'

'Tell that to Sonny Boy,' says Gary. 'God rest his four-legged soul.'

'Marty Finefellow? Here? In person?' Steve claps his hands with relish. 'Good as gold.'

Head against a brick wall. I give up.

Gary lifts his Speight's. 'To round two.' We all take our swigs. 'How's Vanessa and Paulie?'

'Good.'

'They need to be here with you,' he says. 'This is a good place.'

I'm not in the mood for an appraisal of my family life so I turn it around. 'You guys got family?'

Gary is staring out at the trees. 'Not any more.' Whatever he sees, it's way out beyond the darkness, beyond the stars. 'There was a fire.' A last swig from his bottle. 'Couldn't get to 'em in time.'

'Sorry,' I say. 'I didn't know.'

'Why would you?' He prods the food on the hotplate. 'The fish is ready.'

Steve rescues the moment. 'I've got a daughter in Palmerston North. Three grandkids. Gonna visit soon.' He takes the plate of food I pass him from Gary. 'That okay with you? Kids around here for a few days?'

'Sure,' I say. 'Happy families.'

'Let's hope this Marty business is sorted by then,' says Gary.

We all toast the concept.

22

'A skinful of Bundaberg rum.' Marianne Keegan is reading from her computer screen and I can hear her tapping the keyboard as she speaks. 'A bruise around the left eye socket and cheek, unexplained, but consistent with a punch.' More tapping. 'The ligature around the neck. That's about it.'

There are any number of plausible scenarios but in my mind's eye I see Des Rogers answering the door to a fist in the face. He's on the floor wondering what's going on. There's a rope tightening around his neck and his lights go out. A bottle of grog is poured down his throat and he's strung up to a hook in his shed. Game over.

'They find the bottle?'

'In the kitchen. No prints except his.'

'What, not even the kid from Super Liquor that sold it to him?'

'Exactly.'

'The rope?'

'Common as muck, but we're following it up at local DIY outlets.'

'We'll need to check CCTV for those places, and for Deborah's hostel. See who's been hanging around.'

'No shit.'

'How's his telco records?'

'He had a mobile but it's missing. We're going through the call printouts now. I'll keep you posted.'

McCormack is on the phone next. 'Did you charge the silly old coot?'

'Yes.'

'Good.'

'It's a pity you guys can't find a more civilised way of sorting out your differences. You've got a right to harvest your trees. He's got a right not to have his land degraded by the harvesting of your trees. What costs more, the lawyers or the digging of a few extra drainage channels?'

'The principle. I've got plantations right across the Marlborough Sounds. Each of them with their own little Charlie Evans living nearby, whingeing and whining.'

'A bit of goodwill might end up being cheaper in the long run.'

'Goodwill? In with the greenies, I guessed as much.'

'I hear your place got turned over recently?'

'Kids. Looking for money for drugs, or whatnot. Nothing for them here.'

'Trashed the place?'

'Thanks for your interest. The insurance people are onto it.'

*

Latifa is out patrolling SH6, no doubt pulling over miscreants, giving them a talking to, issuing tickets. It's National Earthquake Drill Day the day after tomorrow and a memo has come round explaining, yet again, what is required of us: a calm punter-friendly reinforcement of the drill and explanation of civil defence and evacuation procedures. And here's me thinking I could just run up and down the main street waving my hands and crying, 'We're all doomed, I tell ye! Doomed!' The sun is out and the wind has freshened. I opt for a midmorning walk to show my face, blow out some cobwebs and maybe pick up a coffee from the bakery. Closing the office door I step outside.

Uncle Walter bars my way. 'We need to talk.'

I open the office door and step back inside. 'Take a seat.'

He looks around. 'The girl?'

'Constable Rapata is out on the road. Doing good.'

He nods. 'Somebody's trying to kill my Deb.'

'We're investigating it.'

'And that excuse for a human being hanged himself over in Kaikōura.'

'That's right.'

'You've rattled him.'

'Who?'

'The killer.'

'If I have, then I haven't a clue how or why.'

'We're going to solve this, you and me.' He stands, pats me on the shoulder, and shuffles towards the door. 'We'll get that bastard.'

*

On my way out, I'm accosted again. It's Jessie James from the *Journal* with a new pair of Doc Martens.

'What was that up the valley yesterday? Charlie Evans? The police chopper?' Something beeps on her iPhone and she checks it. 'McCormack?'

'I'd have thought you'd have put two and two together by now.'

'Yep, Charlie's rocking the boat with that petition of his. A lot of people in town work on McCormack's plantations.'

'So you already know what's going on.'

'I hear he shot at McCormack.'

'So you already know what's going on.'

'Help me out here, Sergeant. You owe me one.'

'Do I?'

'The story you got spiked.' She tries coquettish. 'That wasn't very nice.' A strong gust snatches at her tea-cosy hat.

I throw caution to the howling wind. 'McCormack is bringing in the lawyers to close down the petition and the class action.'

'Class action? From what I hear, Charlie's on his own. A crowdfunding of one.'

'Which makes it even more David and Goliath then, doesn't it?' I appraise her: Doc Martens, woolly beret, rebellion chic. 'Back in the day, journalists used to stand up for the little bloke. That's where the story was. Now? It's not so easy I suppose when you've got advertisers to worry about, jobs to protect, all that.'

'That's rich coming from a cop who had a story killed to protect his own interests.'

'Touché.'

She taps her iPhone absent-mindedly against her chin. 'Still. You don't get noticed writing fluff pieces for the machine.' A glance across the inlet at one of McCormack's recent harvests. 'And that view does kinda suck.'

'Right on.'

*

Latifa returns from highway patrol looking flushed and happy. 'Just gave a ticket to this absolutely like hot man. I mean cut, you know? Eyes like Kanye.'

'Who?'

'He's a –' She catches my expression. 'Just joking, right?'

'Good morning's work, then?'

'Ah, yeah.'

I bring her up to speed on Des Rogers and the dodgy crime scene. 'And Uncle Walter paid me a visit. He seems to think we're a crime-fighting duo.'

'Don't write him off. He'll open up a lot of doors that closed when little Prince died.'

'You would have been what, about twenty then?'

She nods. 'Still at varsity, over in Wellington.'

'So law is your second degree?'

'Yeah, did commerce first time round.'

'And ended up a cop?'

'It felt like a calling. They paid us a visit in the third year and said it didn't matter what kind of degree I had, as long as I had one.'

'What do your family think?'

'They think it's cool.' A frown. 'Well, Mum does anyway.'

'Do you remember at the time any rumours going around the community about what happened to Prince?'

'Nah. By the time I got back from Wellington everybody had moved on. Then I was off to police college after that.' She frowns. 'The only thing that stuck was how much we all hated that Rogers bloke. Some even reckoned he was covering up for the one that did it. But nothing specific, you know? Just an all-pakeha-are-bastards kind of thing.'

'Maybe Uncle Walter will dig something up. Batman and Robin, Green Hornet and Kato.'

'He already has a name for you. *Weka-tāne.*'

'Meaning?'

'Weka-man. Like the flightless bird. Running around in the undergrowth, burying your beak in the dirt, digging stuff up and annoying everybody.'

Weka-tāne. I can live with that.

*

The call comes from DC Ford on my home landline later that night.

'SOCA have told us that Martin Stringfellow flew out of Newcastle upon Tyne earlier today to connect with a flight from Amsterdam to Jakarta, and then on to Bali. Paperwork and baggage are all in good order. They don't have any onward details as yet.'

'Thanks.'

I'm outwardly calm but there's a chill in my heart. Maybe Marty is picking up some friends or false papers in Indonesia. Or both. He won't be bringing any weapons like the German hunter-brothers did, anything that requires paperwork and unnecessary attention. He doesn't need to, he can buy a gun here and we know he's good with a blade.

'The offer's still there, Nick. Come in to safety and we move you on somewhere else.'

'No, I need to end this.'

'There's not just yourself to consider here.'

'I'm aware of that, sir.'

How long will Marty be in Indonesia? A couple of days maximum I guess. He's not the patient sort. Or is he? He watched over me for my eighteen months with Sammy and bided his time. No, something tells me he'll be here by the weekend; as far as he knows the clock's ticking on me shipping out to a new country. He'll be in as much of a hurry to finish this as I am.

23

'I can't do this, Nick. It's not going to work.'

Vanessa hates Christchurch. We're stuck in a suburb up near the airport and every time a plane takes off she follows its path with hungry eyes. I've been busy enough the last few months getting trained into the New Zealand way of doing the Job, and coming to grips with the finer points of Kiwi law and order. Paulie has been at school most of that time and settles in well once the teachers and the other kids begin to understand his accent and his sense of humour. Vanessa has sat in our fibro bungalow and seethed.

· 'Maybe if we made some friends.'

'What the fuck for? You're about to get posted to some remote hilltop village where the only crimes are sheep-rustling and incest.'

Paulie looks up from his iPad. 'Can we get some sheep when we go there?'

'Maybe,' I say.

'Havelock. Found it.' He shows us the iPad and Havelock on the map. Googles it some more and finds some photos. 'Looks cool.'

'Can't we just go back to the UK?' pleads Vanessa. 'Scotland maybe. Or Wales. They'd never look there.'

'They'll look everywhere.'

'Then what's to stop them looking here?'

'Who are you talking about?' asks Paulie, still swiping through the tourist photos of Havelock. 'Look. "Greenshell mussel capital of the world." Brilliant.'

A text from my handler in Christchurch HQ. *Check this out.* And a link to somebody's Facebook page. I go through my secure police laptop, which has a VPN making me harder to trace. The link is to a Facebook page in the name of Makkam1973. There's some photographs: our old house, burned down, my mam and dad's house covered in graffiti, windows broken. A caption. *Tut, there goes the neighbourhood.* And last but not least, our dog Buster impaled on a park fence. All the posts have been liked by Marty Stringfellow and a few dozen others.

Vanessa sees my face. 'What is it?'

I lead her into the kitchen, away from Paulie, and show her.

Finally, she gets it.

'Can't they arrest him for that?'

'What? Liking nasty pictures of what somebody else might have done? The kind of legal representation he'll have? Waste of time.' I close the computer screen. 'We can't go home, love. We have to make this work.'

24

If I can just make enough friends to hold the enemies at bay, then I'll probably scrape through. I don't make pals easily, not a good start for an ex-undercover operative for the Serious and Organised Crime Agency. You need topnotch social skills for that kind of work: empathy, intuition, and such. That chameleon ability to turn on the charm and be all things to all people. I don't have it, I rub people up the wrong way. For every Sammy Pritchard who takes a shine to me, there are five Martys sharpening their knives. Still, Latifa sees some redeeming features in me and Uncle Walter has decided I'm the first cop he's prepared to trust in a generation. No pressure. And of course there's Steve and Gary preparing to stand with me to face Marty and whatever he might bring this weekend.

This morning there was a call from Latifa to tell me that Deborah Haruru had woken up. And now here we are at Nelson Hospital and I'm looking into the eyes of someone else who has decided to trust me.

'You're going to find the man that took my boy.'

Not a question, a statement.

Latifa looks at me: give her something back, she's saying.

'I'll try, Deb.'

Deborah believes me, and that will keep her in this world a while longer. There's no CCTV at the hostel, it's not that kind of place. And nobody recalls anybody suspicious hanging around. Deborah herself only remembers dropping off to sleep, naturally. And not waking up until a couple of days later.

'Overdose? Suicide?' She shakes her head. 'Nah. Not this time.' Is there anything she knows that she's holding back? Something a killer might want to stop her telling me? 'Yeah, I forgot to mention his name last time we talked.'

Latifa smothers a smile.

'Give us a yell if you do remember anything, the smallest thing, however stupid it seems.' I leave my card with my home number written on the back. The DC has agreed to post an officer at the door and Marianne Keegan is c.c.d in. We've also agreed with DI Keegan that Latifa and I should be the conduits to Deborah. The last thing we need is some goons trampling in the newly laid flower beds.

It's midweek market day in Nelson. I grab a venison burger and Latifa opts for a whitebait pattie. We hit the winding road back through the hills to Havelock.

'Ready for Drop, Cover, Hold tomorrow?' says Latifa, through a mouthful of white bread and fish.

National Earthquake Drill Day. 'Absolutely.' I'm driving this time and she seems impatient, pushing her foot down on an imaginary accelerator around the sharp bends. 'Have you ever been in one?'

'Not a big one. Felt the odd shake here and there. You get used to it.'

'I can't imagine it.' It's only a few years since the centre of Christchurch was left looking like a war zone, and it seems inconceivable to me that people can get on with things and trust in life again. But of course they do: 9/11, Fukushima, you name it. I share my thoughts with Latifa.

'Shit happens. You dust yourself off and start again. You don't have much choice. Look at Deb.' Her phone beeps and after a quick glance at the screen she squeals in a girlish un-Latifa-like way.

'What?'

'It's Daniel!'

'Who?'

'The gorgeous guy I gave the speeding ticket to on Monday.'

'He's got your mobile number?'

'I wrote it on the back of the ticket.' She presses her lips to her phone. 'Sure thing, honey,' she purrs. Her fingers dance over the screen as she knocks off a reply while we're still in mobile coverage.

*

DI Keegan has sent through an email with a printout of Des Rogers' telco records. In the time between my visit and his death there are no calls received or made on his mobile or landline. On his internet history there are visits to news and sports sites, an adult chat room, and a porn-streaming service. An email from his daughter in Christchurch saying she wouldn't be able to visit this weekend after all because the kids had sports fixtures, one of them was through to the netball grand finals. He has replied: no worries, maybe he'll try and get down there himself to watch the game. Nothing else. He's not on the usual social media networks. If he made contact with his killer during that time it's not evident here. DI Keegan adds in the covering email that there is no CCTV in the vicinity of the bach but they are looking at others from hotels and petrol stations in and around Kaikōura. A doorknock of his neighbours has also thrown up nothing apart from the astonishing revelation that he wasn't well-liked.

I send a query to Keegan asking if it is possible to access any of Rogers' records from when he was still in the job: journals, logs, database entries, whatever.

'Why?' She's on the phone now, businesslike, cutting to the chase.

'I heard a rumour that he was possibly covering up for somebody back then. I'm interested in the company he kept, inside and outside work.'

'You don't think you're overstepping your mark here?'

'Your call,' I say and let the silence hang.

'I'll see what I can dig up.' She tries the meaningful pause too but I've had lots more practice and don't jump in to fill it. 'Don't make me regret this,' she says before hanging up.

*

There's not much else to do for the rest of the afternoon. I put together a goody bag of stickers, badges, certificates, and fluffy toys. I'm due out at Canvastown School in the morning to supervise National Earthquake Drill Day and give out prizes for the best Drop, Cover and Holders in each class. Latifa is doing Havelock School and she's putting together her own goody bag. The sun drops behind one of those many hills and the wind is taking a rest. It's a beautiful and calm evening.

25

Qadim Reza's father, Muhammad, arrived in New Zealand in 2001. An Afghan Hazara fleeing the murderous Taliban, he was on an asylum-seeker boat that foundered in the Indian Ocean near Christmas Island and was rescued by the Norwegian freighter *Tampa*. His timing wasn't good. The Australian government was struggling in the polls and determined to make a vote-winning example of people like Muhammad. After a tense maritime stand-off involving masked and armed SAS troops, weakened and water-deprived refugees, and a stubborn ship's captain – all witnessed by the world's media – a solution was found. The Pacific Solution. It involved Australia offloading its human rights responsibilities onto its mostly poorer neighbours. New Zealand, to its immense credit, was among the first to put up its hand and share the load. Not out of a sense of begrudging obligation but, it seemed to many at the time, more out of a solid sense of right and wrong. And that is where Muhammad's luck began to change. Instead of being caged on a desert island for the next few years, he was able to get on with a new life of peace, security and freedom in the Land of the Long White Cloud. He was a gifted motor mechanic and within six years had saved enough to start his own business in Blenheim. Now the proud holder of a Kiwi passport, he travelled to Quetta in Pakistan where he found himself a wife and, eight years after the *Tampa* rescue, they had a son, Qadim, the first of three.

If any man deserves a break it would have to be Muhammad Reza. But he hasn't seen his six-year-old son for nearly twenty-four hours and we all fear the worst.

The media are all over it and I don't envy DI Marianne Keegan for one second. She looks exhausted. National Earthquake Drill Day got blown out of the water in Marlborough. The call had come in late the previous evening from Qadim's distraught parents. By early next morning, police and Search and Rescue volunteers were out combing the surrounding area. The Rezas live not far from the Wither Hills south of Blenheim and there's a lot of difficult ground to cover. It's now midafternoon and the family and DI Keegan have just done a TV appeal in time for the evening news. Muhammad Reza has this haunted, damned look about him, as if once again he's part of a horrific spectacle way beyond his control.

All morning Latifa and I have been driving up and down SH6 and along the side roads, doorknocking, looking, hoping. If Prince Haruru and Jamie Riley are any guide, then little Qadim has only a few more terrible days to live. Maybe we're jumping to conclusions? Maybe he's just lost somewhere and he'll show up some time soon. Maybe he's fallen in a river or pond and drowned. Maybe something terrible happened in the family home and all this is an elaborate dark hoax to divert attention – but I look at Muhammad Reza's devastation on TV and think: no, somebody else has done this. Studying the photo of Qadim, there's something about him, and Jamie, and Prince. A light that we all see, a light that somebody out there feels compelled to extinguish.

We're obliged now, even while keeping the inquiries separate, to make the links. Too much scrutiny and DI Keegan feels the pressure. What could have been a career-defining case might end up destroying her. I've been there: Sammy P was meant to be my ticket to the top. So the usual suspects have once again been rounded up – the nonces and saddos – and we all know it's a waste of time and resources. The DC and Keegan are in a huddle in the corner of the re-established Blenheim incident room. They summon me over.

'Marianne tells me you've got thoughts on Des Rogers protecting somebody?'

'Just a rumour, sir.'

'We'll be doing all the usual from here but maybe you and that colleague of yours … '

'Constable Rapata, sir.'

'Yeah. The two of you focus on the Haruru link, use Rapata's connections in the community.' He lifts his head to see if anyone is listening in. 'We haven't got time to fuck about, Nick. We need results, not softly, softly.'

Keegan is nodding along in time. I ask about Des Rogers' work records and data entry logs. 'You'll get it by day's end,' she says.

Latifa and I drive from Blenheim back to Havelock and I tell her what we have to do.

'Yep.' She seems flat, drained. But we can't afford that right now, I tell her. We need to dig deep, find some energy and determination. 'Sure,' she says. 'No worries.'

*

The Des Rogers stuff is in our inboxes when we log back on. Reams of it: scanned printouts of his database entries for the two years preceding his retirement, case and incident reports, leave requests, training courses, expenses claims. I don't know where to start.

'How about we dump anything more than six months before Prince's death and more than six months after?' suggests Latifa.

'Works for me.' We reorganise the information accordingly.

'And put aside the training courses, expenses and the leave requests?'

'For now, anyway,' I agree. 'Meantime can you arrange meetings with Uncle Walter and anybody else for asap. Preferably starting tonight?'

'Onto it.' She picks up the phone.

I glance at the camp bed folded up in the corner. It looks like another cricked neck in the morning.

We spend the next couple of hours culling the incident and case reports. It's lucky Des Rogers was a lazy bastard for at least the last two years of his career and didn't generate as much of an electronic paper trail as he could have. Still, it's like wading through Sounds mud at low tide and by sundown we're happy to be grabbing a sausage roll at the supermarket on our way out to a cluster of houses near the local marae. I'm about to be introduced to the Haruru whanau – 'Extended family,' explains Latifa when she sees my blank look.

It's dark by the time we arrive and moths dance around the flames of a fire burning in a drum in someone's backyard. It's a cool evening but there's less of a nip as spring edges into early summer.

'Cuppa tea?' says Uncle Walter.

We both say yes and a younger woman is sent to make it. Uncle Walter is there, flanked by an older woman who looks in her sixties or seventies, another in her forties, and a man who might be her husband. I try to remember their names: Rose the older one, Beth the younger one, and her bloke Peter. The tea returns and the tea maker is dismissed.

'Another one, eh?' Walter shakes his head. 'And now you're ready to listen to us.'

Latifa says something to him in Maori. Calming, placating tones but there is a firmness too. His eyes blaze at her: has she gone too far?

I nod. 'And maybe together we can stop him.' A moth lands in my tea. 'Eh, Walter?'

The other oldie, Rose, turns out to be Walter's sister. Uncle Walter, Auntie Rose to everyone else. She leans across and tips my tea out, moth and all. Hands me another one. 'What do you want to know, sonny?'

It's been a while since I was called that. 'At the time of the little boy's death ...'

'Murder,' three people say simultaneously.

'Some people were saying that the police officer, Rogers, was covering up for someone. That he knew who'd done it.' Latifa tips her head in the direction of the younger woman, Beth. I shift my gaze to her. 'What was that about?'

'Beth,' says Walter. 'Speak up, girl.'

It's clear nobody gets beyond sonny or girl around here until they're collecting their old-age pension. Beth keeps quiet. It turns out she's another of Walter's offspring: sister to Prince's mum, Deborah Haruru. Peter is there for moral support. He nudges her. 'Tell him for fuck's sake, the rugby's on in twenty minutes.'

'Isn't the season finished?' I say.

He looks at me like I walked out of the swamp. 'Replays.'

Beth glares at Peter then straightens in her seat. 'I saw Rogers in town about a couple of days after Princey was found.'

'Blenheim?'

'Well, Renwick, near enough. He was drinking in the Woodbourne Tavern with a bunch of pakeha.' She sniffs angrily. 'I was working there. They were all laughing and carrying on. Plenty of drink inside them. That was the same day we got the medical report on what had been done to Princey.' She pauses, crosses her arms tight.

'Go on,' says Latifa gently.

'Rogers grabs me when I'm going by. Puts his hand on my arse. I'm ready to smash a bottle over his head. This other pakeha tells him to take it easy. She's grieving, he says.'

I wait for more but she's finished. 'That's it?'

She looks affronted. 'Yeah.'

'What'd he look like?' Latifa leans in. 'This other pakeha?'

'Tall, pasty, skinny.'

'Don't they all,' says Peter. 'Except the short, fat ones.' Auntie Rose shushes him.

'Would you know him if you saw him again?' I ask.

She shrugs. 'Doubt it. It was five years ago and I never saw him in there again. I only got to thinking about it months later and wondering if I was imagining things. Looking for something, anything, you know?'

'Imagining what? What makes you think it was anything more than just Rogers being reined in by a pal?'

She's embarrassed. '*Matakite*. A feeling, that's all. I get dreams about that bloke, still. Not him as a memory, but the memory of how I felt when he looked at me.'

I wait.

'*Pōuri*.'

Latifa translates for me. 'Darkness.'

*

I leave Latifa out at the community. She'll stay overnight, maybe try and press Beth for more of a description of the pakeha who exuded darkness. I head back to the office, set up the camp bed, and trawl through more of the Rogers records. A catalogue of incident reports, often sloppy, of drug busts, thefts, assaults, vandalism, domestics. The minutiae of volume crime. Nothing jumps out screaming at me, this is it, this is the key! My eyes glaze and droop, and by just after midnight I crawl onto the creaky camp bed. My last thought before falling asleep is for little Qadim Reza whose time is running out.

26

I've been awake since before five and going through the Des Rogers stuff again. Most of his clients are pathetic low-lifes, dumb-ass recidivists who'd really struggle to exude dark charisma of the type that invades Beth's dreams. I can't see any of them sitting in the Woodbourne Tavern that night with Rogers.

The cafe over the road is the first to open and I treat myself to a takeaway coffee and a bacon and egg toastie. Back at my computer the overnight log reveals the search for Qadim Reza has advanced very little. People have been dragged in and eliminated from inquiries, that's it. Latifa is in by a little after seven looking similarly sleep-deprived.

'Dogs,' she says. 'Yapping all night.'

'Any more from Beth?'

'Nothing. She says it's like his face has deliberately erased itself from her memory. Like a file being trashed, she put it.' Latifa flicks on the kettle. 'That's what you get when you mix Beth's special brand of Maori voodoo and IT know-how. Complete nonsense.' She offers me a tea but I show her my takeaway cup. 'You?'

'I can't see anything in his incident and case reports that excites me.' Latifa is looking over my shoulder at the computer screen. 'Mainly ratbags who find it hard to survive from one fix to the next.'

'I watched the rugby with Beth and her bloke. Slept in their spare room. Beth dropped off to sleep on the couch beside me during the game.' Latifa is rummaging in her backpack. 'Beth said something before she crashed. *Tangaroa.*'

'What?'

She chucks a heavy hardback tome onto my desk. It's a Maori dictionary from the library. 'Look it up.'

I do as I'm told. '*Tangaroa*. God of the sea?'

A finger prod. 'Over the page. Alternative meaning. First line.'

'You have a single word that means "endless wealth personified"?'

She nods proudly. 'Ours is a sophisticated and eloquent culture. Only I don't think Beth meant it in a positive sense.'

'So this faceless pakeha smelt of money.'

'That should impress Detective Inspector Cheekbones and Bobcut.' Latifa plonks herself at her desk. 'Now let's see if we can get a name.'

*

It's as we're going through Rogers' expenses claims and leave requests that something begins to take shape. At this time he's at an address in Renwick, north of Blenheim, hence the session in the Woodbourne Tavern, which would have been his local. Two months before Prince Haruru was murdered, Des Rogers puts in a claim for a meal for two plus sundry cash expenses to the value of four hundred dollars.

'Big meal,' says Latifa.

I point to the code allocated by the finance department. 'It's an informant. Rogers has treated him or her to a feed and slung them some cash.'

Crosschecking with his case and incident reports a week later, we see there is a drug raid on a house in central Blenheim that nets a good haul. Rogers gets the credit. We return to the expenses claim. The dinner partner is given an initial – L.

'L?' says Latifa. 'For the record, it's not me.'

Then there's a leave request three months later. A month after Prince has been found dead. It's for a week in February just after the schools have gone back. Rogers is obliged to give a contact number in case something big comes up and he's needed. There's no mobile coverage where he's going so he provides a landline number and an address for a bach in the Sounds.

'Linkwater. Where Prince was found.'

'Is L for Linkwater?' wonders Latifa. The bach is owned by a property developer, Bernard Webster. '*Tangaroa*?'

'He fits the bill better than the dropkicks Rogers usually deals with.'

Again we crosscheck with the incident reports. A domestic four months earlier. That's a month before the dinner with informant L. Reports of a disturbance at the Webster household in – wait for it – Renwick. Uniforms attend and register a complaint from a bashed-up Mrs Webster. Des Rogers does the follow-up. Mrs Webster withdraws her complaint and the matter is subsequently dropped.

'Look at this.' Latifa swings her screen around to show the licence registrations. 'Webster has a boat.' Sailing around the Sounds, I'm thinking, and hiding in a thousand coves and inlets.

I run him through the database. 'No convictions. But an average of three or four domestic violence complaints lodged per year by Mrs Webster.' The later complaints also allude to violence and inappropriateness with the children.

'Inappropriateness?' says Latifa.

'No details provided.'

Under the circumstances, it's enough for a chat with DI Keegan.

*

There are simultaneous raids on the Renwick home, the Linkwater bach, the Blenheim offices, and the Picton marina berth of Webster's boat, *Prospero*. The Armed Offenders Squad is spread pretty thin. The priority is the boat and the secluded bach. If Qadim Reza is anywhere he'll be at one of these places, out of the way. It doesn't stop us looking for dungeons at the Renwick home though.

Webster himself has his head ducked into the back of a police car and is driven to the Blenheim station. His wife seems bemused but hardly surprised. Maybe she has always had her doubts. The kids are at school so they don't know anything yet. Mrs Webster is allowed to bring them home so they don't hear the news from anyone else first. In the absence of any other leads, DI Keegan is stoked.

'According to the Freaks Hotline, Qadim has been sighted anywhere from Stewart Island to the Coromandel. This ...' she waves at the departing car, 'is good news. Good work, guys.' She pats Latifa on the shoulder and misses the glare it provokes.

We're invited to observe the interview over the video link in the adjoining room. Marianne wants us to feed lines through her earpiece as she hasn't got time to do the usual pre-interview prep. Qadim Reza is on borrowed time.

Webster is tall, thin, and pasty like the mystery bloke in the Wood-bourne Tavern, which is a good start. Apparently his value as an informant was derived from the string of low-end properties rented out by one of his real estate businesses. Half of them subsequently raided as P labs. If any tenants got too troublesome, Webster got his mate Rogers to move them on. Beth from the marae has taken a look at him through the one-way glass and thinks maybe he was among the gang of drinkers with Des Rogers that night. Maybe not. But is he the one who smells of money, *tangaroa*? Is he the one who fills her with *pōuri*, darkness?

'Dunno,' she says, shrugging and turning away. 'It's like *Men in Black* where they have that pen that flashes and makes people forget they've seen aliens, you know?'

Latifa circles her forefinger around her temple. 'Lady Fucken Gaga from way back,' she mutters when Beth has gone home.

DI Keegan is undeterred, she doesn't have the choice to be anything else. She's got Benson beside her and across the table Webster sits with his lawyer, a bloke called Mark.

'Tell us where Qadim is, Mr Webster.'

'Who?'

Mark the Lawyer seems bemused. 'Are you referring to the missing child, DI Keegan ?'

'Yes.'

'And what makes you think my client has anything to do with that?'

'If you stop interrupting you'll find out.'

Mark isn't used to being talked to like this, he reminds me of McCormack's fop, Sebastian something or other. Theirs is more usually the world of corporate law; crime is for the proles. Bernard Webster however, wants to be helpful.

'I'm sorry, I don't know where the poor boy is. If I did, I would tell you. It's dreadful, it really is.'

'Your property at Linkwater. It's less than two hundred metres from where a young boy was found drowned five years ago.'

'I do vaguely remember that, yes. Are you saying the two are linked? And that Riley boy too, out by the fence? My god.'

It's a good performance.

We've got the techs going over the GPS navigators for his car and boat to see where he's been lately. Unfortunately neither go back five years, he only has the latest models.

'Are you able to account for your movements at the following times and dates?' Keegan slides a single printed sheet of A4 across the table.

Lawyer and suspect study it. 'Five years ago is a long time to remember but I can have my PA check my old diaries if you like.' Keegan says yes, she would like. But what about more recently? 'On both of those other dates I was here, in the region, living and working as normal.'

She asks him to give as full an account as possible that will be checked and challenged in subsequent interviews. He gives it. And the clock ticks by. Does he remember Des Rogers sexually harassing a barmaid at the Woodbourne Tavern one night five years ago? Er, no.

'Time for a bit of waterboarding,' says Latifa. 'He's playing with us.'

'All we know so far is that he's a wife-beater who had Des Rogers for a pal. Jumping to conclusions doesn't help anyone, least of all Qadim.'

'Thank you, Obi-Wan.'

Keegan asks Webster about the domestic violence allegations, and the allusions of inappropriateness with their pre-teen children.

'My wife is highly strung. She makes wild accusations one day then retracts them the next. You'll see from the record nothing is ever pursued, and social services don't show any interest.'

'What does she mean by inappropriateness?'

'Ask her.'

The lawyer, Mark. 'Is that all you have? Baseless allegations from a hysterical woman?'

Latifa is right. This is an interview style based on past events which require a reckoning – it's not the way to deal with a current and ongoing threat. According to the clock on the wall it's three forty-five on Friday afternoon. Fair enough, as long as Webster is here in custody then he's not doing anything to the little boy. But if he's the wrong man we're wasting precious moments. Meanwhile, I'm expecting to be visited in the next few days by Marty Stringfellow who carries vengeance in his veins and something sharp in his hand. He dies or I die. Whatever the outcome, I can't see my career surviving. I've got nothing to lose.

'Where's the kid?' It's taken nine steps from the adjoining room to bring me here. I've pulled Webster's chair over backwards and I'm crouched over him with my Glock in his ear. I've found this roar within me that I didn't know existed. 'Where is he!'

The room is quiet, the lawyer has gone rigid. DI Keegan is no doubt calculating how long she can let this run before doing the right thing.

'For the last time.' I start to pull the trigger.

'Oh god,' Webster is sobbing. 'Dear god.'

He pisses himself.

Footsteps down the corridor and it's my mates from the Armed Offenders Squad. From behind his mask one of them says, 'Hang on. Weren't you the fella with the eel?'

I drop my gun, kneel, and put my hands behind my head.

*

I'm suspended. It didn't wash that there were no bullets in the gun.

'At least we can probably eliminate Webster from our immediate inquiries,' I point out. 'He's got questions to answer but I don't think he's our Prince of Darkness.'

'Nice choice of words,' says Latifa, sourly. She's off up to the community to keep on chipping away at fading memories and old resentments.

DI Keegan is philosophical and inclined to agree. He seems too much of a fainty weakling to be doing something this bad. Hardly scientific but we've both been around long enough to trust our intuition. 'It was worth a punt. Not in the training manual but definitely worth a punt.' For her it's back to square one and we all see Qadim slipping away.

DC gives me the same look I got from Sammy Pritchard when he was led out of the dock for his ten-year stretch. How did he get me so wrong? He arrived in Blenheim just as I was having my handcuffs removed by the AOS so I could sign the receipt to get my belongings back.

'What were you thinking, Nick?'

At home there's a message on the answering machine. Vanessa. 'The Chinese VIP arrives tomorrow so we've got to get out.' She sighs. 'I don't think it's going to work, love. I don't feel we're going anywhere except around in circles.' Don't hold back, I'm thinking. 'David has arranged for Paulie and me to get away for a while longer. I can't say where.'

Paulie is in the background saying, 'Is that Dad? When's he coming home?'

There's a crack in her voice. 'The DC is really hoping you and I can work this through. He's got more faith in us than I have.'

Beep, beep, beep. And that's it.

*

I shower and try to keep it down to two minutes to conserve water but it takes a minute to stop being freezing. Out of uniform and into civvies, I pull on the thick TV socks Vanessa knitted for me, the kind that are all the rage in nursing homes. The kettle goes on. Steve and Gary are at the door. Steve has a big grin on his face.

'Daughter's coming down from the North next week, bringing the kids. She's taking them out of school for a few days.'

'Is that a good idea?'

He frowns. 'They're pretty bright kids. They should catch up okay.'

'I meant with Marty due here any time now.'

The grin returns. 'Oh, him. Yeah, we'll take care of him first then she can come down. Sweet as.'

If only it were that simple. 'Great,' I say. 'Cup of tea?'

They come in. Gary wants to know why I'm home early, so I tell him about my adventures with Bernie Webster. He laughs. 'You're out of control.' But we're sharing the same terrible fears for Qadim Reza.

The tea is poured and there are bikkies in the tin. Steve takes three.

'You know, I still think there's something in what that woman from the marae said.'

'Beth?'

He waves his biscuit in confirmation. 'Powerful things, dreams. She's seen the killer alright, she just can't remember who the fuck he is. Give her a while.'

It's something Qadim doesn't have. 'Here's hoping.'

We lift our mugs in a sombre toast.

'So,' says Gary. 'Marty Badfellow.'

I had been hoping for word from the DC that Marty had slipped into New Zealand, perhaps via Oz, after a few days in Bali. That he had been detained at Immigration with a bagful of weapons and a nasty *To Do* list with my name on it. Then we could lock him up and take him out of play. But nothing. Maybe he does have false papers. If so, then he retains the element of surprise.

'Guard duty roster again?' says Gary.

'S'pose so,' I say. 'I'll take first shift.'

We throw some food together and watch the early evening news. The Aussies have progressed from locking up asylum seekers on Christmas Island to locking up bad Kiwis there, prior to deportation back to Godzone.

'Well it was sitting empty after the boats stopped,' says Steve. 'You have to do something. Be a waste otherwise.'

'Send all the bad people back where they came from, huh?' Gary ladles some baked beans onto our plates of fry-up. 'Shoulda done it two hundred years ago.'

We let Richie the mastiff out of his cage for a run. He's used to me now and less likely to tear my throat out, but I still stiffen every time he bares those teeth. We give him the scrapings from our plates but he's not interested. Low energy and no appetite. He seems lost without Sonny Boy, or am I just projecting my own issues onto him? Now the clocks have done their daylight saving thing it's still light well after eight. Nobody is tired. We're all hyper and trying not to show it. Gary takes his axe and chops some firewood. Steve mends some holes in his eel net.

'How old are the grandkids?' I ask him, to fill the jumpy silence.

'Four, seven, and nine. All girls: Scarlett, Ginger and Ruby.'

'Redheads?'

'Nah.'

'Your daughter work?'

'Part-time at that big DIY place. They've got her on this contract that says she's got to make herself available all the time even if they haven't got any work for her.'

'What happens while she's down here with you and the kids?'

'Fuck knows. Breach of contract I suppose.'

'Looking forward to seeing them?'

'Yeah, of course.'

There's a car engine in the distance, somebody coming up the valley. We've all heard it and we carry on like it's probably nothing. But muscles have tensed, knuckles whiten, jaws clench. I recognise the car. It's just the new bloke from up the road.

'How's Vanessa going then?' says Steve. 'And the boy. Seen them lately?'

'No.' He can see from my face that, for me, it's all over.

'Shame. I was going to take you and Paulie out eeling when the grandkids get here.'

'Another time maybe.'

He nods. 'When me and my missus split up nobody was surprised. Especially not us.' He tightens off a dangling thread on his patched net and examines his handiwork. 'Awesome, if I don't say so myself.' He returns his attention to me. 'You don't see it but we do. You and Vanessa, underneath all the shit that's going on, you've got something that's strong.'

'Based on what? The few days you were here before she left me?'

He registers the harshness in my voice. 'We talked sometimes when you were out at work. Yeah, she's angry but only because you keep locking her out.' He puts his hand over his heart. 'What she feels for you and what you feel for her. *Tau o te ate.* Soul mates. It's the truth.'

My eyes have blurred. I really want to believe him but it feels too late, I've already fucked things up too much. 'Getting cold,' I say. 'Going to get a jumper.'

*

The stars are out in their millions and the wind has dropped. It's a half moon but bright enough to cast shadows of the bushes and trees and the edges of buildings. Steve and Gary are asleep and Richie the all-black mastiff snuffles wakefully in the tray of the ute blocking the driveway. I've set the cat trap again as there are still at least two more out there: a large brown-black tom and a smaller grey one. A stoat has stopped by, squeezed in under the trigger bars, eaten the tomcat's sardines and fucked off.

27

'Morning, sunshine.'

Marty.

He's behind me. I twist my head, try to turn. Why can't I move? A bike lock, round my neck and through the boards of the fence. My hands are behind me, cable-tied. I turn as far as I can. I'm wet all over. A smell. Petrol.

'Sleep well?'

There he is, dressed in designer outdoors gear, kitted up like Bear Grylls, and wiping his knife clean on a bit of cloth.

How could this have happened?

I fell asleep. I must have. But more, my head hurts and my left eye is blurred and gummed. Gary is lying on the gravel, over to my right, trussed up and gagged; there is a lot of blood on him. Some will be drippage from the terrible facial wounds. Some may be from his body, I can see tears in the shirt and fresher blood running there. No Steve. The dog? Can't see him either. I feel for my gun but of course it's gone.

'I can see why you like it here.' Marty looks around appreciatively. 'You can yodel through the hills with a knapsack on your back. All that shite.' He nudges Gary with the toe of his hiking boot but there's no sign of life. 'Maori fella? Does he do that war dance they do before the rugby?' He briefly goes into a half-crouch, sticks his tongue out and bulges his eyes. 'Class that. Love it.'

'Is he dead?'

Marty kicks him hard and Gary groans. 'Not yet.'

'Leave him. It's me you came for.'

He shakes his head. 'I'm disappointed. I was looking forward to meeting the lovely Vanessa. And that funny little lad of yours, what's his name again?'

He doesn't need me to tell him. I try again. 'Leave him. He's got nothing to do with this.'

'He's here, he's with you.' Another savage kick. 'He's involved.'

'The other bloke. Where's he?'

'The other Maori lad? Gone to meet his maker.' He takes out a cigarette and fires it up. Lets the flame flicker a while before closing the lighter. I try pulling with my neck at the bike lock, maybe I can snap it through the wooden board, but nothing budges.

'Piss-weak, twat.' The words are for both him and me.

'Steady on, marra,' Marty says.

'You watched me for nearly two years with Sammy but never made the move. No bottle.'

He strolls over and stamps at my head with his top-of-the-range boots. 'And yet here I am, Nicky.'

That hurt. I can feel the other eye closing up.

'Sammy knew he had nothing to fear from you. Not because you're loyal. He just thought you were a bit … how did he put it?' I search for the memory of that summer evening on the cliff top at Marsden. 'Like a poodle, he said. And just as fucking vain.'

That earns another couple of stamps on the head and I feel like I'm going to pass out. But if I'm going to die then I may as well say my piece, get a few things out of my system. That rooster over the road is crowing and the hobby farmers will be up and about soon. The bloke goes off every day to Blenheim to run his website business while she potters around feeding the goats and the chickens. Marty needs to get a move on or they might get nosy and spoil his party. And I need to keep distracting him, because it's all I can do.

'You had your chance to take over when he went down. Why didn't you?'

'Loyalty,' he says. 'You still don't get it. Sammy could teach you a thing or two about that. The number of times he stuck up for you when I told him you were a treacherous bastard.' He snorts. 'He was even putting money aside for that spastic bairn of yours. What a joke.' Paulie's rainy-day fund, boosted by drug smuggling and people trafficking profits. Nice. 'So where are they? Vanessa and Paulie?'

'Safe.'

He shrugs. 'Sammy's a patient man. We'll find them.'

'Sammy wouldn't want Paulie harmed. Vanessa neither.'

'That what you think?' Marty tries looking pensive, it doesn't suit him. 'Aye, you're right, he was torn, conflicted-like. But I convinced him of the bigger picture, the need to set a firm example.'

This is hopeless. They can and will come back for my family after I'm dead and buried. I'm hurting all over and feeling tired, nauseous, whether from blood loss or despair it's hard to tell and makes no real difference.

Marty is behind me again. There's rustling. Stuff being pulled out of a bag. He comes back around, holding a chainsaw in one hand and a phone in the other.

'Sammy wants to see your head in a bag like that Alfredo Garcia bloke. I told him, "Sammy mate, that might be a problem at Customs."' He chuckles. 'So at least a photo anyway.' He holds up his iPhone. 'Pity there's no signal here but I can probably send it from that place down the road, what's it called?'

'Havelock.'

'Aye, like the monument in the park in Sunderland.'

'Same bloke apparently. Some general or other.' Anything to buy time. I'm struggling now, big-time. 'Henry Havelock. Helped put down the Indian Mutiny, a military tactician. Hard as nails.'

'That right?'

'Aye. Kind of bloke Sammy would have loved except he was posh as fuck.'

He's fiddling with the chainsaw mechanism. Not sure what to do with it, there wouldn't have been much need to learn in Sunderland. And I know I'm not going to be rescued by the hobby farmers over the road. I'm finished.

'Really?' Marty flicks the cigarette in my direction but it lands short. He pulls the cord a few times and the chainsaw starts up. Bugger, it's a SmartStart. 'Well there you go.'

The noise is deafening. He steps forward: what's he going to go for first, my head, my legs? I curl up as best I can, a hermit crab retreating into a non-existent shell. Marty is enjoying my terror. He unlocks the safety bar, revs and sets the chain whirring. Through half-shut eyes, as if in a dream, I see Steve running out of the bushes and burying an axe in Marty's skull. Marty drops and the chainsaw skids across the gravel, whining and whipping close to me before the automatic cut-out kicks in. Sparks fly up from the gravel. A blue flame flares briefly on my trouser leg but doesn't catch.

Steve turns the chainsaw off properly and moves it out of harm's way. He digs around for the bike lock key in Marty's pocket and releases me. He picks up Marty's knife and uses it to cut through the cable ties on my hands.

'Awesome,' I say. 'Truly awesome.' I stand groggily upright and nod towards Gary. 'I better go and call an ambulance.'

Steve pats me weakly on the shoulder. 'Good idea, mate. Better make it two.'

Then he shows me the gaping wound in his chest, the blood that still runs freely there as his face turns grey.

28

His real name was Stephen Hemopo and his tangi should really have been a grander affair. There was a short dispute between his daughter and some cousins and uncles who claimed him as theirs, but nobody really wanted to press the matter. Perhaps the row over custody of the body is a way of showing respect. Nor was he ever going to be returned to his own marae on the North Island because there is still some very bad blood there.

Blood. Steve wouldn't stop bleeding and he died five minutes before the air ambulance landed in the paddock over the road. Gary sits beside me now, eyes raw with grief. On the other side of him is Steve's daughter, Lydia, and the three grandchildren. She has been given special compassionate leave from her zero-hours contract at the DIY place so she's not in breach by attending her father's funeral. The traditional three days of lying in state was however curtailed to just one sad and lonely night in the funeral parlour in Blenheim.

Gary has limped to the front of the chapel beside the closed coffin and is speaking in Maori. On my other side Latifa sits, explaining a bit of what's going on, but her heart isn't really in it. Gary is encouraging Steve to return to the ancestral homeland by way of te rerenga wairua, the spirits' journey. Then Lydia takes her turn, and after some tearful words in memory and honour of her usually absent father, she belts out this old Maori song that her dad used to like and the power of it freezes my insides.

Steve has been buried in Deep Creek Cemetery just down the road from our house, in the company of the miners and settlers who have tried to eke a living in this valley the last hundred and fifty years. The hākari is back at our place. About thirty people are in the front yard, picking at the meat and salads on the table, sharing some jokes and stories about Steve, and lifting their faces to the weak sunshine. I'm nervous about having so many strangers on my property but Latifa says it is important, and it was the very least I could do. After all he'd still be here if it wasn't for me. After the burial, the home of the deceased and the place where he died are ritually cleansed and then desanctified with food and drink, in a ceremony called *takahi whare*, trampling the house. I like the sound of that: trampling the house. Maybe they can trample out the touch of evil that kills those who come near me.

'Is it really over now?' Vanessa is by my side, she takes my hand and squeezes it for the answer she needs. Just ten minutes ago the DC asked pretty much the same thing but without the hand squeeze.

'Yes.'

It has to be.

Surely.

The last week has involved a whole bunch of questions, answers, suppositions, evasions and downright lies. Marty had a passport in the pocket of his Gore-Tex jacket. An Australian one held by his younger brother now living in Bali. They look alike. Marty no doubt intended to swap it back for his own on the journey home. He'd left Steve for dead in the hut but underestimated him. Gary was next on the list: tied up and hacked and stabbed over a prolonged period for the drawn-out pleasure of it, while I lay unconscious by the fence. Survival seemingly a lottery. The dog slept through it all. Marty had been on the premises earlier in the day and drugged the bowl of food while everybody was out. That accounted for Richie's sluggishness and loss of appetite. The ambulance crew and first attending uniformed police have questions about the state of Marty's body – the axe in the head is a bit too *Game of Thrones* for them. They don't know the half of it, and it's best they never do.

Paulie sidles up, plate piled high with triangular sandwiches that he swears taste much better than rectangular ones. 'Are we coming home now?' he says through a mouthful of ham salad.

'I'd like that,' I say.

Vanessa looks at me with a mixture of, what? I see hope in there, determination too, but still something held back.

'Okay,' she says finally.

*

It's a week since Steve's funeral. Qadim Reza was found yesterday, in the middle of one of those massive vineyards in the Wairau Valley on the way to Blenheim. He must have endured unspeakable torment before he was released from this world. All I know or imagine is from the news reports, as I'm still suspended. Latifa has tried to fill in a few of the gaps for me but she is on the far fringes of the investigation.

'They have nothing.' The phone beeps, there's another call waiting at her end. 'They're getting so desperate I reckon they might even have you back soon.'

'Thanks. How's it going with Beth and her dreams?'

'There was a camera in the pub at the time but any discs have long since been erased. DI Keegan is wondering if a hypnotist might help.' Yep, things are desperate. Latifa says bye-bye and takes the other call.

Gary is resting up in his room, watching TV shows and movies endlessly on his computer. He's barely spoken since the funeral. Sometimes he'll go for a drive in the ute and let Richie off for a run in somebody's pine plantation. He takes his gun in case there's a pig but always returns empty-handed and, it seems, relieved. We're settling back into a domestic routine here, with Paulie at his old school and Vanessa doing the running around. She thinks I need to stay out of the public eye until Marty's boot marks have gone from my face. We're having a midmorning cuppa on the back balcony. It's windy and overcast so the sandfly count is slightly lower than usual. We're still lathered in repellent anyway, just in case. As we edge closer to summer the river below is diminishing without regular rain, and I've instilled a new mantra in Paulie to help save the water in the tank: 'If it's yellow let it mellow, if it's brown flush it down.' He delights in it, chanting it all day until we yell at him, good-naturedly, to stop.

Vanessa is hanging some washing on the balcony clothes line. 'I want to go home, Nick.'

I put the phone down and hand her some pegs. I've been half-expecting this. 'For good?'

She shrugs. 'I don't know. But I want to see me mam. She's had the chemo, her hair's grown back, she's been through hell and I wasn't there for her.'

And I think about my dad's shoulders shaking during that last hug. I want to see them in their new home, the one they fled to after the previous one was vandalised by Sammy's thugs. There's nothing stopping us now.

Marty is dead. Sammy knows because I sent him a photo on Marty's phone.

Look what I did, I texted, *all by myself.*

Not exactly true but there was a point to be made. Will Sammy take his chances if I turn up on his territory? Maybe, but maybe it's also time to seize the initiative.

Looking at Vanessa I can see that this is one of those pivotal moments. She wants to believe in us again, wants this to work, and she wants something in return. Framed against the trees and the hills, a river mist drifting up the valley behind her, it's like she floats and needs anchoring. Somewhere to call home.

'Okay,' I say. 'Let's go.'

29

Durham, England. Now.

As a uni student I always loved travelling back home from Manchester by train and pulling into Durham over the viaduct high above the city. Just one more stop to Newcastle on that East Coast main line and then home. Durham is a very old city with steep, densely wooded riverbanks and a cathedral dominating the skyline. It's about twenty kilometres south-west of Sunderland. The same River Wear that joins the sea at Sunderland meanders through Durham, enclosing the centre on three sides to form a peninsula that made for good defences in the wars and skirmishes that raged through the ages. Geographically and strategically, there are similarities with my little red-roofed house perched above the meandering Wakamarina River.

The road signs designate Durham as the Land of the Prince Bishops. It all goes back to the early Middle Ages. As the north-east was so far from Westminster, the bishops of Durham enjoyed extraordinary powers such as the ability to hold their own parliament, raise their own armies, appoint their own sheriffs and justices, administer their own laws, levy their own taxes. You name it. They were a fiefdom unto themselves and that was never going to last. In the 1600s, Oliver Cromwell put the boot in to punish Durham for choosing the wrong side in the civil war and it was all downhill from there. Within another couple of hundred years the prince bishops were an officially spent force, even if they did found the esteemed University of Durham on their way out

So, on the one hand you have prince bishops and hallowed academia, but on the other you have the surrounding coalmines (all closed now), the trade unions, and the other assorted riffraff that give Durham its grit and help prevent it being another staid English university city. On any

Friday night down its winding and crowded cobbled streets the pubs will be bursting with academics and ASBOs drinking shoulder to shoulder. But I'm headed to the outskirts to HM Prison Frankland, Category A, population just over eight hundred. It looks like any old correctional centre on a bleak moor – concrete, barbed wire, et cetera – and it's late October, northern autumn, so of course it's raining. The roll call of Frankland's current and former inmates is a who's who of nastydom: Harold Shipman – or Dr Death as the tabloids called him – the Yorkshire Ripper, a former Liberian warlord, and a Loyalist paramilitary who threw hand grenades at a Catholic funeral in Ulster. And, of course, Sammy Pritchard.

I've only just caught him in time. After two years of good behaviour and glowing reports from the parole board he's scheduled for a transfer to a lower category jail. I must be mad. Two years of cowering in my Antipodean bolthole fearing discovery and now here I am waltzing back into the lion's den. But I am mad, crackers, and it feels good. Sammy's waiting for me in a room they've set aside – the privilege of my former high-ranking job in the system. He's put on some weight. A latter-day prince bishop fallen from grace.

'Not taking advantage of the state-of-the-art gym facilities, Sammy?'

'Fuck off, son.' But he says it with a thin smile.

'You got my SMS then?'

He gives the tiniest of nods. He'll never admit to having access to a mobile in here.

'I hear you're on the path to redemption. Expecting to be out in what, four years?'

'Three, if I'm lucky.'

'The new lad that's taken over your trade isn't going to budge easily and most of your troops defected to him. You don't need that grief at your time of life.'

'New Zealand's nice, I hear.'

'Nah, you'd hate it. All that scenery, bitey flies up your nose, and blokes in socks and sandals that can't talk about anything but fucken rugby.' I slide him a printout of that same photo I SMSed him. Marty, post-mortem. 'What say we bury the hatchet?'

'You're a riot, son.'

'I've found new depths. I can thank you and Marty for that.'

'Oh, I think you already had them, Nicky, just waiting to be explored.' He leans forward. 'I spent the best part of the first two years here looking over my shoulder. Given your job, I assumed you'd have me topped.'

'I know the feeling. But that was the difference between you and me. I was never a vengeful bloke, I wasn't the type to have a man killed.'

The past tense isn't lost on him. 'How's Vanessa and the bairn?'

'Good.'

'I'd still like to look after him, he's a fantastic lad.'

'If he's so fantastic why did you send Marty to kill him, and Vanessa, and me?'

A shrug. 'Business, mate. I've an empire to keep together.'

'Fuck you, you sentimental, hypocritical old prick.' I prod the photo of Marty one more time. 'If you make it through the next few years, bugger off to Spain or somewhere, right? This is finished. No more.'

It elicits a murderous black glower which reminds me of Uncle Walter. 'Who the fuck do you think you are and what makes you think I would listen to you?'

'I'm the one who finally managed to get you put in here and nobody expected that, least of all you.' I signal the guard that I'm ready to leave. 'Give it up, Sammy. You can't win them all.'

After a long moment he nods. 'No hard feelings.' He holds out a hand. I study it. Then I shake it. 'Travel safe, Nicky,' he says to my departing back.

I'm still not sure whether I should just be done with it and arrange for the bastard to be shivved in the showers.

*

What with the cranes, the bulldozers and the road diversions, Sunderland city centre reminds me of Christchurch after the earthquake – but without the same fighting spirit and zest for life. I'm meeting Vanessa and Paulie in a Costa Coffee in the Bridges Shopping Centre. Paulie is wondering if we can catch a game at the Stadium of Light this weekend, Sunderland versus West Brom. I dig deep for some enthusiasm. 'Sure. Why not?'

Vanessa has done the rounds of family and friends over the last week. She's reassured herself that her mum is on the mend. I've done likewise with my own folks and the odd mate. It's like we've returned from the grave, they say, and maybe they're not wrong. We're due to fly back to NZ in another week. Or cancel the return and just have our stuff shipped over here. The centre sound system is broadcasting a shite radio station, two likely lads blathering on about nowt, and finding each other really funny then playing some crap music. The peace and quiet of the Wakamarina Valley seems a long way away.

'That's what I was thinking as well.' Vanessa wipes some coffee froth from her lips.

'What?'

'It's all over your face,' she laughs. 'It's like you've got a red hot poker up your arse and somebody's shoved a lemon in your gob to keep you quiet.'

Paulie splutters on his chocolate muffin.

'You're thinking the same?'

'I know,' she nods. 'I'm surprised myself. I was even checking out houses for sale here in that last week before we came back. I just assumed.'

'But?'

'But I've seen me mam and she's fine and she can come and visit now anytime she likes. Right?'

'Sure. Of course.'

'And your folks as well. As long as your dad smokes outside.'

'I'll let him know.'

'And me mates, they can come as well.'

'There'll be some spare blokes in the valley for Petra to try out.' Petra, Vanessa's best friend and notorious man-eating bridesmaid.

'I know. I've already told her.' She shakes her head at the babbling loudspeakers. 'This place is doing me head in.'

'Do we stay Chester or go back to Burgess?'

She shakes her head. 'I've got used to the new name, it's like being married again.' Her hand slips on to mine. 'Besides we don't want to confuse Paulie any more.'

He wipes the muffin crumbs from his mouth. 'I'm not stupid, you know. Just special.'

But it's agreed that we'll stick with Chester.

I'm seeing Vanessa in a new light. We do think the same things, we do share a way of viewing the world. It just gets obscured sometimes. Steve's term. *Tau o te ate*. Soul mate.

Paulie is getting worried though. 'Are we still going to the match?'

We go. They lose.

PART TWO

30

November has turned by the time we get back to the valley and they still haven't caught the Pied Piper – that's what the tabloids are calling him. After a dressing-down from the DC, a black mark on my record, and a promise to Marianne Keegan that I will keep my Glock in my pants, I'm back on duty.

Latifa is happy to see me back and also relieved. 'They had this bloke from Traffic standing in for you. He never took his finger out of his nose. He must have thought he was still in the car on his own in the bushes. Yuk.'

It's a compliment of sorts. I'm happy to get on with the humdrum and once again be gainfully employed earning an honest quid on an overcast Monday. Boy racers. Drunks. Gun-licence applications. Hunting infringements. Petty vandalism. School visits. Vanessa has lined up some part-time and relief work at three local schools. The patchwork enables her to work around Paulie drop-off and pick-ups. Some days our paths cross and we snatch a coffee and a chat in the middle of the day. We've even managed a quickie once, last week, in the car but it left us with cricks in the neck, and sandfly bites. Still, with the shadows of Sammy and Marty dispelled, we have a new lease of life in more ways than one.

But Gary worries us. He stays in that hut on the other side of the drive and we see little of him. The work has dried up and anyway he hardly seems physically capable of it now. To be brutal, it's a real downer, a blight on our otherwise cloudless horizon. I'm contemplating cutting him loose.

Vanessa says no. 'He's been through a lot, love.'

She's right. He put his life on the line for me and he lost a mate. He's still not fully recovered from Marty's savagery. And here I am talking about kicking him out because he's spoiling my second honeymoon.

'Maybe try talking with him?' she says.

There's a thought. I brew up a pot of tea and take that and a tin of cake over.

'Cheers,' says Gary, without much energy.

'How's the shoulder?' Marty's blade sliced deep into the muscle tissue and it's taking a long time to mend. He also lost some teeth and a bit of his ear.

'Sore.' He nods at my uniform which I haven't bothered changing yet. 'Back at work I see.'

'Yeah. It's nice to have something ordinary to focus on after ... everything.'

'Right. It would be. I can see that.'

'Any work coming your way?'

He lifts his shoulder a fraction. 'Not easy right now.' Reaches for his wallet. 'If it's the rent you're worried about.'

I shake my head. 'Not an issue.'

Gary looks up and fixes on me. 'So what is it you want?'

Dusk is my favourite time of day in the valley. The hills loom so close and the light changes rapidly. The river has just fallen into shadow and gone from green to purple-grey. A breath of wind ripples the surface.

'I'm sorry for involving you in my wars.' He shakes his head and tries a smile. I press on. 'I am responsible, I know that. I should have made you and Steve go.'

'We invited ourselves in.'

'Still.'

Gary sips from his mug. 'My dad was in Vietnam. Can you imagine that? Maori fighting these little peasants far away. At the same time Maori were marching in the streets here just to get some basic rights.' He stares at a stain on the rug, Steve's blood never fully washed out but Gary keeps it there anyway. 'They gave my dad a medal. He was real proud of it, showed it around, felt pretty flash for a while.'

'Good on him.'

'He knew it wasn't his fight and he probably had more in common with the Vietcong than the pakeha giving him his orders.' A nibble at the corner of his slice of cake. 'But he was among some mates, and mates are more important than a cause.'

'When I was back in the UK, I spoke to the man behind all this. There'll be no more.'

He nods. 'So you've found peace.'

'I hope so.'

He lifts a hand. 'Your own little corner of paradise. Nice block of land and your family back home with you. Sweet as.' Across the river the pines sway in the evening breeze. 'But I need to have my peace, my reckoning. *Utu.*'

'Forget it, Gary. Unless you get on a plane and pay him a visit, it's not going to happen.'

A shake of the head. 'Not just that bloke. I've got a list that goes way back.'

I study him and get to wondering if I'm on that list. One more pakeha who's taken too much for granted. 'I know it's hard, mate. But we need to look forward.' I place my hand on his arm.

He lifts it off and smiles. 'Thanks for the tea. And that cake.'

*

In the night I hear Gary pack stuff into his ute, close the cabin door, step up onto our back porch and slide the key under the potted tomato plant. There's a brief whistle as he summons the dog up onto the tray. The car door opens and shuts, and the engine starts. There's a crunch of gravel as he goes. I can't tell what I feel. Relief? A new foreboding?

Vanessa stirs, pushing back into me. 'What is it?' she murmurs.

'Nothing.'

31

After several postponements due to either illness or diary clashes from both sides, Beth is going to see the hypnotist today. DI Keegan has asked Latifa and me to pick Beth up from her house near the marae and bring her to Blenheim. Beth is nervous and her cigarette smoke fills the police car.

'I'll be asleep and he'll be like totally in control. He's not going to make me do weird stuff like take my knickers off in public, is he?'

'Just taking your knickers off in private'd be a nice change,' says Pete, contributing to the tobacco fug in the back.

'Shut it,' snarls Beth.

'I'll be with you in the same room,' says Latifa. 'I'll make sure you're alright.'

Instead of the police station, the appointment is at some private consulting rooms around the corner from Marlborough Boys' College. DI Keegan meets us there and we adjourn to the office next door which has a video link, while Beth and Latifa settle in with ponytailed Professor Sumner and his Japanese wall hangings. Meanwhile Pete has gone to the library to watch videos on YouTube.

It's a remarkably low-key transition from Beth's state of nervous wakefulness to the trance-like state we now see. No swinging watches or you-are-feeling-very-sleepy. Blink and you'd miss it. Beth is back on duty serving drinks and meals and collecting glasses that night in the Woodbourne Tavern.

'There's a table just emptied,' she says. 'Boys from the vineyard down the road. Four pots, four plates.' She tuts. 'Ginger kid left half his food again. Fucken waste.' Her mouth goes into a chewing motion. 'Chips are cold.'

Sumner takes her through rounding up the glasses and plates and heading back towards the bar.

'Get off me, ya fucken creep!' She slides her waist away to the left. 'Fucken Rogers, no shame after what you done. Today of all days.'

'Are you saying that?' asks Sumner.

'Thinking it.' She wrinkles her nose. 'He stinks. He wears those cheap nylon shirts and no deodorant.'

'Who else is at the table, do you know them?'

'Three other blokes. Haven't seen the others before.'

'Describe them. Describe the man who is next to Mr Rogers on his ... left?'

'No, right. Left of Fuckface is the carpet. On his right, chubby, with black curly hair. Looks a bit like Pete but with better teeth. Ear stud. Blue polo shirt. Looks like he wants to fuck me. Looks like he wouldn't know what to do.'

'Does he say anything?'

'No, just laughing and staring at my tits.'

'Who else is there? Across the table, maybe?'

She shifts slightly in her seat. 'Younger. Neat, short, brown hair. Dressed nice, his clothes fit well. Those shirts that you wear a tie with. Jacket over the back of his chair. Looks a bit embarrassed.'

'Does he say anything?'

'No, just keeps checking his watch like maybe he should be going. He's wearing a wedding ring.'

'Who else?'

'That's enough, Des. They're grieving.' A pause. 'Leave it, Des. Stop.'

'Describe him, he's straight across from Des, or diagonal?'

'Straight across.' Beth's eyes open, has she woken up?

'Describe him. Tell me about his hair.'

She squints. 'Very short, fair, little bit of grey.' Sumner tries to get her to detail his facial features: eye colour and shape, nose, mouth and such. She's shaking, bottom lip trembling. Tears forming in her eyes. '*Pōuri*,' is all she can say or see. Darkness.

Sumner leads her out of danger. 'His shirt. Tell me about his shirt.'

She steadies. 'White. Short sleeves. Collar. Tennis. Marlborough Tennis Club.'

'Trousers? Shorts?'

'Can't see.'

'Is he wearing a watch?'

'No. There's a band of pale skin around his wrist like he used to wear one.'

'Right hand or left?'

'Right.'

That's enough, Des. They're grieving. 'How does he know?'

'What?' says Keegan.

I repeat the line to her. 'He must know Beth's connection to Prince, that she's related. How? Did Rogers mention it?'

She puts it to Beth via Sumner. All it elicits is a shrug.

'He knows the family,' I insist. 'He's met them or seen them.'

'Shush,' says Keegan. 'You might be right but she's not taking us to him today.'

More questions from DI Keegan's feed through Sumner's earpiece but they come to nothing.

Latifa whispers something to Sumner and he turns back to Beth. 'What is his smell?'

She winces. 'Like when you're walking up the lane and someone's slung a dead cat into the bushes.'

'His real smell?'

'Real enough to me. I don't care if other people can get it or not. I do.'

*

DI Keegan will unleash her hounds to try and track down those boys from the vineyard who were at the adjoining table, even if Beth reckons they were backpackers and long gone. Still, the vineyard might have records. And the other men at the table, associates of Des Rogers in some way. And the Marlborough Tennis Club, the membership lists, club photos and competitions.

'And he's had some previous contact, however brief, with the family,' I remind her.

'Maybe but without Beth's ID of him it doesn't count for much. Maybe someone else from that night will fill out the picture.'

'And he's probably right-handed.'

'The watch?' says Keegan.

'The imprints on the child's neck.' I mime the action of pushing the kid's head under water. 'Maybe that's how he lost his watch? Who knows?'

'Who indeed.' Keegan lets out a sour sigh. 'And not forgetting the spiritual smell of roadkill.'

'Don't knock it,' says Latifa. 'You're a lot closer now because of our voodoo.'

When I'm back at the office, Vanessa calls. She's pissed off with me. 'What did you say to Gary last night? He's gone.'

When I left for work this morning, I didn't mention it. 'Really?'

'No note, no nothing. Just the key under the pot and the place cleared out.'

'He's probably got stuff to think about. Maybe he just needs some time on his own.'

'Stuff?'

'Unfinished business.'

A sigh. 'Men.'

I try Gary's mobile and it goes straight through to voicemail. 'It's Nick. I heard you leave last night. You don't need to go, and you're welcome back any time.' I'm sounding, I don't know, white and well-meaning? 'Whatever, look after yourself. Stay safe.'

Latifa is looking at me. 'Gary gone?' I nod. 'Probably for the best.' She pins up a missing-dog notice on the board.

'You think?'

'Bad thing to go through, being stabbed, and losing your mate. And people only give you so much time, don't they?'

'But I ...'

'Yeah, yeah. You're very concerned for his welfare and you want him to try and move on. Abracadabra, he's done it.'

She has this way of twisting the knife.

The afternoon is spent shuffling electronic paper around and cruising up and down SH6 looking for miscreants. We find three and ticket them. It's only Tuesday of my second week back but already I feel an itch. Maybe it was being back in tenuous connection with the investigation this morning and watching Beth on that grainy video link reliving her encounter in the Woodbourne Tavern. I see this pasty soft-faced man in a tennis shirt, a hand holding a child's head under the water, Prince Haruru facedown in the mud at Linkwater, Jamie Riley propped against the shoe fence, and Qadim Reza among the vines in the Wairau Valley. The Pied Piper has killed two kids in a month yet before that there was a five-year gap. I can't believe nothing has happened during that period but DI Keegan has had people checking and they've found nothing.

Unless, of course, he was doing it somewhere else during that time.

I phone Keegan and put it to her. 'Yes,' she says. 'We've looked into that too. We sent it over to the Aussies, they do a good line in paedos.'

'And?'

'Plenty of creeps but none of them look like ours. There's a couple of unsolveds, one from Queensland two years ago and the other from Perth around the same time. We're taking a second look.'

'But?'

'But I'll keep you posted.'

'Perth,' I say, thinking Patrick Smith. 'What is it about Perth and perverts?'

'Too much sunshine? Both begin with a P?' Her voice drops a notch. 'I hear you're back on track with Vanessa?'

'Yes. I am.'

'That's great,' she says.

Do I detect a hint of regret? I'm not going to ask.

'I don't suppose I could take a look at the Aussie unsolveds?'

'You don't suppose right. Bye Nick.'

Two in Australia, and maybe others elsewhere. Where would you start? Interpol? No doubt DI Keegan has already been down that line too. Besides, Interpol relies on member countries with diligent officers who feed into the system in the hope of solving their mysteries. But I think about Des Rogers and all the others of his ilk out there. What if the investigators don't give a toss because the victim is from the wrong race, wrong tribe, wrong religion, wrong class? What if the investigators are corrupt and deliberately want to bury a case? The Pied Piper. The world is his oyster.

*

DI Keegan might not want to let me into the system officially but it doesn't stop me googling. The search-engine question would have the metadata spooks on my tail but this stuff never was for the faint-hearted. The Queensland case was in Rockhampton, halfway up the coast, during the winter of that year. A child missing for a week before being found floating in the river. Raped and strangled and with evidence of alcohol and drugs in the system. But I understand Keegan's lack of enthusiasm, the victim was a twelve-year-old girl. Why the second look? Then it emerges from later reports that the drug was Rohypnol.

The Perth case was a month later: a ten-year-old boy from the suburb of Armadale, discovered in bushland near a reservoir. The body badly decomposed from exposure to winter rains. Again, rape and strangulation but no mention of drugs or alcohol in the system. This time I don't understand Keegan's lack of enthusiasm. Time and decomposition might account for lower or even no traces of drugs and, even if there aren't any, it doesn't mean there's no connection worth investigating. Maybe the Rohypnol is a later development, a refinement in his MO. Or perhaps Keegan has seen more in the detailed police and forensic reports that makes her think, nah, probably not.

Latifa is looking over my shoulder. 'You need to get a life, Sarge. Get home to that family of yours.'

She's finished for the day. She looks bright, perky, and smells nice. 'Plans?'

'Daniel.' The speedster. Apparently it's going from strength to strength. 'Karaoke night at the Havelock Hotel.'

I wish her well and close down the horrors on my computer screen.

*

After dinner that night, and with Vanessa still frosty with me over the Gary thing, there's a call on the home landline. It's the halfway house in Blenheim saying Deborah Haruru wants me to come and see her.

'Now?'

'No, next Christmas would be fine,' says the warden. 'And bring that girl with you as well.' I assume she means Latifa.

Latifa is on stage in the hotel belting out Etta James' 'At Last' to a besotted Daniel. She has a fine singing voice.

'Sorry to interrupt.' I explain why and she rolls her eyes.

A long lingering tonguey with Daniel and she follows me out the door. 'This better be good.'

It turns out it is.

32

Deborah Haruru seems in a lot better shape than the last time we saw her. Her skin is a healthier colour, the eyes have some life, and her posture is prouder. We're all out on the side verandah in the cold evening air and Deborah has a ciggie on the go.

'You said if I thought of something, no matter how stupid, I should get in touch.'

'That's right.'

Latifa is bracing herself for the stupidity. Perhaps calculating the options of racing back to Daniel and taking up where she left off.

'About two weeks before everything happened.' Deb shakes her head. 'It was a Friday, after school. I was packing the car up 'cause we were heading off for the weekend. Thought it was about time Prince met his uncle. We were headed down to Christchurch.'

Latifa can see I'm struggling to remember who was who. 'Deb's brother is Denzel's dad, the one who's in prison. His name's Travis.'

Deb, Beth, and Travis. The Haruru siblings. I recall somebody telling me something about a son in prison. 'Isn't he still inside? Five years, that's a long stretch.'

'Different offence,' says Deborah. 'He's been out and back in twice during that time. Never learns.'

'Okay.' I promise not to interrupt her flow again.

'We were staying at my dad's place near the marae.'

'Uncle Walter,' Latifa reminds me.

'Prince was off running around with Denzel and some others down the street.' She gives a little jolt. 'I hear a car screech. The kids are laughing so at least nobody's been hurt. I look down the side of the house from where I am out back and see it go past. Real fast.'

'And?'

'It was pretty flash for round our way. One of those ones without a roof.'

'A convertible?' She nods. 'Do you remember the make or colour?'

'White.'

'Make?'

'Nah, I'm not real good with that stuff. I asked Princey what the noise was all about and he said Denzel gave the finger to some pakeha in a car. I asked why and he said why not.'

I wait for her to go on. She doesn't. 'That's it?'

Latifa has the car keys in her hand.

'So I look at Denzel and say, you need to watch yourself, don't go getting my boy into trouble. And he says, sorry, Auntie.' She frowns. 'Thing is, I told all this to Detective Rogers and he wrote it all down. Denzel even remembered part of the number on the plate at the time.'

'Did you hear anything back from Rogers?'

'Nothing.'

'So why have you remembered this now?'

'I think I saw that car today. Same bit of number plate too, it must've stuck in my head and I never knew until I saw it again.'

'Where was this?'

'Straight over the road from here. The Countdown car park.'

*

'FHW something,' says Latifa. 'Round numbers, Deb reckons. Threes, sixes, eights, nines.'

We're running it through the system. It being a convertible helps narrow things down. 'Here we go. It belongs to Ebenezer Holdings, trading as Rent-A-Flash-Bomb.'

He's just down the road from the Marlborough Showgrounds and there's an after-hours as well as a business number. We give him a call and he says, yeah come right over, which is very accommodating for nine thirty at night. He's an Aussie. The name is Joey and, small as he is, he has a voice that doesn't need an amplifier.

'Gen Y, mate, don't you just love 'em? When I was a backpacker, it was a postcard or aerogramme to the folks once a month and I had to sell my blood to a clinic in Kathmandu to get a regular feed. This mob? Hundred bucks to jump off a bridge here, three hundred to skydive there.' He waves at his fleet of flash bombs: retros, convertibles, zippy sports cars and such.

'They'll even lash out for a topless drive over to Rainbow Ski or Harwood's Hole for the weekend to impress some chick. Am I complaining?'

We state our business and he looks up the car in question.

'It's rented to some Pom.' He lifts his eyes from the screen to me. 'No offence.'

'None taken.'

'Jeremy Gibson. Money to burn, that boy. You can tell the way he speaks. I think he might be a viscount or something on the quiet.' He taps a couple of keys. 'Due back, day after tomorrow.'

'How long have you had the car?'

'Couple of years, maybe.'

'Who did you get it from? Do you have the records handy?'

'Easy. One of my regular suppliers. I buy up the best of their old executive fleet every two or three years.' He closes his laptop. 'McCormack Forestry.'

*

'You can't be serious,' says Latifa. We're on our way back to Havelock and I'm driving. She thinks we should pass everything over to DI Keegan and the Pied Piper investigation.

'You've changed your tune. Not long ago you were getting stuck into me for suggesting exactly that.'

'That was different. That was about doing right by the community. People like McCormack, you have to do it all by the book.'

'He plays squash with the DC, he runs the region, it'll get buried. He'll just say I'm running a vendetta.'

'Aren't you?'

'At the moment we have half-memories from Deborah about a car that might have been near the marae five years ago. There's no mention of it in Rogers' case notes. It's flimsy at best.'

'So?'

'If we dig deeper ourselves ...'

'Yourself.'

'And find corroborating evidence, it'll be harder for the DC and Keegan to cover up. McCormack will be obliged to answer questions.'

'So to avoid the appearance of a vendetta, you're going to run your own little unofficial side investigation into this bloke whose guts you hate?'

'That's it.' I cast her a sideways glance while negotiating the racing bend into Renwick. 'You can keep out of it.'

'Too late. I can't unknow something.'

Latifa's right. She's compromised and culpable if I push ahead with this. 'Okay, I'll call Keegan in the morning.'

'Don't have to. I was just sayin', that's all.'

33

The way some of these people live. It must be like falling off the horizon, or one of those ravines in the ranges. There's just a precipitous long drop of loose shale and every move you make loosens your grip. Of course he's seen people living in worse conditions than this but at least things were simpler there – live or die, fuck or be fucked: law of the jungle. There's nothing noble about these savages though. Here survival is a question of how much you can con out of Work and Income, who's left their valuables in an unlocked car, whose livestock you can poach tonight, can you stay one step ahead of Child, Youth and Family who want to take your snotty brat away from you, who's dissing you on Facebook and needs a bottle in the face.

Not long now. She'll strap the ugly little runt into the seat, light up the first ciggie of the day, and gun the stinking rust bucket into town. Lodge her claim, stare in the bargain shop windows at all the shit she'll never be able to afford, come home and find that, yes, things can get even worse in her sorry life.

It's a new sensation for him, feeling this angry, but to have scum like this getting in his way – well, really.

Off she goes. The dog barks. But it always barks and nobody takes any notice. He rolls his car down the drive into the shadows under the tree. There's a shed, not a well-stocked one, mainly empty bottles which will end up in a gully some day because the town tip charges too much to dump shit there. Tools? A chainsaw in need of cleaning. An axe. Nasty, rusty little implements that look like they belong in the Inquisition, plenty of possibilities.

It's like everything has been laid on for him. Then he sees what will do the job. It will work a treat.

34

On my way down the valley to work I call in on Charlie Evans. As usual he's up and about early, attending to the alpacas and chickens.

'Need any eggs?' he says. 'Plenty to spare. Better you have them than the stoats.'

That's a yes and he'll leave a dozen in his letter box for me to collect on the way back at the end of the day. 'Denzel not here yet?'

'No, probably another half an hour before Walter drops him off. Not in trouble again, is he?'

'Just wanting a word. No bother.' I inquire after Mrs Evans.

'Up and down. But maybe more down than up the last few weeks.'

'Sorry to hear it.'

'But I have had a win on another front.' He thumbs at the hill over his shoulder. 'The court has ordered a temporary halt on McCormack logging the other half of the hill.'

'Great.'

'And I'm now a crowd of two. An anonymous donor contributed to my legal campaign.'

'A big one?'

He nods. 'It's certainly levelled the playing field. All came in via some law firm in Auckland.'

The day is shaping up well. 'McCormack must be spitting.'

'I hope so.'

Uncle Walter and Denzel roll up early. That's good. 'Got a moment?' I explain my interest and Walter nods his permission for me to address the boy. 'Remember about a week before Prince died, you and him were playing in the street and there was some pakeha in a sports car?'

He puts on a show of thinking back. 'Yeah. What about it?'

'Your Auntie Deb said you'd been cheeky to the bloke, made him slam on his brakes. She'd mentioned it to the cops after Prince was taken.'

'So?' He's got a glower like Uncle Walter.

'Remember what the bloke looked like? How old, that kind of thing?'

'We're talking five years ago, man.'

'Try, Denzel. It might be useful.'

Walter nudges him. 'Do as you're told, boy.'

A shake of the head. 'He was wearing a baseball cap and shades. Didn't get a good look at him. Just a whitey, that's all. Tend not to look too closely at them unless they're giving me grief.'

'Big bloke?'

'Not especially but he was sitting down in his car so, you know.'

'Fat, skinny?'

'Skinny.'

'Clothes?'

'Yeah, he had clothes on.' Walter slaps him around the back of the head. 'Light-coloured shirt. Pink maybe. Bit gay if you ask me.'

'Anything else?'

'Yeah, nah, sorry.'

'If you think of anything.' I hand over my card and we all go our separate ways.

*

In the office I phone Joey from Rent-A-Flash-Bomb. Does the car in question have a GPS satnav? Yeah, sure, these are flash bombs after all, not your average. Did it come with the car when he bought it? Yep. I send Latifa over to pick it up off him and reassure him I'll cough up for a temporary replacement.

'What's this about then?' he wonders.

I make up some cock and bull story about drug syndicates and he reckons it's cool. 'Mum's the word, eh?'

'Absolutely,' says Honest Joe.

But now I have the problem of trying to access the satnav memory to see where the vehicle might have been five years ago. Normally you just send it to the police IT geeks, but I can't because hush-hush side-run vendettas don't have a valid job code.

'No problem,' says Latifa. A phone call. 'Beth's on her way.'

'Beth?'

'I told you already. She's a whiz at this shit. Did some course at Nelson Tech and topped the class. She would have been eminently employable if she wasn't such an airhead dropkick with everything else in her life.'

Half an hour later Beth arrives with two laptops, some cables, and a pack of cigarettes. We set her up on the back verandah with a coffee and an ashtray and away she goes. While we deal with reports, circulars, timesheets, expenses claims and such, we can hear Beth uttering expletives and breaking for the occasional ugly cough.

'Here's the cunt,' she mutters after about twenty minutes. 'January seventeenth. Driving past Deb's house, just like she said.'

It's up there on the screen, a map of his movements, from McCormack Forestry offices in Nelson, along SH6 and turning off towards the marae where he does a couple of circuits, then out and back to Nelson again via a brief stop off at Havelock Marina.

'Can I get a copy of that?'

'The whole thing? All those backpackers going all over the place as well?' No, I say, just up until the car is sold to Honest Joe. She shrugs. 'Still shitloads. You sure?'

'How about a separate folder, just with the week before and after Prince's murder?' I begin to give her the dates but she lets me know that's not necessary.

'Only my own fucken nephew. Think I don't remember when it was?' Latifa swears Beth to secrecy and I say we owe her one. She waves me away, slightly offended. 'Like I say, he's my nephew. We all want to catch this bloke.' She shakes her head. 'But jeez, McCormack? He's the only one offering any jobs around here, even if it is shit pay. Why'd it have to be him?' Latifa points out that it's all very circumstantial and nobody should be jumping to any conclusions. Beth sniffs. 'Yeah, right.'

So now we have independent corroboration that the McCormack car was in the vicinity of Prince Haruru's home in the week before his murder. But what was it doing there and who was driving?

*

I could happily pore over the downloads Beth has provided and spend the next week full-time tracking McCormack via his five-year-old satnav records, but my job keeps interrupting. A tractor has rolled near Okaramio and the driver may lose his leg. Jessie James is on the scene taking pics and getting in the way. She sidles up to me.

'Back at work, I see.'

'Yes.'

'I heard the air ambulance was called to your place a few weeks back. That Maori bloke that died on your property. And the other one, the Brit. What was that all about? The real story.'

'Bad blood, going back years.'

'Who between? The Maori guy and the Brit?'

'A tragedy and a waste of life. Probably best to let the families grieve in peace.' I change the subject. 'How's your investigative piece coming along?' Her look says, uh? 'The impact of logging?'

'Oh yeah, that.' She tells me she's been invited in to the offices of McCormack Forestry for a briefing by their PR person.

'And?'

'And what?'

'The other side of the story?'

'What other side of the story?'

Journalism School ain't what it used to be. 'Maybe there's a trade union that has another perspective. Or an environmental group. Or an aquaculture business out on the Sounds that's now got silty mussels or muddy salmon. Farmers. Tourism operators. Get my drift?'

'That's a lot of work.' She nods to herself. 'You've really got it in for McCormack haven't you?'

I've a feeling this is going to come back to bite me.

*

On the way back from Okaramio I get a call saying there's been a hunting mishap up the Wakamarina Valley, not that far from home. An ambulance is on its way from Blenheim as the nearer Havelock one is tied up with an accident on SH6 out beyond Pelorus Bridge. It's nearly the end of the day so I make it my last call and grab the free-range eggs out of Charlie Evans' mailbox on my way past. A couple of kilometres short of my house on some clear-felled pasture there's a cluster of shacks built in that spartan style that says not stayin' long. It's where Gary and Steve parked their dogs and guns before I relented and allowed both on my property. There's a bony unkempt horse chewing on tufts of grass, a lamb braying in the undergrowth, and a pig dog that won't stop barking.

'Hello?' I yell, double-checking the address of the call-out. Yes, this was definitely it. 'Hello? Nick Chester, Havelock Police. Anybody home?'

The householder's name is John Fernandez. Johnny to his mates and to the cops he frequently deals with. He exists on a balance of welfare state benefits, occasional labouring work, and miscellaneous windfalls. He's only nineteen and already he has an extensive record for firearms licence infringements, drug possession and supply, firewood and farm machinery thefts, and drinking without a clue. He also has an eighteen-year-old de facto wife and a one-year-old toddler.

'Hello? Johnny? You here?'

The call-out was logged forty-six minutes ago and mentioned a man having his hand caught in one of his own possum traps. That fitted Johnny's MO. The call-out was in his name. There'd be no mobile coverage here. Did he wander in with the possum trap stuck on his hand and call from the landline? Maybe he's since lost some blood and fainted?

'Johnny?' I try the front door.

It's not locked, but that's not unusual up the valley. Pushing it open, I can hear the TV on in the lounge room down the passage. Sounds like a kids show, a cartoon maybe.

'Johnny?' What's his partner's name again? 'Shania?'

I glance in the other rooms on the way along the hall. Messy but empty. I get to the lounge room door and between the yowling pig dog and the TV blare, I'm getting jumpy. I pull out my gun and nudge the door open with my foot.

'Johnny?'

Johnny is there and yes he's got the possum trap on his hand. I doubt he's feeling it though. His skull has been demolished and blood has sprayed up the walls; pinky-grey brain matter glistens on the rim of a coffee mug and drips from the corner of the table. There's a claw hammer on the floor beside him, matted with blood and hair. I hear a noise, a door opening back along the passage, and I whip round, gun levelled.

'What the fuck?' says Shania, dropping her shopping bags and hoisting the toddler into her arms. Mercifully she can't yet see what's in the room behind me. 'Where's Johnny and who the hell are you?'

*

A combination of Blenheim and Nelson dicks are dealing with it. Given the company that Johnny kept, everybody's assuming skanky bogan drug feud and that the emergency call-out was done by the killer, for reasons as yet unknown. Maybe to send some kind of message to someone, or maybe as a twisted kindness to his family so they wouldn't be the ones to find him. Shania and the toddler, Trayvon, are being looked after by her mum down in Seddon on the coast where the earth trembles regularly.

This is becoming something of a blood-soaked valley and people are shaking their heads and saying this place is going to the dogs. I'm with them and feeling pretty shaky myself. There's been some real rage unleashed in that house some time in the last several hours. Personal. From the heart. Terrifying. Yet I've encountered similar levels of violence on a pensioner abandoned in the stairwell of a Manchester tower block, on a teenager who strayed onto the wrong turf. Not personal. Not from the heart. But just as terrifying in its banality. These incidents build and build until one day you snap over the smallest thing – graffiti on the gable end of an old soldier's house, a kid crying about his stolen skateboard.

The rumours catch on the wind and swirl through the gorges. Johnny's linked to the bikies in Nelson, you know. Yeah, but he was a snitch. She's got an old boyfriend, very violent, very jealous. Wasn't Johnny a mate of those Maori from the North Island? Remember the one that died? The cop's place further up, that's right.

No doubt the squad will be investigating these and other matters over the coming weeks. Tonight at home we're eating a mushroom omelette made from Charlie Evans' free-range eggs. It's delicious but I find myself drifting as Vanessa and Paulie try to engage me in conversation. I think pets might be on the agenda.

'What? Sorry.'

'Tune in, Dad,' says Paulie. 'Family time.'

Vanessa takes Paulie's and her plates, and clatters them into the sink. 'Your dinner's getting cold.'

35

A bank of dark cloud looms behind the Richmond Ranges to the south and I'm glad. We need water for the tank and I want to see that river bubbling again. It's early and Paulie is still sleeping. On the back balcony with Vanessa and a plunger of coffee, the sandfly count is low and we're enjoying the moment. Birds flit among the trees, whistling, beeping.

'It's beautiful here,' says Vanessa. 'Another world.'

'It's not Sunderland, for sure.'

'Would you stay here if you were on your own?'

'Probably.' I can see from Vanessa's face that it was the wrong answer. 'You?'

'No. I'd be too lonely. It would be a terrible place to be lonely in.'

'Yeah, I can see that.' I refill both our cups from the plunger. 'Since we came back I've stuffed up a bit, haven't I?' She waits. 'I've upset Gary and he's gone. I've become obsessive about the job again.' She's still waiting. 'Sorry.'

Her hand creeps across the table and folds over mine. 'When we weren't here, me and Paulie, how did that feel?'

'Shite.'

She nods. 'Hold that thought.'

Across the river there's an explosion of engine roars, metallic sounds. A chainsaw. A few moments later a tree detaches itself from the crowd and topples sideways. The crash vibrates along the valley and through the foundations of our home. The pine plantation opposite us is being logged.

I bang my coffee cup down on the table. 'Fuck.'

Paulie comes out of his bedroom, sleep-puffed, anxious. 'What's that noise?'

Vanessa reassures him and distracts him with breakfast. She can see I'm angry, and that disturbs her more than the land being torn apart.

*

According to the recorded message, I'll have to wait until office hours before talking to McCormack Forestry. I seethe all the way down the valley. Passing Johnny Fernandez's house, the crime scene tape is up and the men and women in blue overalls are pottering about. Further down, Charlie Evans gives me a wave in passing and I acknowledge him with an angry nod. In the office the clock ticks around to nine and I snatch up the phone.

'I'd like to talk to Mr McCormack.'

'Who's speaking please?'

'Nick Chester, I'm a resident opposite one of your pine operations.'

'He's busy.'

'Tell him who's calling. He'll speak to me.' Because we both know this is as personal as it gets.

Silence. Some hold music. Split Enz. Yeah, me too. I don't know why sometimes I get frightened either. Well, maybe I can take a guess. A few clicks. 'Sergeant Chester, what can I do for you this fine morning?'

'Mister will do, this is a private matter.'

'You're able to keep these things separate? Well done.'

'The plantation across from my property. Your loggers started today. My understanding is that it's not meant to be harvested for at least another three years.'

'That's right but I've got men standing idle, they were booked to do the other half of my hill behind Charlie Evans' place. Because of his silly legal action that's now on hold, and time is money.'

'You must have other plantations ahead of the queue before that one near me.'

'Not in my backyard, eh?' He covers the mouthpiece and says something to his assistant. 'Yes, there are others which are more mature and would probably bring a better return. This one is cost neutral at best. But I'm happy to forego the profit if it ruins your day.'

He's having fun and I can't do a damn thing about it. 'Enjoy it while it lasts.' I slam the phone down.

'I was going to fetch you a coffee but maybe a chamomile might be better?' Latifa shrugs off her jacket and hangs it on the hook. 'What's up?'

I tell her and she offers a sympathetic smile. 'There, there. You might have to look out of a different window for a while.' I decline the tea and she drags up her chair. 'So tell me about Johnny Fernandez.'

'Blenheim Ds reckon it's drug debts.'

An eye roll. 'They would.'

'Meaning?'

'He's a useless dropkick, too useless to be a player in the drug scene and make somebody that angry. At best he would get a bit of a slap.'

I'm inclined to agree but since when is Latifa au fait with the down and dirty world of Johnny Fernandez?

'Same iwi,' she says. 'Same marae.'

'I never realised.'

'Yeah well, he hasn't got the *moko* on his face so you'd find it hard to pick him, wouldn't you?'

I don't take the bait. 'So you don't think it's drug debts?'

'Grog debts would be more his style. Or an argument with his mates over who's got the best dog or the sickest tatt.'

'He won't be missed then? No big tangi for him.'

'Wrong there. He'll get a fine send-off. Good excuse for a cry and a party.' Latifa returns to my gripe of the day. 'It's not ancient Amazonian rainforest, Sarge, it's plantation pine, the stuff you burn in your fire, you'd be cold without it. What's the big drama?'

How do I explain that the destruction left behind after logging – the splinters, the debris, the dust, the devastated landscape – speaks to me of only one thing: death. It brings to mind war zones, plagues, apocalypse. Having lived in fear of my life for the last two years I'm prone to catastrophising. She'll think I'm nuts and that I really need to find a bit of perspective. Instead I shrug. 'It can't be good for the environment and it makes everything look like shit.'

She takes her chair back to her desk. 'Diddums. You realise your little investigation sideshow just got more difficult?'

I play dumb. 'Yeah?'

'McCormack can say you're just getting back at him for spoiling your view.'

As if I would be so spiteful and petty.

*

Once again my McCormack vendetta is sidetracked by the demands of the job. The Nelson-Blenheim Ds want Latifa and me to help with the doorknocking up and down the valley. DC Ford drops by in person as I'm pulling up to the crime scene.

'Another killing. Must be something in the water over here,' he says. 'You should get your filters checked.'

'It should be a three-day job, sir. Johnny didn't mix with master criminals. Somebody will have left their driver's licence at the scene, or posted pics on Facebook, or told the bloke next to them in the pub. And they won't have had a wash yet so the forensics'll be good.'

'Do I detect a degree of world-weariness in you, Nick? Everything okay at home?'

'Fine, thanks.' I don't mention the logging and don't mention that, in my mind at least, McCormack is shaping up as a prime suspect for the Pied Piper murders. 'How's the Riley-Reza investigation proceeding?' They haven't formally and publicly linked it with Prince Haruru yet.

'Bogged.'

'What about the results of the hypnotism session on the boy's aunt?'

'The vineyard workers at the nearby table were backpackers and they've all fucked off somewhere else. That's going to take an age to work through. The vineyard didn't have them on the books, they were cash in hand. They were kipping in a caravan on site, so no backpacker hostel records of them. There's no CCTV in the tavern going that far back. We know now that Bernie Webster wasn't one of the four blokes at that table and so far efforts to track down the others have failed.'

'Marlborough Tennis Club?'

'Had a break-in a short while back and the place got trashed and a few trophies got nicked. Laptops ditto. Their membership is extensive, a couple of hundred, but we only have this year's list which was on a thumb drive the secretary kept at home for the mailings.'

'The Perth and Rockhampton cases?'

He squints at me. 'For a fringe-dweller you seem remarkably well-informed.'

'Professional interest.'

'I'm not up to date with where they're at.'

But he is. There's been a development, it's written all over his face. I nod at the crime scene. 'DI Keegan isn't interested in this case?'

'Why would she be? Like you said, three-day job at best.' He checks the time on his mobile and feels in his pocket for the car keys. 'All good on the home front? Vanessa and Paulie?'

'As I said. Hunky-dory.'

'Great. I'm glad that Sunderland business is all over.'

'Aren't we all?'

'And I'm glad you're still with us. We need blokes like you around here.'

'Thanks, sir.'

'This is your home now, right?'

'Right.'

*

Up and down the valley Johnny Fernandez's neighbours express shock and horror, but no actual surprise, at his untimely demise. That poor girl and the bub, they say. Shania has been cleared, she was having an interview at the Blenheim Work and Income office at pretty much the time Johnny exited this life. Nobody saw or heard anything unusual. No strangers or unfamiliar vehicles on the road. Nothing. The lead investigator, Detective Will Maxwell, is a stocky ginger-headed Blenheim boy, born and bred, and we've shared the odd wry comment at police socials.

'Those two Maori fellas that were living at your place. Johnny knew them, didn't he?'

'I believe so, yes.'

'One of them got killed by that English nutter?'

'Yeah.'

'The other one, what happened to him?'

'He was badly hurt too. He's gone off somewhere now. Sort himself out.'

'When was that?'

'A few days ago.' We check and confirm exact dates.

'Any idea where?'

'Nah.'

'He didn't tell you? I thought you were mates.'

I lift my face to the pale sunshine. 'He's his own man.'

'Gary. Gary, what was it again?'

'McCaw.'

'McCaw, right.'

'That's what he told me.'

'And you have no reason not to believe him.'

'Like I said, I'm not his keeper.'

'Fair enough.'

'Why are you asking?'

'There's a Gary in the victim's mobile phone records.' He tells me the number and yes, we're talking about the same bloke. 'Lot of calls between the two the last few weeks.'

'They were mates.'

'Including one an hour before Fernandez was killed. A missed call, given that Johnny was out of range.'

'From Gary's number?' A nod. 'Got a location on it?'

'Blenheim.'

I need to have my peace, my reckoning. Utu.

It's hard to believe that Gary could be involved but he was in a very dark place before he left.

I've got a list that goes way back.

I leave Detective Maxwell to his deliberations and we exchange promises: he will keep me in the loop and I will let him know if Gary gets in touch. Only maybe I won't.

*

At home I look out across the river and see they've ripped out about a quarter of the small block they've chosen to log. The pines that once swayed in the wind like a gospel choir are now piled up ready for trucking out. What was green and lush is now brown and dusty, and there are splinters left standing that seem to heighten the devastation, like photographs of First World War battlefields after an offensive or a gas attack.

'It'll grow back, it's only pine, better than logging old growth, surely.' Have Vanessa and Latifa been talking? 'Those hills further down the valley. They've already got green shoots.' Vanessa steers me towards a window where the vista is unscathed. 'Look at that. How glorious is that?'

But I'm compelled to focus on the bad stuff. It's in my DNA. I try to put it into words but they fail me.

Vanessa shakes her head. 'In Sunderland you had brick houses front, back, and sides. Reach out the window and you could touch them. You had a neighbour who drilled and hammered all day long until we wondered what the fuck was left for him to fix.'

'Mum,' says Paulie. 'We'll have to get a swear jar.'

She points her finger at him playfully. 'Bloody shut your cakehole.' He loves it. Back to me. 'If you could put up with that there, how come you're such a precious perfectionist here?'

'Because I'm powerless to stop it.'

'A-ha! The crux of the issue, m'lud. My learned friend is a fucking control freak ...'

'Mum!'

'He doesn't give two hoots about the environment and airy-fairy crap like that. He just wants everybody to fit in with him.'

She's smiling, I am too, Paulie is catching on. 'Busted,' I say.

But later as we're chopping vegies together for the dinner she turns to me with a sharp knife in her hand. 'It's not up to me to salvage your fragile mood every bloody day, Nick.' She chops savagely on a courgette. 'Grow some.'

36

Havelock Marina. It came to me in the night. Yesterday's promised rain didn't arrive until the small hours and as I lay there listening to the patter on the tin roof and to Vanessa snoring softly, I found these things in common. The Havelock Marina is where McCormack's car called in after the circuit of Prince Haruru's marae five years ago and it is where I was summoned by McCormack the day before Jamie Riley's body was found out by the shoe fence. Havelock Marina is conveniently located between where Prince Haruru was found in Linkwater and where Jamie Riley was found on the outskirts of town.

Today I will look for a link between the marina and the murder of Qadim Reza and study again the security CCTV footage sent to me by the diligent IT bloke over there. Derek, that was him, Derek with the tidy emails. The cloud hangs low over the hills and the river has more bubble to it. The clouds and gloom soften the vista of the logged hill. It's a trick of the light here: things that seem ugly under a bright unforgiving sun improve behind the cold veil of a rainy day, and vice versa. Sometimes it's just a matter of attitude. Vanessa eyes me warily over her toast.

'Is today a tick or a cross?'

'We usually do them at the end of a day.'

'New regime,' she says, scraping the last of the marmalade out. 'You get to decide straight away what kind of day you're going to have.' She crunches. 'So what is it?'

Her expression offers little room for manoeuvre. 'A tick, I guess.'

'Good boy.' She reaches for the calendar and hands me a pen. I do as I'm told. 'Have a nice day, love.' She gives me a big marmaladey kiss then goes to sort Paulie out.

I take care on the wet and winding road down the valley. Passing Johnny

Fernandez's house, I give Detective Maxwell's team a wave. Back in mobile range, there's a call from Maxwell himself.

'Did you know Gary and Johnny have a history?'

'What kind of history?'

'Bad blood.'

It doesn't fit with a guy who was prepared to stable Gary's guns and dogs while he lived at my place. You'd assume they were getting on. 'Tell me more.'

He spins me a convoluted tale involving drug debts, Nelson bikies, some Maori gang on the North Island that had it in for Gary. 'Apparently Johnny let them know where to find him.'

'When was all this meant to have happened?'

'About a year ago. And for your information he's not Gary McCaw, his real name is Gary Farr. Two r's.'

'Where are you getting all this scuttlebutt from? The bar of the Trout?'

'Steady on, Nick. This is intelligence from the Nelson drug boys. Rock solid.'

'It's bullshit. Fernandez was looking after hunting guns and dogs for Gary right up until about two months ago.'

'That's the thing,' says Maxwell. 'Gary only found out that Johnny snitched on him about a month ago. You were overseas then, weren't you?'

'So what if Johnny told this North Island mob where he was? Gary's still around, isn't he? They didn't get him. So it's of no account. Not worth murdering for.'

'They firebombed his house up there just before last Christmas. Gary was down at the pub. His wife and kids were inside, never got out.'

There was a fire. Couldn't get to 'em in time.

I have to admit. That's worth killing for.

*

On my way into the office, I try Gary's number. It's switched off or out of range so I leave a message for him to call me, acting official and cop-like and mentioning Johnny's death. I need to be careful about my contact with Gary. There will be questions about whose side I'm on.

The Fernandez inquiry doesn't need me today. Not because there's no work to be done. There are still more doors to knock on but Maxwell would prefer me at arm's-length as speculation builds around Gary. Gary Farr, two r's.

In the office Constable Rapata is bored, tapping her nails on the desk. 'How's the view today?' I can only take so much of Latifa's needling. I tell her I'm off down to the marina but she can give Maxwell a call to see if he can use her. 'Sorry for breathing,' she huffs.

Derek from Marina IT is waiting for me. He has large, blinking eyes, like a possum, and I wonder if he might be nocturnal. I give him some dates relevant to the Qadim Reza case.

'What's your interest? DI Keegan hasn't been in touch regarding these dates.'

'No,' I say. 'I've just had a couple of other complaints about theft and vandalism that have been lying on my desk while I was on leave. I'm tidying up some old paperwork.'

Tidying. I'm talking his language. Derek looks pensive. 'There were no complaints to the marina about theft and vandalism at that time but that doesn't always happen anyway.'

A thought occurs to me. 'Would you have kept CCTV from five years ago?'

'Five years ago? Why?'

'There was a reference to a vandalism case back then when I ran a computer crosscheck.'

Computer crosschecking. He likes that too, he edges his chair closer to me. 'If it was up to me I'd store every last bit of information about everything forever.' He sniffs. 'But my predecessor was Mr Delete and Re-use. Sorry.'

So we stick with the more recent stuff. As a starting point, I'm interested in the day Qadim was found, and anything up to forty-eight hours before that. My focus is on the camera beside the berth for *Serenity II*, McCormack's catamaran. I can see immediately that the tarp has gone and the offending graffiti removed. It looks good as new. In the twenty-four hours leading up to Qadim being found in the Wairau Valley vineyard, there is no movement in relation to *Serenity II*. The boat doesn't move and nobody comes to visit it.

On the day before that, the tarp is still in place and a man in overalls pulls up in a ute around ten a.m. There's a sign on the ute door that tells us he paints for a living. A few minutes later McCormack rolls up in his BMW. He inspects the craftsman's work, declares himself satisfied, and they shake hands after a brief conversation. The craftsman leaves first.

McCormack steps back onboard his vessel and slowly walks its length and back again like he's looking for something. Only he has his head in the air. He's not looking for something, he's smelling for something. He stops. He's found it. He goes inside and opens a window, comes back on deck, sits down and takes out his mobile. He's looking directly at the CCTV camera while he speaks on the phone. Then he gets in his car and drives away.

'What do you make of that?' I say to Derek.

'Nice boat.'

That's the point about the trappings of wealth and success. Folks see what they want to see: the boat, the car, the house, the jewels. It's the things that come to matter and those who possess these things can be rendered invisible, mythic. And that suits some people very well.

So, for all three cases, McCormack is at Havelock Marina in the lead up to the discovery of the bodies. It's pretty loose. He's a rich boatie: why wouldn't he be hanging around a marina? Derek gives me a thumb drive full of the CCTV footage and I call in to the bakery for a pie and a coffee on my way back to base.

In the office there's a yellow stickie from Latifa telling me she's out for the rest of the day. I power up the computer and go back to the original thumb drive Derek sent through for the graffiti call-out. No, nothing has changed. It's early morning and McCormack pulls up in the beemer and the glamour couples emerge: Dickie and Sebastian and two long-legged women. They unpack picnic stuff from the boot while the boys ready the boat. McCormack finds the graffiti and throws his hands up in anger. Everybody looks suitably shocked and outraged. McCormack phones the cops while his companions pack away the picnic gear. Sebastian Ryan, the snooty lawyer, disappears for fifteen minutes and returns with a cardboard tray of takeaway coffees. They get back in the flash car while McCormack deals with the bolshie cop who turns up five minutes later.

I haven't seen the footage leading up to the following day when Jamie Riley was discovered. That was sent to DI Keegan , who found nothing of interest. But she wasn't looking for the same thing. If I call Derek and ask for a copy, will that trigger questions I don't want to answer yet? Probably. Outside, the main drag is deserted as people keep out of the drizzle that has descended on the town. It's easy to imagine grudges festering in this place. I'm running one against McCormack and he's returning the favour, even if it means taking lesser profits on an unmatured harvest just to piss me off. Uncle Walter sometimes seems like he's carrying two hundred years' worth. And Gary. Yep, he's got his list too.

It's early afternoon. I can't move any further on the footage, short of examining it over and over again, and my *utu* is too lazy and ill-disciplined for that. What was DC Ford holding back on the Perth and Rockhampton cases? Those other kids who met terrible fates? I call DI Keegan's extension at Nelson HQ but it rings out. Re-dial and Benson answers one of the other lines.

'She's not here.'

'Where is she?'

'What's it to you?'

I tell him to forget it and he assures me he will. Next, her mobile. She answers, sounding sleepy. 'Late night?'

She grunts. 'My plane was delayed and didn't get in until after midnight and my alarm went off at the wrong time.' A rustling. 'Shit.'

'I'm guessing you're on Perth time?'

'You'd make a good detective.' A hacking cough forces me to hold the phone away from my ear. Maybe she needs to give up smoking. 'What do you want?'

I'm very tempted to share my speculations about McCormack but can't chance it, not yet. 'The DC mentioned there might have been some developments.'

'Did he? To you? Why?'

'I think he's got a soft spot for me.'

'So have I,' she says. 'But this is business.'

'Don't feel like sharing?' I can be flirty too when the need arises.

'No. Tell me about this new atrocity in that dark valley of yours.'

'Fernandez. Low life. Drug thing. Nothing to it,' I lie. 'Quid pro quo, Dr Lecter.'

'Pushy. There was nothing to Rockhampton, I dropped it. But there's a possible link between the Perth case and ours.'

'Possible?'

'They uncovered another dirty old men's club last month. File sharing, chat rooms, live streaming, that sort of thing. The dead boy was linked to one of the people on the membership list.'

'And?'

'There was somebody else further down that same membership list: our old mate Patrick Smith, the schoolboys' friend.'

'Live streaming? I doubt the broadband coverage in the Sounds would be up to it.'

'Admittedly he's dropped off the distribution list since he came to New Zealand. No pings for a long time.'

'So what takes you to Perth? They could email this stuff to you.'

'A confidential chat about what's not on Patrick Smith's record.'

Me and McCormack. Gary and his *utu* list. Uncle Walter and history. DI Keegan and Patrick Smith. And of course there was Sammy and Marty. A magic roundabout of people who won't let go.

*

In the absence of anything better to do, I check the overnight incident log. We're meant to look in at the beginning of each day but I was at the marina all morning and don't know whether Latifa checked it before she went off to help out on the Fernandez doorknock. Scrolling down, there are few surprises. Blenheim is getting a name for cases where young men are caught with meat in their trousers: lamb chops from the Pak'nSave, hot roast chickens from Countdown, sausages from New World. A social scientist would see this as canary-in-the-mine stuff. A warning that society is on the downward slide and that more should be done for the job prospects of ordinary young Marlburians. More firewood thefts: ditto. Another campervan down a ravine. A tourist bashed and robbed. Some forestry machinery vandalised. No, it wasn't me.

My mobile goes. An unidentified number. 'Yes?'

Gary's voice. 'You rang?'

'Did you hear about Johnny Fernandez?'

'Yeah, I heard about that.'

'The investigating officer, Maxwell, would like a word.'

'Yeah, he left a message.'

'So?'

'Bit busy.'

'Did you have anything to do with it, Gary?'

'No.'

'I heard about your family and the fire. If it was me ...'

'But you're not, Nick. I had nothing to do with this.'

'So come in, tell the truth.'

'And justice will prevail, eh?'

'If they have to come looking for you, it'll be worse.'

'Look after yourself, Nick. You and your family. Good people. You mean well.'

He's gone. I try calling back but the phone is switched off.

*

Half an hour later Detective Maxwell is in the office. 'You've been talking to Gary Farr?'

They're either monitoring Gary and his spare phones, or they're monitoring me. 'Yep, I was just about to call you.'

'Is he coming in?'

'Didn't sound like it. But you'd know if you're monitoring his calls. And mine.'

A smile. 'We're trying to get a trace on him, you know how it works.'

'So you know I called him earlier and left a message.'

'Yeah, thanks for that.' Maxwell's got something on his mind. He's wondering whether to share it. 'We've got his DNA in the Fernandez house.'

'You would have. They were mates, at least until a few weeks ago.' Maxwell won't tell me how significant the traces are. 'So where is Gary? Do you know?'

'The last phone contact I told you about was in Blenheim, yesterday. This one today looks like he's over in Wellington.'

'You weren't watching the ferry or the airport?'

A withering look. 'Nah, didn't think of that. He'll have mates with boats. My guess is he's headed to Palmy to sort out the blokes that bombed his house.'

'He told me he had nothing to do with what happened to Fernandez.'

'Fingers crossed? Hope to die? Well that's alright then, good as gold.' He pulls up a chair. 'Nick, some friendly advice. Don't get caught with shit on your shoe. People won't want to be near you.'

*

Heading back up the valley, it's very still and the clouds are lifting. Across the river they've ripped out another couple of hundred square metres of my view and gone home for the day. Paulie and Vanessa are waiting for me with a look that suggests they've been plotting.

'We want goats,' says Vanessa.

'Yeah,' says Paulie. 'Two. Both girls, because boy-goats smell.'

A plate of cake is pushed my way and followed up with a can of beer. 'And chickens.'

'Okay,' I say. The cake is delicious.

Vanessa nods. 'And we want you to take care of it.'

'Yeah,' chimes in Paulie. 'Quick smart.'

I can see it all before me. The job list from hell: fixing fences, sourcing materials and livestock, food, vet stuff, researching what the fuck you do with them. Being outside in the rain, feeding them, finding the lost ones, hanging out with the sandflies. It's another bloody tipping point, I can tell by Vanessa's determined expression.

'Okay,' I say. 'Sounds great.'

Paulie punches the air. 'Woo hoo, get in!'

Vanessa has been to the library and brought back a guide to self-sufficient living. She hands it to me. 'Chapters ten and twelve. You get reading. I'm making a roast for dinner. Okay?'

'Woo hoo,' I say. 'Get in.'

37

It's a clear and crisp Saturday, perfect for traffic duty. Before going into work I stop by the DIY place down by the marina. It's a big list: chicken wire, nails, wood, rope, tarp, chain, guttering, et cetera. Apparently goats are gregarious animals but they don't like rain or cold and they need to be well fenced in. The saying goes that goats spend twenty-three hours a day planning their escape and the last hour executing it. As for chickens, don't get me started. Handing over the credit card, I wince at the damage and load the stuff into the back of the Toyota. They don't have the tarp and rope and advise me to try the marine supply shop on the main street.

There, they have exactly what I need. It's boatie heaven, this is the place to come and splice your mainbrace. There's a bunch of photographs on the wall behind the salty sea dog who's serving me.

'What's that about?'

He glances up at the pics and turns back to me like I've just got a bit personal with him. 'Skippering service. If the boaties want to park up at Picton or Nelson or wherever, we'll bring their boat back here for them. Or if they just want a day with their pals on the water getting pissed, we'll do the driving.'

I've seen a familiar face: McCormack on his catamaran giving the thumbs up with his arms around the shoulder of the designated skipper. 'Did you guys do the repair job on the *Serenity II*, the graffiti?'

He squints at the photo mosaic again. 'Yeah, we did. Only that isn't *Serenity II*, that's *Serenity I*.'

'*Serenity I*?'

'Yeah. Sank out on the Sounds, must have been about five years ago now. We helped him find the replacement.' He shakes his head. 'Serve him right. Should have used one of our pro skippers that day, not some blow-in who didn't know port from starboard.'

*

A quick Google search tells me all about it. There's a report in the *Journal* about a boat belonging to Nelson businessman Richard McCormack, sinking in the Sounds in mysterious circumstances. Mysterious? The weather was fine and the boat was believed to be in good condition. He wasn't aboard at the time, it was being sailed back from a temporary berth at Picton. The skipper was able to escape in the inflatable tethered at the stern and raise the alarm. It all happened within a week of Prince Haruru's body being found at Linkwater.

I write down the name of the 'blow-in' skipper and run his name through the database. He's known to us: Kevin Moran, a petty recidivist from Blenheim, a meat-in-the-trousers type. Except his record in our database stopped about two months ago. Then he turns up in a report from Crash Team instead. His ute went off a ravine in the ranges near Nelson while I was in the UK. Him and a mate. No survivors. As he was a known pisshead, alcohol was presumed to be a significant factor.

Latifa arrives, wan and sleepy.

'Late night?' I inquire.

'Assignment deadline: "The Place of *Utu* in the New Zealand Legal Framework". I got a shitty grade for the last one so this one has to be good.'

Utu. Funny you should mention that. 'I thought you were the swot on the course? Straight A's type?'

'So did I.' She yawns. 'How's your vendetta going?'

I bring her up to speed. The latest CCTV and the satnav from five years ago putting McCormack at the Havelock Marina across the three murders. The mysterious sinking of the *Serenity I* five years ago, just after Prince was found. And the untimely death just a few weeks ago of Kevin the skipper.

'I remember that,' she nods.

'The car crash?'

'No, the sinking. It was in the papers. Everybody assumed it was scuttled as an insurance job.' She gives me this sad look. 'It's not the most compelling of evidence is it, Sarge? Loose coincidences over five years and a drunk driver crashing on a notorious road. If I had this to defend in a courtroom I'd be a happy girl.'

'It's a slow build. But we'll get there.'

'Yeah,' she says. 'Any proper work to do today? Maxwell's finished with me for now.'

'Check the overnighters. Then maybe we can go out on the highway and bring home some bad guys.'

She grins. 'Already got one of them, thanks.'

*

Out on SH6, the conditions are good and nobody is being too stupid. We're heading back to Havelock and I try getting the skinny on the Fernandez investigation out of Latifa.

She stares straight out of the windscreen, focuses on driving. 'I just knock on the doors and do the introductions. The Ds do the questions, they have the theories.'

'Which are?'

'Gary is right in there, centre of frame. I did tell you to watch yourself with him.'

'Why? What had you heard at the time?'

'I heard about the North Island gang stuff. About his family and the fire.'

'You knew all about that way back then?'

'Course. How come you didn't? I thought you were his mate?'

'Well, yeah but, no we didn't talk about that.'

'What did you talk about?'

I try to think. I take too long.

'Sport? The All Blacks? Women? Fishing? What?'

'He said his dad fought in Vietnam.'

'Yeah? Well, there you go.'

A ute passes us going the other way, too fast. Latifa pulls one of her murderous U-eys and the lights and siren go on. I recognise the ute as it slows and we pull in behind. It's Charlie Evans.

'I can't wait for the ambulance.' Tears pour down his face. There's a woman rugged up in the back seat, grey face, short shallow breaths. 'Beatrice's leaving me, isn't she?'

We escort him at high speed to Wairau Hospital in Blenheim, radioing ahead for them to be ready and clearing the road with our lights and siren. Mrs Evans is whisked through double doors on a trolley and Charlie sits in the waiting room staring out the window.

'I don't know what I'll do without her.'

'She's in good hands,' I say.

He smiles, eyes brimming. 'Beatrice said goodbye this morning. She sat up in bed and even ate a bit of breakfast. Gave me a list of jobs, the arrangements for her tangi.'

'Tangi? She's Maori? I didn't know.'

'Why would you? You never met. Her people are from south of Christchurch. We went back there at least once a year. Not so much lately, she hasn't been able to travel.' He scratches absent-mindedly at a sandfly bite on his wrist. 'These battles I have, to try and look after the land. They're more for her than me.'

'How did you meet?'

'Varsity. In Christchurch. Prettiest girl in the room. I knew then, the moment I laid eyes on her. Her folks weren't too rapt at her going off with a pakeha. But they mellowed.' He examines his liver-spotted hands. 'Together forever. Soul mates.'

'*Tau o te ate*,' I say.

'That's the one.'

Beatrice Evans dies an hour later, Charlie at her side.

*

I doubt if it's what Charlie or Beatrice would want but I find myself feeling even angrier about McCormack and the poison he brings to the world. Charlie Evans, I've decided, is a good man and he did not deserve the extra pressures brought to bear on him while his wife was dying. Richard McCormack, I've decided, is a thoroughly bad man and, one way or another, I'm going to make him pay. But I'm mindful of trying to keep his venom from infecting my own life. So driving back up the valley I meditate on practical issues like where to situate the goat shelter and which breed to go for: Saanen or Toggenburg.

38

The new week begins with a nationwide alert out for Gary Farr. Detective Maxwell has named him as prime suspect for the murder of Fernandez and allowed the media to run with his photo and description. The ninjas from the Armed Offenders Squad are scouring the country for him. Gary meanwhile has gone off grid. He's ditched the mobile and he's not accessing bank accounts or government services. I picture him holed up in high country somewhere with Richie the mastiff and a loaded gun, living off the land. I fear the worst. He won't let them take him alive.

Over breakfast Vanessa wanted to know more.

'Did he do it?'

'I'd like to think not but it doesn't look good.'

It's overcast and there's a wind and a real bite in the air: a woolly socks, beanie and duvet day. A day for staying indoors and comfort eating, not a day to be heading out on the Sounds in an open-topped boat. The salty sea dog from the marine supply shop is taking me to where *Serenity I* sank. It's out the far side of D'Urville Island where the Sounds meet the Tasman in deep, deep water. And way off the beaten track between Picton and Havelock. King cormorants and gannets spear the freezing water for food, and a pod of dolphins cracks the surface off to starboard.

Sea Dog nods. 'Insurance job. Course it was.'

'But no inquiry to that effect?'

'I wouldn't know. But those people, they never get looked at, do they?'

'How deep do you reckon it is here?'

He shrugs. 'Fucken deep as it gets.'

I was expecting an accurate sea dog reckoning in fathoms or leagues or something. 'Too deep for salvage?'

'Too expensive.' He sniffs the wind. 'You finished? What's your interest anyway? Not that I'm complaining, a charter's a charter.'

'Cop business.'

'You're a brave man shoving your nose into McCormack's affairs. He doesn't take prisoners.'

But maybe he does. Prince Haruru, Jamie Riley, Qadim Reza. Out in a boat on the Marlborough Sounds where nobody can hear their cries.

*

'Where've you been?' Latifa lifts her eyes from her computer screen and studies my windblown hair and face. 'Not out in the fresh air, surely?'

'I took a ride out to where that boat sank.'

'Should've taken a fishing rod. Made it worthwhile.'

I test my theory on her: the idea that McCormack has the boys on the boat in that week or so before he kills them.

Latifa frowns. 'So you really do think he's the Pied Piper?'

'That's the theory I'm working on, yes. Have you been away somewhere the last few days?'

'Just hanging out with normal people, cop shit notwithstanding. Doing meaningful stuff. It gives you perspective. When people do things, good or bad, there's usually a reason: revenge, jealousy, alcohol, whatever.' She twists in her chair. 'What's McCormack's motive?'

'How about he's a psychopathic paedophile?'

'Yeah, yeah. So one of his cars was out at the marae a week before Prince's murder. Maybe he got lost, drove up the wrong road? Maybe someone else was driving it. Just because he chops down trees and makes more money than you doesn't mean he's a child murderer. Earth calling Sarge.' She switches off her desktop and shrugs on her coat. 'Beattie Evans is lying in state and receiving visitors. I'm going to wish her well on her journey to the hereafter and tell her she needs to give that husband of hers a good talking to before she goes aloft.'

I turn my computer on and wonder whether, as a senior officer, I might be setting a bad example with my dark obsessions. Then I dig out marine charts for the spot where the boat sank and discover that it would actually be feasible to send divers and a mini-sub down there and look over the wreck. Curiosity satisfied, I do Latifa's bidding and perform some normal police duties. The overnight log: nothing of consequence, more meat and firewood thefts, petty drug busts, a drunken brawl, a break-in at a Blenheim shop. After that it's up and down SH6 to ticket five boy racers, one of them old enough at fifty-four to know better. I see goats and chickens along the way. It's like that. You develop an interest in something and you start noticing it everywhere. The big white goats, Saanen, are my favourites, purely because they look cool. That's my decision: two Saanen. The chickens aren't finalised yet but I'm leaning towards Buff Orpingtons maybe, or perhaps Brown Shavers, which apparently give good big eggs.

You develop an interest in something ... A car crashes on a notorious road, a weekly occurrence here. But there have been other deaths since I talked to ex-detective Des Rogers and showed renewed interest in the cold Prince Haruru case: Des Rogers' suicide-cum-murder, Deborah Haruru's attempted suicide-cum-murder, Kevin the blow-in skipper from five years ago dying suddenly in a car crash. What else is ringing a bell? An unexplained break-in at McCormack's offices in Nelson. A break-in at the Marlborough Tennis Club; the logo on the shirt of the man who oozes darkness. Back in the office to check the database. Already there's a coincidental link – both break-ins were in the same twenty-four-hour period. It looks more and more like someone covering their tracks. Latifa is going to love my latest musings.

*

In the absence of DI Keegan, who is still in Perth, I give Benson a ring.

'Yeah?'

'Do you have any developments from Kaikōura on the Des Rogers thing?'

'Not for you, no.' If I had an *utu* list I think Benson would be right up there. 'Why?' A spark of curiosity from Benson? Maybe he's got a performance appraisal coming up.

'Ah, nothing. Just something I heard.'

'Spill.'

I take a punt. 'Something about a white car in the vicinity.'

'Lot of white cars in this country.'

'So it's probably nothing.'

Benson sniffs. 'Who'd you hear this nothing from?'

'Friend of a friend in Kaikōura.'

'Friend of a friend? You mean you have one and a half friends? Sure you're not overselling yourself?'

I could be imagining things, but I might have touched a nerve with

Benson. There *is* a white car in the frame in Kaikōura. It just needs to be the one I'm thinking of. Next, the Marlborough Tennis Club break-in and hopefully an easier ride with the Blenheim volume crime Ds.

'What about it?' The woman on the phone seems to have picked up Benson's social skills.

'Solved? Only I've got similar stuff happening over here and might have someone in mind.'

'Nah, not solved.' She taps on her keyboard. 'Unusually professional, no fingerprints, no Facebook posts. Not your average break-in. Havelock, eh? So you have master criminals over there?'

'Specially inbred. Okay with you if I drop by and talk to the tennis club?'

'Be my guest, plenty on my plate. Keep me posted.'

The Marlborough Tennis Club secretary agrees to meet me in an hour. She's a fit-looking woman nudging sixty and wears her short tennis skirt and ankle socks well. She looks at me like I haven't got enough money or influence.

'The police have already been here and we've told them everything.'

'I'm looking at similar cases over my way in Havelock. There might be a pattern.'

'What do you want to know?'

'How did they get in?'

'Through the back door, they broke a pane of glass.'

'No alarm?'

'Not then. There is now. I mean this is Blenheim, isn't it? We never thought.'

'What did they take?'

'They went through the bar till but we empty it every night. They took some spirits and some beer, cigarettes. The petty cash box in my office. A few trophies.'

'Anything else?'

'The laptop in my office, some photos.'

'Photos?'

She nods. 'They smashed most of them but a few were missing.'

'Which ones?'

'Team tournaments. Competitions.' She sits up proudly. 'We usually win the regionals.'

'Shame. Do you have copies of those that went missing?'

'Somewhere, maybe. We're talking five years ago now.'

'Five years?' A nod. 'The membership lists?'

'On the stolen laptop. But I have this year's on my home laptop. Why?'

'The pattern we have in Havelock: there's been a couple of break-ins at places where you wouldn't expect to find that much cash or stuff worth stealing – sports clubs and such. Then a few weeks later there are break-ins at the homes of people on the membership list.'

She puts a hand to her chest. 'Heavens, no.'

'Maybe you could zap me that current membership list and we can monitor if there are any subsequent break-ins?'

'Well, I suppose so.'

'Thanks.' I hand her my card. 'And if you dig up any copies of those old photos, maybe you could let me know?'

'Why?'

'I promised to keep my Blenheim colleagues in the loop. If you find replacements then it's less important for us to keep on looking.' A smile. 'We're all on the same team, right?'

She studies my business card. 'Chester. Were you in the papers recently?'

'Earthquake Drill Day, Canvastown School.'

'And that terrible incident up the valley. People died.' I look sombre for her. 'You poor man.'

'Time's a great healer.'

As I walk out she's studying my card and I'm not sure she's bought my story.

*

Still, as promised, the email comes through two hours later with the membership list and I go straight to *M*. Yes, there he is, up to date on his dues: Richard McCormack. Next, an online visit to the *Journal* archives for five years ago to check the sports reports. The tennis regionals won once again by the Marlborough club, no team photo but it is reported that the mixed-doubles champions include, you guessed it, Richard McCormack.

Latifa returns midafternoon. She looks like she's had a good cry.

'Did you know Beattie Evans well?'

'Nah, not at all. But it's good to have a bawl now and then.'

'Many visitors?'

'Steady stream. Denzel's keeping a good flow of tea and coffee coming

200

and biscuits. He's a revelation, that boy. Transformed.'

'Just needs a chance, that's all, and Charlie Evans is the kind of bloke who would give him it.'

She nods. 'And it's not as if Denzel hasn't got enough on his plate, what with Johnny.'

'Johnny?'

'Fernandez, the bloke that got killed with the hammer, remember him?'

'What's the connection, apart from same iwi?'

'They used to hang out together when they were younger. Good mates back then, inseparable. But Johnny got into drugs and shit and if it hadn't been for Uncle Walter then Denzel would have gone the same way.'

'What's Walter up to?'

'Watching Denzel like a hawk. Johnny's death seems to have hit him hard. This could make or break him.'

'Fingers crossed.'

'You'll never guess who called in to pay his respects.'

'Surprise me.'

'Your good mate McCormack.'

'Did Charlie show him the door?'

'No, Denzel did. They were having words on the back verandah. Then McCormack left. He'd brought a lovely big bunch of flowers.'

'Sweet.'

'Shame. A bloke tries to redeem himself and all you can do is think the worst.'

I still can't tell whether Latifa really is a McCormack fan or whether she just loves winding me up.

*

Something is building. McCormack is there at every turn but Latifa is right, all I'm gathering is a whole bunch of supposition and coincidence. I criticise Detective Maxwell for doing exactly that with Gary, yet look at me. Hell, Maxwell probably has a more solid case with Gary than I will ever have with McCormack. I'm just picking at the edges. If I really was *Weka-tāne*, I'd be digging my nose right into the undergrowth and tossing everything. I'd be making an unholy mess and pissing everybody off. I'd be getting at the truth.

39

Vanessa and Paulie are happy with my choice of Saanen goats and Brown Shaver chickens, and this weekend I'll put together the sheds and runs and fencing as promised. Vanessa finds my farm talk arousing; it's a bit kinky really, but who's complaining? I feel obliged to warn her of the impending storm. We're enjoying another sandfly-lite breakfast on the back verandah with the gurgling river battling the crunch and drone of the logging machines across the way. Vanessa sips her coffee while I lay out my crazy theory and suicidal plan of attack.

'I'm with Latifa on this one. You're off your trolley. You might well be right about this bloke but the way you're going about it.'

'I know how it looks. But unless it's tested none of us will ever know. And those kids and their parents need …'

'Closure? Resolution? Don't give me that.' She takes a spoonful of muesli. 'You're going to do this anyway, aren't you?'

'Yes.'

'You're big enough to fight your own stupid battles. But don't spoil it for us.' Paulie looks up from his cornflakes at her sharp tone. 'We like it here and we want to stay.'

'What's changed? It's not that long ago you hated it.'

She tilts her head. 'It grows on you, like moss or fungus.' A nod over the river. 'The lumberjacks will come and go, and in between there's acres of peace and that river and those hills. It's addictive.'

'I know the feeling.'

'I wonder sometimes, Nick, I really do.' She pushes her empty bowl away. 'He's powerful, this McCormack bloke. This could get you sacked.' A sideways glance at Paulie. 'It affects us all.' The Paulie Fund, so often it comes down to that. She can see from my expression that I'm hell-bent on doing this. 'After the thing with Marty and Sammy, you said this was all over.'

'It is.'

'No, it isn't. You always need dragons to slay. Why aren't we enough for you? Why are you prepared to jeopardise all this?'

'I was a cop when we got together. Nothing has changed.'

'Everything has changed. That's why we're in New fucking Zealand, for better or worse.' She starts clearing away the dishes. 'I know at heart you're a good man and you want to do what's right. But you also need to know exactly what you're risking.'

'I do.'

'No,' she says sadly. 'I don't think so.'

*

In the office, I start the ball rolling, calling the Nelson volume crime Ds to inquire about the break-in at the McCormack Forestry offices all those weeks ago on the same night as the tennis club.

'Why the interest?' he says. I've met him in the corridor before. Joe, his name is. An affable if wily fella nudging retirement and wanting to keep his life simple.

This is where I can choose to concoct a story that helps prevent the shit from hitting the fan too soon. I can put my family first. Nah. 'Something has come up which makes me suspicious.'

'Care to be specific?'

'It's tied in to the Pied Piper investigation. I think McCormack warrants a closer look.'

'The kid murders?' says Joe. 'You serious?'

'Yep.'

'That woman from Wellington.'

'DI Keegan.'

'Yeah, is she in on this?'

'Not yet.'

'Is anybody from the task force up to speed?'

'No.'

A pause at Joe's end. 'Hold on a wee sec, I'll put you through to my boss.'

I tap on a few keys and bring up the incident report. 'It says here three laptops were stolen, some money from a petty cash tin in the secretary's office, and the place was substantially vandalised, particularly in the foyer area. Right?'

'Right, look my boss has just stepped out, he'll give you a call back, okay? This is all a bit ...'

'And I'm guessing some of that damage was to his collection of photos? Some missing?'

'Right but ...'

'No worries, that's all I need. I'll check with the insurance company.'

'Hang on ...'

I run through the same routine with the insurance company contact mentioned in the incident report. Then it's just a matter of sitting back and waiting.

*

'Get yourself over here. Now.'

I've anticipated DC Ford's call and I'm already on my way. Latifa is keeping her head down. I've warned her of my intentions and promised to try and protect her from what's to come.

'Thanks. They're going to send that bloke from Traffic back in here you know.' She puts her finger up her nose and crosses her eyes. 'This better be worth it.'

Whether it's a leak from the Ds' office or a tip-off from the insurance company, McCormack has already been on the phone to Ford. He's incandescent and threatening to bring in the lawyers.

'He has questions to answer,' I insist.

'What questions?' says Ford.

I lay it out for him: Deborah Haruru and the car in the marae a week before her son is murdered, Honest Joe's Rent-A-Flash-Bomb, the McCormack car fleet, the satnav and the marina. The other marina connections: the sunken boat and the dead skipper. The photographs stolen from Marlborough Tennis Club and McCormack Forestry on the same night.

'That's it?'

'Yeah.'

'You presented this to DI Keegan?'

'No.'

'Why not? She's running the investigation. Not you.'

'I'm aware of the sensitivities. I wanted to try and gather enough to back up my theory so I didn't waste precious investigative resources.'

'My arse. You knew I'd kick it into touch. Our processes and protocols are there for a reason. What you've presented to me today, it's all circumstantial bullshit, mate, a good lawyer could drive a truck through it. And because you've gone off half-cocked they'll do exactly that.' He shakes his head. 'Get out of here.'

'Constable Rapata advised me against this course of action, sir, but I overruled her as her senior officer. She is not culpable in this matter.'

'That's for me to decide, not you, Sergeant. Get out. You're suspended. Again.'

'On what grounds?'

'You're a loose cannon, your precipitous actions may have jeopardised a murder investigation, you've broken several regulations and protocols. I'll get them into alphabetical order and email you.'

I should have expected this but it still comes as something of a shock. My guts are churning and I wonder, too late, whether it's all a huge mistake.

And the thing is, it's only the beginning.

*

I'm driving around aimlessly, afraid to go home. Vanessa will be even more furious than the DC. My career is unlikely to survive this. To add to it, there's a message on my mobile from Latifa.

'I've been suspended. Thanks for that.'

Shit.

I find myself driving by the marae past Deborah Haruru's old house, following that map laid out on the satnav printout. There are kids in the street, kicking footballs, jumping bikes over bumps. Kids that five years ago gave some cheek to a pakeha in a flash car. A man who returned and took one of them away. I'm doing the second circuit now, round the block. What is he looking for, what does he see?

Uncle Walter flags me down. 'Looking for somebody? Need any help?'

'No,' I say. 'Just passing time.'

'You look like you're having a bad day.'

'Do I?' We say our farewells. In the rear view he watches my retreat.

Down to the marina, floating past *Serenity II* and its new paint job. Out on to Queen Charlotte Drive, through Linkwater towards The Grove and that stretch of Sound where Prince's tormented body was found. I get out and stand at the water's edge. The tide is low and herons pick at the mud.

It's still only late morning, the sun is right overhead. I turn and look at the houses. They all face the Sound. Big windows designed to bring that view home, but nobody saw a thing. Nobody saw a car pull up or a boat sail by and disgorge a small boy. Was it the wrong time of day, everybody asleep? Was it one of those cars or boats that's invisible because they blend in to the surroundings? Rich, sleek. I turn around and head back but still can't go home. Instead of turning right towards Havelock and Canvastown, I turn left and drift past the shoe fence. The light is fantastic. There's no wind, just a long still line of battered and weather-worn shoes against this stunning green hill.

And a bunch of flowers where Jamie Riley was found.

Love. Always. Mum. xxx

I can't conceive of that kind of loss. Why not? Is it worse to have your child stolen from you or to lose them to your own vanity and pride? To know that you alone are responsible, nobody else.

Back up the valley, they are waiting to find out what the hell I've done.

40

'Good,' says Vanessa.

I wasn't expecting that. 'So you're not angry?'

'Not surprised; two very different things. You were always going to do it and I was never going to be able to stop you. Blind Freddy could have seen what was going to happen. So we need to focus on the positives.'

'Which are?'

'You can get on with sorting out the goats and chickens.'

And here we are three days later. Fences and sheds erected, water tanks in place, a dozen pullets exploring their new surroundings, and two goats chewing on the blackberry brambles beside the compost bin. Paulie is beside himself with excitement. He got to name the goats and the result was inevitable.

'Spongebob and Squarepants.'

'Which is which?' I'm infected by his grin.

'Spongebob is the big one with the funny eye.'

He was less inventive in naming the chickens. They're all just called 'Chook', except for the single noisy rooster that is named in honour of Steve. It's a glorious day: blue sky, sun carving out the hills, the river shimmering and clear. Vanessa seems happy and, if she's not, she's disguising it well. The phone goes.

'It's for you.' A wary look in her eyes.

Jessie James is seeking comment on a story she's about to run. She gives me the gist: vindictive copper uses local murder tragedy to smear businessman, victims' parents outraged and disgusted, personal dispute over logging behind it, cop tried to solicit the *Journal* to join campaign, likely to his lose job. Et cetera.

'No comment.'

Back outside to my family, the sunshine, and our livestock. A bush falcon glides high along the path of the river in search of prey, catching the updrafts, playing the breeze. Our neighbour drives past in a crunch of gravel and doesn't return my wave.

'Who was on the phone?'

'The *Journal*. It's going to get ugly.'

'Lunch?' She heads back to the house and we follow. Home-baked bread, salad, and cheese are laid out on the pine kitchen table. 'Maybe you should look for another job.'

'I might not have any other option.' I break some bread. 'Any ideas?'

'The mussel factory is always taking people on. Driving. Vineyards.' The rooster yodels. 'Maybe a farmer?'

'None of that pays well or offers much security.'

'As opposed to what you have now, you mean?'

'Maybe we should have taken up the DC's offer of a transfer.'

'Too late.' She slides more salad onto Paulie's plate. 'What are you hoping to achieve?'

'Provoke a reaction, shake the tree.'

'Hoping he'll make a mistake?' I nod. 'A man who hasn't made any so far. And if it's the man you're thinking of, then we're talking about a person who has made a fortune out of being astute.'

I think about it for a moment. 'He's had to do a lot of track-covering the last few weeks since I started showing interest in the Prince Haruru case.' I list it. 'That suggests to me that he is jumpy, that I am onto something.'

'How does he know you're looking at this old case?'

'I think Des Rogers tipped him off. It would fit with the allegation that Des was covering up for him. Maybe Des thought he could make a dollar or two out of it.'

'Blackmail?'

'Why not?'

'So this Des Rogers would have to have something to bargain with, otherwise your killer would just tell him to get lost.' Vanessa starts clearing the table, putting the dishes in the sink. She lets Paulie grab a last bun. 'You can't just shake the tree and sit back. You've put everything into jeopardy. If you really feel you're on the right track, go out and prove it.'

'But you told me to focus on the goats and chickens.'

'And you did. You passed the test. Good boy. Now get out of here and fight for what you believe in.'

*

Coming back into mobile range at Canvastown, I call Latifa, feeling guilty and responsible.

'What do you want?' She does a good line in coldness and distance.

'To say sorry. What's the reason they've given for your suspension?'

'Hanging out with a fuckwit like you.'

'That's insubordination.'

'So suspend me.'

'Why, really?'

'He reckons that by knowing what you were doing and not reporting you, I'm colluding.'

'That's not fair.'

'Since when was life ever? Anyway I'm not a snitch. Now he's got to find somebody to run Havelock police station for him. He'll calm down once he realises how indispensable I am.'

'I'll fix it, I promise.'

'Yeah, well.' There's a murmur in the background. It sounds suspiciously like Daniel the Boy Racer. 'It has its compensations.' A slap and a giggle. 'What are you going to do?'

'Get them to take the accusation against McCormack seriously. Get some more proof.'

'Maybe you should have thought of that earlier.' I can't fault her logic. A sharp and possibly carnal intake of breath. 'No rush about getting me unsuspended, Sarge.'

So I'm back on that glorious drive down the coast to Kaikōura and the sea is shimmering and calm, the sand is still eerily black like the beaches used to be near the long-dead Durham coalmines, and there's still snow on those ranges. It's late afternoon when I get to town and I decide to grab some food first, fill in some time. It has to be nice and quiet and preferably dark before I make my next move.

Twilight cedes to night. The crime-scene tape has gone from Des Rogers' bach and already the For Sale sign is up. There's nobody around. I've parked up the street and walked the last couple of hundred metres with my holdall. It contains gloves, a crowbar, and a torch. It's a flimsy door and only makes a slight crack under the right pressure. Inside,

I close the curtains and flick on the torch. The chemical smell of a recently released crime scene mixes in with old odours of cigarettes, fried food, sweat, and a single middle-aged man on the skids. The place has been tidied up though, probably by family or friends, in preparation for sale. I just hope it hasn't been tidied up too well.

Where to start? If Des Rogers did have a trump card then it's likely the killer has already been through here looking for it and maybe it's already gone. I don't know and can only hope. In the bedroom the double bed has been made up with a new duvet cover and pillowcases, garishly bright and feminine, and not in keeping with the overwhelming sad maleness of the place. The wardrobe and drawers have been cleared out. I'm too late, I'm thinking. Way too late.

The second bedroom, smaller, has had a similar makeover job. Fresh covers on a single bed and furniture emptied. Bathroom and toilet; I check the cistern: nothing. Back to the combined kitchen, dining room, sitting room. There are books on a shelf for show. They look like a job lot from some charity shop with reading material that I would never have credited Des Rogers with: Jodie Picoult, Maeve Binchy, Di Morrissey. I pick them up and flick through but nothing falls out. On the fridge a new set of magnetised coloured letters spelling out W-E-L-C-O-M-E.

Out to the shed where Des was found hanging from the hook on the wall. There's a suspicious dark stain on the ground. The torchlight floats around the walls, tools along one side, rusty and unused; Des would have had little interest in maintenance and odd jobs. Three removal boxes, items cleared out from the house, perhaps awaiting collection or shipping to the dump. I bring the Toyota down and load them in.

On the way out of town. I pass the public phone box a hundred metres down the street. I'm prepared to bet that's where Des rang the number that sealed his fate. Up the coast to Seddon and pull into a motel. I need to get away from Kaikōura but don't want to take all this stuff back to the farm. The young bloke in reception hands me a key for the last unit in the far corner and that suits me fine. I carry my boxes in from the ute, call Vanessa to tell her what I'm doing, and settle in for a long night.

The first box is full of clothes and shoes and I feel like I should be wearing protective gear before handling them. The smell is rank, many of them are unwashed. It would have been kinder to have thrown the whole lot straight onto a bonfire. The second box looks more promising:

envelopes and files, bills, tax returns, receipts, bank and credit card statements, old payslips, superannuation statements, birth certificate, driver's licence, passport. All of these in a single envelope from Kaikōura police, obviously returned after they had finished examining them. Old postcards and letters from the days when such things were still the currency of relationships. Photographs: Des on his wedding day in 1980s fashions writ large, Des in police uniform at the beginning of his career and receiving a commendation when he was possibly still a good bloke, snaps of his children, and then their children. By the time he's a grandad he no longer appears in any more pictures with his progeny. I hope that among these papers is the key to his untimely death but it begs certain questions: if it's here then why didn't DI Keegan's team find it or, for that matter, the killer? Or am I way, way too late?

The chain of events since I spoke to Des Rogers: first he is murdered, then there's an attempt on Deborah Haruru's life, then Kevin the blow-in skipper of *Serenity I* dies in a car crash, and there are mysterious break-ins at McCormack Forestry and Marlborough Tennis Club. All within a relatively short period of time. Prince Haruru is the key, the killer is tidying up loose ends from that case only it seems. With the others he has perfected his MO and left no trail. Any mistakes he made were five years ago. But what were they? The people he has killed, or tried to kill, hold the answers. Those break-ins hold the answers. It has to be McCormack, it just has to be.

The third box has more clothes, outdoor clothes, big waterproof jackets, gumboots, also toiletries, spectacles, knick-knacks, some CDs: Crowded House, Genesis, U2. Who'da thought? I flick through them, check the discs inside. Nothing from Crowded House or Genesis. Then I open up U2's *The Joshua Tree* and there it is: a smaller version of a photograph I've seen before. A song from that CD comes to mind. 'I Still Haven't Found What I'm Looking For.'

Only I have.

41

If New Zealand is God's work, then it is unfinished. It's still finding its shape and place in the universe. In the night in my Seddon motel room, I felt a noticeable shudder. Something has shifted. This is the Ring of Fire after all and in this sleepy little corner of a sleepy little country, the Wairau Fault connects with four others snaking from north, south, east and west into a seismic junction box known as the Marlborough Fault System, which is hard-wired for imminent disaster. According to the email briefing we received before National Earthquake Drill Day, the Wairau Fault is nearing the end of its interseismic period and the current estimated hazard is considered to be relatively high. It's an $E=mc^2$ kind of formula and apparently it means that sometime in the next week to two hundred years we're doomed. That's just the kind of catastrophising that really gives Vanessa the shits. She won't let me watch the news anymore because the medieval-style slaughter around the world lodges itself behind my eyeballs and my lips purse and my mood darkens. I'd like to think it's a saviour complex, I'm Clarice Starling and I have to save the lambs from their fate.

Vanessa sees it another way. 'Control freak.' But she is kind of impressed with my endeavours as I bring her up to speed on my Kaikōura trip. 'That's the kid there?'

'Third from left.' When I first saw this photo in McCormack's foyer, I registered Denzel Haruru and McCormack himself and made the link with the crossbow attack on Charlie Evans' alpacas. What didn't register, because I had never heard of him at that point, was that Denzel's cousin Prince was also in the photo. A little kid with sparks in his eyes and, by my calculation based on the date on the big cardboard cheque, only a few weeks to live. The larger version of this had been stolen in the mysterious break-in at McCormack's office. The smaller copy of this is what got Des Rogers killed.

'Will it be enough to tip the DC over to reconsidering?' We've pulled the small table over to a sunny spot where we can drink tea and watch the chickens. Vanessa is considering buying a .22 so she can shoot stoats if they menace the coop. Talk about a Clarice Starling complex.

'I doubt it. But I know I'm on the right track.'

'So what now?'

I don't know, yet. What I need is for Beth to come out of her trance and say yep, that's the guy in the Woodbourne Tavern. I need the killer on CCTV dumping the bodies of Jamie Riley and Qadim Reza. I need to deliver McCormack on a plate if the DC is ever going to investigate his own squash partner. The newspaper arrives in the mailbox. The headline in block caps is VENDETTA. There's a photo of me underneath and then the whole story as outlined by Jessie James yesterday.

'You've lost weight since that was taken.' Vanessa lays a cool hand on the back of my neck. 'You're in much better shape now.'

The phone goes. I hand the paper over to her and go inside to answer it.

'You're famous.' It's DI Marianne Keegan.

'Back from Perth, I presume?' An affirmative umm. 'Anything worth pursuing with Patrick Smith?'

'Maybe. But I'm just calling to say sorry all this had to happen. I saw the paper. You deserve better.'

'Thanks.' Vanessa has just come in with the empty cups and the newspaper. She raises a quizzical eyebrow and mouths: Who is it?

Work, I mouth back.

'If there's anything I can do.'

'I don't think so. The boss is pretty pissed off.'

'Is there anything in it? Your theory?'

'No, I just grasp these things out of thin air. Make it up as I go along.'

'Testy,' says Marianne. 'Maybe we should catch up for a beer on neutral ground and you can run it past me?'

'No, it'll work out.'

I wrap the call up under subtle scrutiny from Vanessa. 'Was that DI, what's her name, Keegan?'

'Yep.'

'Are you in more trouble?'

'No, she was just ringing to find out what's been going on, she's been out of town.'

'She offered sympathy?'

'Of sorts.'

'Does she know about the evidence you've been gathering? She might give it more weight as she's not connected to McCormack.'

'No, she doesn't.'

'So you've arranged to meet her, to pass it on?'

'No.'

'Why not?'

I hesitate. Only briefly, but enough for Vanessa to register it. 'I need to gather more. I'll present it to her and the DC at the same time so they can't ignore it.'

'Right,' she says. 'Good idea.'

But there's a seed of doubt there now which I fear will germinate over the coming days.

*

I spend the afternoon being a farmer, tending to the goats and chickens, fixing fences and tightening wires. If anything it makes Vanessa even more edgy and suspicious. In her mind if I'm doing good things around the house I must have done bad things elsewhere for which I'm trying to compensate. She's not having any of it. She's gone off to pick up Paulie from school and even though she left with a smile and a wave, it's obvious I'm in for it.

What to do? Go honest and admit to the one-night stand with Marianne Keegan? Or keep shtum and tough it out? It has to be the latter. Or something in between. But the whole unvarnished sordid truth will just bring everything crashing down. I think about that midnight earth tremor in Seddon. That's all it takes. One slip.

*

'Fancy a walk down by the river?'

She doesn't, but we will. We plant Paulie in front of TV *Spongebob* with a muffin and a Milo. We follow the same path I usually take to drown the cats caught in the trap: a feline Via Dolorosa. The river is low and it's that time when the sandflies go into a last-minute feeding frenzy before daylight disappears. We stand at the water's edge slapping at the insects and staring into the deep dark pools where the eddies swirl.

'The answer is yes.'

She turns to me, tears in her eyes. It's like I've just hit her and, in a way, I have. 'When?'

'When you were in the safe house in Nelson. I thought you'd left me, you and Paulie. I thought it was all over. I was drunk and didn't think there was anything left to lose.'

'You were wrong.'

'Yes.'

'You stupid, fucking, selfish bastard.' She walks away along the river's edge. Arms folded, shaking her head.

'It was a mad, stupid time. You'd gone. Marty was coming after me. I was expecting to die any day. Crackers, I was. Off my head.'

'Where?'

'Some motel in Blenheim.'

'How many times?'

'Once. Never again.'

She's heading back up the path towards the house. 'I've finished talking.'

There's a cloud of sandflies in front of my face and this beautiful place feels like hell on earth.

*

It's been a cold, tense evening and Paulie is troubled by the atmosphere. He's clingy and takes a while to settle in his room. In bed, Vanessa puts her light straight out and turns away. I contemplate heading for the spare room but I suspect that may make things even worse.

In the middle of the night I'm woken by a hard punch on the shoulder.

'Was she any good?' Vanessa has her bedside light turned on and shining in my face Stasi-style.

'What?'

'You heard me.'

No more lying. 'Not bad, I mean, aye, canny, you know.'

'Is that "not bad" as in canny good or fucking mind-blowing?'

'No, definitely not mind-blowing. Just alright, like.'

'What about her? Did she enjoy herself?'

'I dunno. Probably.'

'Probably? How do you know?'

'Well she made all the right noises.'

'Noises?'

'Kind of snorting, heavy breathing stuff.'

'Snorting? Like a pig? Like this?' She makes the noise then punches me again. 'Fucking stupid bastard.' She makes me sit up and pay attention. 'You don't fuck anybody else ever again. Even if I do leave you. Even after I'm dead. Never. Ever. Got that?'

'Yes.'

She turns and puts her light out.

And snorts.

42

There's a very slight thaw, enough to hang some hope on. But I'm obliged to get my own coffee and breakfast even though it's her turn. A gusty wind sweeps up the valley shaking the trees and sending clouds scudding across the sky. After the weekend break the loggers are back at work over the river: a constant stream of trucks and other machinery up and down the skid. They start early and finish late, arc lights illuminating their progress during the dark hours – the place resembles an alien landing pad. Or our very own Mordor. McCormack is ratcheting up the spite. In the scheme of things, it doesn't worry me as much anymore. My marriage is still intact, only just. The noose was around my neck and the hand was on the trapdoor handle. Now we're just checking the wording of the reprieve note.

The phone goes and Vanessa eyes me suspiciously from her position at the washing machine. But it's Detective Maxwell.

'Heard from your mate Gary Farr?'

'No.'

'There was a house firebombed in Palmerston North last night. A bloke called Ronnie Parata. He and Gary go back a long way. But not as friends.'

'And?'

'Tragically Ronnie didn't make it out. Luckily he was the only one there at the time.'

'Will he be missed?'

'Well the crime stats will go down in the area so there might be a few redundancies.'

'Sounds like a win-win.'

'Look, to be honest, we're not going to bust a gut investigating Parata's demise, and Johnny Fernandez is no great loss to society either. We'll go through the motions. But if Gary calls, tell him to stop, now. He's made his point. This isn't the wild west.'

Since when? 'I'll pass it on.'

'Do that. Make him listen, for his own sake.'

'Anything else?'

'Yeah, we've been going through Johnny Fernandez's phone and internet in more detail. Did you know he and Des Rogers were buddies? Didn't you have a bee in your bonnet about Rogers?'

'Des has only been retired a couple of years and Johnny's record goes back a while. It's likely their paths would cross professionally.'

'As recently as a month ago?'

*

Maxwell knows I'm suspended – it's all over the bloody papers after all – so he's not prepared to send anything through on email or keep on talking on the monitored phones. He wants me at arm's-length. We rendezvous in the Pak'nSave car park on the outskirts of Blenheim, where the stolen meat handovers usually take place. The gist is that Johnny Fernandez is believed to have been one of Des Rogers' snitches, which fulfills another local rumour about the ill-fated lad. But after Des's retirement the contact continued, less frequent, more sporadic. Maybe Johnny was feeding the odd titbit to Des who would pass it on to colleagues in return for favours, money, spare drugs, whatever. The most recent contact was in the twenty-four hours following my meeting with Rogers in Kaikōura. Coincidence? Who knows.

'Did anything at the Fernandez crime scene jar?' I ask.

'You were there first. You should know.'

Apart from the possum trap on the hand, the head caved in with a hammer, and lashings of blood, nothing had jumped out. The place was a halfway-tidy tip, which is what you come to expect from a useless recidivist with a girlfriend and a baby. Any tidiness was probably down to her.

'I didn't do a detailed examination,' I say. 'I saw the mess and called it in.'

'From what we could see, Gary was trying to find something. The drawers and cupboards had been turned out. The possum trap on the hand wasn't an accident. It was an incentive to reveal information.'

No, I'm thinking. Not Gary. 'Let me know if anything else comes up.' I offer a flag of truce. 'And if Gary calls, I'll have a serious talk with him.'

'Saw you in the paper.' A chuckle. 'Good one, I reckon McCormack's a prick as well.'

*

I drop by Charlie Evans' place. He buried Beatrice a couple of days ago but I was too busy tilting at McCormack's windmills.

'I'm sorry I wasn't there, Charlie.'

'No worries. I probably wouldn't have noticed you anyway.' He seems lost.

'No Denzel today?'

'I told him to stay away for a while. I need some time to myself.'

I leave him to it. Back in mobile range, I call Latifa and ask her to meet me at the marae.

'Okay. And thanks.'

'What for?'

'Putting the word in for me with the DC. I'm back at work from tomorrow.'

It wasn't my doing but right now I need all the friends I can get, so credit gratefully accepted. 'I suspect he's just calmed down and realised he went a bit far.'

'Whatever.'

At his house near the marae, Uncle Walter is in his front yard mending eel traps. Denzel is mowing the lawn while something doofs out of his iPod headphones. 'Got him well-trained these days,' I say to Walter.

He smiles. 'It's that Charlie bloke. He's got a good spirit. Passing it on to Denzel.'

Latifa pulls up in her Subaru. 'Yoo-hoo.' She seems drowsily happy and we both know why. She gives me and Uncle Walter a hug each and brings the sun out from behind a cloud. Throws a wave and a wink at Denzel who doesn't know whether to scowl or blush.

'I need a word with the boy. That okay?'

Walter summons him with a lift of the chin. A supplementary glare from the old man and Denzel realises he needs to remove the headphones.

'You remember Johnny Fernandez?' I ask Denzel. A hawking spit from Uncle Walter.

'Yeah?'

'You were mates.'

'Not for a long time.'

'When?'

'When we was kids. I was, I dunno, eight, nine, ten?'

'And he was about four years older?'

'Something like that.'

'Why'd you stop?'

A nervous look at Uncle Walter. 'He was always gettin' blazed. Got boring.'

'Was he with you that day the pakeha car came through?'

He narrows his eyes. 'Yeah, why?'

'Did he recognise who the bloke was in the car?'

'No.' There's a 'but' in his voice.

'But what?'

'About six months ago he reckoned he saw him.'

'Did he give a name?'

'No. He said it was a secret.'

The 'but' is still there. 'He give you a hint?'

'Like I said, he was always gettin' blazed. I asked him where he got the money from. No job, no dole. Not even doing any stealing or anything since he met Shania. He reckoned this rich bloke was sending it his way.'

'Rich bloke?'

'Yep.'

'You never mentioned this before.'

'And have Johnny thinking I'm a snitch? No way.'

'But now Johnny's dead.'

'Yeah.'

'Good riddance,' says Uncle Walter.

*

Why would this rich bloke tolerate Johnny's blackmail for several months before killing him? More answers raising more questions. Either way it's enough for me to try a second push with the DC but I need reinforcements. I need DI Keegan. I call Vanessa to let her know I'll be meeting Marianne and why.

'Fuck's sake, Nick,' she says. 'Grow up.' But she signs off with another pig snort to let me know I need to lighten up too.

In Nelson, DI Keegan meets with Latifa and me at a coffee shop in Trafalgar Street. She hears me out, looks at the photo from Des Rogers' bach, and agrees it's worth another chat with the DC. I ask about her trip to Perth and the scuttlebutt on Patrick Smith.

'Sordid and sleazy, but in the end a waste of time. He was still employed at his private school in Perth five years ago so he couldn't have done Prince Haruru.'

'Wouldn't you know that before you went over?' asked Latifa.

Marianne isn't used to the lower orders speaking out of turn. 'People go on holidays, they act in concert with others, there were any number of permutations. I needed to see the records for myself and posh schools like that want you to ask nicely. Ask your mate here,' she nods towards me. 'See a wild goose and sometimes you just have to chase it anyway.'

Marianne leaves to lay the ground work with the DC. She'll call us when she's ready. Latifa brings back two more coffees and some ginger slice. 'Body language between you two,' she says, breaking her slice in half. 'If I was Vanessa, I'd be packing my bags.'

Ignore that. 'How's the study going?'

'Not bad.'

'That essay you were doing about *utu*?'

'Haven't got it back yet.'

'Fingers crossed.'

'I think the profs will like it. *Utu*, payback. They love that shit. They've got photos on their office walls: tribal warriors from PNG, All Blacks doing the haka, the Black Panther salute at the Olympics – accessories to go with their lumberjack shirts and skate shoes. None of that is ever going to threaten them and what they've got.' She reaches for my untouched ginger slice. 'You eating that?'

'Help yourself.'

'Heard from Gary?'

'No.'

'If you don't think he did Johnny Fernandez, you're going to have to move fast to prove it.' She finishes off the slice and wipes her fingers on a paper napkin. 'Or they'll kill him, those AOS blokes. Nobody wants a crazy Maori on the loose with a grudge and a gun.'

The call comes through from DI Keegan. DC Ford will see us now.

*

DI Keegan does most of the talking. I think she's already given the DC the gist, but she's running through it again and stopping every now and then to check details with me, bring me back into the fold.

'We can't ignore it, sir. We need to ask him some questions, if only to eliminate him from our inquiries.'

The elephant in the room is the clout that McCormack carries in the nation's capital but this isn't the time to force 'fear or favour' down the DC's throat. He looks at us each in turn and finally gives a terse nod. 'Your call, DI Keegan. You're the one running this inquiry.'

The threat is clear. Her head is also on the chopping block. He hasn't finished.

'I still don't want you anywhere near this, Nick. There'll be a disciplinary hearing next week. I suggest you call the union lawyer and get some good advice.'

Marianne shakes her head. 'All very well, sir, but I need him on the case now, briefing my team. He's the one who has put all this together. We need to be on firm ground with McCormack.' She looks my way. 'As firm as possible, anyway.'

The DC doesn't seem to be enjoying his day. He gets on the phone to his higher command to start the arse-covering.

*

Together DI Keegan and I brief her team and there's to be a consequent revisiting of all the gathered evidence in the new light. There's a nervous hubbub about the Incident Room: renewed focus and a big scary target make for a certain frisson. By video link the Kaikōura-based Ds get a kick up the bum. We really want to know about calls to and from that phone box near Des Rogers' bach and we want CCTV and forensics re-examined.

'Maxwell needs to be brought into the fold too.' I share Latifa's concerns: if Gary didn't kill Johnny Fernandez, we need to settle that and get the AOS dogs off his scent.

DI Keegan is straight on the case and after a one-sided and seemingly tense phone call she arranges for me to call into Blenheim to bring him up to speed.

'He lacked enthusiasm,' she said.

Understandable. It's his murder and he'd no doubt like to keep it that way. I shrug. 'He's the one that brought me the link between Fernandez and Des Rogers. He must have known I wouldn't let it go.'

'He's probably concerned that I'm empire building and that I'll swallow him whole.'

'Will you?'

She grins wickedly. 'Absolutely.'

On the way back through to see Maxwell, I drop Latifa off in Havelock. Before she exits the car she gives me a sideways look. 'DI Cheekbones definitely likes you. Anything I should know?'

'No. Nothing.' She doesn't believe me but it doesn't matter. 'We need to talk to Beth about the Woodbourne Tavern again, without leading her. See if there's any more she can give us.'

'Even if she can suddenly name him, I don't think her dark aura shit will stand up in court.'

'Still, a bit of spiritual reinforcement wouldn't go amiss. And it does tie McCormack and Rogers together if she can have them at the same table that night.'

That fresh wind from this morning has shifted around to the south and blown some bigger and darker clouds our way. A steady drizzle sets in as I cross the Wairau River and look out on to the vineyard where Qadim Reza was discarded. According to Jessie's article in the *Journal*, both the Rezas and Rileys are disgusted by my accusations against McCormack, affronted at having their misery appropriated for my personal vendetta. There was a photo of them all together, united in their hurt.

I'm sorry but that pain isn't over yet. I do promise though that I will catch this bastard, whoever he is.

43

After three days of revisiting the Pied Piper evidence, and the now-associated Rogers and Fernandez cases, things have moved swiftly. A combination of GPS/satnav and CCTV puts either the old convertible from McCormack's fleet, or McCormack himself and his new BMW, at Havelock Marina in the days before Prince Haruru, Jamie Riley and Qadim Reza were found. Now a review of the marina CCTV on Tuesday night – the night immediately preceding the discovery of Jamie Riley's body at the shoe fence – has McCormack's beemer parked nearby and being loaded up with a large sail bag from *Serenity II,* around eight p.m. The loader is an unidentified person with a baseball cap pulled low. That Tuesday morning, I had met McCormack to report the vandalism damage to his boat. They were going nowhere that day. So what was in the bag and why didn't Keegan's team pick it earlier? It was early Tuesday evening they say, a long time before the boy's body was found, and they were focusing on suspicious movements in the middle of the night. Plus it was McCormack's beemer and posh boat. Who'da thought that could be suspicious?

Richard McCormack has been invited in for a chat and given two days' notice – that's the kind of preferential treatment you get when you have money and influence. It's more than enough time for him to bring in his Wellington-based lawyer, a woman with strong family connections in the higher echelons of government.

Fiona Knight has a stare that could sculpt diamonds. She and DI Keegan face off on either side of the desk. To ginger things up a bit, Marianne has invited me into the room to assist with the interview. It's highly provocative and she hasn't sought the DC's approval for the tactic.

'I'm figuring we might only get the one crack at him,' she smiled grimly as we headed down the corridor. 'May as well go for broke.'

McCormack is in the kind of suit you wear for a day's corporate raiding. Or to appear before a parliamentary committee where you intend to let the oiks know who's boss. Keegan has put us opposite each other: Richard and Fiona, Nick and Marianne. A chilled Otago Pinot Gris and some lobster, and it would be a perfect double date.

The recording equipment is running. Fiona Knight begins by establishing that her client is here of his own volition and is keen to assist the investigation in any way he can and to remind us that he can, and will, leave any time he wishes.

'Absolutely,' confirms DI Keegan with a beam.

Knight flicks her fingers irritably. 'You may proceed.'

DI Keegan starts by asking McCormack to account for his whereabouts in the hours preceding the discoveries of the bodies of Jamie Riley and Qadim Reza. His lawyer hands over two A4 sheets, one for each victim, duly accounting for those hours. Keegan then inquires similarly in regard to Prince Haruru.

'Who?' The case has not been linked publicly in the media.

Keegan elucidates.

McCormack frowns. 'That was five years ago, Inspector. But I will check my diaries from then and if I can help I will.'

'Thank you.'

At this stage everything is essentially an unchallenged open account. We want his story first. We hope to tear it apart at a later date. Keegan hands McCormack and the lawyer each a list of stolen or damaged items reported to the insurer after the break-in at the McCormack Forestry offices. She asks McCormack to read out item six.

He obliges. 'Sundry display photographs.'

'Stolen or damaged?'

'Stolen.'

'Strange thing to steal.'

'I don't profess to know what goes through the minds of these low-life morons.'

Keegan hands him the photo I found in Des Rogers' U2 CD: him, a big cardboard cheque, Denzel Haruru and his cousin Prince, among others. 'Was that one of them?'

He studies it in its transparent cover. 'I believe so.'

'Are you able to explain how this image came to be in the possession of a retired and now deceased police officer named Desmond Rogers?'

He frowns. 'No.'

'Mr Rogers was found murdered recently.' Keegan names the date.

He raises the groomed eyebrows. 'Shocking. Do you believe there's some kind of connection?'

Change of tack. Keegan pushes a still photo from the marina CCTV across the table and announces for the tape what it is: an unidentified person, tall and probably male, loading a sail bag into the boot of a BMW the night before Jamie Riley's body was discovered. There's a date and time printout along the bottom. 'Is that your car, Mr McCormack?'

'It's one of our executive fleet, yes.'

'Do you normally drive it?'

'I often drive it.'

'Were you driving it on that night at that time?'

'I'd have to check my diary.'

'Let me help you,' I say. 'It was the evening of the same day you made a complaint about vandalism to your boat. We met that morning down at the marina. Remember me?'

He meets my eye. 'Yes, I do.'

'Around ten hours after this picture was taken, the body of James Riley was found nearby. He'd been tortured, raped and murdered.'

'Yes, it was on the news. Terrible. How can I help?'

'You can let us know if that's you in the photo,' says Keegan. 'And what's in that bag.'

He studies the picture again. 'No, that's not me. And I don't know anything about the bag.' There's a tensing as he looks at it.

'So who could be driving your car?'

'Not *my* car. The executive fleet. We have around a dozen people entitled to drive that vehicle. Eight of them are male, six of them, including myself, are young and/or tall enough to be that person. The other two are a lot older, shorter and perhaps rounder. And this is assuming none of those original six then loaned the car to somebody else.'

Very comprehensive. It's like he expected the question and prepared for it.

'Is there a log of who books the cars in and out?' asks Keegan.

'Yes, you'll have to talk to my PA about that. But I think it's a pretty loose system.' A chilly smile. 'I trust my team implicitly.'

DI Keegan is closing in on what she hoped to achieve from this interview. But she wants it on record. 'Yes, we will need to speak to your PA, and your executives, and to examine company records, including computers. We'll be in touch to arrange an appointment. We appreciate your cooperation in this matter, Mr McCormack.'

'That's it?' says Fiona Knight.

'Yes.'

'Cheap trick.'

'Excuse me?'

She flaps her hand in my direction. 'Having that joker in the room.'

'This is a murder investigation, Ms Knight. Not a game.'

'Yeah, right.'

I'm focused on McCormack as he leaves the room. He's troubled. Either he knows we're onto him, or he knows who we should be onto.

*

The DC is waiting for us in Keegan's office. Not happy about me being in on the interview but biting his lip nevertheless. He seeks reassurance and Keegan obliges.

'Mr McCormack is cooperating fully with our inquiries and is prepared to allow us to interview his employees and go through their files, both paper and electronic. That will happen over the coming days, sir.'

'Anything from the interview itself that adds to, or diminishes, your suspicions?'

'Nothing concrete.'

'But?'

'It's early days, sir.'

'Here's hoping you find something in your trawl.'

We all go our separate ways: the DC to brood about his corporate reputation and his budget submissions, DI Keegan to dish out jobs to her team. And me back to the farm to wait for further developments and instructions from Keegan. I'm deemed too much of a risk to return to normal duties pending next week's disciplinary hearing. The DC has acceded to Keegan's request for me to remain involved with the investigation but on an extremely tight leash.

'I like the sound of that,' Keegan purred jokingly, once the DC was out of earshot.

It elicits a rush of blood down below. The danger hasn't passed in my self-inflicted chaotic love-life.

Driving back from Nelson through Rai Valley, I see more denuded hills. Sometimes I think I'm getting used to it, but today they still look raw and unloved: a wounded landscape. I'm glad my vendetta is unsettling McCormack. He deserves it.

At home Paulie is triumphant, 'Eight eggs today, Dad. Look at them.'

They're big and brown, as promised by the sustainability book.

'Fantastic,' I say.

'Got a joke for you, Dad.'

'Okay.'

'What's a Kiwi Hindu?'

'I don't know.'

'Lays iggs, bro.' We hoot and high five.

Vanessa wants to know how it went with McCormack, so I tell her.

'Miss Piggy did well, then?'

I'm not sure how long this will go on for, perhaps forever. But it could be a whole lot worse. 'Early days, yet.'

'And David still doesn't want you back at work?'

Is her reminder that she's on first name terms with the DC deliberate? A code-cracker could spend years deciphering Vanessa's choice of words.

'No. Except as needed on this case. There's a disciplinary hearing next week. I'm meant to have booked the union lawyer.'

'Have you?'

'No, not yet.'

She hands me the phone. 'Get onto it. Then when you're done, the goat shed needs clearing out.'

'I'll do it,' says Paulie.

'No,' says Vanessa, firmly. 'Your dad will.'

But I let him help anyway.

*

It's Friday evening, and we decide on a family walk up the road before dinner. Past our place, it's no longer sealed and Paulie finds himself sliding on some of the steep gravel turns. He doesn't look like he's too sure about this. It appears the loggers have nearly finished on that small, immature block over the river; McCormack's spiteful little project. It's a beautiful evening, fading sunlight dances on the river rapids, birds dart among the trees, and the air is filled with warbling and clicks and whirrs. Now and then the stench of roadkill or discarded mammals rises from a gully.

'Pooh-ee,' says Paulie, pinching his nose. 'That stinks.'

There are random diggings into the side of the hill where a hundred and fifty years ago men chanced their arms at a gold find, only to discover after a month or two of gruelling bare-knuckle work there was nothing but another empty hole. And I wonder already if we're wrong on McCormack or, even if we're right, that we'll never get enough to prove it in a court of law, and a clever well-connected brief like Fiona Knight will help him walk free. It's the way of things with people of wealth and influence: they rarely end up paying for what they've done.

'I'll show you mine if you show me yours.' Vanessa has stopped by the side of the road, looking back towards our house, a red roof perched on a hill, poking out from behind the trees and bushes. I join her and she links her arm in mine. 'That's ours. This ...' her spare arm sweeps the river below, 'is ours.' Paulie has picked up a handful of gravel and is dropping individual stones into the waterfall scurrying down the hill below us. 'He is ours.' She turns to me. 'Show me what you've got that beats this. Show me what you've got that's worth throwing this away for.'

I show her my palms, they're empty.

'Exactly,' she says.

There's a tightness in my chest. I know she's right. But it doesn't stop me worrying that I'm still capable of throwing this all away.

44

We are woken early by a call from Latifa on the landline.

'Denzel has gone missing.'

My immediate thought is that he's another one of those loose ends that the killer is tidying up. He knows something even if he doesn't yet realise it. But I try to stay calm. 'Give me the details.'

'Uncle Walter says he didn't come home last night.'

'He's fifteen and not unknown for being a free spirit.'

'Not anymore' says Latifa. 'Walter thinks there's cause for concern and he's not a man who would worry unnecessarily about stuff like this.'

We agree that she will pick me up and we'll head out to Uncle Walter's place. No uniforms, her car, not official business so I don't break any more rules. I bring Vanessa up to speed and she hands me a mug of coffee. She looks like she'd prefer me not to get involved but this is a missing boy only a few years older than Paulie. 'Is this going to end badly too?'

'I hope not.'

When we arrive, Uncle Walter tells us he's already checked with Denzel's mates. Nothing. Likewise Charlie Evans hasn't seen him. A worried Walter is a new experience for me. He seems smaller, older, more vulnerable.

'Was anything bothering him? Acting strange, out of sorts?' asks Latifa.

'Since that dropkick got killed up the valley, he's been on edge.'

'Fernandez?' I say.

He nods. 'Denzel's jumping at shadows, locking the door at night. We never lock the doors around here.'

'Can we look in his room?'

'Help yourself. Fucken pigsty if you ask me. Good luck.'

Denzel's room is classic teenager: clothes on the floor and spilling out of drawers, a fug of testosterone and sweat and overdue laundry. A poster on the wall of some shirtless six-packed rapper, another of a young woman wearing nothing but tribal tattoos. We rummage around but find nothing of interest or which seems unusual.

'Is anything missing that you're aware of?' I ask.

Walter nods assuredly. 'His crossbow.'

'We confiscated it.'

'He got himself a new one with his wages from Charlie's place.'

'Charlie's paying him? I thought it was meant to be restorative justice for the alpaca.'

'Yeah, it is *utu*. But Charlie's got a soft heart to match his soft head.'

'Mobile?'

'Yeah, that's gone as well.'

'Anything else?'

'Nah. Don't think so.' He looks at me, there's a plea in his eyes. 'You bring him back safe, hear me?'

I glance at Latifa. We're thinking the same thing. Denzel is probably in hiding. But he's not privy to the kind of information we have about the list of people before him who have been the victim of violence or accident over the last few weeks. Only Johnny Fernandez. It's a big conclusion for the boy to have jumped to. So what precisely made him jump?

*

'Beth,' says Latifa.

'What about her?'

'She's probably been spooking him with her voodoo shit. Telling him ghost stories.'

We pay her a visit. She's a late riser and we find her sitting on her front verandah with hubby Peter having a breakfast cuppa and ciggie. 'Denzel? What about him?' She coughs and the birds fly from the trees.

'Done a runner,' says Latifa. 'Scared shitless about something.'

'So he should be.'

'Why, what have you been saying?'

'*Whakatupato*. Johnny Fernandez was a sign. A warning.'

'Why should Denzel have anything to fear from evil omens, Beth?'

'Our whole family is cursed. *Mākutu* has been sung to us. Cursing song. Look at us. Princey. Deb. Daddy Walter. And Denzel too.'

'What about you?' says Latifa. 'You're a Haruru. Aren't you worried about the curse?'

She nods towards her husband. 'Too fucken late.'

Another cup of tea and a second ciggie and Beth admits that she may have spooked the boy beyond what might have been necessary. But she does seem to have made the connections through police and news reports and word of mouth about the growing list of people associated with the case who seem to be meeting very bad luck.

'You're probably on that list as well,' I remind her.

'Yeah.' She squints at me through a curl of smoke. 'You too, Sergeant, eh?'

It had occurred to me but I'm figuring this bloke prefers softer targets: children, medicated women, flabby drunkards, anaemic stoners. I'll be way down on his list. Or so I hope.

She draws deep on the ciggie. 'I'm going to meet him again, the killer. See him and remember him. No more *Men in Black* shit.' She points at me. 'And you are going to bring us together.'

'Let me guess,' says Latifa. 'This all came to you in a dream?'

'You, my girl, are losing touch with your people and your culture. Probably that coconut job of yours. You need to reconnect, go on a pilgrimage or something like those people do at Mecca.' A parting cough as she heads back indoors. 'Pull your head in, girlie, he's got plans for you, too.'

*

'What does she mean by that? Silly bitch.' Beth has got under Latifa's skin.

'Probably just pointscoring, putting you in your place.'

'Yeah, well. Didn't need to do it like that, did she? Could'a just slapped me or something. You don't use the spirits to score points.'

'Don't worry about it.'

'Easy for you to say.'

We've got a list of family and friends spread around the region, indeed the whole of the country, from Auckland to Dunedin. In this situation, probably the best place for Denzel to hide out would be a big city hundreds of kilometres away. Could he have got on the Interislander with his crossbow? Possibly. Or maybe he's hitched a lift south. Latifa will go into the office and make inquiries. We can't think of anything else. Walter doesn't want to make it official yet. When and if he does, we can call in Search and Rescue, other police regions, the media, and such.

She drops me back at the farm and there's a message for me. I'm to call DI Keegan. I do so and tell her about Denzel, off the record.

'Cause for concern?'

'I'll keep you posted.' I ask if there are any developments.

'Our Kaikōura Ds got a fix on the white car spotted in a petrol station down the road the night Rogers was killed. It's part of the McCormack executive fleet.' She says the last two words with quotation marks in her voice. 'But the driver is wearing a hoodie and big-peaked baseball cap and pays in cash. The young guy on the cash till hasn't got the best memory, he's a pothead. Kaikōura. Who would've imagined?'

'The executive fleet log?'

'Nonexistent. New kids on the team fill it out to impress the boss but after a few months nobody bothers.'

'Satnavs in the cars?'

'The geeks are on it. Will let you know.'

'Office computers and diaries?'

'Ditto. And we're lining the execs up for interviews. All of them, including the women and the shorter, older blokes who don't fit the description. Doesn't mean they don't know anything.'

'Anything else?'

'Traffic took another look at the crash report on the ute that went over the cliff with the dodgy boat skipper in it. Marks on the road and on the vehicle are ambiguous and there was significant damage to the ute as well as rain and alcohol involved.'

'But?'

'One theory puts a second vehicle just behind, ramming the ute over the edge. Impatience and road rage on those twisty turns. Not unimaginable.'

'Theory never pursued?'

'Why would you? Too hard, nobody around, and the dead bloke was a dipstick. Pity about his mate but apparently he was a bit of a loser too. Life's too short, so to speak.'

We're both feeling the same buzz. 'It's taking shape, isn't it?'

'Like a sculpted blancmange.'

*

Sunday. The loggers have taken a weekend break and peace has returned. Paulie is on his Play Station and Vanessa wants to have angry sex with me. If we must. Afterwards, she's less angry. We have lunch on the back balcony overlooking the river and it looks glorious and crystal clear.

'Let's go for a swim,' she says, polishing off her bun.

And so here we are standing on the smooth stones naked in the early afternoon, threading our way into the freezing water where, until recently, I was drowning the last of the feral cat family that invaded our property. Vanessa looks stunning, girlish in a way I haven't seen her for years. I can't take my eyes away from her nipples.

'Water's cold, isn't it?'

She's looking further south on me. 'Sure is,' she grins.

We slip down into the depths, gasping for breath. It seems impossible to remain, but we do. One minute, two, three and then we're swimming and ducking under. At last, enough is enough, and we dry each other on the shore as the sandflies hover around us. There's a loud noise. An engine, approaching up the river, out of sight around the bend. A helicopter. It comes into view, flying quite low, maybe no higher than a hundred metres, its shadow dancing on the hillside. Forestry? Department of Conservation? On a weekend? There are no markings on it. Vanessa doesn't care. Naked as the day she was born, she gives it a cheeky wave. It sweeps off up the river then swings back around and flies over us again on its way back to wherever it came from.

45

It's another beautiful spring day, Paulie is back at school and Vanessa too, called in on relief. I'm at home, reading through the list DI Keegan has emailed to me: the McCormack Forestry executives with access to the company cars. There are four cars and twelve people. Although she has insisted on interviewing all of them, younger and older, male and female, it is already evident that some can be eliminated from our inquiries. Of the two older employees that Richard McCormack referred to, one was in hospital having a colonoscopy and the other was on holiday, whitebaiting over at Haast, on the days of interest. One of the women is clearly too petite to be the figure on the marina CCTV loading the sail bag into the BMW. The other, well maybe, she's taller and more statuesque, but I don't see it. A woman wouldn't do these things to a little boy, surely. Yes, there are exceptions and some famous monstrous couples out there but I'm prepared to believe my instinct here – this is the work of one bad man.

Which leaves eight people, including McCormack himself. Of these, only four, again including McCormack, were with the company five years ago and had access to the executive fleet around the time Prince Haruru was killed. They are Feargal Donnelly, Operations and Logistics Manager; Brian Wheeler, Marketing; and James Onslow, Research and Product Development. All of the others have only joined McCormack Forestry in the last couple of years. So there's a shortlist of four people who have had access to the company cars for all three child murders and the murders of Rogers and Fernandez. Oh, and the suspicious demise of the boat skipper.

DI Keegan has anticipated my next question. Was there an accident or damage report on any of the fleet cars immediately following the boat skipper being shunted over a cliff? No. The offending shunter must have been using a private vehicle, not the company car. The shortlist of four executives has been run through national and international databases and none have thrown up any flags of interest for previous bad deeds. While all twelve will have their telephone, email and internet records checked, the focus resources-wise is on the shortlist and they have also been scheduled for a second round of interviews commencing today. Marianne signs off with a happy face emoticon.

I hear it again. The helicopter coming up the river. Not as loud, flying higher. I step out on to the balcony. It's the same one as yesterday, no markings. Others that come this way – Forestry, DOC, police, Search and Rescue, the Marlborough Sounds tourist flights – I know their markings. Is it McCormack trying to spook me, get me to back off? Is it Sammy Pritchard failing to keep his word, showing that his handshake counted for nothing?

Who the fuck do you think you are and what makes you think I would listen to you?

And his parting words.

Travel safe, Nicky …

But thoughts like that just take me back down the road to ruin. I need to curb the paranoia. It's just a helicopter, a prospector, joyrider, whatever. And if it does turn out to be an emissary of Sammy's, then I really will make that call that gets him shivved in the showers.

*

I take a drive down the valley in the Toyota. I'm on edge and need to be out doing something. The Fernandez house has been cleared as a crime scene and I stop for a nose around. The lamb is still bleating so I take it some food and fresh water. It doesn't work; it's a dedicated bleater. The pig dog has gone. The door is locked but it doesn't take long to locate the key, which is under the nearest plant pot; it's like that in these parts. Inside are the same residual crime scene chemical smells I encountered at Des Rogers' place. Less of the single-man fug here and more of the meaty tang of a recently cleaned bloodbath. I'm really not in the mood for searching for clues. Detective Maxwell's team has already done that and I have reasonable faith in his abilities. Besides, I'm no longer obliged to convince people that McCormack needs to be looked at.

But still I find myself floating through this shabby ghost house with its echoes of a nascent family life. Might Johnny and Shania and their bub have eventually made something of themselves? A halfway decent, if often tough, existence. People do that, don't they? They change and grow. They give life a go even if it's a life many of us might shudder at.

I'm closing the front door and locking it when the phone goes inside. The landline. I open up again, and rush to grab it.

'Hello?'

'Who's that?' Denzel's voice.

'It's me, Nick Chester. Where are you, Denzel? People are worried about you.'

The phone clicks and hums. Why would he be ringing Johnny Fernandez? He knows he's dead. It must be Shania he wants to talk to. There's something she knows or can do for him. I call Detective Maxwell and tell him what's just happened.

'Yeah, weird,' he agrees.

'Maybe I could talk to Shania, try and find out what it might be about?'

'Not a good idea, mate. She's a victim of crime and you're suspended.'

'Not fully. Talk to DI Keegan. If she clears it, you're covered.' He does and a few minutes later he calls back with the address of Shania's mum in Seddon. Back to earthquake central. I thank him.

'No worries. DI Keegan and I agree, if there's any wild-goose chases then you're the best man for them: resource and cost neutral.'

'So I can't claim the petrol and a pie for lunch?'

'Yeah, nah, sorry.'

Shania's mum lives in a cute weatherboard place on the outskirts of Seddon. It's well-kept, the lawn is mowed, and there are flowers here and there. I begin to see where the halfway respectable flourishes at Johnny's house have come from. Shania's mother seems an open and good-hearted woman, forgiving of her daughter's flirtation with the dropkick end of town.

'Lovely accent you have, Geordie isn't it?' I nod confirmation. 'Had a fling with a boy from Newcastle when I was young. He was very funny and surprisingly good in bed.'

'I'm from Sunderland meself. Good in bed? Newcastle? You sure?'

She chuckles. 'Shania's out back with the bub. Go through. Tea, coffee?'

'Tea'd be great, thanks.' On the back verandah Shania is breastfeeding the toddler and modestly pulls a blanket up at my approach. I introduce myself.

'Yeah, I remember. You're the one that found Johnny.'

I ask how she's going and she says not bad considering she's been widowed at the age of eighteen. There's a toughness about her, but it's not bitter. She doesn't embrace victimhood or seem to be at the mercy of tempestuous fate. Mum appears with the beverages and leaves us in peace, and Shania switches the child over to the other breast.

'I was at the house this morning, taking a look around.' Shania doesn't question it, she assumes that because I'm a cop I can do exactly that. 'The phone rang while I was there. I'm pretty sure it was a kid called Denzel, Denzel Haruru. Know him?'

'Yeah, he and Johnny were mates when they were kids.'

'Have you seen him recently?'

She shakes her head. 'I'd never heard of him until about maybe a month ago. Then he was round our place a few times after that. He was working further down the valley, at the alpaca place.'

'Did you talk to him, or do you know what he and Johnny talked about when they were together?'

She tilts her head at the toddler. 'I was usually getting dinner together or feeding her. They laughed, talked about old times, trouble they used to get into. Smoked some dope. Drank some beer.'

'Nothing specific come to mind? Nothing you wouldn't have expected to hear?'

'No, what's this about?'

I tell her about the alternative theory on Johnny's death. That it wasn't drug-related, nor was it tied into old grudges with Gary Farr and North Island gangs.

'Those kid murders? No way.'

'It's a possibility we're exploring. He might have known somebody who had or has a link to them.'

'Who?'

'Exactly. Did Johnny mention anything to you, anything about people from his past?'

'Nah. All he had was schemes about how to score the next lot of easy money. Never ever came to anything.' There's a look in her eye, opaque.

'Except?'

'Except he heard about some cop that he used to know, dying down in Kaikōura. He said it gave him some ideas about where to get a few bucks for next year's firewood.'

I wait but there's no more. 'That's it? Nothing else?'

'Another easy money scheme.' She tears up, extracts the bairn from her nipple, rearranges her clothing.

'Denzel would have known about Johnny dying, so I'm thinking he must have been ringing you instead. Any idea what about?'

'No. Sorry.'

I'm obliged to leave it there and believe her. But there's something she's holding back. Shania takes the toddler to her bed and Mum shepherds me towards the front door. 'It's a blessing in disguise,' she murmurs. 'I have my daughter back. Now we can start over.'

*

What was Denzel after? He's afraid and in hiding. He needs something that he thinks will protect him. Johnny kept guns on the property even though he shouldn't have with so many infringements against his name. Did Denzel want more firepower than his one-shot crossbow? If so, he could probably have just gone up there, broken into the shed and taken something. Or did he believe that Johnny held some other talisman that would protect him from evil spirits?

I'm driving through Blenheim and the petrol light has come on, so I stop to fill up. Is Denzel in danger? If Shania is now the holder of the talisman that got Johnny killed, is she also in the line of fire? Two blocks away from where I stand, Deborah Haruru, Prince's mother, is still recovering from an overdose that she didn't take. Her mind and memory are on the mend and she has given us the lead on the McCormack car that drove by the marae a week before her son was taken. Surely she is still in peril? I ignore the warning sign about mobiles and petrol tanks and call the iwi home, asking after her.

'Yeah, she's good,' says the warden. 'Good enough to move on soon. Plenty of people lining up for a spot here, unfortunately.'

I thank her. A car horn toots. Someone wants me to get a move on. 'In a hurry? The petrol only pumps as fast as the machine lets it.'

'Oh, it's you,' he says. 'The policeman.'

I recognise him too. It's McCormack's lawyer, Latifa's tutor, Sebastian Ryan: in the job just nine months according to the personnel files. Unfortunately he's not on our shortlist of four as he really does deserve a going over with a telephone directory to the kidneys. 'Not at work today? You're a long way from Nelson.'

'None of your business, I'm afraid.' He smiles falsely and thumbs at the next car behind him. 'There's a queue forming.'

Those class-war hackles of mine are on the rise again. Us and them. The Shanias and Deborahs and Denzels of this world, we can't take all of them into protective custody. I study Ryan in my rear view. The best thing is for us to lock Richard McCormack away, quick smart. Lock him away so tightly that all the money and the best lawyers in the world can't get him out again.

*

In my absence, Latifa is ensconced with Traffic Man again.

'Get me out of here,' she pleads quietly into the phone. 'Before he drags his brain out through his nostril.'

We arrange to meet up in the Havelock Town Cafe where I order a flat white and a chunk of rocky road while I'm waiting. Some backpackers are there stretching out their drinks while they access the free wi-fi. I think about the German brothers, about whether their careers as assassins have recovered from the early setback. I think about that helicopter floating up through the valley, following the path of the river to our house. I think about Sammy Pritchard and try to recall whether or not, behind the badness, he was an honourable man. But then he has profited hugely from trading in human misery; what do I expect? No. It's paranoia, nothing more. But with good reason, people have been dying around me. Axes, claw hammers. I'm wading through a gore fest. Who wouldn't be jittery?

Latifa interrupts my dark reverie by taking a bite out of my rocky road. 'Yeah, I'll have one of those and an L&P.'

I go to the counter and place the order. 'Any news on Denzel?' I ask on my return.

'Nothing. Uncle Walter is getting frantic, ringing me every half hour. None of the mates or family knows anything.'

I tell her about the phone call at Johnny Fernandez's house and about my subsequent visit to Shania in Seddon.

She rips open her L&P and gulps down the sugary water. 'For somebody who's suspended, you're putting yourself about a bit.'

'It's this or twiddling my thumbs at home.' Which reminds me, I need to clean out the chook shed at some point and feed everybody, livestock included. I talk to her about my underlying concern: Denzel, Beth, Deborah, all of those Harurus theoretically in danger. Should we be looking after them more?

'Denzel's taken matters into his own hands. Deb's in the halfway house and their security has improved since last time. Beth's big and ugly enough to look after herself and Peter's no shrinking violet when it comes to the biff.' She polishes off her rocky road and casts covetous glances at mine. 'Maybe you should add yourself to the list. You'd have to be getting up his nose more than anyone.' She makes a grab for my slice but I'm too quick. 'Speaking of noses, I'd better get back to my colleague in the office.'

Her phone goes and from her face I can tell it's not good news.

'Shots fired out on the Sounds. Patrick Smith's place.'

*

I shouldn't be here but nobody was going to stop me. Traffic Man never gave me a second glance. Initiative isn't his strong point: infringements and road rules are his world; people are complicated. We've commandeered a boat from the marina and Traffic Man is driving. The wind has picked up, as it often does on the Sounds, but it's a much nicer day than the last time I was here. Even from a distance, we can see that there's quite a commotion around Patrick Smith's place, both on and off the water. The AOS ninjas are on their way by helicopter; they're probably getting a bit sick of Patrick Smith by now. Join the queue.

Two vessels are moored to Smith's jetty – Patrick's new boat, *Caravaggio II*, and another containing four men: Uncle Walter and three young sturdy blokes from the marae. The boys in the marae boat are shouting and swearing but they're not game to get up onto the jetty. The reason is that Patrick stands above them with his gun aimed. The one I approved the licence for. Patrick's orange tent is pegged just along from the jetty with the fly flapping in the wind. He has a table and chair set up outside with another for his stove and a tarp rigged over the top for shelter. There's a figure sitting glumly in the camp chair.

'Looks like we've found Denzel,' says Latifa.

'Who?' says Traffic Man.

'Never mind.'

We join the party. 'Mind if we tie up here, Patrick?' I say. 'And we're going to come up there so you'll need to put the gun down.' The chopper is audible in the distance. 'AOS. We don't want those blokes getting nervous do we?'

Patrick waves the barrel of his gun at the men in the boat. 'They stay where they are.'

There's a further explosion of curses from Uncle Walter's crew. I turn to the man himself. 'What's this all about, Walter?'

'This pervert has kidnapped my boy. He's got him prisoner.'

'Denzel,' I shout. 'Are you a prisoner?' I don't hear the subdued reply. 'What?'

'Nah, not really.'

'See? He's fine.' The other men glower behind Walter. They're good at it. 'Let us handle this?'

Walter gives a curt nod. Patrick gives one too. I climb the steps onto the jetty and Latifa comes with me. She lifts her chin at Patrick's gun. 'Put that thing down, you silly old bugger.'

Pointing up at the helicopter, I ask Traffic Man to send them away. Radios. He's good with radios. He likes that.

Patrick hasn't put the gun down, he's backing slowly, I fear he'll hit a loose plank and blow us to smithereens. Latifa has pulled out her own gun. 'Put it down, I said.'

The boys in the boat are impressed, lots of woo hoos and 'go girl'. We need to calm things down. 'Is Denzel okay here, Patrick?'

'Of course he is. He was scared, needed to take time out.' He thumbs over his shoulder. 'Check the sleeping arrangements. My bag is outside, his in.'

'Hear that, Walter?' I say. 'Nothing untoward.'

'*He's* fucken untoward.'

'That doesn't help at all, mate. We all need to calm down and walk away from this. Denzel's fine, aren't you, Denzel?'

'Yeah.'

'Patrick's a mate, isn't he, Denzel?' He doesn't want to reply to that but he has to. 'Isn't he?'

'Sort of.'

The chopper's not going anywhere while Patrick still has his gun levelled at me. A red laser sight dot is dancing on the side of his head. 'You need to put that down, Patrick.' I point skywards. 'They'll shoot you if you don't.'

'That doesn't worry me as much as it probably should.'

The red light is just above his ear.

'Put it down, Patrick.' It's Denzel, walking our way. 'It's alright.' He turns to Walter. 'He's okay, Grandad. I just want to stay here for a while, right? I'm fine.'

Patrick lowers the gun. The red dot disappears.

'You one of them, boy? Like him? That what you're saying?'

'Nah, not like him. I'm me.'

'You're coming home with us, boy.'

'No, I'm not.'

Walter nods at one of the younger men beside him. 'Go and get him.'

Patrick's gun goes back up, and Denzel runs and retrieves his crossbow from the tent. The red dots are dancing again, one each for Patrick and Denzel.

I step between the warring parties. 'I think that's a no, guys.'

Walter glares at me. 'You gonna let this happen?'

Denzel has his crossbow levelled now. 'I'll come home when I'm ready, Grandad. But not yet. That guy that's doing all the killing. I'm on his list. Have to be.'

'Auntie Beth been scaring you? Don't listen to her stupid ghost stories.'

'He's real enough. Johnny knew him and now he's dead.'

'Denzel's right,' I say. 'He is in danger and this is probably the best place for him. If he comes back home who knows what might happen? Could you live with that, Walter?'

He stands his ground.

'You've already lost too much, Walter. No more, eh?'

He exchanges some words in Maori with the younger men and they cast off and chug away. Walter looks back, I guess he wants to be angry in order to keep face. But he just looks sad and a little scared.

'What did they say?' I ask Latifa.

She shakes her head. 'Our business, not yours.'

*

With everything calmer, we sit down outside Patrick's tent and have a nice chat.

'Both of you: I don't want to have to say this again. You don't wave those weapons at people, they're for hunting only. If I have to take them off you, I will.' The words pass a few centimetres over their heads as I thought they might. 'Denzel, you rang Johnny's house. What were you after?'

'Nuthin.'

'Shania? You wanted to speak to her?'

'Nah.'

Latifa leans in. 'Listen, we're trying to help you and the best way we can do that is by putting this bastard away. If you know something, tell us.'

Patrick taps him on the knee. 'Tell them what you told me.'

Denzel looks past us into the distance. The sun is dropping and the hills are making new shadows. Dark folds, like secret places in the flesh. 'Johnny had a second phone, for his deals and other dodgy shit. He told me the guy's photo was on it. The one he saw in the car that day.'

'Photo?'

'Yeah, he'd seen him a few months back in Nelson. Took a sneaky pic so he could take it home and check. But he was sure it was him.'

'Did he give a name?'

'No.'

'McCormack?'

'He wouldn't say. He just knew he could get a bit of money out of it.'

'Kids are dying and he wants to make a buck?' Latifa is disgusted.

Denzel nods. 'That's what I told him, but Johnny's been a piece of shit from way back.'

'What makes you think the phone is still available? That it hasn't been found and destroyed?'

'I rang it a couple of days ago and it just kept on ringing. If it was destroyed you wouldn't get that, would you?' He frowns. 'Besides, if this psycho dude didn't know his picture had been taken how would he know what he was looking for?'

Des Rogers, I'm thinking. Johnny talks to Des, the money man and go-between and probable partner in blackmail. Des tells the killer and brags about the proof he has in order to up the ante and the price.

'The killer didn't know who took, or had, the photo?'

'Dunno. Johnny just got his cut off the cop, Rogers.'

And once Rogers had been dispatched and the killer scrolled through his mobile he knew to come looking for Johnny. No more blackmail, no more payouts, no more loose ends. But that now begs a new question. If the killer is McCormack, why would he worry about somebody having his photo? He's in the newspaper every other week. Such a photo would only be of concern to someone who shuns the limelight.

46

At the end of yesterday I shared my new theory with DI Keegan. 'It's exasperating, you're exasperating,' she tells me. She's only just got used to the idea that we should be nailing McCormack to a tree and now I'm telling her to save her nails. But I can tell she's not that exasperated, she just likes giving me a hard time.

'As it happens, it's a fluid situation,' she says. 'Other candidates are emerging.'

Over breakfast of some of the nine eggs we got this morning – 'Count 'em, Dad, count 'em,' – I tell Vanessa I'm spending the day with DI Keegan. She gives no outward signs of discomfort but that's just like her, I'll probably cop it later. Instead she sends me on my way with a peck on the cheek and a snort when my back is turned. McCormack and his operations manager, Feargal Donnelly, are up for re-interview today and I'm able to watch over the video link from the adjacent room. While waiting, I pore over the DVDs and transcripts of yesterday's re-interviews with Brian Wheeler from marketing and James Onslow, the R&D guru. For blokes working in go-getter fields, they have to be the dullest men on God's earth. When pushed, it emerges that Brian has a secret vice: he's a twitcher. He loves birds and he can impersonate them quite well, although I do take issue with his tui. It's not that he deliberately flouts the car log booking rules, it's just that he's too excited about what he does in the company car out of hours to remember such trivialities.

James on the other hand seems dangerously dull to the point of coldness and I'm guessing a touch of Asperger's. He's the kind of bloke who invents those logging machines that grab a tree by its throat and chop it off at the knees in one clean movement: the transformer from hell. But is he killer-cold, or just wired differently? Like Brian from marketing, he's single at an age where it raises suspicions and it certainly doesn't help when you're grasping for alibis – then again you could say that about half the blokes who live up the valley. But within the transcripts there's nothing I can point to except that Brian probably should be kicked loose to follow the birds and James needs careful watching, whether he's our killer or not.

Now for today's live action: enter Feargal Donnelly, operations and logistics, plus his lawyer, some bloke from Nelson I've never seen before. Donnelly's about forty and loosely fits the vague physical descriptions we have so far of a man of above average height and slim build with a pale complexion and short fairish hair. I recall our excuse-me-you-first dance in McCormack Forestry reception as I stormed out of the building after one of my run-ins with Dickie. He's a real Irish charmer full of twinkle and mirth and craic. He's flirting with DI Keegan and she's responding with a shy smile: either she's not immune to it or she intends to do him slowly. They talk about the weather, he picks up on her accent and asks whether she follows Liverpool or Everton. The latter apparently. They go through his previous interview and his whereabouts on the days and times in question. It's not easy going back five years, so the focus is on more recent events like the night before Jamie Riley was found by the shoe fence.

'So you were working until,' she checks the transcript, 'around six?'

'Aye.'

'And then you went to Countdown on Waimea Road in Stoke, bought some groceries, took them to your home in Richmond, not far from the pool, and made dinner for yourself and your wife ...'

'Fiancée. Megan.'

'Who was on a late shift at Nelson Hospital until ...'

'Eleven-ish.'

'That's right.' The file again. 'And you used one of the company BMWs for the shopping excursion?'

'Yes.'

'But you're not in the log.'

'Nobody bothers with that. Dickie is cool about these things.'

'Mr McCormack?'

'Yes.'

'There are two BMWs. Which one did you have?'

'The white one.'

'They both are.'

He shrugs. 'Can't remember the rego number, I just took the keys off the peg, pressed the button and jumped in the one that flashed.'

Keegan reads out a plate number. 'It must have been that one because someone else had the other BMW then.'

'I'll take your word for it.'

'And the satnav for that car confirms you were in the supermarket you mention at that time, as does their CCTV.'

'Well there you go.'

'And then there's no satnav record for the next twelve hours. It's turned off and the chip and battery removed.' Bingo, I'm thinking. The emerging candidate Marianne mentioned.

'Really?' He does a good impression of bewilderment.

'Why did you do that, Mr Donnelly?'

'I didn't.'

'Your fiancée, Megan, didn't get home until just after midnight, did she?'

'Was it? I lost track of time, fell asleep in front of the idiot box then took myself to bed. Left her dinner in the fridge.'

'You were there when she got home around twelve-fifteen?'

'Yes.'

'So where were you between six-forty three when, according to the satnav, you arrived home and the time when Megan got back from work? Approximately five and a half hours.'

He's getting agitated. 'Like I said, home and telly.'

'Alone?'

'Yes, of course.'

'So nobody can vouch for you?'

'No. But ...'

'What were you watching?'

'Netflix. *House of Cards.*'

Keegan pushes the CCTV photo from the marina across the desk. 'That's the car there, the one you say you were using.' She stabs the photo with her finger. 'And that's you with the big heavy bag isn't it?'

'No way.'

'This photo is taken at Havelock Marina at 8.03 pm. Ample time for you to get there from Nelson. It's what, a sixty-minute drive at most? The weather and roads were good that night so probably nearer forty-five.'

'Other people have keys to that car.'

'Who?'

'Dickie. He has a spare set.'

'So you're saying Mr McCormack took the car from outside your house for a few hours and then returned it?'

'Why not?'

'And fiddled with the satnav to incriminate you?'

He rubs his forehead, he wants all of this to go away. 'Again, yes, why not?'

And that's the crux of the matter. More proof is required to nail it but there's enough to do a formal arrest and a taking of DNA and other samples, as we have already done with McCormack. Feargal will be put into the cells and brought before a magistrate at the earliest convenience, probably tomorrow, so he can be held in custody for longer. His home and office now become secondary crime scenes and forensics will be all over them. Maybe Beth Haruru will pick him as the man in the Woodbourne Tavern that night. Maybe Denzel will remember him driving by the marae. Maybe we'll find phone and internet links between him and Des Rogers. Maybe we'll locate Johnny Fernandez's second drug-dealing phone, and Feargal's photo will be on it. Donnelly is led away for processing. He'll be put into a paper suit so we can also test the clothes he's wearing. The twinkle and the craic have evaporated.

'So, McCormack's up next. Is he off the hook now?'

Keegan is flushed. She's close to a result. 'He's due in this afternoon. I don't see any harm in keeping the appointment unless Feargal confesses in the next hour or two.'

I'm a bit disappointed. Was that it? So soon, so easy?

*

To kill time before McCormack's interview I head down the road to a cafe and grab a sausage roll and a coffee. The investigation feels like it's once again out of my hands and DI Keegan well and truly has the initiative. A man not on my radar, Feargal Donnelly, is in the frame and it's shaping up well. I can just sit back and let DI Keegan wrap up the case, then it's so long Marianne. So why do I feel cheated? Vanessa would provide the answer instantly: control freak. There's a text on my phone from the DC telling me my disciplinary hearing is tomorrow morning, here, at ten. And I haven't organised the union lawyer. I give her a call and she's pissed off at the short notice, it's not like she hasn't got enough on her plate with all the hundreds of other errant Tasman District officers trying to wriggle out of trouble, but she'll see me half an hour before the hearing and we'll take it from there. They do good sausage rolls here, huge chunky things that these days would probably be called artisan by some, and lethal by others. I slap on some tomato sauce and go for my life.

There's a familiar face at the cafe window; a familiar face with an unfamiliar expression. It's Sebastian Ryan, McCormack's company lawyer, and he's smiling and looking friendly. He's coming inside.

'I thought it was you.'

'You were right.'

He puts his hands up in mock surrender. 'How about a fresh start? I know I rub people up the wrong way. I blame my parents. I sometimes come across as …'

'A smug snooty prick?'

He laughs. 'Possibly. Look, I'd be lying if I said this was an accident. And I don't expect you to believe for one moment that I'm suddenly Mr Nice Guy.'

'No danger there.' What does he want? The answer's no, let me eat my sausage roll in peace. Get lost.

'It's Richard.'

'Dickie?' I say, through an open mouthful of food, being deliberately gross.

'He's under a lot of pressure. I don't know whether you're aware, but McCormack Forestry is up for a public flotation next month and it's not going as well as planned.'

'Logging not what it's cracked up to be?'

He hides his irritability well. He's really trying. 'This investigation business.'

'The child murders?' A flinch. Must I be so blunt when we're talking about the poor man's profit margin? 'What about it?'

'Richard has been over-stressed of late. Between you and me …' Suddenly he's confiding in me. 'Richard's judgement has been a bit off …'

'Target?'

'Exactly. He realises he should have kept a tighter rein on the car log. And now that Feargal's in trouble.'

'News travels fast.'

'His solicitor called me. They're bringing in the big guns, so I'm assuming the worst.'

'Good idea,' I say.

He nods grimly. 'Anyway, my focus is on making life easier for Richard. So I'd like to know what we can do to assist your inquiry, and perhaps redeem the McCormack brand a little?'

I look at him like he's nuts, in fact I'm aiming for the shit-on-the-shoe look that his social class do really well. The server brings over my bill and Ryan intercepts it and hands him a twenty dollar note.

'Allow me,' he says. 'My treat.'

*

I recount my Ryan conversation to DI Keegan.

'Redeem the McCormack brand?'

'Yeah, that's what he said.'

'Tosser. How does he propose to assist our inquiry?' The last few words with finger quotes. 'Like it's a grace and favour he dispenses rather than our fucking job to do as we see fit.' Marianne's childhood Liverpudlian accent strengthens the angrier she gets. Class war can do that for you. It's a magical thing to be cherished and held close.

'I told him it'd be a good start for the brand if Dickie answered all our questions truthfully and stopped pissing about.'

'So let's see if he's passed on your advice,' says Marianne.

I'm back in on the interviews. It's not that I'm needed, it's just that DI Keegan wants to send a message to McCormack and his lawyer that she is in charge, not them. Fiona Knight looks up at me and smiles thinly. The death stare has warmed up a fraction. Even McCormack meets my eye without wanting to stick a dagger in it. I don't like this friendliness and civility one bit. They're up to something.

Ms Knight slides a new sheet of A4 towards us, one each. It's a full account of Dickie's movements from five years ago. It seems that on the relevant dates, Dickie was at a Forestry and Land Management conference in Dunedin. She follows up with an envelope for DI Keegan.

'Conference registration, hotel and travel receipts, photographs of Mr McCormack at the gala dinner.' So McCormack wasn't around to kill Prince Haruru. By implication he hasn't done any of this.

'Why have you waited until now to hand all this over?' asks Keegan.

'It's only in the last week that you have decided to investigate my client

250

officially.' Fiona Knight casts a glance at me on the last word. 'There has been no need, until now, to account for his movements. The appointments schedule for five years ago had been archived and the record-keeping systems had been disrupted by the burglary and vandalism in the office last month.' That frosty smile again.

'Anything else?' says McCormack, finding his helpful face.

DI Keegan closes her file. She's ready to give up on him and focus on Feargal Donnelly. I'm not. A grudge is a grudge after all. 'The car Feargal's been driving. That's your favourite isn't it?'

'Come again?'

'We all do it. Favourite armchairs. Favourite coffee cup. Favourite table at our favourite restaurant. You have your favourite beemer, right?'

'What of it?'

'There's a spare set of keys for that one and you keep it all to yourself. The collegiate brotherhood all-mates-together thing goes out the window for this one.'

'Is there a point here?'

'You don't live that far from Feargal. A few blocks, is that right? If you fancy driving that car and he's got it, you take it back off him. Maybe you drop the other one in its place, maybe not. You're the boss, after all. Who gives a fuck?'

Fiona Knight frowns at my language and loads up her briefcase. 'I think we're finished here. My understanding is that the person who did the killing five years ago is the one doing it now. Mr McCormack was out of town five years ago. Ergo.'

DI Keegan is giving me the look. The don't-do-something-stupid look. She's right. If the paperwork in the Fiona file stacks up, then it can't be Dickie. Focus on Feargal, nail him. Don't be distracted by your feud with McCormack. But I so want to punch him, I really do. I hand the floor back to DI Keegan.

'Thanks for your time and your cooperation,' she says.

'If there's anything else,' says McCormack. 'Please, don't hesitate.'

I won't.

*

'What was that about?' DI Keegan has moved on and doesn't seem that interested in the answer. She's looking at her whiteboard, assigning tasks that will help wrap up Donnelly and the Pied Piper murders.

'Nothing. Me and my grudges. I find it hard to let go.'

'The second-key thing was worth establishing. Thanks for that.'

'Pleasure.'

'You're not convinced?'

'Like I said, I need to let go.'

Keegan gives me a distracted smile. 'You need to head back up the valley and spend time with that family of yours.'

Everybody keeps telling me that, over and over. It's feeling like an ending and I'm not sure I'm ready for that yet. A dangerous complicit look passes between us and I know I'm capable of doing something stupid today. There's a knock on her office door. It's Benson.

'Just the man,' she says. 'Can you summon the troops for a briefing?' She checks her watch. 'Half an hour.'

'I'll be off, then,' I say.

She turns back to the whiteboard. 'Cheers, Nick. Thanks.'

47

Their own little Garden of Eden: the cop and his happy family, honest folk making a go of it. The woman pegging out the washing, the sunlight haloing her hair. She looks his way as if she can see him but he's sure she can't. They need to learn to mind their own business – all of them.

The water rushing below. Birds flitting among the trees across the river, their crystal clear chimes. So much life. Yellow pollen floating in the breeze. The boy collecting eggs from the hen coop. Tiny enough, when viewed through a distant lens, to crush in the palm of a hand.

48

Wednesday is my day of reckoning. Well I seem to have lots of them lately. This one is my disciplinary hearing. In some ways it's a pity the Sammy Pritchard thing has been resolved, because that would have made it harder for the DC to sack me. Now there's nothing stopping him. Except that previously he seemed to have quite liked me, or at least liked my wife, and expressed the opinion that I was an okay cop and he'd like me to stay on his team. It's a long way for me to have fallen but never let it be said that I'm not an ambitious over-achiever. I can fall further and faster than anybody out there.

The union lawyer has read through the 'show cause' letter that was emailed to me at the end of yesterday and moaned again about the short notice. I find myself defending the DC to her.

'Well we've all been a bit busy with these murders and stuff. And the boss has his budget submissions.'

'But according to you he's been pissed off for weeks now. Yet you only got the letter last night?'

I shrug. 'So what do we say to them?' 'Them' being the review panel: the DC, another bloke of a similar rank, and a woman from Human Resources.

'Tell them why they shouldn't sack you.'

'Any thoughts?'

She sighs. 'Did you have a good reason for doing the bad things they mention?' She lists them again: unauthorised access of classified information, abuse of certain regulations and protocols, pissing off rich powerful folk, that kind of stuff.

'Yeah, I wanted to catch the prick who's been murdering the kids.'

She writes that down. 'Good. Anything else?'

'Not really, sorry.'

In the meeting we're all sitting around a boardroom table and the DC asks if I've received and read his letter.

'Yes, thanks. Sir.'

He turns his attention to the union lawyer. 'You have a prepared response?' No, she tells him, because of the extreme short notice. 'Would you like a postponement?'

'Yes,' she says.

'No,' I say.

'Which is it?' asks Ford with a frown.

'No. You know the reasons why I did those things on your list.'

'We need to maintain the highest possible standards, Sergeant, and stick to regulations. We're under public scrutiny. We ...'

'We wouldn't be in the position we are now without me jumping the gun. We weren't making any worthwhile progress, sir.'

A mobile goes off, then another. Then mine. The only ones that don't seem to be ringing are the union lawyer's and the woman from HR's; either they're good sorts and turn theirs off for important meetings or this doesn't concern them. I suspect the latter. Mine stays unanswered; under the circumstances it might be more polite. The DC takes his call and his face turns even grimmer. He's looking at me all the time and then ends it.

'It seems Mr Donnelly's managed to hang himself this morning before we could get him ready for court.'

'Bugger,' I say.

*

In some ways it makes things easier. Enough evidence can be gathered to close the case to everybody's satisfaction, except maybe the victims' parents, without having to undergo the rigour of the defendant's day in court. Aspersions can be cast so the media dutifully paint it as a win. Justice prevails, the rightful order is restored, and it's back to business as usual. The DC and his colleagues on the disciplinary panel adjourn briefly to discuss me, but really he's got bigger fish to fry.

The woman from HR gives me the news. 'Back to work on Monday and keep your nose clean. This is your second strike.' A smile like she's just been nice to me. 'Between you and me, I think the DC is quite pleased about this.'

So I have the rest of the week and the weekend off and then it's back to the fray. No doubt during that time DI Keegan will have parcelled up

Feargal Donnelly and be heading back to Wellington as the conquering hero. Meanwhile there's some holes in the chook run to patch, and the goats' water supply needs connecting. Dropping by the DIY superstore in Nelson to pick up the stuff needed before heading home, I notice the staff all seem happy enough with their zero-hours contracts. Happy in a North Korean citizenry kind of way. Climbing into the ranges, I see the clouds have come in from the south and rain has appeared as if from nowhere and the bright spring day was never here. The hairpins glint wetly in the headlights and my windscreen wipers struggle with the sudden deluge. Water gushes along the roadside drainage channels and out of the culvert pipes into the dark ravines hundreds of feet below. Behind me some dickhead has his lights on full beam, blinding me in the rear view. He's halfway up my arse; any closer and we'll have to get married. My knuckles and jaw are aching from the tension and I need to do something about it. I pull into the next passing place and the moron goes on his way with a middle-finger salute. It would have been easy for him to shunt me over that edge to be swallowed by the bushes and not found for days. Easy and imaginable. For an otherwise laidback and laconic place, New Zealand seems to have more than its fair share of impatient four-wheeled tosspots.

*

At home Vanessa and Paulie are huddled by the stove nursing mugs of cocoa.

'What's with this weather?' Pulling up a chair, I bring Vanessa up to date, selectively edited for Paulie's sensibilities.

'So it's all over and you're back at work next week?' I nod. 'Fantastic.' Vanessa hands me my cocoa. 'I've got some news, too.' It seems Vanessa has some work at a local school every day until the Christmas break. Maternity leave cover. She anticipates my next question. 'Paulie can stay on at his school at their after-hours care club until I get there at four.'

Paulie seems happy enough. 'Great,' I say. The weather is no good for any outside work today so I offer to make a curry for dinner and Paulie looks worried. 'Not a hot one, I promise.'

'Okay.' But he's not convinced.

'Any other gossip around here today?' I say, chopping chillies.

'The helicopter came through again. The one I showed my titties to.'

'Mum!'

'And?'

'It went away again. I had my clothes on this time.'

'Gross!'

Repeat after me: I will not worry about stuff like this, I will not worry about stuff like this. It's just a helicopter.

'And Paulie got ten eggs today.'

'Ten? Far out.' I high five him twice, so they add up.

'And I think we've got a perv.'

Jesus. 'Tell me more.'

'This morning. Across the valley in that logged block, somebody with binoculars. I saw them glint in the sun.'

'How do you know he's a perv? Could have been just looking for some trees or markers or whatever it is forestry folk do.'

'Thanks a lot. But I was hanging out my knickers and that's worth staying around for.'

'Mum!'

'Joke.'

It's the valley. You get all sorts up here, I'm thinking. Usually harmless – unless they're sent by Sammy Pritchard. Or they're looking for something Johnny Fernandez may or may not have. Vanessa is watching me. 'What?' I say.

'It's nothing, the binoculars thing. It was just a joke. Remember them?'

I smile and try to act normal but the moment has evaporated. Vanessa looks sad and I chop more chillies than Paulie will be able to cope with.

*

In the night I'm lying awake like in the days when I was still waiting for Sammy and Marty to find me. Nothing has changed. I pad over to the window which looks across the river. Clouds obscure the stars and wind tears at the treetops, but the rain has stopped. Further down the river there are flashlights fanning across the hill and the sharp cracks of a pig hunter's gun. These things I have come to know and understand and no longer fear. The people coming for me and my family will not be so clumsy and loud.

There, I have admitted it to myself. Somebody out there has not finished with me.

49

It's Friday. I've been back on duty a week. A week of driving up and down SH6 and ticketing boy racers. A week of issuing infringements to blokes for chasing pigs through the backyards of other people's homes, and nicking their firewood stash along the way. A week of digging gladwrapped packages of meat out of the pants of young Marlburians. Latifa is happy to have me back, she prefers my company to that of Traffic Man any day. She's neck-deep in her law exam revision and finishing off her assignments, and she's contemplating taking the first six months of next year out of the job to try and break the back of her degree.

Feargal Donnelly will be cremated this morning. Not too many questions have been asked of the police station custodial supervisor about the circumstances of the suicide – shit happens. New evidence of Donnelly's probable guilt has emerged in the last seven days of digging by DI Keegan and her team. It seems that more of the alibis provided by him relating to the disappearances and discoveries of Jamie Riley and Qadim Reza have fallen apart. They mainly relied upon his fiancée, Megan, and she isn't backing him up. Also, in each of the two recent child murders, Dickie McCormack is adamant that he did not have the BMW in question and that Feargal did at the relevant times. Preliminary forensics have traces of Donnelly in the suspect BMW but then again he never denied that he sometimes used it. His work schedule as operations manager had him on the road a lot and able to spend time with his victims during their final week on earth without anyone wondering where he was. Even the Garda came to the party – the Irish police sent through details of a teenage conviction for public indecency: an encounter with an underage lad in the toilets in Phoenix Park in Dublin. Lastly, the stoned casual on duty at the Kaikōura petrol station on the night of

Des Rogers' murder has identified Feargal Donnelly as the driver of the beemer that called in there for fuel. At least he's pretty sure anyway. Thin and circumstantial still, but it's looking like it'll be enough, and it will never have to be challenged in court, so the investigation is winding down and DI Keegan will be heading back to Wellington any day now.

I wonder about Feargal's resilience though. This is a man who has supposedly coolly dispatched three children plus Des Rogers, Johnny Fernandez, Kevin the boat skipper, and finally tried to kill Deborah Haruru. This is the Prince of Darkness, the *taniwha* monster that slithers among us. Yet at the first sign of overdue interest in him he kisses the world goodbye. Then again some people are like that. I've arrested enough of them in my day. Men who will terrorise their rivals, their neighbours, and their family, but fold like wet cardboard when called to account.

There have been no more helicopters up the valley, no more binoculars glinting in distant bushes, and Vanessa and I are back on an even keel. Paulie has annexed the hen coop as his personal fiefdom and the goats are keeping the blackberry brambles and gorse under control. The weather is usually more good than bad, and life, in general, is sweet.

A slight cough announces another presence. I must have been miles away in my thoughts and Latifa is out back printing something off. Jessie James makes herself comfortable in the visitor's chair.

'Jessie. How can I help you?'

'I owe you an apology.'

Gen Y apologising. It doesn't get any more intense than that. 'What for?'

Latifa pokes her head around the door, sees who it is, pulls a face and goes back to her printing.

'The article I wrote saying mean things about you.'

'Apology accepted.'

'I owe you.'

'No, you don't. Sorry is fine.' I tap the fascinating circular I'm reading about health and safety. 'I've got a lot on my plate so, much as I appreciate you dropping by ...'

'I went to that bastard's funeral today.'

Donnelly, I assume. 'And?'

'Those poor parents. They were there. It was so sad. I asked them for comments, and do you know what was on their minds?'

'No.'

'They were feeling guilty for criticising you in that piece I wrote. They were sorry: if it wasn't for you going out on a limb none of us would have known.' Tears are streaming down her face. 'They wouldn't have their closure.'

It's doubtful they'll ever have it but I appreciate the thought.

'They insisted I pass on their thanks to you,' Jessie says, 'and their apologies. So here I am, and I'm adding mine too.' She reaches across and clasps my hands. 'You're a good man, Sergeant Chester.'

'Thanks.'

'His fiancée wasn't a bad sort either, you know. I think she's well rid of him. Shame, really, she's a lovely woman.'

'Can't blame her for what he did.'

'No. She thought it was funny, though.'

'Funny?'

'Him being accused of keeping the kids on that boat. He hated boats, she said, apparently he got seasick standing on a jetty.'

'Must've taken some Sea Legs.'

'Must've,' says Jessie. She stands up and sticks out a hand for shaking. 'No hard feelings?'

'Life's too short and this town's too small.'

Latifa comes out of the printing cupboard as the door closes behind Jessie James. 'What'd she want?'

'To apologise.'

'What for?'

'Besmirching my good name.'

'Must want something off you.'

'Cynic.'

'Mark my words.'

*

The next morning it's Saturday and we've had a lie in and now we're having a late family breakfast. Vanessa blessed me with a bout of pre-brekky raunch while Paulie watched re-runs of *Spongebob* downstairs. She nudges me playfully with her hip as she refills my mug from the coffee plunger. Paulie is on to his second pancake. A vehicle crunches over the gravel driveway and I go to take a look. It's a ute.

'Gary!' I shake his hand and he accepts hugs from Vanessa and Paulie. He's carrying a holdall which he eases to the floor. We gather around the kitchen table and recharge the plunger. Gary seems healthier and brighter but there's a look in his eye I can't work out. Like he's squaring for a fight. 'Detective Maxwell off your case, now?' I ask.

'Pretty much, he's got somebody in the frame for Johnny Fernandez apparently.'

I know all about it, thanks. 'What about that fire in Palmerston North, Ronnie somebody?'

'Parata. Mystery, huh? Who could do such a thing?' Neither of us is going to pursue it. He takes the coffee that Vanessa offers him. 'Cheers,' he says. 'Been doing some thinking. I'll be needing the shack again. That okay with you?'

'Sure, no worries.'

'But I won't be paying any rent. Finished with that crap.'

This could get interesting. I can feel myself bristling. 'How long did you have in mind?'

'As long as it takes.' He takes a sip of coffee and winks at Paulie before he fixes back on me. 'You said before I left that you figured you owed me over that psycho Marty bloke?'

'I'm listening.'

'You want to be my friend, that's great, but we need to even things up a bit.' He thumbs over his shoulder. 'The far paddock. You don't run animals in it, you don't grow anything. You're not using it.' He rummages in the holdall and brings out a plastic shopping bag. 'Down payment. I'll build my own place, live in the cabin while I'm doing it.' I can see there's a lot of money in there and he knows I'm wondering where it came from. 'None of your business.' He gulps down another mouthful of coffee. 'I know the market rate. I know what that block is worth. I'll pay a fair price for it. Deal?'

I look at Vanessa and she nods. She's good in these situations. Decisive. And it all goes towards the Paulie Fund anyway. 'Okay, but ...'

'Sorry. No buts. No conditions on how I live my life on my own property. If I choose to be happy Farmer Giles next door then it's your good luck. If I'm the neighbour from hell then that's the way it goes. You have no control over that. You'll just have to trust and hope.'

He's been thinking alright. 'What if I say no?'

'I'll say goodbye.'

I'm tempted by that. But in order for things to even out I do have to give something up. We shake on it and Paulie takes him out to introduce him to the chickens and the goats.

50

Monday comes around and Paulie is back up at Pelorus School while Vanessa is off in the opposite direction filling in at Havelock. It's late November and people's minds are turning towards summer. There's more traffic up and down the valley, more campervans at Butchers Flat, and during the nights more cracks and flashes as the pig hunters take advantage of the milder weather. With less rain, and the water in the tank a finite asset, Paulie has resumed his yellow and brown mantra of rules for toilet use.

In the office there's an email waiting for me, inviting me to farewell drinks for the Wellington contingent tomorrow in Nelson. It's a long drive back through those ranges with a beer or two inside and Vanessa won't like me socialising with DI Marianne Keegan, so on balance I'm inclined to decline.

'If you need skippering back from Nelson I can oblige,' says Latifa handing me a coffee. 'We've gotta say a proper bye-bye to DI Cheekbones, eh? Make sure she leaves.'

And I'll probably be in as much trouble if Vanessa learns I've declined so as not to upset her. Damned if I do ... Latifa sinks her coffee and grabs the keys for our morning drive along the highway when the phone goes. After some umms and yeahs and notes on the pad she lets the caller know we're on our way.

'Break-in down at the marina, the Menz ...' she highlights the 'z' with a slash of her forefinger, '... shed.'

'Much taken?'

'Dunno yet. They found the door kicked in and a bit of a mess. Maybe some womenz wanted to join and weren't allowed.' She turns the sign on the office door to *Closed* and hands me the keys. 'You driving?'

*

Raphael is the convenor of the Menzshed and he isn't happy.

'Bloody kids. That's the third time.'

I cast my mind back through the local crime stats: third time in about as many years, if I'm right. Not bad going really. I recall places in Manchester and Sunderland getting broken into three times in one day. 'Anything taken?'

'Paint. Some tools, a drill. That kind of thing.'

'You can buy that stuff dirt cheap in Bunnings,' says Latifa. 'Have to be a real sad bastard to steal it.'

Raphael clears his throat. 'These were top of the range.'

'Maybe you can give us a list, and any photos or serial numbers would help,' says Latifa.

There's something familiar about Raphael but I can't place it. 'And there's this too.' He shows us the damage.

'Youse are all handy blokes. Should be able to fix that yourselves.' Latifa taps the details into her iPad. 'Hammer and nails, lick of paint.'

Raphael shakes his head. That's who he is: he's the bloke who painted over the graffiti on *Serenity II*. He was on the CCTV footage, the proud posture, the dashing mane of black curly hair. He's caught me giving him a funny look. 'What is it, Sergeant?' He rubs at his face. 'Something there?'

'No.' I explain the CCTV connection.

'Ah, right. Yeah, I sometimes get some contract work for the marine shop in the high street. And Mr McCormack has taken a shine to me. He told me he likes the idea of a Raphael painting his boat.'

'Pay well?'

'No, he's a stingy bastard, but that's probably how he got rich, eh?'

I remember from the CCTV, after the inspection of Raphael's repair work on the graffiti, McCormack walking over the boat sniffing for something. 'Did you notice a funny smell when you were working on the boat?'

Yes, he'd been asked about it by one of the task force detectives. At least some of my CCTV observations had been followed up then.

'Describe the smell.'

He wrinkles his nose. 'Like roadkill but also a bit vomity. I think a rat or something must've died down there. Way ripe it was.'

Vomity.

Was that the bad breath odour I'd caught a whiff of as I interviewed McCormack? Maybe Feargal had indeed been onboard and failed to clean up properly after a bout of seasickness. 'Did it get stronger or weaker over the time you worked on the boat?'

'Weaker definitely, by the time I finished you had to try hard to catch it. But that first day or two. Yuk.'

'How long did the job take?'

'A couple of weeks. I was fitting in with my other commitments. McCormack wasn't in any great hurry.'

So something had died on *Serenity II* but the smell had diminished over the following several days. If the thing had been removed after a day and propped against the shoe fence then that would account for it.

*

'You never did a full forensic on *Serenity II*?'

Keegan muffles the phone while she talks briefly to somebody at her end. 'It was on the list while McCormack was in our sights but then Donnelly topped himself and saved us the budget expense.' DI Keegan seems distracted. In her mind she's probably halfway across Cook Strait already. 'We did the basic, which proved that Jamie Riley probably died onboard, but it was inconclusive on Donnelly being present.'

'Inconclusive?'

'He's in the beemer with the sail bag but there's nothing of him onboard the boat. But there could be any number of good reasons for that. Maybe he wore special pervo overalls which he later discarded.'

Or maybe he wasn't even there because he gets seasick standing on a jetty. 'Who *is* onboard, forensically?'

'McCormack obviously, it's his boat.'

'But he's got his alibi. What about his other employees?' I'm back in the office, worrying down the phone while Latifa's at lunch. 'We still don't have detail on precisely how and where the kids were killed. The sail bag. Did we ever find that? And where was Qadim Reza before he died?'

'Jesus, mate. Feargal took him off in the beemer, did his horror show in a dungeon somewhere, then dumped him. End of story.' She's getting snappy. I'm raining on the homecoming parade. 'The job's finished, Nick. No need to do anymore. We go stirring things up now and we'll have more political flak from McCormack. We need to leave him alone. It was Feargal Donnelly, in the BMW, with the Rohypnol.'

'And that's what you're putting in the file to close it?'

'Signed off by the chain of command, today. Sleeping dogs, Nick. He's even got a record of it in Dublin.'

'A quickie in the park toilets when he was sixteen? Doesn't make him a killer.'

'It helps build the picture, Nick. For fuck's sake.'

There's nothing so far to say it definitely wasn't Donnelly and that, it seems, is enough for everybody else. But it's not enough for me. 'Fucking amateur hour. I can't believe this.'

A chill descends down the phone line. 'The DC told me about you over a farewell dinner with the brass last night. The nitty gritty on how you ended up here. You're no stranger to amateur hour yourself. Two years undercover and buckets of money and you score, what, an overdue library fine and a slap on the wrist? If I were you I'd count my blessings.' She changes the subject, brightens her voice. 'Let it go, Nick. Join us for a beer tomorrow night, old time's sake. It might not be a perfect result but it's the best we're going to get.'

I need to give a little. She's taken risks to back me up and follow my flights of fancy. There's no harm in sending her on her way with a smile, a wave and an ale or two. 'It's a date. See you then.'

It's not Feargal Donnelly. He's just an affable Irishman who thought he was everybody's best friend until he found himself tied to the tracks in the path of a runaway train. A man who gets seasick isn't going to spend a week on a boat getting his twisted jollies, he'll get them on terra firma. And he's not going to drive down to Kaikōura to kill a bloke for a photograph that means nothing to him. But if the killings stop now, will that be enough? If I was the Prince of Darkness, the Pied Piper, I'd be considering my options – I've come dangerously close to being found, close enough for me to get worried and take action to cover my tracks; now a dead man is being blamed and the heat is off. I'd call it a day, maybe get my kicks somewhere else. Count my blessings as DI Keegan might say.

So can I live with that? Let Marianne's sleeping dogs lie?

*

Back at the farm, Gary has pegged out his claim on the far paddock, and a bobcat and pallet of building supplies are blocking my driveway. Paulie is chatting to the chooks and Vanessa is watering the vegies. It's Little House on the Prairie except we're in the feral hills of the Wakamarina.

'How many eggs?' I ask Paulie. He lifts two hands and splays his fingers, then curls one in. 'Only nine? They're slipping.'

'I think they're a bit tired.'

'Slack, more like.' I glance over at Vanessa. 'Roast chook for dinner?'

'Dad! No!'

I let him know I'm joking and he shakes his fist at me good naturedly. Vanessa is by my side, handing me an empty bucket. 'Fill that up, one more line of beans to go.'

'As you wish, m'lady.'

'Paulie, tell Dad about school.'

A grin creases his face. 'I'm getting a certificate tomorrow. And a prize.'

'What for?'

'Being brilliant, as usual.'

'Fair enough. Anything specific?'

'I dunno, kid of the month or something?'

'Fantastic!'

'Can you come to assembly tomorrow? Mum's working and doesn't love me enough.'

'Paulie!'

'I'll be there, son. I love you even if Mum doesn't.'

'Thanks Dad, love you too.'

Vanessa punches me in the shoulder. 'Stop ganging up on me and go fetch the water.' Then she starts singing. 'Food glorious food, roast chicken and stuffing ...'

'Mum!'

While I'm filling the bucket something is buzzing in a little corner of my brain. I can't get hold of it though. Instead of roast chook we opt for frozen pizzas for dinner, Paulie's choice as a reward for winning something at school. The sunset sky is a spectacular swirl of orange rays, vivid blues, broiling purple clouds, and black silhouetted hills. If somebody painted it that way you'd tell them to never give up the day job and ease up on the wacky baccy.

'Stunning,' says Paulie and we all agree. The end of another day in paradise.

51

Vanessa has to go in early to Havelock School because the teacher she's covering for is usually on the early start roster on Tuesdays. It's her job to make sure the kids don't get run over by parent drop-offs, or logging trucks, or blazed mussel-shuckers coming off the night shift. It's my job to take Paulie to school, attend the prize-giving, and pick him up at the end of the day on my way back from showing my face at DI Keegan's farewell do in Nelson. Paulie is digging into his Weetbix and I'm topping up my mug from the plunger when the phone goes. It's Shania, Johnny Fernandez's de facto widow.

'Somebody has been in our house.'

'Yeah, the detectives have been there, and forensics, and I've had a look round too.'

'Not the valley. Here, my mum's house in Seddon.'

She gives me the details. She and Trayvon had stayed over at an old school friend's place a few blocks away. Mum meanwhile had a sleepover with her boyfriend in Blenheim.

'I got back half an hour ago and found the place trashed.'

'Notice anything taken?'

'My iPad, that's it really.'

'Money? Other valuables?'

'Nah, not much of that stuff around here.'

'Could just be kids or whatever?'

'S'pose.'

'But you don't think so?'

'They went through my undies drawer, slashed the mattress, the couch, mum's bed. Kind of thorough the way kids aren't, you know?'

'What were they looking for, Shania?'

'Probably Johnny's phone.'

'The one you didn't tell me about last time we met.'

'You know already?'

'Denzel told me. Do you know where it is?'

'No. He used to keep stuff in the shed in an old tin behind some tyres.' Genius, I'm thinking. Not. 'But I checked, nothing there.'

'So somebody thinks you might have it.'

'Will they come back?'

'Maybe. Some advice, Shania. Don't hold anything back from us. There are bad people out there.' I tell her to phone the local cops and put in an insurance claim. 'Maybe you and your mum should leave town for a bit. Go and visit some friends or relatives?'

'You reckon?'

'Yeah, I reckon.'

If Feargal Donnelly is the Pied Piper then he just came back from the dead to give Shania a scare. But I know that won't be enough to mar the celebrations and bon voyage to the task force this evening. I wrangle Paulie away from his third bowl of cereal and into the Toyota and we hit the road for Pelorus School.

*

I'm really proud to watch my son get his certificate and a book token. I've not been around for many of these kind of events, that's been Vanessa's domain. I've always been off doing something which seemed more important at the time. Paulie tips me a wink as he receives his award for a drawing he did recently. He holds it up for the assembled throng – him, Vanessa and me on the farm with some chickens and the weirdest looking goats you could imagine. It's nothing special, I'm thinking, but Paulie is well due his place in the limelight. Of all people, it's Sebastian Ryan who, on behalf of the prizes sponsor McCormack Forestry, shakes hands with my son and poses for a pic for the newsletter before making a quick speech.

'McCormack Forestry is proud to be the sponsor of the Pelorus School Awards and to continue the strong community partnership forged over the years.' He leans forward over the lectern. 'The daily news is full of doom and gloom and now more than ever we need some light, some heroes.' A sweep of the arm taking in the audience. 'The Pelorus–Havelock school cluster has produced some great leaders, thinkers, scientists, sportsmen and women. Even politicians.' He pauses for the good-hearted snickers and boos. Gestures towards my son. 'And I can foresee the day when we'll be queuing up to admire and buy the great art of Paul Chester. I only hope I can afford it.'

It's jarring seeing that prick up there but the town sign is the symbol of a sawmill blade, and logging is the main employer in the area. I bite my tongue, applaud, and accept an invitation from the principal to join her, her staff, and the other prize-winning parents for tea and cake. She introduces me to Ryan.

'We've met,' I say, shaking his hand anyway.

'And we meet again.' Ryan is good at this: transformed from snooty twat to Sebastian Smooth-as-Fuck. He's got the principal blushing and the eyes of a few mums and teachers on him. 'Great kid.'

'Paulie? Yes, he is.'

'Paulie?'

'Another few years and we'll dignify him with a simple Paul. But for now it works.' I sip from my tea and crunch on a bikkie. 'This part of your job description? School prizes?'

'We share it around among the executives. Sometimes it's Mr McCormack, sometimes it's PR.'

'And you'll be one short now too.'

He nods and looks troubled. 'That's right. Poor Feargal.'

My phone goes. Latifa. 'You need to come to the marae. Now.'

I make my excuses and nip over to where Paulie is enjoying the adoration of his peers. 'Pick you up at the end of the day, on my way back from Nelson, okay?'

'Sweet as, Pops.'

*

'I had a dream.'

I look over at Latifa. Normally when Beth says something like this there will be a roll of the eyes or a snort of derision. Not this time. Latifa is taking this seriously.

'Go on.'

Beth is sitting cross-legged on the floor like a guru and we're down there with her. She stares straight ahead, as if she's in a trance, but she's not. She's just recounting a story. 'The *taniwha* is swimming up the river, looking for a feed.'

'Monster,' says Latifa, quietly in my ear.

'Yeah, got it.' It's the same word Gary used when he read the story to the Russians about the eel. Seems a long time ago.

'The moon is full,' says Beth.

'That's this Wednesday,' whispers Latifa. 'Tomorrow.'

'Yep.'

'He rests in a deep, dark pool. He smells blood.'

I check my watch. Latifa glowers at me.

Peter pops his head around the door. 'Anybody got any smokes?'

'Fuck off,' says Beth, out the corner of her mouth.

'Just sayin'.' He disappears.

'There's a child at the riverbank. Scared. Alone. Crying.'

I'm listening now. Is Beth foreseeing another abduction?

'The *taniwha* swims over to him.' Beth's looking directly at me now, there are tears in her eyes. 'There's a woman at the boy's feet. She is still. The *taniwha* can't decide which one to eat.'

I shake my head. It's just a dream, mumbo jumbo. And yet I'm feeling cold and scared and alone like that child she sees by the river. Snap out of it.

'Latifa,' I say. 'Why did you bring me here?' I'm angry, my precious time has been wasted.

'Wait,' she says. 'Please.' She gestures for Beth to continue.

'The *taniwha* can see the house on the hill behind the child. A red roof. The moon shines on it.'

My home. She's talking about my home. 'That's it?' I ask.

'Yeah,' says Beth.

'Thanks.' I turn to Latifa. 'Can I have a word?' We adjourn to the Toyota. 'You've called me away from my son's school assembly for this woman's dream.'

'It's important, can't you see that?'

'It's a dream. She drinks, she smokes weed. Maybe she eats cheese at the wrong time of night. We need to stay level-headed here, it's our job.'

'Usually I'd agree with you but there's something building with Beth, we can't ignore it.'

'I can.'

'We care about you. We don't share this stuff with anybody.'

I can see she means it. 'Yeah, thanks, sorry.' She's getting out of the car, looking hurt. 'Heading back to the office?'

'In a while.'

'Okay, see you there.' I gun the engine and drive away. It's bullshit I tell myself. But it's got under my skin.

*

The atmosphere is cool for the next few hours. It's too small a station for that kind of tension so I take a walk around town, grabbing a ham roll in transit. There's a text message on my phone from Vanessa saying she'll be able to pick Paulie up from school after all. It's not from her number; maybe the battery ran out and she borrowed a colleague's. Back at the office Latifa seems to have withdrawn her offer of skippering us to DI Keegan's leaving do in Nelson. There's a terse note instead – *Got a headache and need to study tonight.* Meanwhile she's out on the road looking for bad drivers until home time.

By midafternoon it's back on the road to Nelson. Passing Pelorus School, I can see the kids heading home and I know Paulie will be biding his time in the after-school care club until Vanessa picks him up. Why am I driving seventy ks in the wrong direction to drink with people who, for the most part, I don't like, in order to celebrate the end of a mission that I don't think is accomplished? Because it's the done thing. Because Marianne Keegan is, at heart, a good sort who stuck her neck out for me. As is DC Ford. As for Benson and Hedges? They can go fuck themselves. As the car climbs into the ranges, the sky closes in and drizzle spits from the mist. My neck and shoulders are tensing on the hairpins as logging trucks roar past and impatient utes try to climb up my arse. Passing the spot where Kevin Moran was nudged over a ravine, I get to wondering what was so incriminating in that boat he was paid to sink.

And if McCormack was out of town on business, who hired Moran? Where did they find him? How did they know he was their kind of guy? Des Rogers again, the pet cop with the useful address book. But McCormack can't have been too impressed having his precious boat sunk by a dipstick. And I've been too distracted to ask him about it. Maybe now, with the passage of time and a rock-solid alibi, he'll feel like answering a few more questions? I doubt it, he'll be on the phone to Ford straight away. Who could I ask without ruffling a few feathers? Of course, my new best mate, Sebastian Ryan. I ring Pelorus School on the hands-free to see if they have a mobile contact for him. Why? Oh, I just want to thank him for the book token he gave my son today, unfortunately I had to rush off. Sure, they say, no problem, and they give me it. I'll call him when I'm back in the office tomorrow.

Half an hour later at Nelson HQ the bar is open and DC Ford is giving a speech in praise of DI Keegan and her team. She is looking slightly flushed, perhaps half a bottle of Cloudy Bay ahead of me. Benson and Hedges look glazed with a Speight's in each fist and will probably have a fight later on. Ford is eyeing me warily as he pauses to take a sip from a glass of water.

'Glad you could make it, Nick.' Marianne's got a dangerous twinkle in her eye and her voice has dropped an octave or two.

'You've done a good job,' I lie. 'You can be proud.'

'Do you really think that?' She smiles and puts her hand on my arm, squeezes it. 'No. You don't. But you're a good man.' Another squeeze. 'Very good.'

I should tell her about Shania's place being trashed and how, if that means what I think it means, then Feargal Donnelly was the wrong man and our killer is still out there. But I don't. This is her party. 'When do you ship out?'

'In a hurry to see me go? First flight tomorrow.' A sip from her Cloudy Bay. 'Tonight's my last night.' She gives me that look I last saw across the table in a Thai restaurant in Blenheim.

My pocket is throbbing again but this time it's my phone. Vanessa. 'Are you two on the way back yet? We need some milk.'

'No, I thought you were picking him up?'

'Me? But we agreed this morning.'

I'm cold. 'You didn't send me that text?'

'What text?'

52

During the long drive home all I can think about is Beth's crazy dream – the *taniwha* coming up the river to our house in search of its next meal. The text on my phone supposedly from Vanessa turns out to be from a pay-as-you-go mobile. The same number must have sent the text to Paulie's phone which he showed to the after-school care supervisor. It said, *Paulie take the 4pm school bus and I'll pick you up at the hotel at Canvastown, Mum x.* So the supervisor had put him on the four o'clock run and arranged for the driver to drop him at the Trout Hotel. The driver remembers Paulie giving him a cheery if nervous wave. Then, in the rear view in the distance, a car rolling in to pick Paulie up. What colour? White. Make? Not sure. It doesn't matter. It wasn't Vanessa. Somebody has Paulie.

'He'll be terrified.' Vanessa is buried into my chest. 'It's *him* isn't it? You've provoked him into doing this.'

'Love …'

'And all that time you're out drinking with her.' She lifts her head and unfolds herself away from me. Her eyes are filled with disgust.

Marianne's party folded not long after and her trip home and cele-brations are postponed. Everybody is out doorknocking, manning phones, checking CCTV. Search and Rescue are combing the area. Spotter planes, helicopters, boats. Patrol cars on the lookout. But there's no sign. The white car disappeared east and south along SH6 according to drinkers in the Trout, but if it got as far as Havelock it merged into the slightly larger crowd. McCormack has come back swiftly and said all of his fleet is accounted for, he's oozing sympathy and offering whatever resources we need: extra people, extra vehicles, his plantation chopper. It doesn't stop us pulling him and all of his executives in for another chat. Somebody in that select group is behind this.

I want to be there. I want to shove a gun in their nostrils until they tell me where Paulie is and give him back to me. I don't care if some of them are innocent. And that's why DC Ford and DI Keegan won't let me be within cooee.

'You're best here, mate. Vanessa needs you.'

No, she doesn't. She blames me and she's got a point. I've pushed and pushed and sacrificed my own son to my pride and my ego.

When we weren't here, me and Paulie, how did that feel?

Shite.

Hold that thought.

Vanessa turns from staring out over the valley and the encroaching blackness as day gives way to night. 'You're still here?'

I phone Latifa and ask her to come up and be with Vanessa. No need, Vanessa says from the window behind me. Latifa tells me she's on her way. I grab the keys and head for the door, turning for a last look and a last word but there's nothing there. Gary is out somewhere, word has it he has a new girlfriend in Havelock. He's cleared the pallet from the driveway and parked his bobcat behind the shed. I skid on the gravel road outside the house. I'm driving angry and need to pull myself together for all our sakes.

Havelock main drag is empty as it should be on a midweek evening. As my mobile comes into range, a message comes through.

See how easy it is?

It's from the same number as earlier. I text back, *I'm going to kill you*

That won't get your son back

I don't reply. The ball's in his court. I phone Keegan. 'The executives. Have they accounted for their movements?'

'Yes, they have. We're checking them now.'

'All of them?' I explain that the killer has been in touch. We need to be looking at their phones.

'We're focusing on the shortlist, the ones who had access to the company cars five years ago. Going through their phone records first.'

'That's not good enough. We need to put them all through the mincer.'

'I'm trying to prioritise. We're doing our best, Nick. You need to be with Vanessa.'

I cut her off rather than say what I'm thinking. I need to reserve my rage for myself and for the man who has my son. We're the only ones who deserve it. I know where I'm headed now and I don't care whether or not I'm welcome.

*

'Who the fuck is it?'

I slap the door with my hand again. 'Me, Nick Chester. I need to talk to you.'

'Fuck's sake.' Beth opens up and a swirl of smoke fouls the cool night air. She's in a t-shirt and knickers and has a mug of what smells like rum and coke in her hand.

I push past her. 'He's taken my son.'

'Who?'

'Your fucking *taniwha*. I need you to remember who he is.'

Her face softens. 'Not that easy, love.' A cough. 'The poor boy. Jesus.'

'Come with me.'

'What?'

'Get your clothes on. Now.'

Peter lifts his head from under the duvet. 'Mate, we were just getting started. First time in months.'

'Fuck off,' I tell him.

'One of these days I might just do that.'

'Where are we going?' says Beth.

'You'll see.'

She gives Peter a wave and a girlish smile and hooks her arm in mine. 'Don't wait up.'

*

The Woodbourne Tavern is closing for the night but I flash my ID and tell them not just yet. On the way over I've phoned DI Keegan and acted less angry. She's keen to help so I've asked her to do me a favour.

'What do you need them for?'

'I'm going to post them on Facebook and call them bad names.'

'Nick.'

'Just do it, please.'

'This place has changed,' says Beth, taking in the décor.

'A lot?'

'Nah, the layout's pretty much the same, just had a lick of paint and been freshened up.'

'Where were they sitting?'

'This isn't going to work you know.'

'Show me.' She does and we arrange a table and some chairs just so. 'Rogers?'

She points to a chair and I ask a member of staff to sit in it. 'Do I get overtime for this?' he grumbles.

I chuck a hundred on the bar. 'A round for this table. Whatever they're drinking.'

That elicits a few more volunteers. All the chairs are quickly filled except one, I reserve that for myself. I get Beth to stand exactly where she was standing when Rogers grabbed her arse and the Pied Piper asked him to stop. Beth smiles apologetically and sips from her double rum and coke. 'It's not happening, love. Sorry.'

I bring up the photos on my phone, the ones Keegan sent me of the McCormack executives. The boss first. 'Him?' A shake of the head. Donnelly. 'Him?' Same again.

'Like I said, *Men in Black* and the magic flash pen.'

She's not scared enough. She needs to feel the same kind of scared she felt that night. I take out my Glock and press it into her cheek. 'Think.'

The barman playing Des Rogers splutters his drink. 'Fuck mate, no need for that.'

I look into Beth's eyes and summon all the *pōuri* there is within me. 'If I have to hurt you I will. This is too important.' I want to add sorry, but in truth I'm not. I've no doubt broken a whole bunch of psychiatry taboos as well as several police regulations and human rights articles. Professor Sumner wouldn't approve. Nor DC Ford. Marianne Keegan? Maybe.

Beth peers closely at me, is it me she's seeing or the Pied Piper? Has my cold dark rage triggered a memory? She touches my face with her ciggie-smelling hands. She's back there, I can see it, and this time she's fighting her fear, trying to shrug it away after all these years.

She shakes her head. 'That's enough, Des. They're grieving.'

'You know him,' I say. 'And he knows you.' That shrug again. I'm in danger of breaking the spell. I stay focused on oozing out my *pōuri*. I take up the killer's refrain. 'Leave it, Des. Stop.'

Sweat forms on her brow, she leans down over the table, peers hard into my eyes. Her hand grips my arm, fingers dig in. I think about what I will do to the Pied Piper when I find him and I try my best to seep it through my pores into Beth's grip.

'That's enough, Des,' I say again. 'They're grieving.' *Tangaroa.* Endless wealth personified. Power. Privilege. I focus on those things that make my class-war hackles rise and feed my darkness. I stare into her bloodshot and slightly jaundiced eyes. Bring him forth. He's in there. Find him. Bring him to me.

Beth's head tilts. It's like she's just recognised somebody in the street. Somebody she hasn't seen for a while. Not sure if it's really them.

Find him. Bring him to me.

After a moment she straightens up, picks up my phone and thumb scrolls through as if she's looking for a date on Tinder. 'Him.' She prods the picture. 'But his hair was much shorter then.'

I look. Of course. I should have known earlier.

'Thanks,' I say. 'And sorry, about the gun.'

She lifts her drink. 'No worries. I'd have done the same to you.'

The Pied Piper.

All I have to do now is hunt him down.

*

'It's Sebastian Ryan.'

I'm on my way to Nelson, racing back up through the ranges and the rain has returned.

'The lawyer?' DI Keegan doesn't buy it. 'How do you know? He wasn't even around five years ago.'

'Beth Haruru identified him.' I don't offer any details of the circumstances. 'We need to bring him in. I'm on my way over, I'll meet you at his place.'

'Nick, we have nothing on Ryan except this woman's five-year-old recollection of a conversation in a pub. What makes you so sure?'

'I believe her. There'll be more, we'll find it, just bring him in.'

'I'll send somebody round there.'

There's a taxi on its way to take Beth home but with a few dollars left on the bar tab she's in no hurry. I'm suddenly afraid for Vanessa and Latifa. There's no answer on the landline and both their mobiles are out of range. I've left a message for Vanessa suggesting she get out of there just in case Ryan comes calling. Still, as backup, I try Gary. Again it goes through to voicemail.

'Gary, it's Nick. Not sure where you are or if you'll get this but I need a favour.'

I finish my plea and chuck the phone onto the passenger seat. Now it's me climbing up people's arses around the hairpins and flashing them to move over. The rain pounds the windscreen and the wipers are working overtime. Tuesday ticks over into Wednesday as I descend back into mobile range on the outskirts of Nelson. My phone again. Keegan.

'He's not there.'

No. Of course he isn't. The disappointment is like a hard slap. I'm fuelled solely on adrenalin – for some people that means cold, hard focus. For me it's working like Red Bull and vodka with a couple of truckie's pills thrown in – all charged up with nowhere to go. 'Known associates? Other addresses? A bach?' Pied-à-fucking-terre.

'Go home, Nick. We'll have people out looking for him.'

I close her down and sit by the side of the road staring out over the dark waters of Nelson Bay as rain drenches the windscreen and a freighter passes on the horizon. Within a minute there's another call. DC Ford.

'Mate, you're not helping anybody, least of all yourself.'

'That right?'

'We're pulling out all the stops, we've got people out everywhere looking for Paulie, we're exploring all angles. But we're trying to stay methodical and professional. Focused. That's where the results come from. You're firing off like a Catherine Wheel that's lost its nail. Go home and be with Vanessa.'

Rain pelts the windscreen, it's one of those deluges you get here, it can turn solid earth to swamp in no time at all. 'That's what everybody's saying but she doesn't want me there.'

'She does,' he says gently. 'Believe me, she does.'

*

I'm on my way home. The rain is easing. Sebastian Ryan. Why haven't I seen it earlier? I've thought he was a prick since day one and that's usually enough for me to place a guilty tag on a man. But his boss was a bigger prick so my focus was on McCormack. If I'd seen it earlier would I still have Paulie now? Yes. Ryan was onto me long before I was onto him. He's had my family in his sights for some time now. Following us, no doubt – me to my job, Vanessa to hers, Paulie to school. He sent that text to my son, he even knew to call him Paulie because that's what I told him at school assembly. A charming and concerned inquiry to a teacher about the after-school care arrangements for the delightful special-needs boy would elicit all Ryan needed to know. I can imagine the exchange.

'Normally his mother collects him but today it's his dad. The chap you met at morning tea. The policeman, that's right.'

Was that him in the helicopter? Was that him staring at Vanessa through binoculars from the plantation? Was that him rummaging through our property back when I'd only been thinking about Sammy Pritchard? That's how he could have found all the mobile numbers he needed: there's a list on the fridge, written up there for Paulie's benefit, it's visible through the glass door. Ryan, ahead of me all the way.

Suppose I make everything add up and find the connection between Ryan and McCormack from five years ago; simple enough, they were buddies long before they were colleagues. Where's he been the last five years? He's Latifa's tutor, she mentioned he'd been to PNG. No doubt he's left a trail of tears in the Highlands which nobody has cared to follow. He fits the loose description: tall and skinny and pasty with short, blondish-greyish hair, even if he has let it grow a little since. It will be his photo on the missing mobile. But there are no traces at the crime scene, and any on *Serenity II* can be explained by his association with McCormack. Any incriminating traces perhaps on *Serenity I* will be at the bottom of Marlborough Sounds. Say he insinuated his way into these lives by giving out prizes at school sports day or whatever. I can see it: we can join the dots and they'll lead us nowhere. This man will walk free.

Why is he prepared to kill over a photo of his boss with some Maori kids? Or a blurry pic on a teenager's mobile? Because the people who had those things knew who he was, wanted to blackmail him, and could draw attention to him. But none of it would work in court, the photos alone count for nothing without the accompanying testimony of Rogers and Fernandez who knew the story behind them. But now they're dead and anything they knew died with them. This man will walk free.

His is a world of assumed privilege; he knows all the right people, all the best lawyers. *Tangaroa*, endless wealth personified. And all we can assemble are blurry pictures on CCTV and fuzzy memories from the damaged and deranged that nobody wants to listen to. Except now he's gone feral and taken my son. He must know he could have walked away if push came to shove, but he's taken this action. Why?

And then it comes to me. He's no longer concerned about loose ends. He doesn't care anymore. I've spoilt his party. He's not used to that. This is revenge, pure and simple.

53

Back at the house all the lights are out. Well, it's nearly two a.m., so it shouldn't come as a surprise. But something doesn't feel right. Latifa's and Vanessa's cars are there. Still no sign of Gary. The gravel on the driveway is stirred up like somebody has arrived or left in a hurry. That could have been me leaving or Latifa arriving. But the lights should be on, Vanessa should be there at the window, watching, brooding, crying. Latifa should be checking who's just arrived or fussing around making yet another cup of tea, or on the landline for an update. I retreat to the shed to find my torch. When I flick the light switch, it's not just the lights in the house that are out, all the power is off.

I take my gun out, grab the torch and head for the junction box. The main switch is off, I turn it back on. Immediately several lights go on in the house but there's still no sign of life. I slide the door open and edge my way through.

'Anybody home?' There's a trail of blood along the kitchen floor. 'Hello?'

Around the edge of the partition wall into the lounge room I can see feet. Vanessa's. I approach, wrapped in dread.

She's alive, breathing, but only just. She's on her side, hands cable tied behind her and a roll of electrical tape over her mouth. I cut the ties and tape and try to wake her but she won't come to. Examining her eyes it's obvious: she's been drugged. There's no other sign of injuries. The blood trail isn't hers. I put her in the recovery position and call an ambulance. Then, with trembling hands, I put the phone down. 'Latifa?'

I try the other downstairs rooms, upstairs, outside to Gary's hut. She's not there.

Ryan means to hurt and take away all those I care about. But why did he leave Vanessa? Maybe he thought he'd done enough to kill her. Or maybe he's worked out that I've already lost her.

*

The ambulance folk arrive and start checking Vanessa, readying her for the fifty-odd kilometre trip to the hospital in Blenheim. What the hell are we doing in this stupid, remote, savage place? There's a water bottle on the table nearby. The paramedic sniffs it.

Rohypnol.

'Is she going to be alright?'

'Hopefully. Good job you found her early. An overdose of this and after a while you just give up on breathing. Was that the idea?'

'Who knows?' Ryan certainly didn't give a fuck either way.

The paramedic holds open the ambulance door. 'Are you coming?'

'No.' I need to find my son.

They leave and I phone Ford and bring him up to date. 'We need to know from McCormack, or any of his other colleagues, the places Ryan might take Paulie and Latifa.'

'Latifa?'

'He's got her too. And she's injured, her blood's on my kitchen floor.'

'Jesus. We'll get a crime-scene team there.'

'Whatever. I'll be in and out of touch.'

'Nick …'

But I've finished speaking with him. Back in the Toyota and down the valley road again. It was obvious really. We should have had a checkpoint at the bottom of the valley: one road in, same road out. He wouldn't have been able to get at Vanessa and Latifa. Twenty-twenty hindsight. Then again we don't have the manpower to cover all the eventualities for Sebastian Ryan and what he might think of next. I phone Keegan.

'Nick, I'm sorry, I've just heard.'

'I need maps of all McCormack's plantations and any buildings or sheds on them, starting with the one over the river from me on Tapps Road. I need them on my phone before I go out of range again. I'll sit outside the Trout for half an hour, after that I'll be gone.'

'On it. We'll have AOS and a chopper do a flyover on all of them with the thermal camera looking for signs of activity.'

'And it's a bit late now, but I need a block on Wakamarina Road in case he thinks of heading back this way.'

'Yep.'

I park up by the Trout Hotel and wait. It's after four and the eastern sky is getting lighter behind the silhouette of another of McCormack's shaved hills. Perhaps if I hadn't been blinkered by my disapproval of McCormack's loggers spoiling my precious view I might have seen things more clearly. And yet, my grudge against him helped turn the whole investigation in the right direction. A ute turns off SH6 to head up the Wakamarina. I recognise it and flag him down.

'Nick?' Gary looks drowsy and confused. I bring him up to speed. 'Christ.' On the back tray Richie gives a grumpy woof at being woken.

My phone beeps with the incoming maps. A thought occurs to me. 'The spare phone you used when you were on the run. Do you have it?'

A frown. 'Yeah. Why?'

'You got it from Johnny Fernandez's place, right?'

'Right. How do you know?'

'Lucky guess.' He hands it over and I scroll through the photos. Sure enough. I show it to Gary. 'This is the man who has Paulie and Latifa. We need to find him.'

'Any ideas?'

'You hunt around here, know any huts or buildings on or near that plantation over the river from us?'

'Yeah, I can think of a few.' He smiles. 'Need company?'

'Sure,' I say. 'Why not?'

*

Instead of crossing the bridge to follow the mainly unsealed Tapps Road up the other side of the valley, Gary takes us back in the direction of home.

'Trust me, it's a quicker and smoother road this side. We can cross the river upstream. Anyway, I need to collect some stuff first.'

I've downloaded the maps so they're readable offline. The covering email from Keegan has a warning:

> We've run Ryan through the system. Don't be fooled by the private school ponce act. He did a stint in the army in his 20s. Assume he can handle himself.

But that comes as no real surprise, his dispatching of Des Rogers and Johnny Fernandez was not for the faint-hearted.

Back at the farm Gary puts a GPS collar on Richie, tunes in his receiver, and selects his best pig gun. He also takes some binocs and then straps some anti-prickle armour on to his legs and arms. I'm getting impatient.

'Woolly mittens in case it gets chilly? Check. Nice thermos of cocoa? Check.'

Gary smiles. 'You'll see, tough guy.' And he flicks his fingers at the maps I'm studying on my phone. 'You won't need them.'

He has his EPIRB and I have my personal police alarm clipped on, which serves a similar purpose. In the absence of mobile and radio coverage in these hills, it's all we have and even they aren't infallible. Alternatively you could let people know where you're going to be for the next while. It's like signing the hiker's log on the way to the OK Corral and saying due back in two hours or send help. As an Occ Health and Safety issue, the union isn't impressed but this is Marlborough and you learn to live and die with it.

The river is predictably icy but only thigh deep, thank goodness for El Niño. The track is steep on the far side. Two years here and I haven't been this way, yet it's less than two hundred metres from my doorstep. The pre-dawn chorus is in full swing. Richie hangs close, tail wagging and ears pricked: alert and excited for the hunt. Gary leads on, I suspect that if he had a tail and doggie ears he'd look similarly excited. Me, I just want Paulie and Latifa back safe and sound.

The clouds that held the rain earlier are breaking up and the moon shines through. Almost full, like the one Beth Haruru dreamed about but it's dropping fast, yielding to the new day. Back in the gloom of the forest all around us are beech and other native trees and they are full of life. Weka cooee and thump in alarm at our passing. Possums scramble up the trees they've been eating. Moths dance in the light of Gary's head torch. Mosquitos whine and bite. Gary was right about the prickle armour: the blackberry vines and gorse bushes tear at my legs and arms and it's bloody painful. There's movement in the foliage nearby, something big, and Richie has the scent of it as the wind shifts. Is Ryan waiting for us, one step ahead again? The bush breaks open to our right and a figure rushes through with a terrifying grunt.

'It's a fucking pig,' laughs Gary. Richie is going ape and barking to bring the valley down. 'Shush.' The dog settles into a low growl and crouches, holding position while the pig makes up its mind what to do.

And so we stand there for a long minute, and another. The pig looks like it wants to charge us and stick one of those yellow tusks in deep. Gary murmurs something to it in Maori. Soothing. The pig stares us out then gives a final snort and disappears back into the bush.

'What did you say to it?'

'I said on your way, we're not going to eat you tonight.'

'You can communicate with pigs?'

'All the time, mate.' He throws me a grin and switches off his head torch. 'Some listen, some don't.'

Another twenty minutes of bush-bashing and excruciating tearing at my limbs and we reach a clearing. It's where the pines once stood. It would have been dead enough then – they don't support much in the way of flora and fauna – but it's desolate now. Tendrils of mist hang in the air. New Zealand is good at this stuff, any day of the week can look like the dawn of time itself. That prehistoric awakening as the swamp bubbles and an ugly bug-eyed fish takes its first faltering steps onto land, evolving before your very eyes. We back off a few paces into the cover of the surviving trees. It's like I'm about to be sent up from the trenches across No Man's Land. Gary hands me his binocs. I hadn't seen it at first because it merged in with the surroundings. About five hundred metres away on the far side of the clearing there's an old cedar hut, boards weathered grey, a rotting windowless frame, and a flimsy door. Just visible to the right, the edge of a white car parked there.

54

Gary sends Richie off around one side of the clearing and the mutt is smart enough to hug the tree cover. Meanwhile we skirt the other side. The dog's collar is transmitting and the receiver maps where he is. Gary presses a button which sends a signal through to Richie to stop.

'Nifty,' I say.

'If we put these on you pakeha two hundred years ago, the world would be a different place.'

We're within two hundred metres of the hut now. The sensible thing to do is trigger our alarms and EPIRB and call in the AOS to clear this up professionally. I voice this to Gary.

'But then he gets arrested and spends the next few years stuffing you around in the courts. I've been in the system, seen the rich white boys get bail 'cause the judge is an old mate of their dad's. Then what, he vamooses off to Vanuatu to take up where he left off? You want that?'

There's a muffled noise, a yelp, from within the cabin.

No. I want Paulie back: safe, sound, now.

He ratchets his pig gun and I check my Glock. We aim to get as close as we can within the tree cover but the last fifty metres has to be across open clearing. Richie is our backup. If Ryan makes a move before we're ready, then the dog will be signalled to rush in. If he tears Ryan's throat out that's a bonus, but if he at least distracts him it'll help. It ain't much of a plan but it's all we've got. The sun glances off the top of the hills and I can see the red roof of our house from here through the beech trees. The river is running through a gully below us and for a moment, time stands still. It's the same river I marvel at every day from my balcony across the way yet, here, it feels like we've crossed over into Hades, the anti-world of the one I believe I inhabit. The world that Ryan, and his buddy McCormack, call theirs: darkness in place of light, death instead of life, destruction over creation. Am I about to join it by resolving things their way?

Sometimes you don't have the luxury of choosing.

It's that last fifty metres. No Man's Land. Gary needs to stay in the tree cover until I get to the side of the hut. He has a wider view of what's happening and if Ryan shows himself then Gary will signal the dog. I brace myself and rush over, crouching as low as possible, reach the gable end of the hut and wait. Gary has just broken cover and is running the first ten metres when the cabin door opens. I see Latifa, Ryan right behind, gun in the back of her neck. It looks like her Glock. Her face is puffed and beaten.

'Chester! Show yourself and throw your gun down. And tell your friend to drop his weapon as well.' I do, and Gary does as he's told too. 'What's your name?'

'Gary.'

'Call your dog in, Gary. Then shoot it.'

'Nah.'

Ryan pulls Latifa's head back and pushes the muzzle of the Glock further into her neck. 'I won't ask again.'

Gary presses the button on his gizmo and Richie comes bounding in. Gary calls the dog to heel and reaches for his dropped gun. Hesitates. 'I can't do this.'

Ryan's finger tightens around the trigger and he tugs tighter on Latifa's hair. Wind drifts across the clearing.

'It's only a fucken dog,' says Latifa. 'Do as you're fucken told!'

'You heard her,' says Ryan.

Gary lifts his rifle. And lowers it again. I feel for him but I see the bigger picture. I take the gun out of his hands and shoot Richie for him. The shot echoes through the misted hills, the dog yelps and collapses, blood seeping and spreading beneath the prone body.

'Fuck, mate. What'd you do that for?'

'I'll buy you another.' I give him back his rifle.

'Put the gun back on the ground,' says Ryan.

Gary does so.

Latifa can't help herself, she bursts out laughing. This isn't what Ryan expected. It unsettles him and he drops his guard. Latifa lashes her head back into his face and there's the crunch of breaking nose. It's not enough to stop Ryan from blindly pistol-whipping her and she slumps to the ground. He wants to kill her but he has Gary and me to deal with. Gary is bending for his gun so Ryan shoots him first. He drops like a stone. Then Ryan shoots me. In the leg. It hurts like fuck. He walks over and stands beside my head. He kicks it a couple of times.

'Stand up.'

'I can't.'

'Do it.'

'No.'

He walks back over to Latifa and places his gun against her temple. 'Now.'

Gary probably dead. Latifa next? I manage to get to my feet. 'Where's my son?'

'Where I left him.'

'Is he unharmed?'

'Not telling.'

'You're not as smart as we thought you were. The heat was off with Feargal in the frame. You could have taken a sabbatical, maybe take up again in pastures new, or old. PNG, somewhere like that?'

'You worked it all out.' He's back before me, gun held loosely at his side. 'Congratulations.'

'Bilateral aid, I'm guessing? The law and justice program?'

A wink. 'Hands across the water, that kind of thing.'

'How many kids did you kill in PNG?'

'I lost count.'

'So why didn't you take your chance?' My leg is going numb, the bottom half is drenched in blood. I'm having trouble standing, focusing, thinking. 'Why are we still here?'

'A balancing of accounts. Have you heard of the term *utu*?'

'Oh, you're one of these people Latifa talks about, with *National Geo* pictures on the wall, noble-savage stuff.'

'Insightful girl. She did a good essay on it. A plus. She understands that justice isn't justice without some taste of revenge, however subtle. *Utu*, Sharia, Old Testament, Talmudic law. The way I see it, they're all variations on a theme. It's really just a simple matter of double-entry bookkeeping.'

'So, what now?'

He lifts the gun back up, levels it at me. 'You're going to watch your son die before your eyes.' A rabbit scampers across the dead clearing. 'Then Latifa. Then I'll finish you.'

I'm struggling – my head is swimming with the pain. But I see Latifa stirring behind him and I have to keep him talking. 'If you're going to do that, I can't stop you.' Latifa is still again. Has she passed out? He notices me looking at her. Glances back and I edge closer. 'Bright girl,' he says. 'Such a waste.'

'Tell me something. Was there anything meaningful about those locations?'

'Does it matter?'

'I'm curious.' I tip my head towards his gun. 'Indulge me, one last time.'

'The shoe fence? The vineyard?'

Latifa coming round again, she shakes her head groggily. 'Yes. Why there?'

'Aesthetics, playfulness. Nothing deep.' He shrugs. 'Sorry.'

Nothing deep. Just vacuous and self-obsessed, always and forever.

He reacts to the rustle of Latifa moving behind him and I throw my weight on him. He goes down and we're rolling around in the pine needles and cold, damp earth and I'm trying to stop him from shooting me. He's strong, and I'm dizzy and weak. With all I have, I pull my head back and nut him, my thumb finds his eye and I gouge – a Sammy Pritchard special. He lets out a roar, spitting blood in my face, and I can feel the barrel of the Glock scraping my side.

Latifa comes down hard on him, with a knee on his head and prises the gun off him.

I grab it from her, examine it, test its cool weight in my hand.

Even with his head in the dirt under Latifa's knee, there's a gleam in Ryan's eye. 'Go on,' he says. 'You know you want to.'

'Sarge.'

I press the muzzle against his nostril. 'Release you from this cruel world that you've made a whole lot crueller?' He nods. My knuckle tightens on the trigger. 'Where's Paulie? No Paulie, no favours from me.' His eyes go towards the hut. 'Is he unharmed?'

'Yes. You have my word.' He looks at me. At the gun. 'So finish it. Have your *utu*.'

'Sarge?' Latifa frowns. 'What are you doing?'

'What does it look like I'm doing, Latifa? He's scum.'

A shake of the head. She nudges me aside. 'Not your call, boss.' She picks up and checks Gary's pig gun and fixes a beady on Ryan. 'Don't go appropriating our culture, it's our *utu*, you twisted creepy fuck. Not yours. Hands off.'

'Latifa,' I say, 'keep out of this.'

'You need to have more faith, Sarge. Trust me, this fella is going away for a long time.' She unclips handcuffs from her belt and pulls Ryan's wrists into position. 'Ten, fifteen, twenty years from now people will say: who's that sad, grey, fat nobody with the bowl of slop that people keep spitting in? Oh, him? He used to be the Pied Piper, the sick fuck who killed those kids way back when. And somebody will slap him in the showers yet again and say not so fucken flash now, eh?' She clicks the cuffs on him. 'Hey, did I really hear you say I got an A plus for that essay? Sweet as.'

I drag myself towards the hut. Paulie is in there on a mattress, breathing, unharmed, but out cold from the Rohypnol. I trigger my GPS alarm. I'm shaking and my vision has blurred. I lie down, holding him.

EPILOGUE

Both Gary and Richie survived, although the latter's usefulness as a pig dog is limited by his tripod status. My leg fared better but two weeks later it's still pretty sore to walk on. Gary's prickle-armour managed to take the oompf out of the bullet meant to kill him but he needs a few weeks under observation. His new girlfriend from Havelock happens to be a nurse at Nelson Hospital, which works out well.

'I still can't believe you shot my dog,' he says, shaking his head.

'I think Latifa is still pretty dark with you about some of your life choices too.'

'Yeah, well.'

Latifa is just along the corridor with Daniel the spunky Boy Racer in attendance. She shows me the finger, her ring finger, and grins through the injuries Ryan inflicted on her. 'Engaged. And me with a face like a kumara.' She squeezes Daniel's hand so hard he winces. 'Isn't he a sweetie?'

'Sure is. Back in the office next week?'

She shakes her head. 'Exams. Make it the week after.'

It looks like it's me and Traffic Man for the foreseeable. 'You're still pursuing the legal career then?'

'Course, why wouldn't I? And the field has thinned out now that Ryan is gone. One extra job vacancy in this region is always welcome.' She sees the look of regret I fail to hide. 'Don't worry, I'll be in the job a while yet.' She grins. 'We need to complete your cultural training first.'

*

At Nelson Police HQ, Keegan and Ford are in conference. There's some tidy footwork needed. They need to extract themselves from the innuendo they created around Feargal Donnelly, and the civil action his de facto widow may well take, and build a new legend around Sebastian Ryan.

'All of the parents of the kids recognised his photo,' says Keegan. 'He'd presented prizes or donations at the schools and sports clubs where their kids were. Or he was tagging along when McCormack was on duty.'

'And five years ago?'

'He was a tennis buddy of McCormack's. Not as good as Dickie, so his name doesn't get mentioned in dispatches but he was on a social photo at the tennis club Christmas do. He wasn't actually based in the region but visited often enough. Hung on McCormack's coat tails.'

And once Ryan knew we were talking to the ex-barmaid Beth Haruru, that tennis club photo had to disappear as did any others placing him in the narrative. The cardboard cheque photo with Denzel and Prince and the other neighbourhood kids? A Family Fun Open Day at the marae. It turns out Des Rogers was there, supposedly doing some Blue Light police and youth community work. In truth, facilitating Ryan's introduction to the Haruru *whanau* and access to young Prince. It was Ryan who took the infamous photo and Rogers knew that, stored it away for a rainy day – a witnessed connection, however loose, between Ryan and the boy. But there's another name right at the centre of all this, from day one. 'McCormack has known all along hasn't he?'

'He says not,' says Ford. 'It would be best for all if we believe him.'

'Yes sir,' I say, but we all know I don't mean it.

Something's nagging at me. 'So why did Feargal Donnelly kill himself? He knew he was innocent, he could get a good lawyer.'

'He got a visit from one,' says Keegan. 'Ryan looked in that morning. Must have put some words in his ear about how they were going to hang him out to dry. Ryan was the one who took the car from outside his house and was helping to put him in the frame.'

'But all Donnelly had to do was spill.'

'Would we have listened?' She looks at me. 'Well, maybe you would have. But the sealer was Donnelly's health background, which Ryan must have wheedled out of him long before that. He hasn't shown great resilience over the years: a suicide attempt at uni before his final exams, another one when a girlfriend left him. All craic and no ticker, poor bloke. Ryan knew which buttons to press: family shame, ruin, whatever.'

Loose ends remain for the paperwork and the prosecution brief, but that's their problem. We bid our farewells. Ford shakes my hand, hopes my leg gets better soon, and Keegan mouths au revoir.

*

One more stop before home. I know he'll see me. He invites me to take a seat and admire the view of the river.

'How long have you known?'

'Known what?' McCormack lifts a water bottle to his mouth and takes a swig.

'Ryan. Don't fuck about.'

'I'm as shocked as everybody.'

'He often borrowed your boat. Sank the first one five years ago, which must have made you think. Then he borrows it again for Jamie Riley. He's kept the boy on there and you spoil his plans by deciding on a pleasure cruise before he's ready. He did the graffiti, maybe while he was still out at sea so the CCTV didn't catch him, and let you find it so you'd call that day trip off, giving him more time to dispose of the boy. Pity about that nasty smell he left behind, eh? It didn't bother you?'

'You tell a good story. Maybe you should have looked closer at the boat that day, Sergeant, instead of standing back and being snide. You might have caught the scent of something.' He stands and offers me his hand. 'I wish you well for the future, Mr Chester. These have been very difficult times for all of us.'

I ignore the hand. 'What makes you think they're over? When I give evidence at the trial I'm going to make sure everybody knows what kind of man you are.'

*

On the way back up the valley passing Charlie Evans' place, I see that he and Denzel are feeding the alpacas with the straw bought in for a long dry summer. I hear that Patrick Smith is still out on the Sounds. Every day his campsite seems more and more permanent and Denzel drops by sometimes for a cuppa. I give him and Charlie a wave and notice the hill behind them is still intact. Logging suspended while McCormack deals with the imminent public float of his company and the need for positive community relations that entails. It's a beautiful day with fluffy clouds scudding across a blue sky and vivid flowers dancing on the roadside verge. The livestock look relaxed, the fields are green and rolling, a bucolic paradise. Does it feel like home? The jury is still out.

Paulie is triumphant. 'Twelve today, Dad. Twelve eggs!'

'A record.' We high five twice and then add two.

He hasn't mentioned the time with Ryan and we haven't pressed him on it. We don't know whether that's the right or wrong thing. The experts have differing views as experts are wont to do. We'll keep our fingers crossed and move to fix it if it shows signs of being broke. Vanessa has fully recovered from her Rohypnol overdose. She summons me out to the balcony with a pot of tea. I'm not so sure, the sandflies are fierce today. She chucks me the repellent.

'Lather up. I won't take no for an answer.'

'You never do.'

I don't know why she's forgiven me. Maybe she has this infinite capacity. Maybe she felt sorry for my leg wound. Maybe she likes messing with my mind. Probably all three but either way I have to be the luckiest man in the world. Across the river, the hill is scarred from the logging but I'm getting used to it. This valley has had some atrocious things done to it in the last hundred and fifty years in the name of commerce and progress, but the wounds scab over and it keeps fighting back with all the beauty it can still muster. Vanessa has learned to love this place and to bring Paulie and me along with her. She hands me my new mug, a present from Uncle Walter, it's got a picture of a weka on it. *Weka-tāne*.

'What's new?' I ask.

'I've been offered a full-time contract at the school for next year.'

I slap a sandfly and sip some tea. 'Great.'

'Say it with meaning.'

I reach across and grab her hand. 'That is really great, love.'

'Again. Louder.'

'That's fantastic. Woo hoo!'

She grins. 'That's better. You can have some cake now.'

She goes to bring some and that's when we hear a familiar noise. It's that chopper coming up the river again. Same chopper? It rounds the bend, low, and scoots up towards Butchers Flat. Yes, it's the same one.

Vanessa returns with the cake. 'What is it?'

'That helicopter again.'

'Must have liked my tits and come back for more.'

But I'm afraid and she can see it. She knows I'm thinking Sammy Pritchard. He's the only enemy left out there and he hasn't given up on me after all.

Who the fuck do you think you are, and what makes you think I would listen to you?

The chopper comes back around the river bend and disappears behind the tree line. He's going away again. It's just a surveyor or something. It's just my stupid paranoia. And then it rises above the tree line about a hundred metres from our balcony and I'm thinking Bond villain thoughts. This black chopper is about to blow our house to smithereens. The noise is deafening and Paulie runs in and grabs his mum. He's terrified.

I'm sick of all this. I rush to the balcony rail, willing him to do it. I'm smacking my chest and gesturing 'come on' with my hands. It's like the prelude to a drink-fuelled barney in a pub in Sunderland. Go on, Sammy, just fucking finish it. Do your worst. I'm spoiling for a fight with a bloody helicopter. I've completely lost it.

The phone must have been ringing but I didn't hear it. Vanessa brings it out on to the balcony. Taps me on the shoulder. 'It's for you.'

'Hello?'

'Mr Chester, we meet again.' It's Andrei the Russian, Bond villain voice and all. Is this revenge Chechnya-style? He opens the chopper window, leans out, smiles and waves. Stupidly I wave back. It doesn't seem like he's being unfriendly.

'What can I do for you?' I have to shout over the noise of the chopper.

'We have looked all over the district and decided that this suits our purposes the best.'

'What?'

'Your property, we want to buy it.'

'Why?'

'To launder mafia money. No, just joking. We like it. We want it.'

'Are you the money behind Charlie Evans' class action?' I shout back.

'Who?' he says, but I can see the smile on his face from here. It makes sense, you see a place, you like it, you want to preserve the natural beauty of the area. And you can afford to do exactly that. 'How does two million dollars sound?'

It sounds like more than four times what this place is worth. It would help set Paulie up for quite a while after we've gone. 'Can I think about it?'

'Sure, you have two minutes.'

I look at Vanessa and Paulie and they look back.

'What?' they say.

ACKNOWLEDGEMENTS

All characters appearing in this work are fictitious. Any resemblance to real persons, living or dead, is purely coincidental.

This book was completed shortly before the earthquake of November 2016, which devastated the area around Kaikōura. Many people have lost a lot, some their lives. It is a beautiful part of the world and I wish you a speedy recovery.

I'd like to thank Beau Webster and Neil Kitchen from Tasman District Police (Blenheim and Nelson offices respectively) for their advice and clarifications on NZ police procedure. Tracy Farr and Gaby Brown for early readings of the manuscript and words of wisdom on New Zealand culture and turns of phrase. Any mistakes are mine alone. A.J. Betts is to thank/blame for supplying me with the 'Kiwi iggs' joke.

Thanks also to the team at Fremantle Press for all their support, efforts and encouragement to spread my wings in this temporary conscious uncoupling from Cato. In particular my wise, generous and patient editor, Georgia Richter. Thank you too to my agent Clive Newman for working hard to try to ensure that I can give up the day job and still pay the bills.

Finally, my beautiful wife and muse, Kath, who continues to lead me into more adventures and shares the precise soul of an editor in her early readings of my manuscripts.

NICK CHESTER IS BACK

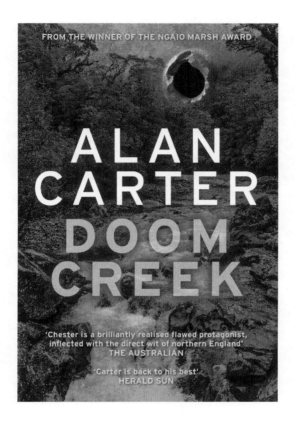

Sergeant Nick Chester has dodged the Geordie gangsters he once feared, is out of hiding and looking forward to a quiet life. But gold fever is creating ill-feeling between prospectors, and a new threat lurks in the form of trigger-happy Americans preparing for Doomsday by building a bolthole at the top of the South Island. As tensions simmer in the Wakamarina valley, Nick Chester finds himself working on a cold-case murder and investigating a scandal-plagued religious sect. When local and international events reach fever pitch, he finds himself up against an evil that knows no borders.

AVAILABLE FROM FREMANTLEPRESS.COM.AU AND
ALL GOOD BOOKSTORES

THE CATO KWONG SERIES

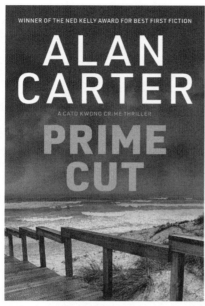

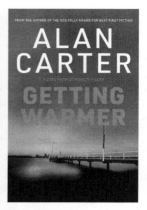

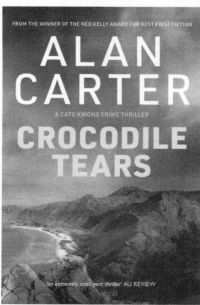

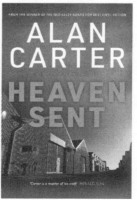

AVAILABLE FROM FREMANTLEPRESS.COM.AU AND
ALL GOOD BOOKSTORES

'Ladies and gentlemen, we have a new entrant into the higher echelons of Australian crime fiction writing.' *Sun Herald*

'An excellent read.' *The West Australian*

'A confident, witty, entertaining and gritty tale with an interesting, multicultural cast.' *Sunday Times*

'A gripping read. So real I had to wipe the blood off my fingertips.' *Dave Warner*

'Prime tale.' *Herald Sun*

'[The characters] all speak with that authentic voice which you only find in the best crime novels.' *Courier-Mail*

'A very strong and enjoyable read ... there are many layers to this story, genuine "aha" moments and a very strong cast of main and supporting characters. Four stars.' *Books+Publishing*

'Riveting reading.' *The Examiner*

'A deadly debut, ambitious and multi-layered.' *Allan Guthrie*

'The only disappointment is the end because you want to go on being part of these people's lives.' *Adelaide Advertiser*

'A promising new talent in Australian crime fiction.' *Australian Book Review*

'Plenty of dismembered corpses and a dark sense of humour ... an enjoyable debut.' *Sydney Morning Herald*

'What I really enjoyed ... is the novel's sense of humour – the way Carter has balanced the grisly reality of the crimes and the attendant commentary on mining development and migrant labour with the genuinely comic and witty self-deprecations of the characters ...' *Weekend Australian*

'A rollicking good read for those who enjoy a thrilling story.' *Minestyle Magazine*

'Accomplished and entertaining.' *Sydney Morning Herald*

'*Getting Warmer* is a winner.' *The Saturday Age*

First published 2017 by
FREMANTLE PRESS

Reprinted 2017, 2020.

Fremantle Press Inc. trading as Fremantle Press
PO Box 158, North Fremantle, Western Australia, 6159
fremantlepress.com.au

Cover design by Nada Backovic, nadabackovic.com
Cover photograph by Enzo Amato/ImageBrief.com
Printed and bound by IPG

 A catalogue record for this
book is available from the
National Library of Australia

ISBN 9781925164534 (paperback)
ISBN 9781925164541 (ebook)

 Department of
Local Government, Sport
and Cultural Industries
GOVERNMENT OF
WESTERN AUSTRALIA

Fremantle Press is supported by the State Government through the
Department of Local Government, Sport and Cultural Industries.

Fremantle Press respectfully acknowledges the Whadjuk people of the
Noongar nation as the Traditional Owners and Custodians of the land
where we work in Walyalup.